THE SECRET MISS RABBIT KEPT

A NOVEL BY
ROBIN CAIN

Print ISBN-13: 978-0984289882.
Print ISBN-10: 0984289887.
eBook ISBN-13: 978-0984289899.
eBook ISBN-10: 0984289895.
Cover photo by Andrey Bondarets through shutterstock.com.

ACKNOWLEDGMENTS

For my daughter's birthmother whose tremendous courage and faith made extraordinary love a reality, the real Emma Jean who taught me 'skin color ain't got nothing to do with nothing', and the wonderful seniors who shared their final journeys with me. I will never forget any of them and I hope you won't either.

Lucky for me, no writing buddy greater than James Lockhart Perry exists. I thank him, along with the many talented writers at www.internetwritingworkshop.org, for sharing their valuable time and priceless wisdom. I am forever indebted.

CHAPTER 1

My mother was murdered.

That's what I told nosey old Penny Parker, anyway—mostly because she always acted like she was better than me, but also because the truth was much worse. I'm sure she would've loved to hear how my real mother didn't love me, how she'd thrown me away like an old bag of clothes, but I refused to give her the satisfaction. Penny would say, "She actually *dumped* you like garbage? Wow, glad I'm not you."

Heck, I wished I wasn't me, but Penny didn't need to know that either. No one did. So to make myself feel better, I made up the story about my mother being murdered—anything sounded better than rejection—and she bought it.

Unfortunately, Penny Parker had a big mouth.

"Why on earth would you tell Mrs. Parker's daughter that your birthmother was murdered?" my mother asked the very next morning. Although she'd waited until she'd sung me Happy Birthday and lit the candle on my birthday muffin, her question turned my wish into one for Penny Big Mouth's murder.

"Good Lord, So-So," she said, using the moniker I'd been given years earlier by a relative who'd curiously decided 'Sophie' was too difficult to say, yet hadn't considered its possible long-term affects on my self-esteem. "Making up a story about your birthmother being murdered? That's just wrong. Reminds me of the nonsense folks made up back in the fifties. Girls suddenly sent off to live with relatives, parents hoping no one would be the wiser when their daughter reappeared nine months later, everyone acting like nothing happened. You know my dear friend Linda? She reached adulthood before her parents even told her she'd been adopted."

Sixteen years old and my birthday celebration reduced to a lecture and a muffin.

"Things have changed in the last twenty years, So-So. Putting babies up for adoption is an act of love. If you aren't comfortable telling people the truth then tell them it's none of their business, but don't just make up stories. Especially not awful ones."

A long silence followed, leading me to believe she might've finally exhausted her subject matter.

"Do you suppose she ever thinks of me?" I asked.

"Does *who* ever think of you, dear?" She tilted her head to view me above the eyeglasses perched upon her nose and which had come precariously close to falling into her sink of sudsy water. "And stop playing with your food. You're making a mess all over my floor."

"My birthmother." I swept the remaining muffin crumbs off the table and onto the floor when she looked the other way.

"No matter how many times you ask, my answer isn't going to change. I don't know."

"Come on. Isn't it normal for me to wonder about something like this–especially on my birthday?"

"Yes, of course it is. It just seems that you've been asking for as long as I can remember–and not just on birthdays, either." She tossed the towel she'd been using to dry the dishes on the counter and faced me. "I don't want to seem heartless, but I can't change the facts. I don't *know* the answer." She removed her glasses and held them up to the light. Once satisfied her view was unimpeded–acknowledged with an imperceptible nod of her head–she put them back on. "Enough now. Go get ready for work. Seeing as this was the only job you could get, you better not start off being late."

Lie number two I'd told in as many days. The nursing home wasn't the *only* place I could get a job. It was the only place I'd *applied*. Assuming the residents were unloved toss-aways like me, I figured we'd have something in common. This idea—spawned by the anniversary of my birthmother's choice—made near perfect sense, but my mother didn't need to know as much, seeing as she'd just busted me for one lie.

Instead, I left the story intact and dressed for work. The required shapeless polyester uniform, paired with the white rubber-soled shoes, looked ridiculous and only added to my already-sour mood.

Happy birthday to me.

THE SECRET MISS RABBIT KEPT

CHAPTER 2

With only ten minutes to spare before my first shift began, I pulled into the parking lot of Sterlingwood Manor Nursing and Rehabilitation Center. One of the prettiest structures in town, it had been built on an oversized parcel of land and fashioned after an old southern plantation with two-story-high columns and a sweeping porch. Its large windows, adorned with hints of lace curtains, took their places between stately, tall black shutters. An expansive lawn, dotted with River Birch trees, and rose bushes proffering shades of crimson, peach, and the palest of yellows, surrounded the building. This bucolic scene, offering an inviting welcome at the end of a long driveway, only added to the illusion of an ideal place to live. Had it not been for the sign out front, one would have never guessed the city's elderly came there to die.

Inside the lobby, a middle-aged African American woman approached me. Built like an army tank and possessing skin the color of midnight, her physical presence not only shrunk the room, but also caused me to take a backward step when she wrapped a strong, intimidating arm around me.

"Hello, child! Nice to meet you. You sure be a sight for sore eyes."

She introduced herself as Emma Jean Baker, Head Nurse's Aide, stringing all the syllables together as if one word, and explained she would be in charge of my training. Showing me where to stow my things and how to punch the time clock, she grabbed a pile of sheets from a nearby laundry cart and started down one of the hallways. "C'mon now. These people ain't getting *themselves* up today."

With no time for anxiety to fester, I could only try to keep pace with her and the massive amounts of information she shared over the course of the next couple hours. We performed duties I hadn't imagined were necessary or possible. She spewed facts—names, room numbers, medical conditions, habits, and schedules—as we moved what felt like hundreds of bodies in and out of wheelchairs and beds. Changing bandages and linens, we logged liquid intake and urine output for people whose entire lives were tattooed on their bodies by scars, wrinkles, and folds. The words 'incontinent' and 'dementia' were repeated more times than I could count.

Much of what she said went in one ear and out the other, but just when some of the chores began resembling a routine of sorts, she led me to a room at the end of one of the halls, opened the door, and announced that she wanted to introduce me to a special lady.

A tiny woman sat in the bed, her lower half covered by a quilt. Slightly graying hair left in its naturally curly state framed a heart-shaped face. Her nearly translucent skin resembled a shade of black the opposite of Emma Jean's—like coffee brewed without enough grounds. Round wire-rimmed spectacles befitting a scholar sat on the end of her nose. Her lips moving silently, she studied a Bible opened on her lap, and never looked at us.

"Good morning, Miss Rabbit. How you doing today, hon? This here be my new helper Sophie."

Emma Jean's booming voice startled the woman, but she proceeded to give me the once-over with espresso-colored eyes nearly swallowed up by lids long ago grown heavy from age. She studied me a long time before returning her focus to Emma Jean.

"Miss Rabbit here doesn't much like to talk," Emma Jean explained. "She understands plenty, though. Don't you, Miss Rabbit?"

The woman remained silent.

"For some darn reason, Miss Rabbit here decided she just ain't got nothing good to say. Ain't that right, Miss Rabbit?"

"Hello, Mrs. Rabbit." I used the incorrect title on purpose. "Nice to meet you."

She took my hand and turned it palm side up. Tracing the lines there with one long, knobby finger, her tattered nail scratched its way across my skin. Mysterious task complete, she squeezed and let go. Her eyes met mine and she smiled for the first time in my presence.

"Well, lookie there," Emma Jean said. "Seems you got yourself a new friend."

Uncertain to which of us she referred, I smiled at a still-silent Miss Rabbit.

"Okay, hon, let's get you up and ready for the day." Emma Jean led Miss Rabbit through dressing then settled her into a wheelchair. We pushed her into the dining room where, as Emma Jean explained, Miss Rabbit liked to look out over the grounds until breakfast was served. She never asked for a thing or complained, which seemed unusual based on what I had seen from others.

Once we left her and reached an adequate distance, my curiosity got the best of me. "What's her story? How come she never talks?"

"Beats me. She just don't. Been here four years, too."

"Is she able to talk?"

"According to her chart, yes. Just chooses not to. Nice change, though, after all the yelping souls here."

"But how can she never talk? That's impossible."

"I reckon she just don't feel the need."

I thought of the times I'd been mad, particularly at my mother, swearing I'd never speak to her again. Those silences never lasted more than twenty minutes. How could anyone not talk? It wasn't normal. There had to be a better explanation.

"Hurry up," a heavy-set woman in a wheelchair hollered from a few doors down. "I gotta pee!"

"Hold on, Gertrude. We're coming," Emma Jean said, and gestured to me. "This here is Sophie. Sophie, meet Gertrude Steiner. You're going to help her onto the commode this time."

We had transferred people onto the portable toilets all morning. Believing I could now master this task, I followed them into the room.

Emma Jean stood at a distance, reminding me to loop my gait belt around Mrs. Steiner's waist in case she lost her balance. The only other instruction consisted of Mrs. Steiner's repeated requests for me to hurry.

My feet between Mrs. Steiner's legs, I grabbed her belted waist so she could stand and pivot—a task complicated by her substantial weight. Milliseconds into the transfer, she shuddered and went limp. As I locked my knees to prevent us both from collapse, her urine cascaded down my legs and over my new white shoes. The gravity of the situation didn't move Emma Jean into action until Mrs. Steiner began choking.

In what would have been a clumsy comedy routine in any other setting, Emma Jean grabbed Mrs. Steiner from the back as I struggled in the front. When our counterproductive efforts collided, all we could do was ease the fall. Mrs. Steiner slid to the floor, unconscious in her own puddle of urine, with half of Emma Jean's body trapped beneath her.

"Go get Scofield," Emma Jean hollered, referring to the on-duty nurse.

Likely having heard the commotion from a nearby room, Scofield appeared in the doorway and knocked me aside in her haste. "What happened?"

Certain I'd created trouble, I let Emma Jean answer while I slinked out of the room.

After a multitude of medical professionals had come and gone, Emma Jean found me still frozen in the hallway. "There you are."

"Did I kill her?"

Emma Jean laughed. "Is that what you thought? Good Lord,

you ain't did nothing wrong. She done had a stroke."

"Then she's alive?"

"No, child. Gertrude's gone." She put a tender arm around me. "It was just her time, though. Nothing you could've—we could've—done different."

I supposed Mrs. Steiner had all kinds of ailments, but she'd been alert and functioning. She'd spoken her last words to me—a stranger. All her years, all her experiences, the sum total of Mrs. Steiner, gone in the time it took her to pee down my leg. I couldn't stop my tears.

Nurse Scofield joined us in the hallway, her expression all business. "Tough thing on your first day. No doubt. Take some time. Punch out and go home. We'll see you—if and when you come back." She walked away before I could respond.

"That be a good idea, child," Emma Jean said. "Your young self probably seen enough for the first day. Go on now. Get your stuff and get on home."

She walked a few feet then turned. "This really what you want to be doing, hon? It's sad work—even on a good day. You might want to think about that some."

My instincts telling me to run, I retrieved the things from my locker and went home.

I arrived to an empty house. The aroma of a meal I'd missed still lingered—a welcome relief after the nursing home stink. I stripped off my uniform and urine-soaked shoes, piled them in a heap on the bathroom floor, and took the hottest shower of my life before crawling into bed hours before my usual time.

I dreamt of zombies with pleading eyes and gnarled fingers. Their pained voices echoed. I ran up and down hills, through crowded streets, and empty alleyways, but they kept pace. Stumbling through my terror, I turned another corner. A hand grasped my shoulder and I startled awake to the sound of my own cry.

My mother, perched on the edge of my bed, caressed my arm. "Bad dream? You were yelling."

I rubbed my eyes and the creatures slithered into the dusk outside my bedroom window.

"It's okay. It was just a dream," she said. "You must be overtired. Get a good night's sleep or you won't be able to get up for work tomorrow."

I could all but see her mother antennae raise at my lack of response.

"What's the matter, So-So?"

I didn't feel like talking, but her need for discussion outranked my need for silence. As the arch of her eyebrow urged me on, I mustered all the drama at my disposal. She'd never let me be a quitter without good cause. "I don't think I can work there anymore. A person died in my arms today–literally in my arms."

Her crinkly-eyed, about-to-cry expression contorted her face. "Oh, that poor woman."

"Poor woman? She *peed* all over my leg."

"Shame on you."

"But Mom, she died!"

"Yes, and you were the very last person to help her, so she wasn't alone. All those people need care for whatever reason. You and your coworkers are likely the only interaction they'll have in any given day. But for the grace of God that woman could've been me, So-So. Wouldn't you hope someone would take care of me instead of just walking away?"

Tempted to point out my birthmother had done the very same thing, I thought better of it. Even I knew it was too soon to bring that subject up again, but in the long silence, my guilty conscience whispered and left me no choice.

"I'll think about it."

The next morning, my freshly washed uniform hung from my bedroom doorknob, patiently awaiting my answer.

CHAPTER 3

I showered and once again dressed in the ridiculous uniform before plodding down to the kitchen. My father, sitting at the table, greeted me with a smile.

"Good morning, Sunshine," he said, glancing at the wall clock. "Well-rested after, what... sixteen hours of sleep?"

"I could sleep sixteen more, too. I feel like I've been run over by a truck."

My mother set a plate of waffles in front of me. "Here you go, So-So. Special just for you because of your hard day yesterday." She turned to my father. "Sure you don't want any, honey? I'd be happy to make you some."

"Thanks, but I've got to get moving. Besides, you know heavy breakfasts on a workday don't suit me. These cornflakes are fine." He put a spoonful into his mouth and spoke while he chewed. "Sophie, did you survive your first day okay?"

"Barely. Did Mom tell you what happened?"

"Yes, I'm sorry to hear that. Must've just been her time." He wiped up milk he'd spilled on the table. "You know, you're going to experience a lot of those kinds of things working there. I don't think you realize what you've gotten yourself into."

My mother set a dish on the counter with a loud clank. "Honey, we've discussed this. Just let So-So eat her breakfast now."

All about not ruffling her feathers, my father gave me a look that said, "We'll talk about this later", and refocused on eating his cornflakes.

"So-So, are you sure you don't want to have a party with your friends this weekend?" my mother said. "I feel bad we didn't get to celebrate yesterday. Sure wasn't much of a birthday." She gestured to a covered dish on the counter. "We saved your cake."

"Thanks, but that's okay. Besides, I'd have to invite Penny and I really don't want to." I still hadn't forgiven her for ratting me out.

"She's a good friend to you. Don't talk that way."

"Some friend."

"So-So, don't blame her for your lies."

My father must have sensed the conversation taking a turn for the worse. He shoved his chair from the table, took his bowl to the sink, bent my mother over in his arms, and planted a big wet kiss on her lips. They stayed locked together for so long I had to look away. When he finally let her go, her cheeks resembled an overripe peach. He winked at me as he headed out the door. "I'm off to work. Enjoy your day, ladies."

His kiss proved to be the perfect distraction. She didn't say another word while I finished my breakfast, then only offered a preoccupied goodbye when I left for work.

At Sterlingwood, Emma Jean and I arrived in the break room at the same time to punch in. Her big grin and slap on my back baffled me. I'd just walked past people mindlessly calling out from their beds, others pacing the hallway oblivious to their own drool, and the stink of the place had already attached itself. How could anyone smile?

"Ha, I win the five bucks," she announced.

"What five bucks?"

"Scofield said we'd never see you again. I win."

Co-workers betting against me? I think not.

Emma Jean punched her time card, waited for me to do the

same, and then gave my arm a squeeze. "Good girl. Now let's go. And get ready to work hard because I been up all damn night loving on my man and I ain't got me a lick of energy."

The blunt admission and devilish laugh left no room for commentary. Like a puppy-in-training, I walked beside her on an invisible leash as she recited more facts about Sterlingwood. I recalled some of the information from the previous day, but a do-over suited me just fine.

"We're in A-Wing today. The wings are A thru D. A has twelve rooms of residents, two to a room, and they need the least help. They mostly mobile and continent—meaning they can hold their business until they get to a toilet. Most still have their wits about them. They just need help with dressing and getting to meals." She paused, as if making sure I could keep up. "You'll learn to appreciate A-Wing; it be our break before we get D-Wing. D has less folks, but they tougher—all bedridden and so confused they don't know if we're their mommas or their maids."

The more she talked, the less I retained. The less I retained, the more her instructions scared me. I kept nodding anyway.

From time to time, in various rooms, she wrote on a pad of paper she pulled from her pocket. If she couldn't keep track of things, how did she expect me to?

"What are you writing?"

"Unusual stuff. Nurses so busy they can't notice everything. Our job be to let them know if something ain't right."

"What was wrong in the last room?"

"Mrs. Finder kept scratching between her legs. Could be infection."

I just thought the woman had an itch. How would I ever know what defined 'unusual'? I made a mental note to carry a big pad of paper in the future.

With most of the residents now on their way to breakfast, Emma Jean announced it was time for break. She dropped her armload of sheets on the nearest chair and headed for the front porch. "Rain or shine, I need the fresh air and change of scenery. You welcome to join me, but do what you want. My butt's going in the sun."

Earlier that morning, she had pulled a resident chart from a carousel in the nurse's station. She'd explained how aides were encouraged to access the charts if they had questions about a resident's history or medical condition. Guessing I could find the secret to Miss Rabbit's silence in her chart, I passed on the fresh air and sunshine.

The nurse's station empty, I located the file and took a seat. According to the records kept, a brother, Emery Rabbit, admitted Mable Rabbit, born May 24, 1900, to Sterlingwood Manor on May 1, 1971. He was listed as her only living, and nearest, relative. A name listed as her sister's had been crossed out. Emery's address, unchanged or updated since Ms. Rabbit's admission, placed him in an Atlanta retirement community a good hour away in the best of traffic.

Admitted after a stroke and broken hip resulting from a fall, Miss Rabbit had been at Sterlingwood for four years. Medical history included a heart murmur, high cholesterol and blood pressure, as well as a prior bout with breast cancer. Follow-up examinations noted her medications were keeping her blood issues in the normal to normal-high range. X-rays indicated her hip had healed as well as could be expected for a woman of her age and condition. Physical therapy, ordered to replace past occupational therapy, had been terminated a couple years prior.

A sentence on the last page caught my eye: Patient continues to be verbally non-communicative. No medical diagnosis for same. Psychiatric consult recommended.

Nothing in the chart indicated Miss Rabbit had ever seen a psychiatrist, but multiple entries by a Nurse Smith, whose chicken scratch I could barely read, indicated she'd spent a great deal of time with Miss Rabbit. By the looks of what I read, unless I'd missed something, Miss Rabbit just didn't want to talk. If she had done so in the last four years, there weren't any notes to prove it.

How could anyone not talk?

My grandfather used to bet me a nickel I couldn't keep quiet for five minutes. I'd take the bet, but within seconds, no less than five hundred topics—all urgent—popped into my head. I never won the nickel, and here, Miss Rabbit had stayed silent for years. How had she managed? More important, why would she? I had to find out.

Break nearly over, I returned Miss Rabbit's chart to its slot and found Emma Jean in one of the hallways, looking remarkably refreshed after her fifteen-minute break.

"C'mon child, let's move. We're behind now. This is our next room and these two ladies never made it to breakfast."

She introduced me to Viola Barnes and Ethel Johnson, both of whom were dressed, though Viola appeared to be having a little trouble with a zipper. Recognizing a task I could handle, I walked over to help.

"Honey, have you seen my son?" Viola asked.

I glanced at Emma Jean for an answer, but Ethel spoke up. "Now, Viola, you know he only comes on Saturdays. Today is Friday."

"But he didn't come last week."

"Well, maybe he'll come tomorrow," Emma Jean said. "You two get on now. You're already late."

Viola shuffled out the doorway, her walker hitting the floor with each slow step. Ethel followed, using her own walker and moving just as slow. Emma Jean and I made their beds, grabbed their laundry, and moved on to the next room where, according to Emma Jean, 'the sisters' lived.

Caroline and Ruby Hathaway shared more than just a family name and a room. Both sported identical pixie haircuts and eyeglasses, as well an oddly shaped mole on one side of their face or the other. I assumed they were twins.

"Good morning, ladies. This our new helper, Sophie." Emma Jean gestured to each woman as she introduced me.

Caroline sat on the edge of her bed, clothes for the day neatly stacked beside her; the covers of her bed pulled up and smoothed out as far as her arm could reach. A wheelchair sat bedside, locked down and ready. "Good morning, dears," she said. "It's so nice to meet you, Sophie." Her pleasant voice seemed all the more lovely once Ruby's booming voice filled the room.

"You sure took your time getting here. My back is killing me from lying in this bed. I need to get up—now. I'm soaking wet and someone needs to change me. I rang and rang. No one came to help, so I had to go."

"Come on, Ruby," Caroline said. "These girls are doing the best they can. A little patience would be nice. Besides I told you not to drink all that soda pop last night before you went to bed. You know it makes you pee."

"You just hush, Caroline. You have no idea what it's like to lay in a wet bed for hours. Mind your own damn business."

"I'm just saying—"

"Shut up. I don't even want to talk to you today."

Caroline frowned and glanced at us.

"Now this ain't no way to start the day." Emma Jean walked to Ruby's bed and gestured for me to help Caroline. "And look here, Ruby, your help light ain't even on. How we supposed to know you needed us?"

We all looked at the call light above Ruby's bed.

"Well, it was on. I turned it on myself. Must've turned it off when I got so disgusted with you all. Just never mind now. Hurry up and change my clothes."

Emma Jean dressed Ruby and helped her out of bed, but Ruby continued to complain. She hated the food. She didn't understand why she even bothered getting up. She couldn't stand all the crazy people. Her back and neck were killing her. She just wanted to die and she deserved better. While Ruby's energy fueled her constant stream of complaints, Caroline put on her socks and shoes, buttoned her housecoat, and combed her own hair.

Once both ladies were seated in their wheelchairs, Caroline waited for Emma Jean to push Ruby out of the room before she followed, as if she knew her place was second to her sister. I stayed behind and changed the sheets on Ruby's barely wet bed, then finished straightening Caroline's. Following Ruby's rants down the hallway, I caught up with Emma Jean.

"Go on to the next room while I get these girls down to breakfast," she said. "Martha Applebee. Nice lady. She'll tell you what she needs. I'll be back in a minute."

Though reluctant to be on my own, I did what she asked.

Martha Applebee sat upright in bed when I entered. "Well, hello dear. It's so nice to see you again."

"Hi, I'm Sophie."

"Of course you are, dear. Come, we need to talk." She motioned for me to sit beside her. "Now, when you see Fred you have to tell him he must remember to feed the cats. I forgot to feed them before I went to bed last night and I fear they must be starving." She glanced at the ceiling, as if mentally checking off her day's list. "And you need to cancel my lunch date with Clarissa. I just don't feel up to it today, dear."

"Clarissa?"

"Yes, dear, you remember. My sister. She called last night."

None of the residents had phones.

"Okay, Mrs. Applebee, will do. How about we get you up for some nice breakfast now?"

"Oh, that sounds just delightful, dear. Where shall we go?"

"Um...how about downstairs?"

She wrinkled her nose. "Well, alright then. If that's what you prefer." Popping out of bed, she began rifling through her closet. "What shall I wear, dear? Is it casual or formal?"

Was this woman serious?

"Mrs. Applebee, I think you should wear whatever makes you happy."

"Then I shall wear something nice." She held up a blouse emblazoned with sequins. When sunlight streaming in through the room's only window hit the beads, a prism of light danced across the far wall. Her eyes lit up and she clasped her hands to her chest. "Oh my, how lovely. A rainbow just for me." Without missing a beat, her mind bounced back to the task at hand. "My new black trousers would look marvelous with this, don't you think?"

"Marvelous, Mrs. Applebee."

Upon my approval of her clothing selection, she stripped off her nightgown. Completely naked, she couldn't have weighed a hundred pounds. Her slender arms and legs hung onto their last vestiges of muscle tone, but her shapeless bottom lay like a pancake. Her chest was marred by decades-old incisions where her breasts had once been. Between the lack of meat on her ribcage, the slender build, and missing parts, she could have easily been mistaken for a young boy. The slight remains of her pubic hair only added to the illusion. Her complete lack of both modesty and embarrassment astonished me.

"Honey, reach up on that top shelf and get me my hat, will you? I can't go to brunch without a hat. What *would* people think?" She shook her head at the mere suggestion.

Dressed and hair combed, she placed the cabbage rose embellished, purple creation on her head. Emma Jean arrived in time to witness the finished product.

"Why, Martha," she said. "Don't you look nice today."

"Yes, dear, my assistant here and I are off to Sunday Brunch. Would you like to join us? I'm sure they would all love to see you again."

Emma Jean winked at me and smiled. "Martha, I need to borrow your assistant for awhile. We have us some other business to tend to. Follow the folks heading down and we'll catch up with you later, okay?"

"Oh, such a pity. This place has such a lovely brunch." Mrs. Applebee straightened her hat, hugged us both, and left the room.

With her out of earshot, I turned to Emma Jean. "Is that unusual enough for the notebook?"

"No, child, that be her normal–crazier than a hoot owl, but always pleasant. Still living her grand life in high society, she be used to wearing fancy clothes and such."

"If she's always so confused why is she in this wing?"

"Some days she better than others, but most the time her mind just likes the past better, I reckon. She ain't no bother to no one and takes good care of herself. Did she ask you to remind Fred to feed the cats?"

"How'd you know?"

"She asks every morning like clockwork. No one's ever seen Fred or the cats, but to Martha they be real as you and me."

"What happened to her breasts?"

"Cancer, but I ain't never heard her complain or talk about them none. Guess them boobies weren't that important in the scheme a things."

Not important in the scheme of things? Mine had taken nearly forever to show up, and I'd stuffed my bra with tissues for months before that. The thought of them cut off made me cringe. No boobs? No, thank you.

Someone yelling in what sounded like Italian interrupted my thoughts.

The Secret Miss Rabbit Kept

CHAPTER 4

Emma Jean and I located the source of the commotion in the hallway. A woman no taller than my shoulder, her face flushed beet red with anger, yelled and gestured at something or someone I couldn't see. Spittle accompanying every word out of her toothless mouth, she directed her cries to a place high on the wall.

"Mama, hush...it's okay," Emma Jean told her.

The woman kept up the rant, slapping her forehead and stamping a foot to annunciate her points. A taller woman, standing inside a doorway further down the hall, shouted. "Yes, yes, yes! No, no, no!"

"What's happening?" I asked.

"This is Mama. Her roommate Polly Stern is the one in the doorway. Mama's real name is Mary, but ain't no one here calls her that. She only speaks Italian, and from the words we've figured out, seems she be cursing a blue streak. Polly only says two words and you just heard them both."

"But who's Mama shouting at? There's no one there."

"There never is, child. She walks up and down the hallway,

hollering 'til it's all out her system, then she'll start up again later. Pretty obvious she be madder than hell about something, but ain't no rhyme or reason."

"But—"

"Don't go trying to figure it out. Most stuff here you have to just let go. Mama just be Mama. She ain't hurting no one and unless you know Italian, the words don't mean nothing."

Mama disappeared around the corner and the same ten-or-so words she repeated echoed off the linoleum floors and bare walls. Polly Stern shouted, "Yes, yes, yes", turned on her heels, and went back inside the room.

"C'mon now," Emma Jean said. "We have to finish up these rooms. It'll be time for these folks' lunch before long."

"Lunch? Some of them are just now having breakfast."

"Yep, but we're behind with you being new and all. You'll get the hang of it. Don't worry."

Feet throbbing and back aching, I had no energy to worry. I could only pray the day would be over soon.

A little before noon, Emma Jean asked me to gather the residents unable to take the stairs and line them up by the elevator for transport to the dining room. "I'll ride down with them. You just keep the peace while I'm gone," she said, wheeling the first four people into the elevator. "It's called crowd control." She laughed as the doors shut.

Sounded simple enough. I headed to the Day Room.

Though quite large, the room held no furniture. Bland yellow paint and pictures of green pastures and calm seas covered the walls. Residents in wheelchairs, parked toe-to-toe or back-to-back wherever space allowed, swallowed up the available floor space.

An evangelist's voice blared from a ceiling-mounted television. "Out of great suffering have come the greatest expressions of gratitude. Rejoice and praise the Lord! My children, can I get an Amen?"

None of the residents answered his call. Most just stared— and from the same spots they'd been left to sit. Like every other aid, I imagined, Emma Jean and I had likely spent no more than ten minutes with any one resident all morning. At this rate, I would never find more time to spend with anyone, much less Miss Rabbit. How would I ever get her talking?

Motivated to move faster, I started with the nearest wheelchair and, one-by-one, lined them up at the elevator. Everyone now gathered in place, I waited for Emma Jean. When the doors opened, I wheeled a woman inside. Emma Jean bent to adjust the footrest on the chair.

"Does a Nurse Smith still work here?" I asked as nonchalantly as I could.

"Yep, do you know her?"

"I didn't recognize her name in one of the patient charts." Guessing my fascination with Miss Rabbit would seem foolish, I left that part out.

"There be loads of folks you haven't met, child. She's off this week. Due back tomorrow, I think." She loaded the last resident the elevator could hold. "She been here a long time. Nice, but she don't take to any silliness. Spent time in the military and don't talk much. Just goes about her business. Mind yourself when you work her shift."

The elevator doors closed.

The noise level around me had grown. Like impatient kindergarteners at recess, every able body budged to the head of the line. Those in wheelchairs shouted at the trespassers. Perhaps propelled by instinct when unable to grasp the turn of events, others fussed. I returned one resident to the line and another shoved them out of the way.

In the midst of the chaos, a man approached from the end of the hallway. With more long gray whiskers on his chin than hair on his head, he resembled my grandfather's old horse left out for winter pasture. Unlike that horse, this man trotted like a three-year-old colt. Dressed in a baggy pair of stained trousers and threadbare t-shirt, he'd have been mistaken for a homeless man if he'd been out in public. The erect penis protruding from the fly of his pants announced his lack of common sense. His palsy-afflicted hand, beating relentlessly on his right leg, punctuated his condition like an exclamation point to an unspoken sentence.

None of the orderlies for the male residents in sight, the problem became mine. Erection Man now a spectacle, the other residents began yelling. One old woman let out a long, loud wolf whistle and dissolved into laughter. The able ones stepped out of line to gawk or escape and the hallway bottlenecked. Wheelchairs collided as more people hollered and fussed. Oblivious to the commotion he'd caused, Erection Man unconsciously used his penis to part the crowd. In the middle of a stampede of sorts, I lost all control.

The ding of the elevator preceded Emma Jean's roar. "Oh good God, Roy! Get that damned snake back inside its cage! Ain't we told you enough times to keep them pants of yours zipped?"

Either deaf or defiant, Roy grabbed Mama as she passed, pinned her against the wall, and began dry-humping her over her housecoat. Now with an actual target for her rage, Mama let loose, and in spite of the language barrier, made it quite clear she wanted no part of Roy's invitation.

Emma Jean shoved or climbed over everything in her way, pulling Roy and his erection off Mama. An orderly arrived and managed to get Roy's fly zipped. Roy trotted off and Mama followed, still hollering and slapping her forehead.

"You get an education here, child. That's for sure," Emma Jean said, trying to regain control of the line.

"No kidding. Did you *see* that thing?"

"Probably going to ruin you for life, too. They just don't make 'em like that very often. I been with a lot of men, child, and I ain't never seen one that big. Seeing as I only been with black men, that be saying a lot."

The 'borrowed' copies of my mother's poorly hidden Cosmopolitan magazines provided all I knew about the supposed size of black men. With no first-hand experience, and having now seen Roy, Emma Jean's statement sounded like good news.

The remainder of the shift passed with relative ease, but punching out for the day still arrived as a relief. Sliding my card in the time clock, I let out a loud sigh.

"Is there a problem?"

I turned. The question had come from a tall, slender woman with hair pulled back in a tight bun. Her lack of makeup revealed skin the color of that which never sees sunlight. Her clothing–tan pants, a plain brown t-shirt, ugly functional shoes, and no jewelry–spoke of a person too busy to bother with style. The outfit offered no clues to her identity or purpose, but the name on the envelope she held suggested a possibility.

"Nurse Smith?"

"Yes?" She gave me the once-over.

"Hi, I'm a new aide here."

"New aide, you have a name?"

"Oh, sorry. I'm Sophie."

"You coming or going?"

"Going. I just punched out."

"Well, go then." She turned on her heel and walked out of the break room.

A flush of heat rose from my belly.

How had Emma Jean described her? Nice enough? I think not.

Hurrying to my father's car I'd driven to work, I took off my shoes and threw them in the back seat. Even outside in the fresh air, I could still smell the old-people odors clinging to my uniform. The day had been a huge improvement over the previous one–no one had died–but the thought of doing this job forty hours a week for the rest of the summer overwhelmed me. Breaking Miss Rabbit's silence might make this work worthwhile, but between nurses betting against my return and a bitchy, rude one who wouldn't give me the time of day, my odds of survival didn't look good.

The question my mother asked the previous night nudged my conscience. *Wouldn't you hope someone would take care of me instead of just walking away?*

Damn it.

Well, I'd show them all *and* I would get Miss Rabbit talking.

Throwing the car into gear, I peeled out of the parking lot. A bunch of blackbirds gathered in the grass scattered in all directions. At least *they* knew enough to get the heck out of my way.

CHAPTER 5

I slammed the back door and stomped into the kitchen. My mother looked up from the table, removed her glasses, and set them on her abandoned crossword puzzle. Ignoring her raised eyebrows, I flung my shoes into a far corner and walked to the refrigerator.

"You want to tell me what's wrong?" she said. "Or should I guess?"

"Nothing."

"So-So..."

"Mom, I'm just in a bad mood, okay? It was a tough day. I'm tired."

"But not too tired to slam the door or throw your shoes?"

I filled a glass with sweet tea and guzzled it. What missed my mouth trickled down the front of my uniform and joined the other spots and stains already there. My mother's eyes bored holes into my backside as I wiped my mouth with the back of my hand and set the empty glass in the sink. She obviously wanted an answer and I was out of tea.

"Sorry I slammed the door." I refused to apologize for throwing my shoes. As bad as they stunk, she'd have thrown them, too.

"You don't have to apologize, but at least tell me what's wrong." Her voice oozed sweetness, which irritated me even more.

"I just had a crummy day, okay? Why can't you just let it be?"

"I'm your mother is why. If something is troubling you maybe I can help."

"You can't help with this. The woman is just a bitch and— "

"Watch your mouth, young lady. I won't have that kind of language used in this house."

I had to acknowledge her admonishment before she'd continue.

"Now, who are you talking about?"

"This nurse at the home. She doesn't even know me and she was a bitc— She was rude to me for no reason."

"She doesn't know you? Then I'd have to guess that you don't know her either."

"No, I never met her before today."

"Then you don't know why she did what she did. If you didn't give her any cause to be mean, then it must be something else. Don't be so quick to judge others, So-So. People don't always do things for the reasons you think. Like they say, 'Don't judge a man until you've walked a mile—"

"Mom, stop." I wasn't ready for another one of the Wise Old Man quotes she habitually dispensed. "You don't even know her."

"And my point is neither do you. Give her another chance."

My father once described my mother as a woman who'd give the devil the benefit of the doubt. I could see why. Her quick-to-forgive attitude drove us both crazy. People would cut her off or speed past her in traffic and she'd say they must have needed to get there faster than she did. A few months prior, when someone had stolen our newspaper from the driveway for an entire week, she explained it away with their not being able to afford their own; they obviously needed the paper more than we did. In her mind, everyone–including my birth mother–had a good reason for everything.

No point in arguing, I left the kitchen. Climbing the stairs to my room, I glanced back as she walked to the sink, no doubt to wash the dirty glass I'd left on purpose. I'm sure she thought I'd had good reason.

"Oh, So-So?"

I paused on the step. "What?"

"I almost forgot. Penny called again while you were at work. She wants you to call her."

I hadn't spoken to Penny since I'd told her the story about my birthmother being murdered. I assumed, since our mothers talked to each other all the time, she knew the truth, but I wasn't sure. I'd been avoiding her calls.

I grabbed the phone from the table in the upstairs hallway, pulled it into my room and, stretching the cord as far as it would go, shut the door. Penny picked up after the first ring.

"Well," she said. "You finally decided to call me back. I've only called about a gazillion and ten times."

"Sorry, I've been busy. I started my new job, you know."

"God, I can't believe you took a job in an old people's home. Are you crazy? Yuck, that'd make me puke for sure."

"It's not so bad." I refused to let her think she knew everything. "Some of the people are actually kind of funny."

"You are so weird. And, by the way, thanks for lying to me. Your real mom wasn't murdered. You made up that whole story. I can't believe I actually believed you."

"Well, maybe she should've been murdered."

"Yeah, my mom made me promise not to say anything, but I know your real mother just dumped you. All I can say is wow."

I took a deep breath while she blew a bubble with her gum. A loud pop assaulted my ear.

"I mean, don't you wonder what she was thinking, just leaving you like that? Makes you wonder what kind of freak she was, doesn't it? Don't people in the south know any better?"

A couple months prior, Penny's family had moved from California into a house down the street. Our mothers became fast friends. We didn't go to the same high school–her parents electing, of course, to send her to a fancy private one. We shared none of the same interests, but that mattered little to our mothers. They had forced us onto each another in hopes we'd be new best friends just like them.

Pigs would have to fly first.

From the moment we met, Penny made it clear that being from Los Angeles made her smarter and better. Only hicks lived in the south and they didn't know from nothing. If not for our mothers, I'd have never spoken to Penny and, right then, I wished I never had. "I'm sure she had her reasons. I have to get off the phone now."

"But I wanted you to come over and listen to the new Elton John record I bought." She snapped her gum again. "You *have* heard of Elton John, haven't you?"

"Yes, Penny." I could have choked her. "Thanks, but I'm too tired. I just want to stay home now."

"But I called all my other friends. It's Friday night and you're the only one around."

"Sorry." Not the least bit sorry, I hung up.

The next morning, Mrs. Kowalski greeted me as I walked into the nursing home. "Piece of bread and a cold potato. Please. Come on, I'm hungry. Just a piece of bread and a cold potato. Come on, I'm hungry."

She had begged me for food multiple times the previous day. At first, I thought she hadn't gotten enough to eat, then I'd watched her eat lunch and, not twenty minutes later, she had begun chanting again for food. Emma Jean's theory involved a life of poverty and a never forgotten hunger.

I handed Mrs. Kowalski one of the pieces of candy I kept in my pocket. She stuffed the butterscotch into her mouth. "Piece of bread and a cold potato. Please. Come on, I'm hungry. Just a piece of bread and a cold potato. Come on, I'm hungry." Her words slurring around the candy, she continued to ask for food as I headed in another direction.

I had arrived early to prepare for D-wing—the toughest one according to Emma Jean. Having already experienced what I considered 'tough', I guessed this wing had the potential to kill. When Emma Jean explained we'd only be assigned eight single rooms instead of twelve doubles, the difference scared me. What could only eight people require that would fill an entire shift? I'd fretted all night, staying in my bedroom instead of watching television with my parents, and I'd barely slept. My silence during breakfast had only served to deepen my mother's worry lines.

Emma Jean stood outside our first room, her trademark smile absent. "Okay, child, don't say I didn't warn you. If you make it through today, you just might survive."

My gut reeled.

"This here room belongs to Mr. Monsanto. He got hisself a bad case of throat cancer. Only the good Lord knows why he ain't in some hospital where he should be."

She opened Mr. Monsanto's door and The Odor wafted out. Struck by a solid wall of the foulest air imaginable, I imagined a rotting corpse. Something horrible waited on the other side, and Emma Jean's words hadn't prepared me.

"Oh my God..."

"I know, child. Takes a bit of getting used to."

I pulled up my uniform to cover my nose and breathed through my mouth for the first few minutes. The stench attached itself to my skin.

"Let's get this done." She gestured me to the opposite side of the bed.

Mr. Monsanto lay on his back, eyes shut and lashes caked with a crusty discharge. His face, frozen in a grimace, sported random patches of stubble. The remaining strands of his white hair, greasy from neglect, lay plastered to the sides of his head. A feeding tube protruded from the center of his swollen and scarred neck. A yellow-tinged slime oozed from its edges.

We rubbed him with lotion, but his skin, the color of ash, remained cold to the touch. If it hadn't been for his breath–short staccato gasps that caused his chest to rise and fall–I'd have thought his heart had stopped. Even in his semi-conscious state, though we were as gentle as we could be when we turned and cleaned him, he moaned in pain.

The scene reminded me of a dog I'd had as a little girl. A very playful thing on a normal day, she had begun throwing up all the time. One night, I went to bed with her at my side, woke up the next morning, and she was gone. My parents told me she had been put to sleep so she wouldn't suffer.

Could her suffering been worse than *this*?

We finished cleaning Mr. Monsanto as best we could. Emma Jean grabbed the pile of dirty linens and motioned for me to follow. Outside the room, she stopped, took a deep breath, and closed her eyes. "I tell you, that there hurts my heart."

My throat closed up like someone had put a noose around my neck.

"You okay, child? You's looking a little pale." A second passed and she chuckled. "I mean, paler than normal."

Not in the mood for her white girl jokes, I headed for an exit in search of fresh air.

"Good idea," she called after me. "Get some air. I'll be in the next room."

For the second time in three days, I wanted to run away.

Outside on the porch, I collapsed onto one of the benches. Its splintered wood bit through my pant leg, leaving a sliver in my thigh. "Damn it."

"Now, is that any way for a young'un to talk?"

The voice startled me. I hadn't noticed the old man sitting in one of the chairs. His face unfamiliar, he wore a rumpled, faded suit coat and sported a hat just like the kind my grandfather wore. Gramps always made me laugh when he had called the hat his pork pie.

"Sorry, sir. I thought I was alone." My mother would've killed me for cursing.

"Ah, you ain't never alone in a place like this. I come out here to get some quiet, but the commotion always follows me."

"Do you live here? I'm Sophie."

"Live? Is that what you call it? Ain't really living tho, is it now?" He studied my face. "Ah, you're too young to know of such things."

Unsure of how to respond, I focused on the sliver lodged in my pant leg.

"A girl young as you ought to be somewhere else. Seeing all

this day in and day out sure to wear on you some. You got folks?"

"Excuse me?"

"Your mama and paw. They want you working here?" He removed his hat and scratched his balding head.

"They didn't stop me, if that's what you mean."

"Well, if nothing else, I reckon you get yourself an education here."

Emma Jean had said the same thing after the incident with Roy and his erection. Did all black people think the same way?

"Yes, sir. I'm definitely getting an education."

"If'n you learn just one thing, Miss Sophie, learn this: Don't get old. It ain't nearly all it's cracked up to be." He shook his head, mumbling something, and pulled a handkerchief from his pants' pocket.

The sliver removed and nothing more to distract me, I was unsure of what else to say. He had replaced his hankie and leaned back in his chair, appearing to be lost in his own thoughts. Manners prevented me from saying nothing.

"Nice talking to you."

When he didn't answer or look my way, I went back inside. Halfway down the hall, I realized the man had never told me his name.

THE SECRET MISS RABBIT KEPT

CHAPTER 6

In our next room, Emma Jean arranged bottles and medical supplies on a table. A woman lay motionless in the bed, on her side, with eyes closed. The mattress underneath her, swooshing as air automatically pumped and released, sounded like someone gasping.

"I just spoke to a black guy out on the porch and didn't catch his name. Do you know who he is?"

"Only black men I know wouldn't set foot in this place," Emma Jean said.

"Hmm, must have been a visitor then. Could've sworn he lived here."

"Smith—the nurse you asked me about—is back at work today. She's coming to help us with her." Emma Jean gestured to the woman in the bed.

"Why? What are we doing?"

"This is Mrs. Riggler. Brought here to heal after surgery to fix her broken hip. Thanks to some of our staff, she got herself a bedsore now."

"A bedsore?"

"Ulcer. Comes from lying in one spot too long. Skin gets no

blood and dies. Just like they say: if you don't move it, you lose it."

Smith breezed into the room. "Okay, let's do this."

Speaking directly to Emma Jean, she must have felt our introduction the previous day had been sufficient. Pulling the table closer, she re-organized the items Emma Jean had placed there then motioned for me to get on the opposite side of the bed.

All of us positioned, she spoke as if reading from a textbook. "The treatment for a decubitus ulcer involves keeping the area clean and removing necrotic—or dead—tissue," she said, pulling back the sheets. "This is a breeding ground for infection. Therefore, we use antibiotics as part of the treatment. Additionally, because the ulcer is so deep, debriding the necrotic tissue is necessary."

Afraid of sounding like I'd walked into the wrong classroom, I didn't ask what debriding meant.

"These pillows tucked under Mrs. Riggler stop her from rolling. The ones wedged between her knees and ankles are prevention measures to keep the bones from pressing against each other for too long."

The lifted hospital gown revealed a large, stained gauze pad covering the woman from waist to thigh. When Smith peeled off the pad and the full smell of decaying flesh hit me, I had to avert my eyes and take deep breaths.

Emma Jean looked at me sideways. "You okay, child?"

"Leave the room if you're going to be sick," Smith said, tossing the soaked pads onto plastic sheets Emma Jean had laid out on the floor.

I bit my lip, hoping the pain would distract me.

Mrs. Riggler's buttocks resembled a hollowed out melon—only if one overlooked the black tissue and mucus. At the sight of what must have been bone, I refocused my breathing. My knees began to shake.

Neither Smith nor Emma Jean spoke as Smith started the debridement. Gesturing for this or that, Smith snipped away at the inside of the wound and poured in the hydrogen peroxide, which fizzed and bubbled like carbonated soda. Soundless up until then, Mrs. Riggler moaned.

Emma Jean stroked the woman's matted hair. "It's okay, hon. We almost done."

The peroxide's bubbles slowing, Smith stuffed handfuls of cotton pads back inside the wound and taped on a fresh pad. "Clean her up and reposition her," she said, bending to help Emma Jean pick up the discarded waste. "And you," she pointed at me, "Go get some air. You look like you're about to topple over." She gathered the trash and left the room.

"Wait. Before you go," Emma Jean said. "We need to sponge her down, lotion her up, and put her in a new gown."

I steadied my knees and we finished our work.

Emma Jean touched Mrs. Riggler's limp hand. "Okay, you're all set now, hon. You can finally get yourself some rest."

As if cued, the mattress refilled with air.

"You know, she shouldn't be like that," Emma Jean said once we left the room. "Those lazy-ass night shift folks are to blame for this. Never moving her, never tending to her backside–a damn crime, I tell you. Well, I say good riddance."

I struggled to keep pace with her angry footsteps. "Good riddance?"

"Smith had them fired, every last one of them. Should've had them arrested, but don't know if'n that would've worked. And to think, that poor woman could've been out of here once her hip healed. Now it looks like she ain't never going to leave–least on her own two feet. All cuz some folks don't got the good sense God gave them. I tell ya, just makes me want to spit." She slammed the door to the supply room. Several people in the area turned and stared.

"I've never seen anything like that bedsore," I said.

"And, pray to God, you never will again, child. That be a sin, what you just saw. A *mortal* sin." She rubbed her eyes, as if trying to erase the image. "Now, go get some air. I'll be in the next room. There's a new patient coming in."

At this rate, I'd be taking a break every half hour.

"Go on now, child. This'll get easier."

I doubted her, but went out to the porch anyway. All the chairs sat empty.

When I returned and Emma Jean wasn't in the next room, I finished making the half-made bed. At the sound of her voice in the hallway, I stepped out of the room. Standing with the admissions director and two other people, she waved for me to join them.

The director leaned over to me. "I'm sorry, I've forgotten your name."

"Sophie."

"Sophie, this is Cynthia Messina and her husband."

The woman in the wheelchair had to be younger than my mother. Her unblemished skin, stretched tight over high cheekbones, lay as unwrinkled as the sheet I'd just used to make the bed. Her blond hair matched mine. With unfocused eyes, she twitched and mewed like a newborn kitten. She had to be the new resident, but her starched, buttoned-down blouse, tailored jacket, and pleated skirt implied otherwise.

Mr. Messina's bad comb-over, and clothing which may have recently doubled as pajamas, spoke of a man who didn't have time for himself. His eyes, the same shade as his wife's, looked like they'd been open for days, but they held a certain warmth.

"Hello, dear. It's nice to meet you. Isn't it nice to meet these girls, Cynthia? Yes, we are glad to meet you, Sophie and Emma Jean."

As near as I could tell, Cynthia couldn't communicate, so every sentence Mr. Messina spoke arrived in duplicate. After several minutes of this, the admissions director politely excused herself. Emma Jean's patience faded soon thereafter.

"If you won't be needing our help with anything, Mr. Messina, we'll be on our way," she said.

"Oh no, we're fine. Aren't we, Cynthia? We don't need a thing. Do we, Cynthia?"

Cynthia continued her mewing as we headed down the hallway.

"Why is she going into D-wing?" I asked. "She doesn't look sick."

"Only bed we got. They tell me Mr. Messina be taking full responsibility for her care. We just have to bathe her. From what I see, that's enough."

At the nurse's station, Emma Jean stepped in front of one of the other aides and grabbed Cynthia's chart. Scanning the contents, she read aloud. "Stroke. Brain damage. Says here she only fifty-three."

Fifty-three sounded too young.

"How old do you think her husband is?" the other aide asked.

"I'd say he be getting a hell of a lot older by the minute," Emma Jean said, studying the chart a moment longer. "Aw shit, child, let's go back, make sure they getting settled okay."

Mr. Messina's singsong voice drifted out of the doorway as we approached. "You'll be just fine here, won't you, Cynthia? Yes. I think you will. I'll unpack your things and then how about we take a nice walk around the property? Would you like that, Cynthia honey? Yes? Okay, let's do that then." He turned and addressed us. "We've decided to go out for a little walk after we unpack. Isn't that right, Cynthia?"

I imagined he'd gotten accustomed to the solitary banter at some point, but I hoped Cynthia might answer him this time.

"Would you like these nice girls to show us around? Hmm? Oh yes, you're right, dear. They probably have plenty of others who need their help. Right again, darling. Okay then, we'll just finish up here and be on our way."

Emma Jean joined the game. "Well, you folks enjoy your walk and we'll see you at lunch in about an hour or so. Cynthia, do you remember where the dining room is?"

"Of course she does. Don't you, Cynthia? Yes, we're fine for now, but thank you. We'll see you ladies later at lunch."

Leaving them to their conversation, we backed out of the room. Halfway down the hall, when Emma Jean failed to note the obvious, I spoke up. "Wow, that's sad."

"There's a lesson to be learned there, child. His glass be half-full."

The night before, my parents had an argument about my job choice. I'd already gone upstairs, but I could hear them in the living room.

"I don't like it," my father had said.

"I don't like it any more than you do, but we agreed to let So-So make the decision. That's why I interrupted you during breakfast. She's been so negative lately. This job might make her realize her life isn't so bad after all. You know she told Penny Parker the reason she's adopted is because her birthmother was *murdered*?"

"I don't see how being around dying people will cheer her up any."

"She might start seeing the glass as half-full for a change. I mean, there are far worse things than having to tell people you're adopted, for heaven's sake."

When my father didn't comment I pictured him with his face buried in his newspaper, more interested in what President Ford was doing for the economy than in any lie I'd told Penny Parker. I could hardly blame him. Mr. Messina wouldn't have been interested either. Nearly losing a wife probably changes one's priorities. His worries made mine seem pretty stupid.

"Lady, piece of bread and cold potato?" Mrs. Kowalski said, now in front of Mama and refusing to let her pass. "Come on, I'm hungry. Just a piece of bread and a cold potato, please."

Mama raised her arms and shouted at the ceiling, as if pleading for intervention from a higher power. Not easily put off, Mrs. Kowalski stayed put and asked again, though louder this time.

When Mama slapped her forehead and stomped off in the other direction, I guessed that my glass wasn't the only one sitting half-empty.

CHAPTER 7

The next two rooms Emma Jean and I worked weren't as difficult–not like Mrs. Riggler's bedsore, or even Mr. Monsanto's throat cancer, whose stench still clung to my uniform like glue. A stroke victim and another in a coma made little impression. Had I already become numb to the sights and smells, which had earlier repulsed me? Or was I just in shock?

By ten o'clock, I'd taken so many 'catch my breath' breaks that I didn't feel a need for our scheduled one. While Emma Jean set her butt in the sun, I visited Miss Rabbit, whom I found in her room, contemplating something beyond the window.

"Good morning, Mrs. Rabbit. Remember me? I'm Sophie. I met you the other day."

She looked at me, but didn't say a word.

"Beautiful day outside. Weatherman says it's going to be a warm one."

She pointed to the bathroom.

"Need to go?"

She nodded and I wheeled her to the toilet.

Grabbing the wall-mounted bar with her one able hand, she steadied herself upright on her one good leg. Small breaths of exertion accompanied each effort and one wobbly pivot later, she landed on the toilet. I stepped out to give her some privacy.

Not long after, the toilet flushed. She used her good leg to push herself out of the bathroom.

"I'm impressed, Mrs. Rabbit. You sure can get around."

She scooted to her dresser and pulled out a pen and pad of paper stored underneath some folded clothes. Scrawling words on the paper, she furiously underlined one and held the note up in front of my face. Emma Jean hadn't mentioned Miss Rabbit communicated this way. Could we be making progress?

"*Miss* Rabbit," I read aloud. "Ha, I hoped you'd correct me sooner or later. I got you to say something, though, even if it was only on paper, didn't I?"

She threw the pen and paper on the floor, motioned me out of her way, and wheeled out of the room.

I caught up and walked beside her until we reached the large bay window in the dining room, then lowered my voice so none of the others in the room would hear. "I didn't do it to make you mad."

Her eyes met mine before she dismissed me with her good hand. Determined to make things right, I sat down next to her.

"You finally write a note, but you still won't speak. I've read your chart, so I know you can talk."

She pursed her lips and raised an eyebrow, as if to say "Why should I care?"

"I like to learn about people, Miss Rabbit, and I'm a talker, so I can't believe you have nothing whatsoever to say."

Her gaze focused outside, beyond the panes of glass. With her paralyzed hand lying limp atop the knitted afghan on her lap, her good hand worked loose one of its threads.

"Isn't it awfully lonely inside that head of yours, day after day, with no one else to share your thoughts? If you talk to me, it can be our little secret if you want. You don't have to speak to another soul as long as you live, but will you please talk to me?"

Her jaw muscles knotted. Like Mama, she could have been silently cussing a blue streak.

A shout from somewhere down the hallway turned our heads.

I left Miss Rabbit and hustled in the direction of the noise, winding up a few paces behind Emma Jean. We found Polly Stern, pinned up against the wall by another one of Roy's erections.

"Yes! Yes! Yes!"

Seemingly encouraged by her limited vocabulary, Roy pushed harder, and the harder he pushed, the louder she yelled.

Emma Jean grabbed Roy, I grabbed Polly, and we pulled them apart.

"No, no, no!"

Emma Jean laughed so hard she ran off to the bathroom with her hand between her legs like a toddler about to wet her pants. I waited outside the door until she rejoined me.

Wiping the smeared mascara from under her eyes, she shook her head. "Child, these people just tickle me. My old lady bladder can't take it. I swear, if anyone doubts the good Lord has a sense of humor, they ain't *never* worked in a place like this."

Although I had ample opportunity, I didn't tell Emma Jean about Miss Rabbit's note—not then or at any point the rest of the morning. Something about the gesture struck me as private, like the note should be our little secret. What might have been a waste of time felt like progress, so when the residents' lunch period ended, I went to spend my break with Miss Rabbit. A little quiet sounded good.

"Yes, I'm coming back to bother you, Miss Rabbit," I said, shutting the door to her room. She shook her head in what I guessed to be disgust, but I sat down anyway. "I've been thinking. It wasn't right to make you so mad and I'm sorry. Now I realize I've been going about this all wrong. Why *would* you want to talk to a stranger? You wouldn't, right? So the way I figure, you have to get to know me better. That makes sense, doesn't it?"

Her expression didn't change.

"Okay, let's see. Where should I start? Born here in Georgia, I've never lived anywhere else my entire life. Never traveled west of the Mississippi, never even been on an airplane. I'm an only child and I'm sixteen."

Miss Rabbit set her Bible on the bedside table.

"This is my first job. I took it because...well, I just figured I'd have a lot in common with the people here." I knew enough not to share my 'toss-aways' theory. "I thought a medical career might not be so bad, but I have to tell you, I've sure seen a lot of terrible stuff."

She offered an encouraging nod.

"No offense intended, but some of these people are real challenges. It's just so sad. Until I worked here, I had no idea what a nursing home was like. I don't know where I thought old people went, but this is all new to me. And you know, Miss Rabbit, I hear some of these people never have visitors—*ever*." I caught my slip too late. "Gosh, I'm sorry. Maybe you never have visitors."

She didn't flinch or frown or act like my words hurt in any way, but I wanted to kick myself for being so thoughtless.

Another subject came to mind. The intimate detail might draw her out.

"You know what else about me, Miss Rabbit? I'm adopted. I don't tell too many people that, either. Not often you meet someone who's adopted, I bet."

Her fingers worrying the thread of the afghan, she once again fixed her gaze outside the window.

"Yep, adopted as a baby. I know nothing about my real mom or dad." I leaned in and lowered my voice. "And you know what? They left me on the steps of a church."

Knowing she wouldn't repeat what I confided gave me confidence. The story, just like my adoptive parents had told it to me, rushed out in one long, uninterrupted stream. "A priest at Our Lady of Perpetual Help Church heard a baby's cries. He found a basket with me inside, and a note pinned to my blanket. The words were addressed to God and asked for forgiveness. Isn't that something, Miss Rabbit? What kind of parent just leaves their baby on church steps?

"When my parents told me this story, I stayed angry for a long time. Parts of me are still mad if you want to know. Just the other day, I even told a friend of mine I'd been adopted because my real mother was murdered. Can you believe it?" My pulse sped. "I mean, murder only makes sense, doesn't it? What kind of monster just leaves their baby?"

I'd asked that question a million times and the answer still eluded me.

"Now, don't get me wrong. I love my parents and they love me, so it's not like I wound up in a bad deal or anything. I just sometimes wonder what my real parents were thinking. I mean, wasn't I worth anything?"

Miss Rabbit's eyes filled with tears.

"Oh geez, I didn't mean to make you cry."

Offering a handful of tissues from the dresser, I waited until she wiped her eyes and blew her nose. Focusing on anything but her, I spotted a nest of baby birds on a limb outside. I nudged Miss Rabbit and pointed.

The mother bird had just returned, her beak full of nourishment for her small brood whose shrill peeps penetrated the glass. With mouths wide-open and undeveloped wings flapping, they strained to get the handouts. Once relieved of her load, the mother left. The babies' little heads, barely visible above the edge of the nest, hunkered and huddled together.

Miss Rabbit's smile gave me an idea. "Would you like to go outside? The fresh air might feel good."

She blew her nose again and nodded.

The summer breeze carried a child's giggle and the aroma of newly mowed grass. As we traveled down the sidewalk, Miss Rabbit patted my hand. Although I still had no explanation for her tears, I sensed the change of scenery had made her feel better.

The circle of the grounds completed, I brought her back inside. Emma Jean met us at the doorway.

"Well, Lordy, what is the special occasion that got you outside, Miss Rabbit?"

"I just thought she'd enjoy it." I prayed Emma Jean couldn't tell Miss Rabbit had been crying.

"Hmm...how nice. Well, come on now, child. Smith wants us at the nurse's station."

With a quick kiss to the top of Miss Rabbit's head, I left her by the window to watch for the mother bird.

At the nurse's station, Smith began without so much as a hello. "Mrs. Kramer hasn't had a B.M. all week and the laxatives aren't working."

Up until a few days prior, I not only had little idea what B.M. meant, but had never once considered its importance. Since I'd stepped foot in the place, bowel movements seemed to be all people ever discussed.

"That woman has shitting problems the likes of which I ain't never seen," Emma Jean said. She took a sip of the soda she carried everywhere and turned to me. "Mrs. Kramer. Remember her?"

Smith looked at me and my brain froze. Many of the residents' names hadn't yet begun to register. In most cases, I still thought in terms of labels: the lady with no hair or that woman with diarrhea. I shook my head.

"Wheelchair? Stroke victim?" Emma Jean said. "We put that yellow housecoat on her and she yelled at me when I transferred her."

The yelling I remembered. Ethel Kramer had fought with us when we tried to move her.

"No B.M. in a week–that's why she be hollering. Didn't you see her blowed up stomach? She *really* be full of shit."

My brain knew 'fat' and 'pregnant'. I hadn't considered shit.

"Eww..."

Smith leveled her glare at me. "I'll make sure I call you in to help."

After she'd gone, I turned to Emma Jean. "Why does she hate me so much?"

Emma Jean took a big slug of her soda then unsuccessfully tried to stifle a belch. "Oh, don't mind her. She just don't take to any foolishness. She's used to the young ones up and quitting all the time. You white folks worry too much anyway."

"You white folks?"

"Yeah, none of you can just let things be. Like Miss Rabbit. You ain't fooling me, child."

"What do you mean?"

"Just thought she'd enjoy the walk? Didn't happen to be because you think you can get her to talk, did it? You have to get all up in her face, worrying something's wrong. Why can't you just let her be? Ever think maybe she just don't want to talk?"

She walked away, shaking her head and muttering.

Once certain she wouldn't turn around, I stuck out my tongue.

I'll bet she hasn't written you a note.

THE SECRET MISS RABBIT KEPT

CHAPTER 8

Near the end of our shift, Nurse Smith decided that not only had the time come for Mrs. Kramer to have a B.M., but Emma Jean and I would assist. A nagging sense of dread accompanying me, we followed the briskly stepping taskmaster.

"What exactly are we doing?" I whispered to Emma Jean.

"She's going to explode if'n we don't help her."

"Help her? What does that mean?"

"An enema, child, and she won't like it."

Mrs. Kramer started hollering the minute we entered the room.

"Ethel, don't fight us now. You know we have to get that out of you," Smith said, setting the enema and KY jelly on the bedside table next to the portable commode.

"Nooooo!" Ethel Kramer lashed out with flailing arms and dug her nails deep into my flesh. Emma Jean struggled to undo Ethel's grip and a wrestling match ensued.

"Ethel Kramer, you let go—now!" Smith's tone meant business.

Losing some steam upon Smith's command, Ethel released the tender flesh of my underarm, but the bloody gash she'd left couldn't have hurt worse had someone pressed a lit match to my arm.

"Hush now, Ethel," Emma Jean said, grabbing her around the waist. "I reckon you'll feel better when that block's out of you."

With Emma Jean holding a nearly spent Ethel above the commode, Smith gave the enema—which took less time than the battle we'd waged. Smith gathered her supplies, told us to keep her posted, and left the room. I went in search of first aid for my arm. By the time I came back, Ethel was grunting.

"That a way, Ethel. Go on and push, honey," Emma Jean said, nodding when I showed her my bandaged arm.

Ethel's already red face darkened as she fought her burden. I wondered, not for the first time, what had possessed me to take the job. Her struggle—far more education than I needed—appeared endless. While Emma Jean kept up an incessant stream of chatter I prayed for an end to the nightmare so I could go home.

Smith reappeared at exactly what should've been our quitting time to check Ethel's progress. The basin's contents must not have pleased Smith because she shook her head. "Sorry, my friend." She pulled on two pairs of rubber gloves and lathered up to her wrists in KY jelly.

"Nooooo!"

We lifted Ethel and Smith worked on manually removing that with which Ethel's aging body refused to part.

My butt instantaneously clenched. Ethel's screams nearly peeled the paint from the walls. Anyone in the vicinity, certain we were beating the woman, would've called the police. No wonder the windows were never open.

An eternity later, and what I'm sure seemed far longer to Ethel, Smith finished. She told me to empty the now-filled commode basin and I did so, with one hand over my nose and my eyes fixed on the ceiling.

With Ethel quiet, her pressure relieved, and the blockage gone, exhaustion settled on me hard. My legs, like quick-setting concrete, could barely move as we resettled Ethel in her wheelchair.

Leaving the room, Emma Jean turned to me. "Child, you look like you done been beat up. I been trying to tell you this be hard work, especially for a young'un. You got the strength and all, but I ain't seen enough to know if you got the heart. You going to make it okay?"

"I won't lie. This is tough."

"Ain't never *not* going to be tough."

"Then why do you do it? Minimum wage for all this work seems crazy. Plus you take the bus every day. How do you make any money?"

"The way I figure, if God's keeping score–which I 'spect He is–then I's getting me enough points for Heaven. I ain't going to that other place, child. Nope, not after all I been through in this joint. You can take that," she snapped her fingers, "to the bank."

"Is that how it works?" I thought I knew better, but Emma Jean had lived a lot longer. Maybe she had some secret.

"Well, that's how it should work, child. You gets what you give in life."

"How do you explain all the suffering then? Mr. Monsanto's throat cancer? Mrs. Riggler's bedsore?"

"No explaining that. Good Lord must have a plan is all. Ain't for me to judge, but I know I ain't doing nothing to get Him fired up at me."

"You religious or something?"

"Ain't no atheists in a foxhole, child."

Before I could ask what she meant, the admissions office door opened and the director walked out.

"Ladies, come see me before you leave today, please."

"We be on our way out right now," Emma Jean said. "What'd you need?"

"Just wanted to give you a heads up. There's a new resident joining us in the morning. In D-wing—"

"There ain't no room in D-wing. Cynthia Messina took the last bed."

"I'm having the next shift move some people around. We have to take this one. His name is Tommy Chilton. You'll meet him in the morning." She turned, hesitated for a second then turned back. "Prepare yourselves, ladies. He'll be our youngest resident yet."

Neither of us spoke after she closed her door. I guessed we were lost in our own thoughts, wondering just what 'the youngest' meant. With Emma Jean having a bus to catch and my needing to get home, we punched out and headed for the front door. I didn't notice the man I'd spoken to earlier on the porch until he stood directly in front of us.

"That's him," I said, nudging Emma Jean.

"That's who?" She glanced from me to him and her face lit up. "Well, ain't you a sight for this tired old lady's eyes."

"I thought you said you didn't know any black men in this place?" I said, but she ignored me and wrapped her arms around the man. Nearly squishing the hat he'd taken off to greet her, she hugged him so hard she could have snapped his lean body into halves.

"Ah, Miss Emma, I's missed that big 'ol smile of yours." He held her face for a moment then kissed her on the cheek.

"I ain't seen you for a long while. Where you been at?"

"You know. It's hard." He rubbed the whiskers on his face. "I was here just this morning, but I didn't see you. Thought maybe you were off today. I left for a spell. Had an appointment in town. About to head back home, but thought I'd give it one more shot today."

Emma Jean nodded. "Wish you'd come found me earlier so we could've sat and visited. There's someplace I got to be soon."

"Sorry. You know I would've liked that." He looked at me then, like I hadn't been standing there the whole time. "Well, hello. Miss Sophie, ain't it? You still here I see."

"You two know each other?" Emma Jean said.

Had she gone deaf?

"This is the man I asked you about."

As if I hadn't spoken, she focused on him. "Well then, we'll visit next time, I reckon. Take good care now," she said, patting his arm. "And good luck to you."

"Thank you kindly. Will do." He nodded at me before

heading down the hallway.

Trying to absorb what I'd just witnessed, I hurried to keep up with Emma Jean. "Who was that man?"

Now halfway down the sidewalk, she waved me off. "Child, I's in a hurry."

"Stop walking so fast. Your bus isn't even here yet. Why didn't you tell me you knew that man when I asked?"

"How'd I know who you was talking about? I know lots of black folks. I can't count for every last one of them."

I grabbed for her arm, but she pulled away. Several steps later, she stopped and took a deep breath, the quick pace winding her.

"Okay, child." She wiped her brow and thought for a second. "That there was Emery. Emery Rabbit." She held up her hand to shush me. "Don't be getting any ideas. He ain't here very often. Leave the man be. He got his hands full with his sister. They don't need you poking your nose where it don't belong. You understand me? Let this be."

When the traffic light at the intersection up ahead turned green Emma Jean's bus approached in the long line of moving cars. She pointed at me before walking to the curb. "I's warning you now. Let the man be."

The bus squealed to a stop and she boarded without a backward glance. I waited until the bus disappeared around a corner, then I hightailed it down the sidewalk and back into the building.

THE SECRET MISS RABBIT KEPT

CHAPTER 9

The front desk clerk raised her head when I entered the lobby, but distracted by her ringing phone, she only nodded. I hurried down the back stairwell to Miss Rabbit's room and, hoping I'd hear Emery's voice, pressed my ear to the door.

Down the hall, Mrs. Applebee waved her arms and shouted. "Someone has stolen my fur! I've looked everywhere. I'm afraid it's gone. We have to call the police, file a report with my insurance agent. That fur cost Henry over $10,000." Her eyes tearing up, she wrung her hands as she paced.

I hurried closer and hushed her. "Mrs. Applebee, your fur has been sent to the cleaners. Don't you remember?" I could now count improvisation among my many talents.

"The cleaners?" She stopped pacing. "Of course. Silly me. Well, make sure Henry picks it up before this Saturday. We've tickets to the opera, you know."

"I'll remind him." I directed her back inside her room.

"Oh my goodness, what would I do without you, dear? We must speak to Henry about a raise. You're such a godsend."

"Thank you. Now, stop worrying. Isn't it about time for your

Bingo game?"

"Why, yes it is." She glanced down at her watch-less wrist then grabbed the hem of her housecoat. "But for heaven's sake, I can't wear *this* old thing. What will they think of me?" She rushed into her room. Pulling pants, tops, and dresses from her closet, she laid them across her bed. The discovery of her purple hat brought a smile. "Ah, there you are. Now I will be the Belle of the Ball."

Crisis resolved, I resumed my listening post outside Miss Rabbit's room. Two residents, waging an argument nearby, disagreed on the day of the week. Neither one of them correct, I leaned into the doorjamb.

"Mable, I can't leave it like this 'tween us," Emery said. "We ain't getting any younger, you know."

I pictured Miss Rabbit worrying the threads of her afghan as she stubbornly ignored him.

"We need to let the past rest now. Whatever happened–and I already done told you my actions was wrong–needs to be buried now. We were young'uns. I didn't know better—" His last words snagged up somewhere deep in his throat.

A long silence followed by a sigh.

"I don't want to go to my grave with this. C'mon now. I's begging you."

The ache in his voice hurt my chest, a knot of anxiety pushing hard against my heart. Miss Rabbit's unnecessary willfulness made no sense. Why wouldn't she talk to her own brother? At the tail end of life, what could possibly cause such a quarrel?

Emery's footsteps approached. Scooting into the room across the hall, I hid just inside the shadows as Miss Rabbit's door opened wide. Emery stood with his back turned, the hem of his suit jacket wrinkled and riding high, his scuffed boots worn down at the heels.

"You's one stubborn old girl, Mable Rabbit. Always been. I should've known not to come back here today, to try again. Granddad always said there weren't no sense in beating an ol' mule. Now I knows he was right.

"I won't be back for a spell. If'n you need anything, you

knows where to find me." He paused then lowered his voice to little more than a whisper. "I loves you, Mable. Don't forget that." Hat in one hand, he rubbed an eye with the other before walking away, shoulders hunched, head hanging low.

Emma Jean's words at the bus stop played in my head: *Let the man be.* Unable to witness any more of his pain, I did just that.

Though my heart ached for Emery, my feet and back plain ached. Anxious to get out of my uniform, jump in the shower, and collapse on my bed, I drove home. Too tired to bother opening the garage door, I parked in the driveway and entered the house through the front door.

"Surprise!"

My parents, a handful of relatives, and a few school friends—not to mention Penny Parker and her parents—stood in the front room, wearing goofy grins and even sillier party hats. Streamers and an overabundance of balloons hung from the ceiling. Music in the back yard blared through the open windows. My mother, owning the biggest smile in the crowd, rushed forward.

"Surprise, So-So!"

"M-mom..." I twisted my mouth into a 'gee-I'm-so-thrilled' smile.

"This was the only time we could surprise you. Happy late sixteenth birthday, sweetie!"

Everyone swarmed, offering me hugs and pats on the back—until they got closer. Their noses wrinkled at the nursing home smells. Hugs turned brief and polite. I eased my way to the stairs, hoping the stench would follow.

"We have a nice barbeque planned out back," my father said. "Why don't you go freshen up and change your clothes? We'll head outside. You come out when you're ready."

"Yeah. You smell like shit—literally," Penny Parker chimed in, pinching her nose.

First tortured by Emery's pleas, then cut to the quick by Penny's gross stupidity, my day had gone straight from rotten to rancid. As I struggled to hold back tears, all my real friends—the ones who didn't have the pleasure of knowing Penny—stood in stunned silence.

"It's obvious she needs to freshen up, Penny. You didn't need to so rudely point this out," Mrs. Parker said, intervening only, I'm sure, to prevent her daughter's behavior from ruining her own social standing in the neighborhood.

Penny turned on her heels and went outside. My school friends, huddled together in a corner, whispered to each other. By the looks on their faces, I guessed Penny had probably said a lot more than 'shit' before I'd arrived.

"Come on, everyone. I need help carrying things outside," my mother said, motioning everyone to follow. "Then how about we play a game of horseshoes?" Her buoyant step and chirping voice ignored all evidence of Penny's remark. My father kissed me on the forehead then nudged the others to heed his wife's directions. A millisecond before the first tear slid down my cheek, I ran upstairs and threw myself across my bed.

I hated surprises, I hated my birthday, and most of all, I hated Penny Parker. She'd find a way, if she hadn't already, to tell my friends about my being adopted. None of them knew and I wanted to keep it that way. Penny's strong points, if such things existed, weren't tact or secrecy. She had to be little Miss Knows Everything.

With no choice but to join the party, I wiped my tears, took a shower, and rifled through the contents of my closet. Although my mother would prefer I wear something 'frilly', that wasn't going to happen—not from my closet, anyway. An outfit we'd actually agreed on during a recent shopping trip—a 'not-too-short' skirt and peasant blouse—would have to do.

A whiff of nursing home assailed me as I dressed, leaving me to wonder if the odor had embedded itself in my skin. My aunt, who fancied herself a bit of psychic, had sent perfume for my birthday. Making a mental note to ask her what had inspired her vision, I blasted myself with the stuff and went downstairs.

"There's our party girl! Come join us." My mother's joy, as obvious as the overabundance of my perfume, had no chance of wearing off on me.

The group had divided itself between the horseshoes, my father's smoking barbeque, and my mother's carefully set but over-decorated tables lining the patio. A mound of presents sat off to the side. Signs announcing my birthday, along with more balloons and streamers, festooned the backyard. I couldn't have felt like a bigger heel.

"Dad's got burgers and dogs on the grill. I made lots of side dishes and Mrs. Parker was nice enough to bring this beautiful gelatin mold," my mother said, gesturing to the over-sized, green speckled dome on one of the tables.

"This is great, Mom. Thanks." At her coaxing, I added, "Thanks, Mrs. Parker."

"My pleasure, Sophie. The recipe came from my latest issue of Bon Appetit, you know," Mrs. Parker said, as if the reference vindicated the use of nuts and mayonnaise in gelatin. She wobbled as her spiked heels sunk deeper into my father's lawn. Likely tired of trying to balance, she moved over beside me on the patio, lifting one foot at a time to wipe off the Georgia clay. "Oh, my poor shoes! These cost me an absolute fortune back in L.A."

She would babble to anyone willing to listen and, not being one of them, I wandered over to my school friends. They'd claimed a spot under the crabapple tree at the far edge of the yard.

"Wow, who's the bitch with the attitude?" Mandy whispered a little too loudly when I sat down on the grass next to her. Count on the Italian girl with seven siblings not to mince words. Her jet-black eyes shooting lasers across the lawn at the back of Penny's head reaffirmed what I already knew: Mandy Siglione made a better friend than enemy.

"That's Penny Parker, a neighbor kid my parents forced on me. Our moms are friends."

"She always act like that?" my friend Cindy asked.

"Actually, yes. Did she talk to you guys at all while I was upstairs?"

"No, she's been right by her mother's side most of the time," Mandy said. The speed of her reply set off an alarm in my brain. Several seconds passed before Betsy chimed in.

"She talked to me a little right when we were introduced, but

I walked away when all her bragging got to me." Though normally prone to constant chatter, Betsy stopped and focused her attention on re-tying the laces of the only pair of shoes she owned. I hated Penny even more for the way her boastfulness must have hurt my friend, a poor preacher's daughter.

My uncle's booming voice rose above the music. Standing with some of my other relatives over by the game of horseshoes, he delivered the punch line from one of his oft-repeated jokes. He'd never admit being nearly deaf or completely absentminded, but the group politely humored him. My family was nothing if not polite.

My friends sat quiet, eyes averted.

"What's up with you guys?" I asked.

No one moved.

"Come on. I know something's wrong. Spit it out."

Mandy, of course, found her courage first. "Sophie, it's just that I...we...didn't know you were adopted."

Penny Parker had struck.

"It doesn't matter, Soph. We're just surprised you never told any of us. I mean, we're your closest friends." Mandy looked to the others who all nodded.

"How did this subject come up exactly?" I needed to know the details before I punched Penny in the face.

With Mandy up to her neck in the deep end, Betsy must have felt the need to wade in and save her by speaking up. "While Penny was talking to me she made some comment about how weird it was–'how gross' is the way she put it–that you were working in a nursing home. She said your mom and dad had to throw this surprise party for you after work. Then she said, 'I mean, her adoptive parents.'"

I sensed Betsy's discomfort, but I had to know what else Penny Big Mouth had divulged. "Is that all she said? Is that what's bugging you guys?"

"Well, no..." Mandy said.

"She said your real mother was murdered," Cindy blurted, the suspense obviously killing her.

All eyes locked on mine. Cheryl, the most emotional of our

group, squeezed my arm. The ensuing silence hung in the space between us, and just like the time Gramps farted at the dinner table, no one knew what to say.

These were my friends and I'd kept my adoption a secret from them for years. Their concern told me they'd understand any truth as long as it came from me. Though tempted to keep my mouth shut, I recalled Miss Rabbit's frustrating silence. Maybe the time had come to open up.

"I lied to Penny on purpose."

Cheryl gasped. "You mean you're not adopted?"

"No, I am adopted, but my birthmother wasn't murdered. I lied to Penny and she knows it. She just wanted to cause more trouble."

Penny still sat huddled with her mother on the other side of the yard. I guessed she'd had all the interaction with my friends she'd needed for the moment.

"That bitch," Mandy said, a tad too loud again.

"Your being adopted is no big deal. Honest," Betsy said, crossing her heart. "We're your friends–unlike Penny. We were just surprised you kept this a secret for so long."

I forced a laugh. "We were all surprised today, weren't we?"

The music shut off suddenly. All heads turned to investigate– except Mrs. Parker, whose exaggerated giggle drew attention to the fact she'd just spilled her drink on the man standing beside her.

Ignoring the show her friend put on, my mother directed us all to the patio. "Come on, everyone. The food is ready. Let's eat so that So-So can blow out her candles and open her presents."

I turned to my friends. "I'm sorry, you guys. I guess I just didn't think my being adopted was important. It's hard for me to talk about."

Everyone nodded. Cheryl patted my arm.

We joined the group at the picnic table. Penny scooted over on the bench, but when none of us chose to sit there, Mr. Parker sidled in beside her. My father served up his burgers and hot dogs while my mother held court over the vast array of side dishes.

During dinner, my uncle retold one of his jokes, loud enough this time for any uninvited neighbors to hear. Mrs. Parker regaled us all with some story about an acting career she hoped to revive one day. I stayed quiet, aware that if I didn't, I'd wind up hitting Penny Big Mouth. Sometimes silence is a good thing.

Everyone finished with dinner, my mother dashed inside to get the cake. She paraded it around like a prize-winning science project, then set it in front of me and asked my father to light the candles. Before a drop of wax fell, she chirped, "Make a wish, So-So!"

I wished for the same thing I'd wished for the last couple of years. *I wish I knew why my mother left me.*

CHAPTER 10

The next day, I arrived at work to find a note taped to the time clock. I had less than a minute to get to the Day Room for a mandatory meeting of all first shift employees.

The night nurse, Scofield, acknowledged me with a nod as I took a seat in one of the few empty chairs at the side of the room. I scanned the crowd for Emma Jean and spotted her in the back of the room next to a woman whose inflated Afro, overdone sparkling blue eye shadow, and enormous hoop earrings better suited a dancer on Soul Train. When I raised an eyebrow at Emma Jean she gave me her 'bout time you got here' look. I stuck out my tongue at her and refocused my attention on Nurse Scofield.

"Okay everyone, I'm sure you're all wondering why we called this meeting, so let's get started. Tommy Chilton, our new patient in D-Wing, arrived last night. He's twenty-four-years old and in a complete vegetative state." The group's collective groan completed Scofield's sentence.

Nurse Smith stood against the far wall. Based on the dark circles under her eyes, I guessed she'd already worked one or two shifts.

"Listen up, people." Scofield waited until the chattering stopped. "This is a very unusual set of circumstances. Mr. Chilton's social worker told us the wife prepared a letter, requesting it be read verbatim." She held up a piece of pink stationary. "This is a first, I know, but so is having a twenty-four-year-old resident. I'm sure it's the wife's way of avoiding numerous questions. I'll tell you now, it's a bit dramatic, but keep in mind who wrote the letter and why. Remember, the more information we all have, the better." She put on her glasses, took a sip of water then began to read aloud.

"To the people who work at Sterlingwood Manor and don't yet know my husband Tommy." Scofield cleared her throat. "Last September, Tommy and his friends were out celebrating the birth of our son. They'd been drinking and one of Tommy's friends insisted he could drive them all home. Somewhere between a bar and town, on a deserted road in the countryside, the car careened into a ravine and slammed into a tree. Due to the late hour, weather conditions, and poor visibility, no one spotted the car. It was hours before any of them were pulled from the wreckage.

"The driver and front seat passenger were declared dead at the scene. They raced Tommy to the hospital with severe head and spinal injuries, but he lapsed into a coma and didn't open his eyes again for weeks.

"It's now been several months since Tommy came back to us and, in spite of intense therapy, he's not the same man I said goodbye to that night in September. He can no longer speak and has no control over his movements. No one can tell me if he recognizes anything that goes on around him, but I'm convinced my Tommy sees and understands. As long as his heart continues to beat, he will be my husband and the father of my son. I thank you for any kindness and respect you can show us while Tommy is in your care. Sincerely, Tommy Chilton's wife Sarah."

Scofield folded the letter, removed her glasses, and waited for a distant ringing phone to be answered.

"There you have it, folks. It's now our job to keep Mr. Chilton alive and comfortable. Particulars can be found in the chart. The night shift has gotten him settled. His wife, here most of the night, left to get what I suspect is some much-needed rest. Let's remember to provide them both with the respect they deserve." She glanced at Nurse Smith. Something unspoken passed between them before Scofield turned back to the group. "And one more thing. We don't want another Mrs. Riggler, so let's stay on the repositioning."

Her last words—part admonishment, part warning—triggered an eerie silence in the room, but curious about the woman seated with Emma Jean, I couldn't sit still any longer.

"This here is Sophie," Emma Jean said as I approached. "The one I been telling you about. Sophie, this is my sister Tanya."

Tanya's cold eyes gave me the once-over before she mumbled a curt greeting and walked away. I couldn't decide if her enormous dimpled rear-end straining the fabric of her uniform resembled an overinflated water balloon or the hips of a rhino.

"Emma Jean, when did you get a sister?"

"When'd I get a sister? You silly fool, she been my sister all along."

"You never mentioned her. Did she just get a job here?"

"She been on vacation. Worked here long as me. Now, c'mon, we got work to do and I want to take a quick peek at the new guy."

Tommy Chilton's air mattress whispered as we entered the room. With the curtains pulled shut, gray shadows painted the walls behind where Tommy lay on the bed curled up in a fetal position and covered by a blanket. His eyelids flickered. Spittle ran from the sides of his mouth. His face, peppered with acne and a greasy sheen, affirmed his youth. The tracheotomy tube in his neck and catheter snaking out from under the covers screamed of something normally reserved for those who'd spent more time living. The scene struck me as a spectacular illustration of an only previously imagined hell.

Emma Jean stood at the edge of his bed, staring at him. "Oh Lordy, he the same age as my son."

As I hung back at the doorway, unsure what to do or say, she stroked Tommy's arm. His eyes awkwardly ill-aligned on some distant place, he tightened into a spasm, his bony shoulders stabbing against the thin hospital gown.

Claustrophobia gripped me. Let Emma Jean have her moment. I had to leave the room. Tommy Chilton was a tragedy, no doubt, but no worse than some of what I'd seen in the last few days. Honestly, were there varying degrees of hell?

A loud cry for help interrupted my thoughts. Hoping my question hadn't prompted God to offer another example of degrees, I ran to find the source.

"Help me!" Beatrice Walker lay tangled between the toilet and her wheelchair crammed against the wall.

"What happened?" I grabbed her under the arms and lifted her into the chair.

"Oh, thank God you came." Her chest heaved with deep straining breaths. "I thought I was going to die. Someone just left me here. I wasn't strong enough to get back in the chair by myself." She rubbed her arm, which had been pinned by her body weight in the fall. Settling into her chair, she straightened her housecoat.

Tanya appeared in the doorway, her hands perched on her massive hips. "What are you doing in here? This is my room."

"You're the one who left me here," Beatrice said, pointing a shaky finger. "I kept calling and you never came."

"What are you talking about, old woman? I've only been gone a few minutes. I can't spend all my time in here. You aren't the only person I have to take care of in a day." Tanya grabbed the wheelchair and yanked Beatrice out of the bathroom, nearly running over my toes in the process.

"Tanya, don't you think—"

"Don't I think what?" She glared, daring me to finish my sentence.

I wanted to say that 'old woman' wasn't a very nice term, or leaving Beatrice alone on a toilet for however-long might not be safe, but Tanya was Emma Jean's sister and, with the hundred-some pounds and twenty-plus years she had on me, I didn't have the nerve to take her head-on. I patted Beatrice's hand and asked if she was okay.

"She's just fine," Tanya said. "Now, go on. Your people need you, not mine."

When Beatrice silently hung her head I shot Tanya the dirtiest look I dared and went in search of Emma Jean. Ruby's yelling had me stop in the sisters' room.

"I told you to stop talking, Caroline," Ruby said as I entered the room.

Caroline sat up in bed, her short gray hair sticking up every which way. "Hello, dear."

"What are you two arguing about now? I could hear you from the hallway." I opened the curtains to let in the morning sun.

"We aren't arguing. Caroline just doesn't know to mind her own business. And close those damn curtains. The sun is too bright."

Ruby's attitude clawing at my patience, I closed one side.

"I'm just saying, I think it's time you thought about joining in," Caroline told her. "You're turning into an old grump."

"Mind your own damn business!" Ruby picked up a book from the nightstand and hurled it at her sister.

"Stop, Ruby. Calm down." I returned the book to its place on the dresser. "What has Caroline done to get you so mad already?"

"I simply suggested she come to Bingo with me," Caroline said. "Instead of staring at the television all day. It would do her some good."

"She's been nagging me since daybreak. I'm going to have to switch rooms. I can't take her nonsense." Ruby threw back her covers. "Now get me the hell out of bed so I don't have to listen to her anymore."

"Okay, but you need to be nicer to your sister." Their room wasn't my assignment, but I hated subjecting Caroline to any more of Ruby's anger.

"That's okay, I'm used to her bossy ways," Caroline whispered.

"Why don't you want to go to Bingo, Ruby?" I said. Someone had to side with Caroline.

"I don't like Bingo and Caroline knows that. We have this same goddamn argument every single week."

"Maybe Caroline would just like your company."

"Well, then maybe she should watch television with me."

No sense in arguing, I dressed Ruby and helped her into her chair. When she wheeled out of the room Caroline didn't even ask her to wait.

"My goodness, that woman could make a nun curse," Caroline said.

"Maybe you should think about switching rooms."

"But what would we do without each other?"

I shrugged. What indeed?

"I mean, she is bossy, but she's my sister and all I have left in the world. I worry about her. She eats too much, watches too much television, and she's never nice to anyone. It's hard not to say anything. If I don't watch out for her, who will?"

"I don't have a sister, so I don't know what it's like, but you do bicker a lot. Have you always argued like this?"

"Gosh, I never thought about it. She's always been bossy, but she's gotten worse with age." She leaned closer and whispered as I helped her with her shoes. "I think that's why she never got married. No man could stand her always wanting to wear the pants, if you know what I mean."

"Neither one of you ever married?"

"No, but it was different in my case. I was going to get married once, but he was killed in the war. Just broke my heart. No man could take his place."

"I'm sorry."

"It was a long time ago. We weren't officially hitched yet, but I knew he planned to ask. He just never got the chance. Now Ruby, she never got close enough to any man. In fact, I don't think she ever had one who cared enough to stay with her."

"I suppose some people just don't want to get married."

"Maybe so."

"Neither of you had any children?"

"No, our brother had some kids, so we got to be aunties, but we haven't seen any of them in years. Think they all live out west somewhere. Our brother passed years ago."

I couldn't stand around all morning while Caroline

reminisced, and my mind still festered over what Tanya had done. "Ready for breakfast?" I helped her into her chair and gave her hair a quick combing. "You're all set."

"You married, dear?"

"I'm only sixteen."

"I was seventeen when my Harry went off to war."

"Too young for me, Caroline. Now, you go on off to breakfast. Ruby is probably saving you a spot."

"Oh pooh, I doubt that." Caroline rolled her eyes, but headed towards the elevator.

Mr. Messina passed, head down, walking at a fast clip. His clothes still had the slept-in look.

"Good morning, Mr. Messina." I averted my eyes from his unzipped fly.

"Oh, excuse me," he said, tending to his zipper. "I'm getting here a little late today, I know. Cynthia will be very upset with me." He wore his worry in crinkled eyebrows and tightly set jaw.

"I'm sure she'll understand. She was asleep when I walked past awhile ago."

"Oh, good. I wouldn't want her to wake and me not be there."

I recalled the music he'd turned on in her room the previous day, the way he'd carefully arranged her perfume bottles on the dresser and organized her shoes on the closet shelf. Now as he rushed to her side, I wondered for whose benefit he really did these things. I guessed Cynthia hadn't noticed his efforts, much like she wouldn't note his absence, but his concern touched me. I could only hope, for his sake, Cynthia would still be asleep when he reached her room.

"Where you been at?" Emma Jean hollered from the end of the hall.

"Sorry, Beatrice needed help, then I had to get Ruby out of her room before she took off Caroline's head. Where've you been?"

"Tommy Chilton's room. His parents showed up. I wanted to introduce myself. Damn shame is what that is." She wiped the sweat off her brow with the back of her arm. "Phew, I's starting to stink already and the shift ain't barely begun."

She always smelled of baby powder, no matter how hard or long she worked. I guessed she kept a supply in her pocket.

"How were the parents?"

"His mama didn't talk much. Father seems like a real nice fella. Obvious they still pretty broke up about this, but I's thinking they wrapped their heads around it now. Not much can be done. Their son, so ain't no choice. Not like they can just leave him."

What would Emma Jean think of my birthmother leaving me?

"C'mon, things to do." She grabbed sheets from the linen cart and motioned for me to follow. "You on your own tomorrow. Smith thinks you ready."

"She does?" I didn't know Smith thought anything about me.

"Yep. Don't take long around this place to get your own people. We figure between folks dying on you, others shitting on you, and most about killing you, you seen enough now to figure it out for yourself. This is what you get for coming back after your first day." She laughed. "You ready?"

"I don't know."

"Ah, don't you worry none. I's here to watch over you, help if you get in a pickle."

In the next room, still dressed in her nightgown, Mama stood in the center of what looked like a puddle of urine.

"Mama, what happened?" Emma Jean pointed to the floor.

Appearing to care little about her wet feet, Mama rifled through the top drawer of her dresser and pulled out a handful of photographs. Polly, sitting on the edge of her bed, used one of the two phrases she knew. "Yes, yes, yes."

Mama sat beside her and set the pile of pictures on her own lap. She picked up one, said something, and then handed the photo to Polly for her inspection.

"Well, look at that," Emma Jean whispered. "I ain't never heard Mama have a normal conversation."

"How do you know it's normal?"

Emma Jean laughed and, ignoring the puddle of urine for the moment, we edged closer. The photographs, all odd-sized and sepia toned, with curled edges and age-old cracks, captured unsmiling people with stiff postures and haunted eyes. Mama and Polly, like two old friends sharing memories, paid no attention to us. After they had gone through each photo, Mama tucked them back deep inside her drawer.

"Yes, yes, yes," Polly said. "Thank you."

"Prego," Mama said, walking straight through the puddle of urine. "Ah, affanculo!" She slapped her forehead and marched out of the room, leaving wet footprints behind.

Emma Jean shook her head. "Mama is having conversations. Polly is learning new words. Looks like Crazy Sunday has begun."

"Crazy Sunday?"

"It's Sunday and there's a full moon tonight. Get ready. You ain't seen *nothing* yet."

Oh, Lord. I thought I'd seen it all.

THE SECRET MISS RABBIT KEPT

CHAPTER 11

With each passing hour, Emma Jean's warning about Crazy Sunday made more sense. As residents' family members arrived, lugging gifts, grandchildren, and the occasional pet, the noise level increased and, one by one, the residents acted up. Mama cursed incessantly at invisible evils and children running down hallways. Mrs. Kowalski, adept at stopping everyone to beg for food, turned hostile when she couldn't keep up with the crowd. Martha Applebee, convinced these new arrivals represented an imminent party, broke down in tears because neither Fred nor her fur would arrive in time. As Emma Jean and I moved from one crisis to another, I wondered if Murphy had coined his expression after a Sunday visit to Sterlingwood.

The madness continued right up until lunch when Emma Jean and I walked into our last room and found Margaret Bjorn in tears, babbling uncontrollably. A tall Scandinavian woman, she appeared completely normal, but lived in the maze of dementia. Emma Jean explained Margaret relied on routines and when these were disturbed, it was as if she were lost in a dark, unfamiliar room. All the visitors confusing her, we led her to the dining room in hopes things would feel more familiar. She didn't settle down until a cafeteria aide placed a food tray in front of her. Eating she remembered.

Moving on to help others, I stopped at Caroline and Ruby's table. Ruby's chicken sat untouched. "Do you need some help?"

Ruby shoved her plate aside. "This is shoe leather. I can't eat this goddamn garbage."

"I think it's delicious," Caroline said. "Can I have yours if you aren't going to eat it?"

"No, you cannot. It's mine." Ruby pushed her plate out of Caroline's reach and dug into her pudding.

"You don't seem to have trouble eating sweets," Caroline said.

"I have to eat something."

Caroline smiled at me. "She's always preferred sweets."

"Mind your own business," Ruby said, talking around her mouthful of pudding.

In keeping with the Crazy Sunday I'd witnessed so far, Caroline stuck out her tongue. I left them and walked through the dining room, looking for others who might be in need of help.

Stopping to assist Viola Barnes, I glanced over at Mr. Messina and Cynthia. With a magician's sleight of hand, he pulled a flask from his suit pocket, filled his cup, and returned the flask to its hiding place. He then went on to spoon feed Cynthia as if he'd never missed a beat. I located Emma Jean at another table and told her what I'd seen.

"Oh child, that's old news. That flask of his gets more action than a whore on Saturday night. He drinks all day. Can't you smell it on him?" She confided that Mr. Messina had offered her a 'snort'. "Don't judge the man 'til you've walked in his shoes. If a little hooch gets him through the day, so be it."

Refilling his cup two more times while he fed Cynthia the rest of her meal, Mr. Messina kept up a constant stream of one-sided conversation; laughing at his own jokes and smiling when she mewled. His life on display, the truth in Emma Jean's comment became clear. Who was I to judge what helped a man through his days?

Sunday noon meal finished, the residents scattered like ill-mannered children, leaving their plates and messes behind them. Emma Jean and I loaded the first group, which included Margaret Bjorn, into the elevator. She had chocolate pudding smeared down the front of her housecoat, all over her face and hands. Emma Jean instructed me to send the elevator back down, and to go get Margaret showered.

Upstairs, the able residents piled out, pushing and shoving as if chased by an invisible demon. Margaret fought me all the way to the shower room where she then engaged me in a full-on wrestling match. Getting her undressed and showered, while fighting her for control of the shower hose, required the arms of an octopus. A strong centipede might even have had better luck. We both wound up soaked.

All the way to her room, my waterlogged shoes squeaked and squished as if laughing at me. To make matters worse, Margaret kept stopping the chair by putting her feet in front of the wheels. By the time we reached her room, I'd had enough. I gait belted her onto the toilet and removed her dentures. Once the mesmerizing qualities of the toilet paper roll calmed her, I went in search of denture cleaner.

Nurse Smith walked out of another doorway, her hair uncharacteristically messed up and nurse's cap askew. "This place has gone to hell today," she said, straightening her cap.

"I know what happened to me, but what happened to you?"

"Damn Mr. Lowenstein. Out of the blue, he's fussing over his meds. Come help us a second. We need more hands."

Mr. Lowenstein yelled when we walked into the room. "Get the hell out of here. I don't want those son-of-a-bitching medicines."

A frowning orderly stood against a far wall. Mr. Lowenstein's roommate grinned like he'd won a front row seat to a prizefight.

"You get your meds every day. Stop behaving like a child," Smith told Lowenstein.

The orderly and I each grabbed one of the flailing man's arms. Smith, lifting his shirt, quickly injected him in the stomach.

"God damn it!" He broke free from our grip and took a swing at Smith.

She scooted out of his reach. "Better luck next time."

Mr. Lowenstein gave her the finger. Only the roommate had the nerve to laugh.

Suddenly remembering Margaret, I raced back to her room. In the same place I'd left her, she once again had chocolate pudding smeared all over her face and hands. A moment passed before reality hit me: Margaret had worked her toothless gums into a frenzy around something that *wasn't* chocolate pudding.

I vomited my last meal all over her bathroom floor then yelled for help. Smith came around the corner and pushed me aside. To her credit, she didn't hesitate.

"Oh my God, Margaret. Spit that out–now!"

I didn't hesitate either, scurrying out of that room as fast as my feet would take me. My stomach emptied, the vision of Margaret's 'pudding' eventually passing, I walked to the nurse's station where I found Smith washing her hands.

"Heard Margaret wanted more pudding," Emma Jean said, leaning over the counter and giggling. "I warned you. Crazy Sunday–even pudding turns to shit!"

Smith dried her hands and tossed the towel in the trash. "Margaret's all cleaned up. She'll be fine."

Before Emma Jean could make another comment, I asked if she wanted to go on break.

"Sure. You could probably use some fresh air. I'll get a soda pop, meet you there. Should I grab you a pudding?"

I hoped she'd laugh hard enough to wet her pants.

Out on the porch, Tanya reclined on a step, smoking a cigarette. I took a seat in a nearby rocker and watched her blow smoke rings until Emma Jean joined us a few minutes later.

"Damn," she said, flopping down next to Tanya and motioning for her to move the cigarette. "I ain't never going to last the day at this rate."

"I hear ya," Tanya said. "These fools act like they ain't never seen Sunday."

"You hear about Margaret's chocolate pudding?"

When Tanya shook her head, Emma Jean told her the story. They both howled with laughter, but Tanya never looked in my direction.

"What wing you got today?" Emma Jean asked her.

"Mixed nuts," Tanya said, leaning her ample backside up against the railing.

"What's that mean?" I asked.

"Means what wing don't matter," Emma Jean said. "They all a bunch of nuts today."

"Amen to that. Beatrice Walker's even acting crazy," Tanya said. "I 'bout smacked her upside the head. Tell lies on me? Ha."

"Beatrice did seem upset," I said, hoping Emma Jean would come to my defense if Tanya decided to slug me.

Emma Jean looked from me to Tanya. "What'd I miss?"

"Beatrice fell off the pot right after I set her there, said I'd left her. She got to her first," Tanya said, pointing to me. "Crazy old Beatrice just be lying."

Only because Tanya wasn't looking at me, I shook my head at Emma Jean.

Her eyes grew round as dish plates. "Tanya, who you kidding? You famous for not getting off your big old lazy ass to help anyone if it ain't convenient."

The 'I'm going to kill you' glare Tanya leveled at me nearly stopped my heart.

Emma Jean smacked Tanya's arm. "Don't you go blaming this on that child. I know Beatrice don't make things up–even on Sundays, full moon or not. I's warning you. I stuck my dang neck out to get you this job, help you get your kids back, but I ain't going down on account of you." She stood, hovering over her sister. "You hear me? You ain't fooling me twice."

Tanya waved Emma Jean out of her way. When Emma Jean didn't budge, she took a deep drag on her cigarette, puckered up like she wanted a kiss, and blew the smoke in Emma Jean's face. Taking her sweet time to snuff out the cigarette on the railing, she tossed the butt at Emma Jean's feet. She stood and they locked eyes. A long silence followed until Tanya turned and went back inside.

"Now that there's the crazy bitch," Emma Jean said, kicking Tanya's cigarette butt off the porch. "Woman got no sense. Never wants to work, hangs out with fools, loses her kids. I try to help her. Look what I get."

"I didn't mean to cause a prob—"

"Ain't your fault. I know how she is. Almost got herself fired over the same nonsense."

"What do you mean?"

"Ain't like she mean to the folks, but she's just so damn lazy. Does just enough to get by. She was one of them working nights when Mrs. Riggler got her bedsore. Only reason she weren't fired be because she my sister. Smith moved her to days, expecting I'd watch her."

"How'd she lose her kids?"

"She weren't taking care of her babies, so our mama took 'em. I would have done it, but I got five of my own." She took a long swig of soda. "We just wanted her to straighten up. It's like she had them kids then threw 'em away. All because they was too much work."

Despite my desire to ask more questions, I said nothing. We sat on the porch, watching traffic, lost in our own thoughts until Emma Jean crumpled her soda can and stood.

"C'mon, child. Thinking about worries don't make 'em disappear. How 'bout we go help them folks who *do* appreciate us?"

Recalling the day we'd had so far, I couldn't imagine who 'them folks' might be.

CHAPTER 12

Emma Jean put her arm around me as we walked back inside. "I didn't mean to lay all that on you, child. Sorry. Tanya gets me spewing like a teakettle."

"That's okay. I understand. My parents make me crazy sometimes, too."

"Naw, ain't the same thing, but I appreciate you listening. I forget you just a child yourself. How old are you again?"

"Sixteen."

"Damn, why ain't you hanging out with boys or something? I know I ain't never asked 'til now. Figured you just needed a job or something."

"Ever think maybe I'm working on points for Heaven, too?"

"At this rate, you'll be running Heaven when your time comes." Glancing down at my feet, she shook her head and pointed. "What is you thinking? You can't spend the rest of the day in them wet socks. C'mon, I'll hook you up with Dorothy."

"Dorothy?"

"Just follow me."

She led me downstairs to a room I'd never noticed, at the very end of the hall past the laundry area, and rapped on the partially closed door. A woman's voice beckoned us in.

"Hey, Dorothy. Got a new customer for you," Emma Jean said.

Inside the room, soft music played from an old record player propped on a table in a corner. A jungle of potted plants swallowed up the far wall and its window. Framed black and white photographs stretched from one side of the room to the other, their reach broken only by the bed sitting high off the ground like a throne and covered in a patchwork quilt and multitude of pillows. Another entire wall, lined with floor-to-ceiling shelves, served as a storage unit of some sort; every surface crammed with boxes of various shapes and sizes.

Had I tumbled down the rabbit hole?

"Sophie, meet Dorothy Crumble, Sterlingwood's shopkeeper."

My gaze followed the trail of smoke to the room's occupant. In a wheelchair off to one side of the bed, Dorothy sat at a small table littered with papers. A mountain of cigarette butts supported by an ashtray rested near her right hand, where a lit unfiltered cigarette dangled between two knobby fingers. Emma Jean had cautioned me to never to let residents smoke anywhere but in the Day Room, and never were they allowed to have their own matches or lighters. Dorothy must've been the exception.

"Hey, nice to make your acquaintance. Pull up a chair, take a load off." Her heavy New York accent, combined with what must have been years of smoking, coated each of her words.

"What's all this? How have I never seen this room before?"

"Child, you just started a few days ago," Emma Jean said. "You ain't seen everything yet."

"Has she been up to the third floor?" Dorothy asked.

"I was saving that surprise for later," Emma Jean said. She giggled and looked at me. "We's just teasing, child. There ain't no third floor. Just our little joke. We always say there ain't no nuts here. The *real* crazies live up there." She pointed to the ceiling.

Pretty certain I'd seen crazy, I didn't get the joke.

"Seriously, what is all this?" I gestured to the overstuffed shelves.

"This here is Dorothy's store. She got everything from cigarettes to candy to socks."

"Whatever ya need," Dorothy said, breaking into a coughing fit.

"You ever think about cutting back on them things?" Emma Jean asked.

"Ah, shit," Dorothy said, once she'd caught her breath. "What's the point? I got to die of something."

Emma Jean nodded as if the statement made all the sense in the world. "Sophie here needs some socks. She had an unplanned shower this morning."

"Are you fussy, Sophie? I think I only have white ones. Oh, wait a minute." Dorothy balanced her lit cigarette atop the mountain of tamped-out others and wheeled over to the shelves. Grabbing an unmarked box from the middle of a stack of others, she rifled through it and pulled out a pair of brightly colored Christmas socks with tiny jingle bells on the edges. "Here you go, sweetie. Something cheery."

"I don't th—"

"Oh child, those are perfect," Emma Jean said. "This way I can hear you coming."

Tired of wet feet, I guessed Christmas socks wouldn't be so bad. "How much?"

"Special for you today–and today only–two bucks," Dorothy said. "I only take cash."

Hardly a fair price considering my hourly wage came in only ten cents higher, but with no other choice, I took the socks. "Can I pay you at the end of my shift?"

"Sure, but I got an Uncle Dom who'll put you in concrete if you don't pay."

I had no idea what this crazy woman meant, but I took the socks and removed my shoes. "Where do you get all this stuff?"

Dorothy rolled back to her table and re-lit her cigarette. "I take the shuttle into town every week, stock up for those folks who can't get out. I charge enough to make it worth my while. My motto is if I don't have it, you don't need it."

Emma Jean sprawled across Dorothy's bed. "She's saved my

life more than once. Sold me overpriced plugs so many times, I can't even tell you."

"Plugs?"

"Plugs. You know, woman products. For when my friend surprises me."

Not a visual I needed, I walked over for a closer look at Dorothy's plants. Bells tinkled with each of my steps.

"Ha, that's better, child. Little music for my ears as we work," Emma Jean said.

Dry feet did feel better and this short break in Dorothy's little oasis, despite all the smoke, had rejuvenated my spirits. Something about the cozy room shut out all the other stuff. I bent down and examined a potted cactus on the floor.

"You get Miss Rabbit talking yet?" Dorothy asked.

I almost fell over. "Excuse me?"

"Miss Rabbit. I heard you in there the other day."

"Oh, I forgot to mention," Emma Jean said. "Dorothy ain't just the shopkeeper. She also got the biggest set of ears in this place. Dorothy don't miss nothing."

"Yep, and I only sell secrets if the price is right. So, you going to tell us or not?"

"Yes," I said. "I was talking to her, but I talk to everyone."

Emma Jean and Dorothy exchanged rolled–eye glances.

"If I want to get Miss Rabbit to talk, what's the big deal? Shouldn't we all want her to talk?"

Emma Jean shook her head. "I been telling you to leave that one alone. Sometimes you just got to mind your own business." Stretching her arms overhead, she grunted and stood. "Okay, I got to get me back to work. You two visit for a minute if you want. Child, meet me upstairs when you done."

"I'll see you later, honey. Thanks for the referral," Dorothy told her.

"I should be going, too," I said. "Thanks for the socks."

"Sophie, hold on a minute." Dorothy motioned for me to sit beside her. "I don't know you, so pardon me for saying this." She lowered her voice. "I don't think you need to be telling Miss Rabbit some of the stuff you were telling her."

I guessed what she meant, but my unfamiliarity with her kept me mute.

"Now, I'll never apologize for being nosey. It's what I do. Believe it or not, things I've heard around here have saved lives and worry." She took a deep drag from her cigarette, letting the smoke curl up into her nose. A hazy exhaled cloud surrounded her face. "That's why I'm speaking now. You don't know Miss Rabbit. She's an old woman, lived a good long life. If she wants to leave this world not speaking to anyone, she's earned that right. You don't need to be saying things to upset her."

Whatever gave Dorothy the right to make what I said or did any of her business eluded me, but a lifetime filled with my mother's lectures on courtesy wouldn't let me say as much.

"Lot goes on around here you don't know about. When Emma Jean tells you something, trust that she knows what she's talking about. Her and Miss Rabbit are like this." She crossed two of her fingers. "I heard what you told Miss Rabbit about your being adopted and, just so you don't think I'm heartless, I'm going to tell you something here, stick my neck out a bit." She waited for me to acknowledge her statement then she nodded. "You want to know about Miss Rabbit? Get Emma Jean to talk."

The needle on the record player reached the end of the song and didn't return to its cradle. Its repetitious skipping, like these unwelcome words from a stranger, grated on my nerves.

Dorothy wheeled to the turntable and, cigarette dangling from her lips, exchanged one record for another. "Now remember," she said through the corner of her mouth. "You didn't hear any of this from me."

The smoke, the haunting music, the mysterious warning, and the advice raised inexplicable goose bumps. All part of Crazy Sunday?

"I have to get back to work. Thanks again for the socks. I'll stop by with your two dollars before I leave today."

"You need anything else—socks, advice, plugs—you know where I am."

When she laughed and broke into another coughing fit, I hurried out of the room.

THE SECRET MISS RABBIT KEPT

CHAPTER 13

Upstairs, jingle bells marking my every step, I searched for Emma Jean. By the end of the wing, I still hadn't located her, but at the nurse's station, I found Tanya. "You seen your sister?"

"Who wants to know?" Her gaze didn't lift from the magazine sitting atop her splayed legs.

Probably just too fat to cross them, I thought, but bit my tongue. "I do. She told me to come find her when I finished downstairs."

"Sounds like you better find her then." She licked her finger, flipped a glossy page, and then grabbed one of the two soda cans on the table beside her. When an empty candy bar wrapper fell to the floor she slurped at her drink and continued reading her magazine.

Now in front of us at the counter, one of the male residents held an unlit cigarette between two yellow-stained fingers. "You got a light?"

"Um, no." I turned to Tanya. "You have a light for this guy?"

Head still in her magazine, she pointed in the direction of the bank of drawers under the desk. I located matches in the first one, leaned across the counter, and lit the man's cigarette. His t-shirt sported several pinhole-sized burns.

"I'm Sophie. What's your name?"

He sucked on his cigarette until the end glowed red then inhaled deeply. "Pete. Pete. My name's Pete." Another raspy smoker's voice, but clipped and monotone.

"Nice to meet you, Pete. Remember, you need to stay in the Day Room." I gestured across the hall in case he needed a reminder.

"Yes. Yes. Thanks." Puffing on his cigarette like a thirsty dog going after water, he turned the end into ash before he even stepped away. He kept one hand on his shirt pocket stuffed with a pack of Camels and headed down the hall.

"Hey, Pete, you need to stay in the Day Room. Go the other way," I said.

He shrugged and turned, his cigarette ashes falling on the floor. How had the place not yet burned down?

Tanya tossed her magazine onto the table and belched. "He'll head the other way soon as you ain't looking." Not a warning, but a dressing-down. She finished her soda and sashayed away, empty cans and wrapper left behind for someone else to clean up.

Pete entered the Day Room and paraded around the residents parked in wheelchairs. His cigarette down to a stub, he dropped it in the big communal ashtray then walked back toward me. Pulling out his pack of cigarettes, he asked if I had a light.

"Pete, you just had one."

"Yeah." He forced an odd snicker. "You got a light?"

Like a comedy routine, the scene replayed.

"Pete, go into the Day Room."

Shrug. Turn. Repeat.

I couldn't keep lighting his endless stream of cigarettes. Nor could I keep my eye on him. No wonder Tanya had walked away. I shoved the matches back in the drawer and resumed my search for Emma Jean. With the shift almost over, I didn't want her to think I'd abandoned her and left early.

"Hey, Sophie." Nurse Smith had never before used my name. "You interested in pulling a double?"

"A double what?"

"A couple aides on swing shift, as well as Nurse Ross, called in sick awhile ago. I convinced Emma Jean to stay, but I need one more. You interested?"

"You want me work another shift?" I tried to keep the surprise from my voice. "Did you ask Tanya?"

"No." Her tone indicated she had no intention of doing so.

"I need to call my parents and ask if it's alright." I didn't have the nerve to tell her no.

"Please call."

Pretty certain I had imagined the 'please' part, I called home from the nurse's station. As I waited for someone to answer, I looked around for Pete. I could only hope he hadn't escaped the Day Room with a lit cigarette. My mother answered the phone, sounding like she'd just climbed a mountain.

"Mom, what's wrong?"

"What do you mean what's wrong? You called here. What's wrong with *you*?"

"Why are you so out of breath?"

"Oh, am I, dear? I was just out back, visiting with Mrs. Parker. When I came in for the phone, I saw I'd forgotten the potatoes I'd left boiling on the stove. Then the front door bell rang and when I went to answer it—"

"Mom, just listen." I explained the situation, expecting her to tell me another shift would just be too much, I'd be too tired, she had dinner waiting–anything.

"Oh, isn't that nice of you, So-So. You go ahead, dear. Mrs. Parker is here anyway. She's a bit upset about something, so maybe I'll just invite her to stay for an early supper. Your father went—"

"Okay, Mom. Thanks. I'll see you later." I hung up before she could start again. My mother could ramble, no doubt, but whenever Mrs. Parker visited, something shoved my mother into a higher gear. Staying to work another shift might not be such a bad idea after all.

Emma Jean met me in the hall. "Where you been at, child?"

I had to blink twice to make sure I wasn't seeing things. Her hair was...cockeyed. I'd never suspected. "That's a wig?"

She felt around the top of her head and broke out in a big grin. "Damn. The old cat tried to jump off the porch." She tugged a strand on one side, then the other, shifting the balance until, I guess, it felt right. "It straight now?"

"I had no idea that was a wig."

"Quit acting the fool. Course it's a wig. You think I's born with hair like this? You crazy white girl, my hair's just like Tanya's."

I couldn't imagine Tanya's grossly inflated Afro atop Emma Jean's head. "Show me."

"Show you what, child? My hair?"

"Yeah. Now that I know it's a wig, I want to see your real hair."

Without further prodding, she grabbed the top of the wig and lifted. The mop now high above her head, she threw her hips sideways, tilted her chin, and flashed a big smile. Her surprisingly short hair, saturated in sweat, lay in flattened curls. The transformation, on Crazy Sunday no less, made perfect sense.

"Quite the magic trick, huh?" She winked. "But don't be waiting on me to pull a rabbit out my ass now."

"Wouldn't surprise me if you did."

She wiped the sweat from her forehead and resettled the wig on her head. Tugging a few times on both sides, she looked to me for final approval.

"Why are you such a mess, anyway?" I said, smoothing down some stray hairs in the back.

"Lucy."

"Who's Lucy?"

"Crazy old lady you ain't met yet. Meaner than a snake. If she ain't hollering or swinging, you know something's wrong. Need combat pay to deal with the likes of her."

"What happened?"

"I hear all this hollering in her room. I find her on the commode, with Mama all up in her face yelling. Well, that dang Lucy reaches for the first thing she can find to throw." She gestured to her stained, wet uniform top and shook her head in disgust. "Her business misses Mama and hits me. I tell ya, closest I ever come to smacking that fool upside her head."

"Oh yuck, and now you're working another shift?" Her stamina amazed me.

"What's the difference? All the animals out their cages now. You staying, too?"

"I guess so. My mother seemed to think it was a nice idea when I asked if I could stay."

"Well, your mama sounds like a nice lady. Like to meet her some day."

Emma Jean and my mother? I couldn't imagine what they'd have to say to each other. Emma Jean and Mrs. Parker on the other hand? Or Penny? I'd pay to see that show.

"Smith know you staying?"

"No, not yet, but she's the one who asked. And guess what? She called me by name for the first time. And she said please."

"See, child, you making progress." She laughed and slapped me on the back. "Oh, ain't no buses running later. Think you could see fit to give me a ride home? I hates to have my husband come back out to get me."

My parents wouldn't be keen on the idea of my driving all over town late at night, but figuring what they didn't know wouldn't hurt them, I agreed to drive her home.

"Okay, let's go get us something cold to drink, take a little load off, and sit outside for a spell. Never make it otherwise."

"I better go get Dorothy's two dollars before I forget."

"I'll tell Smith you staying. Meet me on the porch."

Moments later, my back turned, she shouted from down the hallway. "Meeeerrrrry Christmas!" She had cranky old Ruby Hathaway wrapped in a great big bear hug.

Crazy Sunday was now official. Everyone had lost their minds.

THE SECRET MISS RABBIT KEPT

CHAPTER 14

Dorothy's room empty when I went to pay her for the socks, I left the two dollars next to her overflowing ashtray and went back upstairs. In the main hallway, Ruby argued with Caroline yet again. Emma Jean's holiday greetings must not have thawed her heart. Passing Mrs. Applebee who questioned a visitor if he'd fed her cats, I quickened my pace before anyone could stop me. The front door shut behind me just as Polly began the second chorus to "No, no, no."

Emma Jean, in her regular spot on the porch, pulled off her shoes. "Ain't had a day like this one in a long spell."

"You weren't kidding about Crazy Sunday. What's with these people today?" I rolled my shoulders, trying to unkink my neck muscles.

"Quite the pissers, ain't they?" She rubbed the sole of her foot. "Dang, my dogs is aching."

As she ministered to her flat, shoebox-shaped feet, I held one of her ice-cold sodas to my neck. Though sweating worse than me, the chilled can gave momentary relief to my hot skin. The outside air, sweltering and muggy, offered no breeze, but large cotton candy clouds overhead provided some shade. We would be at the mercy of the afternoon sun's hot rays all too soon.

A city bus pulled to a stop at the corner, reminding me of Emma Jean's request to drive her home. The prospect, after working two shifts, didn't excite me, but curiosity about where she lived did. Beyond her fondness for wigs, a bitchy sister, and her working toward points for Heaven, I knew little about her.

"What you thinking 'bout so hard, child?"

I shrugged. The knot in my neck, now spread to my shoulders, burned.

"C'mon, I need me a good chuckle. What do you teenager white girls think about?"

"Why do you always say that white girl stuff?" Like a persistent mosquito, her question irritated.

She poked me in the ribs and giggled. "You has noticed I's black and you white, right?"

"Yes," I said, slapping her hand. "You keep reminding me. What's skin color got to do with anything?"

Scratching her cheek, she thought for a moment. "Fair enough, child. You's a new generation. Okay, what is it you *young'uns* think about?"

I considered the phrasing of my answer, but facts were facts. "All we do here is run from one thing to the next." I spread my arms. "This is the only place we ever get a minute to just sit."

"We ain't getting paid to rest."

"But all we do is work!"

"That's why they call it work." She laughed almost as hard as she had about the chocolate pudding.

The lid to my emotions blew off despite the lack of breeze. "When does all this craziness stop so I can take a breath? These people are just so...so...damn needy."

"Ah, you's just having a bad day, child." She dismissed my comments with a wave of her hand.

Frustration bubbled up from my chest, like soda in a shaken can. "How do you ever have a *good* day in this place? One thing after another, it just never stops. You get one person taken care of and someone else needs something. Poop, pee, insanity, erections. No, no, no. Yes, yes, yes. Can I have a potato? Did you feed my imaginary cats? This stuff never ends."

The whites of Emma Jean's eyes grew large as I ranted.

"Do you even know it was my birthday the day I started working here? That Mrs. Steiner died in my arms on *my* birthday?"

Emma Jean stared like I'd just grown horns. "Why in the hell would you start a job like this on your birthday? You done lost your mind or what?"

I wiped my eyes with the back of my hand. "It just seemed...I thought—" A loud sob replaced my words.

Alarm clouding her face, she patted my arm. "Hush now, it's okay."

The tenderness surprised me. I didn't dare risk a glance in her direction. If our eyes met, my heart would burst. Taking the big breath she'd suggested, I slowly exhaled. The pounding of my heart against my ribcage slowed. Just when I thought I'd gotten control, my voice took on a life of its own. A whisper I could barely hear spoke on my behalf. "My mother left me. Dumped me like garbage the day I was born."

Emma Jean's hand froze on my arm. A sharp intake of breath and nothing else. Her silence offered all the encouragement I needed.

"And you know what? I've told people my real mother was *murdered* just so I wouldn't have to tell them the truth. That's why I took this job. Figured the people dumped here were toss-aways like me."

Her eyes closed and, like there wasn't enough air to carry them, her words arrived in slow motion. "Oh, child..."

"But these people...I just can't—"

"Hush now. Listen." She squeezed my hand and wiped a tear from my cheek. "I can't be speaking for your Mama and I sure can't be speaking for how you feel about what she done, but I do know you ain't no garbage. If she done what you say she done, well, she must had her reasons. Stepping away ain't always about not loving. Most times, it be about loving too much."

"Ha, that's a joke."

"Ain't meant to be no joke, child. Look at my sister. The good Lord done blessed her with beautiful kids and she don't take care of 'em none. They was hungry, ignored, left in dirty diapers all damn day. Dang, she weren't fit to raise a dog, much less a baby." She shook her head. "Now, my mama's seeing that they getting to school, they clean, they polite. Little Dion even won hisself the Spelling Bee in his class. Things just better for everyone now."

"What's this got to do with my mother?"

"Oh Lordy." She tapped the side of my head. "Your white skull just too thick or what?"

"You mean my young skull, right?" I swatted her hand, but she grabbed mine and squeezed until I looked at her.

"Listen to me now. Your mama could've been a Tanya. Don't you get it? Maybe she weren't fit to be no mama. Maybe she knowed in her heart she couldn't love you like you supposed to been loved." She took a deep breath and let go of it slowly. "What I's saying, child, is maybe she loved you too much to stay."

The curtain of clouds overhead parted then, providing me with good reason to shield my eyes.

She snorted and gave me a little shove. "You think you're garbage? I ain't heard anything that crazy since, well, since before I came outside." She laughed and reached for her shoes. As she bent, straining over her stomach, a loud fart escaped her. Our eyes met before either of us laughed.

"Ha! Welcome to the Church of Emma Jean, where all preaching comes with a free toot!" She laughed so hard she farted again. "Now, unless you want more of my sermon—or my toots—we better get on back inside. Smith be sending the crazies out here if'n we don't show our faces soon. You think you's okay now?"

I shrugged, uncertain I'd ever be okay. "Sorry about all that."

"I's glad you told me, child, but don't you be comparing yourself to these folks none. They's lived their lives. You just starting yours. Some might've been dumped here, but the rest here because their families can't give them what they need. There be all different kinds of love. I reckon your birth mama knowed that."

I nodded, only because she'd hound me otherwise, and took a sip of my lukewarm soda. When she stood I reached for her arm. "Hey? Why doesn't Miss Rabbit talk?"

"I done told you, child. She just don't talk. Leave it be."

"Dorothy told me you and Miss Rabbit are good friends. If that's true, I'm guessing you know something you're not saying."

"Dorothy's an old busybody. Never you mind her nonsense. Now, c'mon, we need to git," she said, opening the front door. Polly, still in the lobby, had moved on to yeses. I couldn't let Emma Jean get away.

"She wrote me a note, you know."

Emma Jean shut the door and turned. "Mable wrote you a note?"

"Yep, yesterday. I kept calling her Mrs. Rabbit and she got mad. Wrote Miss Rabbit and even underlined the word Miss. She ever write you a note?"

The muscles of her jaw tightened as she chewed on the idea of answering. "Not that I can say."

Scooting inside, she let the door close in my face. By the time I caught up with her, she was leading Polly over to a group of residents in wheelchairs.

"C'mon, old girl," she told Polly. "You can help me wheel some of these folks." She placed Polly's hands on the grips of one of the wheelchairs and gestured for her to push. "Giddyup."

Polly did just what Emma Jean asked, but I'd be darned if I'd do the same. "Emma Jean!"

Her head flipped around so fast I thought it might fall off her shoulders.

"You going to tell me if she's ever written you a note or not?"

Polly's yeses played in the background.

"Child, you got no more sense than the good Lord gave a puppy. Poking your nose into a hive where it don't belong, you soon be wondering why bees be stinging your sorry ass." Frustration, more than anger, shaped her words.

Mrs. Kowalski approached, hand extended. Waving her aside,

I tried one last time. "Has she, Emma Jean? Tell me. Please."

She wiped the sweat from her forehead and closed her eyes. "Oh hell, child. You fixing to be the death of me."

I held my breath. Even Mrs. Kowalski put her pleas on pause.

Emma Jean lowered her voice. "We has to get to work, but if you promise to quit your carrying on for awhile, I promise to talk about this on the way home. Fair enough?"

Fair enough. I'd found just the energy I needed to carry me through the rest of the shift.

CHAPTER 15

For the next several hours, like she knew Miss Rabbit's name rested on the tip of my tongue and the slightest encouragement would initiate a landslide of inquiry, Emma Jean hardly said a word. When she grunted yet another response as we were taking a couple of the residents to dinner, I finally lost my temper.

"You don't have to stop talking to me. I told you I wouldn't ask any more questions."

"Who you kidding? You 'bout to bust." A pointed finger accompanied her words. "You done made me a promise. You better keep it." She poked her head inside Mrs. Applebee's room. "Time for dinner, Martha. Giddyup, old girl."

Martha turned, eyebrows knitted. "Oh, dinner. Yes...yes, of course. I wondered where everyone was off to." She walked to her closet, flung open the doors and rummaged through a pile on the floor. A large brown handbag now in tow, she started toward us. Midstride, she returned to the closet. Tossing aside one thing after another, she located a smaller black purse and held this one up for our inspection. "Far better suited for evening, don't you think?"

Upon our nods of approval, she strolled past us and down

the hall.

"You know she'll be back any second for her purple hat," I said.

"Yep."

"Think she'll eventually figure out she's heading the wrong way?"

"Maybe."

I'd had it with Emma Jean's one-word answers. After I helped her load the residents into the elevator, I took the stairs instead of waiting for her return. My promise didn't include talking to Miss Rabbit. I could beat Emma Jean at her own game, but I had to move fast.

Most of the visitors had left and, due to the big meal earlier in the day, many residents had skipped dinner. Miss Rabbit should have been easy to spot. I found her halfway to her room.

"Hey, where you off to?"

Had there been a cartoon bubble above her head, it would have read, "Oh, not you again. Did you forget I don't talk?" but absent dialogue, she pointed down the hallway and lifted her one good leg onto the footrest. I guessed she wanted me to push her chair.

"Aren't you wondering why I'm still at work?" I said as we proceeded down the hallway.

She looked down at my feet, shook her head, and smiled.

"Are you laughing at my jingle bells? My feet got all wet in the shower today."

No answer.

"Dorothy sold me some socks. Only ones she had were—"

Talking for the sake of talking, I had turned into Mr. Messina. At least Cynthia made noises. Miss Rabbit just sat there. Even Emma Jean had begun grunting answers. What was the point? If no one wanted to talk to me, fine. I pushed Miss Rabbit the rest of the way in silence, parked her in the doorway to her room, and turned to leave. She grabbed my wrist and pointed. When I didn't move, she rolled her chair a few inches and pointed again. Eleven hours of work had stolen my patience.

"You know, this would be a whole lot easier if you'd just tell me what you want."

When she motioned again, I pushed her chair until she signaled for me to stop in front of Dorothy, who sat in the doorway of her room.

Dorothy spoke around the lit cigarette dangling from her lip as she adjusted the ashtray on her lap. "Hi'ya girls. Joining me for a little after-dinner smoke?"

Miss Rabbit pointed to the inside of Dorothy's room.

"Ah, here for business? Very good. Come on." Dorothy backed up and motioned us inside. "Sophie, thanks for paying your bill and saving me a call to Uncle Dom. You enjoying your holiday socks?"

"Some people seem to be enjoying them."

Miss Rabbit made little effort to hide her smirk.

"Good. Nice little Christmas—" Breaking into a phlegm-filled cough, Dorothy set her cigarette and ashtray on a table.

Miss Rabbit offered a piece of candy from the pocket of her housecoat. Dorothy stopped hacking long enough for a gravelly thank you then popped the candy into her mouth. She caught her breath, took a sip of something in a nearby cup, and cleared her throat. "Okay." One little bullfrog remained. "What can I get you?"

Miss Rabbit gestured to something on the shelf. Dorothy wheeled over to retrieve it. One item at a time, they managed to conduct the entire transaction without a word. The pile of items now in her lap, Miss Rabbit pulled out a five-dollar bill.

Dorothy waved her off. "No, Emery gave me some money for you. We're good."

Miss Rabbit slapped her money on the table—hard enough that Dorothy's ashtray skittered to the floor, scattering ashes and butts—then scooted out the door. I crawled under the bed to retrieve Dorothy's lit cigarette and shook it in front of her face. "You smokers are going to burn this place down one day."

"Hell. Might do us all a favor." Dorothy picked up the five-dollar bill and called to Miss Rabbit. "He told me you'd refuse, Mable. Fine by me, but you're just running up a credit, you know." She slipped the five into her pocket. "See how she is?

And you think she'll talk to you?"

I went after Miss Rabbit, stood in front of her so she couldn't move. "What's the matter with you? Your brother just wants to make sure you're taken care of. Why are you so angry at him?"

The effort to propel her chair with one good foot and hand had puckered her face in concentration, but something behind me caught her eye. Her eyebrows climbed a fraction of an inch.

"God dang it, Sophie," Emma Jean bellowed.

Miss Rabbit's eyes said, "Ooo, you're in big trouble now."

Emma Jean pushed me out of the way and grabbed the handles of Miss Rabbit's chair.

"Emma Jean, I—"

"Don't you Emma Jean me nothing, child. I done told you we'd discuss it after work." She wheeled Miss Rabbit into her room and yelled over her shoulder. "Now, git before I change my mind." She kicked the door closed.

As I considered what to do next, Nurse Smith came around the corner, the dark circles under her eyes worse since last I'd seen her. "Sophie, go take your break now while things are quiet." She stopped a few feet from me, her shoulders sagging like the air had been let out of them. "Ugh, I just know that statement will come back and bite me."

Not sure she'd directed the last line to me, I asked, "What will come back and bite you?"

"Never ever say it's quiet. All hell will break loose." She walked away before I could tell her it already had.

On my way to the break room, I found the door to the supply room open and the linoleum floor littered with cigarette butts and burnt matches. A heap of trouble awaited someone, once I told Nurse Smith, but before I could head in her direction, a screeching alarm sounded. I ran back the other way, nearly knocking Emma Jean over as she left Miss Rabbit's room.

"Some dang fool opened the fire door," she said. "Bad enough we have to deal with these folks inside. Now we have to chase them outside."

We almost made it to the exit when shouting erupted from a nearby room. "Help me! They're killing me! Call the police!

Ahhhh!"

"What the Sam Hell is it now?" Emma Jean said, running toward the calls for help with me close behind.

Inside the room, Nurse Smith, along with an aide I hadn't yet met, stood against the wall. A woman flailed around on the floor. No one close enough to touch her, she screamed like the still-screeching fire alarm. "Ahhh! Get away from me! Don't touch me. Help!"

Smith yelled over the noise. "We thought she'd run out of steam, but she hasn't. Stay with her. Make sure she doesn't hurt herself while I go get her meds."

"No! Help me! They're trying to kill me."

Emma Jean approached the woman. "I already been round the block with you once today, Lucy. I ain't going there again. Now, hush."

As if on command, the alarm stopped—and Lucy spit in Emma Jean's face.

The other aide and I gasped.

In a single movement, Emma Jean scooped Lucy off the floor and flung her onto the bed. The metal headboard slammed against the wall with a resounding bang. A stunned and silent Lucy, her eyes round as the upcoming full moon, lay there frozen.

A glob of Lucy's saliva running down her cheek, Emma Jean leaned over the side of the bed and to within an inch of Lucy's face. "Don't...you...*ever*...do that again. You hear me?" She'd whispered the words, but her delivery made clear that Lucy's life hung in the balance.

Lucy blinked.

"Damn right," Emma Jean said, and then marched out of the room.

Nurse Smith walked in carrying a syringe. She looked at Lucy, then at us. "What happened here?"

The other aide spoke up. "Lucy sp—"

"Emma Jean put her on the bed, got her settled down." I hoped my rushed words didn't lead to any more questions.

Smith's gaze ping-ponged between us while I held my breath,

praying the other aide kept quiet.

"Okay, come help me," she said.

She didn't need our help. Lucy obediently rolled over. Smith gave her the shot and left. Lucy lay there, staring at the far wall.

Once we were outside the room, the other aide said, "I've never seen a woman do that."

I didn't know if she meant Lucy or Emma Jean, but I nodded. In all the commotion, I hadn't noticed she walked with a limp.

"I'm Cindy, by the way."

"Sophie."

"This is actually my last day here, but nice to meet you."

"How long have you been here?"

"Too long." She laughed. "I'd worked here a little over four months when this happened." Lifting her pant leg, she pointed to the brace she wore. "I was in a car accident a couple months ago. Doctor said I could finally come back, work part-time as a helper, but no lifting."

My healthy-but-tired legs couldn't imagine being saddled with a brace.

"They're always so short-handed here, I thought I better, but it's just too hard—Crazy Sunday and all. Well, you know how it is."

"This is only my third day."

"Oh geez. Sorry."

I thought about telling her just how sorry I was as well when the intercom system clicked on.

"Please tell me someone located whoever went out the fire exit." Smith's voice reeked of exhaustion.

Emma Jean, in no need of an intercom, yelled from somewhere. "Good Lord Almighty, we done lost one."

CHAPTER 16

I ran toward Emma Jean, but Cindy's brace prevented her from keeping up. "Just go," she called after me. "I'll tell Smith you went to look."

Emma Jean popped out of a room ahead of me and threw her arms in the air. "I'm telling you, this place is turning me into a nut. Can you believe we forgot what we was doing?" She pointed toward the nearest exit and started to run. "I'll take this one, you go out the other one."

"Do you really think someone left?"

"Hell, I'm surprised they all ain't left."

I passed a slow moving Cindy and, once outside, I searched the parking lot and sidewalk. The remaining daylight was on our side, but I couldn't see anyone who belonged in Sterlingwood. In the little time since the alarm had sounded, a walking resident could have gone pretty far, but with few of those, likely candidates were limited.

Emma Jean turned the corner of the building. "Anything?"

I shook my head.

"Okay, you go that way." She pointed down the sidewalk. "If you see anyone, ask them if they've seen one of ours." She took off in a sprint. I ran the other way. A block later, I stopped a man mowing his lawn and explained the situation.

"Ya'll lost someone?" He wiped the sweat off his forehead with a handkerchief he'd pulled from his pants pocket. "Golly, no. I ain't seen anyone, but I been busy doing yard work now that's it's cooled off a spell. The wife's been nagging at me all day, but—"

I thanked him and ran.

I asked a few other people sitting in their yards, but they all looked at me as though I'd brought news of an escaped convict. One older woman even asked if she should go inside and lock her door. A block or so farther, I walked up to an idling police car. The officer rolled down his window as I approached. Blond with pudgy cheeks, he appeared too young to be addressed as sir, but I added it anyway.

"Ma'am?" His gaze shifted from me to our surroundings.

Explaining as best I could, I left out the part about Lucy. He didn't need to know about Emma Jean losing her temper.

"So, ya'll don't actually know if there is a missing person?" His precisely spoken words indicated I might be wasting his time.

"Um...no, but—"

"I suggest you take a head count or whatever it is you folks do to keep track of your guests. In the meantime, I'll circle the neighborhood. If I see anyone, or something gets called in, I'll let you know."

He was right. By now, someone at Sterlingwood might have already figured out who, if anyone, was missing. We could be on a wild goose chase. "Okay, but if you happen to see a frantic black woman dressed like me wandering the neighborhood, stop and tell her we spoke, alright?"

"Roger that, but if you do find someone is missing, call us right away." He waited until I stepped away from his car before he pulled out from the curb.

I crossed the street and hurried back in the direction of Sterlingwood, scanning new yards as I passed. The old lady who'd asked if she should go inside and lock her doors peeked out at me from behind drawn curtains.

A police car pulled up beside me at Sterlingwood's driveway. The passenger window rolled down and the same officer called out. "We got a call from the Quick Stop a few blocks over. From the description, it appears we might have located your missing guest. Jump in."

The thought of any possibility my mother might see me had me hesitate.

"Come on. I just need you to provide a positive ID. If it's him, I'll bring you both back."

My mother, likely still tied up with Mrs. Parker, should be the last thing on my mind. I reached for the passenger door handle.

"Sorry, you have to get in the back. Department regulations."

The wire shield separating the front and back seats resembled a cage. I couldn't have looked any more like a criminal. I slid down in the seat as we pulled out of the driveway. Police radio chatter played in the background.

"I'm Officer Lessons, by the way." He glanced at me in the rearview mirror. Dimples dotted the corners of his smile.

"I'm Sophie."

He picked up the radio microphone, spoke words interspersed with numbers and letters, and refocused his gaze on me. "So, y'all lose people often?"

We were nearing the Quick Stop, but not quickly enough.

"No, sir. This is our first one, far as I know."

He turned, eyebrows raised. "Far as you know?"

The car's air conditioning did nothing for the beads of sweat running down the center of my chest. "I just started working there."

He studied me and I looked away, aware of how bad I must have smelled. Brushing the bangs from my eyes, I discovered a glob of something brown stuck in my hair. Pudding or 'Margaret's pudding'? I shuddered at the thought as we pulled up to the store.

"You stay in the car while I go see what's happening. I'll walk the person up to the window. If it's your lost guest, give me a thumbs-up." He spoke into the microphone again. Response received, he grabbed his nightstick and clipboard off the seat, and stepped out of the car.

The possibilities for our escapee included Mrs. Applebee, but she would likely have stopped at the first neighbors' house, believing she'd come for a party. Mrs. Kowalski would have been hounding the mower man for food when I arrived. Mama was a possibility, though anyone within earshot would have heard her rants. Someone in a wheelchair was unlikely; the fire doors were too hard to push open from a seated position. If it were Roy, I could only hope the old lady stayed locked behind her doors until we got him back home.

Officer Lessons appeared in the store's big plate glass window. He pulled on an arm until the rest of Pete materialized. Dressed in pajamas and slippers, head hanging like a rag doll, Pete looked like a child who'd just been rousted from a good night's sleep. I gave the officer two thumbs-up and nodded. The two of them disappeared from sight for a few minutes before the front door opened. Officer Lessons walked out of the store leading Pete by the arm. He opened the passenger door, placed his hand on Pete's head, and guided him in next to me. I slid over to give him plenty of space.

"What happened, Pete? You okay?"

"Those sons a bitches wouldn't give me a cigarette." Dried spit caked in the corners of his mouth.

"Why didn't you ask at the front desk? You know how to get cigarettes and a light."

"She took away my cigarettes." Eyes averted, he rocked back and forth in his seat.

"Who took them away?"

"The lady."

"What lady, Pete?"

"The lady. She took away my cigarettes. Can you give me a cigarette?"

Officer Lessons and I exchanged a quick glance in the mirror.

"We're almost home, Pete," I said. "I'll get you a cigarette soon."

We pulled into Sterlingwood's parking lot. Lessons opened my door and we helped Pete climb out. Lessons put his hand on

Pete's shoulder. "Sir, you can't wander off any more. Can you promise me to do that? If you can, we can let this matter go."

Pete averted his eyes and nodded. When he started to shuffle away, I grabbed his hand. He tried to pull away and I tightened my grip.

"Ma'am, you're free to go. Please keep a better eye on your guests. This could have been far more serious."

"Yes. Thank you, sir," I said, too embarrassed to make eye contact.

Pete tugged on my hand. "Can I have a cigarette now?"

"In a minute." I guided him inside the building to the nurse's station. No sign of Emma Jean, I slid open the top drawer and grabbed the pack of cigarettes kept there. I shook one loose, handed it to Pete, and dug for the matches.

"Can I have two cigarettes?"

"Pete, you made it back." Emma Jean said, turning the corner with Smith. She wrapped him in a big hug, which made him squirm like he he'd been slobbered on.

When Smith broke into a lecture on the dangers of leaving the building, Emma Jean turned to me. "Smith called the police once we knowed it was Pete missing. They told us where he was, that you were on your way there. Was everything okay at the store?"

"I think the slippers and pajamas gave him away. The officer warned us to watch our guests better."

Emma Jean laughed.

Pete sat down in one of the chairs along the wall. Smith hovered over him, finger in his face. "You leave like that again and I'll take away your cigarettes for good."

He tuned her out in his haze of smoke. Did he even remember a time when the world allowed him his own cigarettes and lighter?

"He says he left because someone at the front desk took away his cigarettes," I said.

Smith stopped her lecture. "Did he say who it was?"

"The lady. You know Pete. Who would take his cigarettes?"

Smith locked eyes with Emma Jean. "I heard him pestering

Tanya for a light several times earlier today." Her words hung in the air like a bad smell.

Emma Jean threw her soda can in the garbage. "I'll talk to her." She walked away shaking her head.

"Can I have another cigarette?"

"Pete," Smith said, "how about you come help me in the Day Room? I could use a big strong guy. How does that sound?"

"Okay." Pete took one last drag and tamped out his cigarette in the ashtray. "Can I have one when I'm done then?"

"Yes, Pete, after you help me." Smith looked at her watch. "Sophie, once we get everyone to bed, you and Emma Jean take off. It should be quiet by then."

Had she already forgotten we had lost Pete the last time she said something along those lines?

Mrs. Kowalski approached me, hand extended. "Hey lady, piece of bread and a cold potato? Please. Come on, I'm hungry. Just a piece of bread and a cold potato, huh?"

Leaving Smith to deal with cigarettes and cold potatoes, I headed back to my wing.

CHAPTER 17

Nurse Smith's prediction cursed us again. No matter how hard Emma Jean and I tried, Crazy Sunday refused to let us out of its grasp. Though Pete stayed put, every other resident caused one problem or another. Two hours after Smith had given us the okay to leave, the residents of Sterlingwood finally gave up their battles and called it a day.

Agreeing to meet Emma Jean in the Day Room, I punched out and collected my things, but couldn't find her upstairs. She'd have to find me if she wanted a ride home. I took a seat in one of the now-empty wheelchairs. Mr. Messina hovered over Cynthia against the far wall. He hadn't yet engaged me in chatter, but Cynthia's fitful mewling coaxed me across the finish line of my marathon day.

"Mr. Messina, when Emma Jean shows up, would you tell her I'm waiting outside?"

"Oh dear, I didn't even see you. Why are you still here? I thought you worked days."

"Worked a double. Just leaving now. Will you tell Emma Jean I'm in the car?"

"Oh yes, we'll tell her, won't we, Cynthia? Yes, Cynthia will make sure I won't forget, won't you, Cynthia?"

I left him, mid-soliloquy. A long ten minutes later, Emma Jean joined me on the porch.

"Where have you been?" I said. "We were in a hurry to get out of here, remember?"

"Don't get yer knickers in a twist. Couple things I had to do."

I led the way to my car. We threw our stuff in the back seat and climbed in.

"You sure you ready to go to my side of town?"

"What do you mean?"

"Not a whole lot of white folks there, child. You going to stick out like a virgin in a whorehouse."

"I'll be fine. Won't I?"

She nodded, but continued laughing.

What could happen? I started the car.

Settling back in her seat, she pointed. "You know how to get to the highway? Head that way and I'll tell you what exit when we get there."

We traveled in silence, decompressing after the long day. The road held little traffic. I had fifteen, maybe twenty minutes tops, to get some answers. Now or never.

"So, you ready to tell me something?"

"My feet hurt, my back aches, and it feels good to just sit here a spell. That's what I'll tell you." Gazing out the window like she was out for a Sunday evening drive, she pointed to a building ahead of us on the right-hand side. "Look, that there's the new restaurant I saw advertised in the paper."

"You plan on telling me about Miss Rabbit or not?" The long day had sapped my energy and patience.

"Oh child, you is a ornery donkey. Ain't you hungry?"

"No, but I can stop and leave you there." Sharper words than I'd intended, I winced, waiting for her to haul off and slug me. She shrugged and turned her attention back to the window.

"We had quite the day," she said, the restaurant now a distant spot in my rearview mirror. "I's surprised you still upright."

"Barely, but at least no one spit at me."

Her spine stiffened. "Lucy's lucky I didn't slap her upside her head."

"Looked like you came close." I kept my focus on the road ahead.

"People like her got no business being in Sterlingwood," she said, pointing at me as if I needed to be convinced. "She should be locked up in a loony bin."

I snickered. "Isn't she already?"

"Ha! You gots a point there."

Her shoes off now, the stink from her feet drifted my way. After two shifts, her baby powder had failed. Certain I smelled no better, I cracked a window when she started massaging her foot. I waited until she switched feet. "So?"

"So what?"

"Stop messing with me. We're here to talk about Miss Rabbit."

She sighed and laid her head on the back of the seat. "Why's this so dang important to you?"

"Just because."

"Because why?" she asked, raising her head.

"Because she won't even speak to her brother. Because I made her cry. 'Why' is because you know something and you're not telling. This whole thing stinks like your feet."

Smiling, she wiggled her toes in my direction. "My feet fresh as daisies."

I shoved her and her stinky foot away. "Quit fooling around and answer my question."

"I was hoping you'd let this go."

"Not a chance."

Crossing her arms over her chest, she twisted in her seat to face me. "Okay, tell me what you said made her cry."

I repeated my conversation: the church, the priest, the note left by my birthmother, the blanket I'd been wrapped in–everything I had shared with Miss Rabbit.

"Oh my, child. That be quite a story."

She pulled at the top of her wig a couple times, like her head had overheated. I rolled my window down farther to give her more of a breeze and focused my attention on passing a car ahead of us. Once in the clear, I glanced over. Her head back and eyes closed, I'd have thought her asleep had it not been for her jaw muscle working.

"And what made you bring all this up?" she asked, eyes still closed.

"I figured if she knew more about me, she'd tell me about herself." The logic sounded stupid in the retelling. "You know, if I opened up, maybe she would."

"And you ain't said nothing more?"

"No. Well, not about all that anyway."

"Roosevelt's the exit after this one."

I had thought long and hard about Miss Rabbit's tears. There was only one thing that made any sense. "Do you think she put up a baby for adoption or something? Maybe that's why she cried?"

"I still think what Mable did, or does, ain't nobody's business."

"So are you saying—"

"What I's saying, child, is ain't no one knows how heavy something be until they done picked it up they self. You ain't lived long enough to understand such things. The exit's coming up here."

"I understand a lot, Emma Jean." I put on my turn signal. "And I can read the sign."

"But you can't understand why your mama left you."

"Nothing explains that."

"Take a left at the stop."

Four blocks and another left later, manicured lawns and single houses stepped out of the way for apartment buildings and concrete. A group of men drinking from paper bags gathered under a nearby streetlight. Their vacant stares followed my car as we passed. Up ahead, a strip mall, its storefronts covered with graffiti-embellished boards, marked the next turn. Beat up cars— one up on blocks, its wheels missing—littered the next street. I lived less than a half hour away, but we'd somehow crossed into another world.

"Is this your neighborhood?"

"Around the next corner."

"So we're almost there and you still haven't told me anything."

"I said I'd talk to you. I's doing that, ain't I?" She pointed to an alley up ahead. "Turn here."

I stepped on the brake.

The car now at a complete stop, she turned to me. "What is you doing?"

"You made a promise. I'm not moving 'til you keep it."

"For your information, child, I is keeping my promise. We just ain't there yet. Now git before some crazy fool sees us out here. I don't need no more allocations today."

"Allocations?"

"You know. Problems."

"You mean altercations?"

"Yeah, that's what I said. I don't need any of them." She motioned towards the alley. "Now go."

I drove until she pointed at a small, two-story brick house with bars on the windows. One of two back porch lights on, the other hung like its neck had been broken.

"Pull up to the fence, right there where the links is missing. We can keep eyes on your car from the kitchen window."

My mother made an appearance in my head just then, asking me what in the world I'd gotten myself into. Crinkled eyes about to cry, hands on hips, she shook her head at me. I closed my eyes to shut her out.

"You coming or what?" Emma Jean, now outside the open car door, reached back in to collect her things. "There be a whiskey inside with my name on it. Giddyup, child."

I locked the car and followed. The back door to the house opened as we approached.

"Where you been at, Maw?" A tall, thin boy with an Afro rivaling Tanya's stood in the open doorway. His eyebrows rose. "Oh, I didn't know you was with someone."

"Darnell, this here is Sophie," Emma Jean said, slipping off her shoes and setting them on the porch. "Sophie, my son Darnell."

He studied me like I was an alien, then looked behind us to the parked car. "She brought you home?"

"Mind your manners and say hello. I done raised you better than that."

He mumbled a greeting and turned back to his mother. "Ain't no food in the house. Did you bring something to eat?"

Emma Jean pushed past him. "Get out the way and help Sophie in, boy, and let me get settled before you start hounding me."

Darnell held the door, motioning me inside "Maw, I'm hung—"

"Where's your daddy? Didn't he feed you nothing?"

Darnell glanced at the stack of dirty dishes and pans piled in the sink. "That was hours ago." He stretched out each syllable as if in pain.

Emma Jean rummaged through her purse and handed him some money. "Here. Go down to the corner, get yourself some food. Just leave us in peace for a spell." Darnell took the bills and started to walk away. Emma Jean pulled him back by his shirtsleeve. "You forgetting something?'

He stood there, embarrassment rolling his eyes, then leaned in to give her a quick kiss on the cheek. "Thanks."

She kept her hold on his shirt. "What else?"

He mumbled a 'nice to meet you' in my direction and skipped out the door.

Emma Jean called after him when the screen door slammed. "Don't you be going anywhere else." She set her purse on the table and opened one of the cabinets on the wall. Pulling out a bottle of whiskey and a glass, she gestured to one of the chairs. "Take a load off, child. You want a soda pop or something?"

"What am I doing here, Emma Jean?"

"You's watching me make myself a drink. Then we going to sit down and discuss this business 'tween you and Miss Rabbit."

"Alright, I'll take that soda then." I sat down in the chair by a window smudged with greasy fingerprints. The kitchen smelled of fried food. A large clock, its hands stopped at quarter to three, couldn't hide the peeling wallpaper. One cabinet door hung cockeyed. Mismatched handles decorated a couple drawers.

"Here's to ya, child." Emma Jean raised her glass, tipped it back and drank.

I pointed to the crayon drawings tacked to the front of her refrigerator. "You an artist in your spare time?"

"My grandbabies don't like it none if I don't show them off a little." She finished her drink in one last gulp, shuddering after she swallowed. "Alright, child. I's ready. Be back in a sec."

Distant stairs creaked. Muffled conversation overhead preceded the flush of a toilet. More footsteps. Doors opened and shut. I'd finished my drink by the time the stairs creaked again and Emma Jean walked back into the kitchen.

"What took you—" The worn leather-bound book she carried, the name Mable Rabbit scrawled across its cover, turned me mute.

Emma Jean placed the book on the table between us and sat down. "Don't even think of flapping your jaw 'til I say what I gots to say." She laid a hand on the top of the book. "This here is Mable's. She done wrote it all by herself." Before I could ask how or why, she held up her hand to silence me. "I's holding onto it for her. I thought about this all day and the only reason I's repeating any of this is because I thinks I now knows why she wrote it, why I has it."

"Can I read it?"

"No. I's going to read to you, bits at a time. Too much for your young self to hear all at once."

"Emm—"

"Ain't going to be no argument, child. My way or no way."

Did she honestly intend to read me a story every night? How far could I get if I just grabbed it and ran?

Her eyes bored holes into me. "I's serious as a heart attack, child."

"This is crazy."

"Crazy Sunday, child. Just one more reason to explain why we's here."

I let out a sigh and agreed to her conditions. She put her feet up on a chair, opened the book, and began to read.

The Secret Miss Rabbit Kept

CHAPTER 18

My name is Miss Mable Rabbit and I's 73 years old. Good Lord, where has the time gone? I been living in Sterlingwood for the past two years now.

I think this here is where I's supposed to say I of sound mind and body. I done had a stroke a few years ago, can't get around much anymore, so the body ain't sound like it used to be, but my mind still good.

I ain't exactly sure why I's telling my secret now, but the lady on the television the other day said souls need to be cleansed. It got me to thinking. I got me lots of time to think in this place. I don't know nothing about no soul cleansing, but I been living with this burden these last sixty-odd years and that's just too long. To tell the truth, I feel downright silly writing all this, but most my relatives is dead, I don't have no friends, and ain't no one here with time to listen, neither. I reckon no one cares, but I'll just keep writing and hope for the best. Maybe this here soul cleansing will help pass the time.

When this be found after I pass on to wherever the good Lord sees fit, someone besides me will finally know the truth. Ain't nothing can make up for what was done to me. What's done is done. I'll just trust the good Lord was taking notes.

I already said this, but I don't want no one doubting me. My name is Mable Rabbit and, though I done spent most my life trying to forget what it is I's about to say, I ain't senile. These ain't the kind of memories that had anywheres else to go.

I ain't never told this story before, but I reckon no one be understanding it if I don't give a little history first. Me as a young'un be long gone now, but this soul cleansing really be for her, so that's where I'll start.

I was born in 1900. My mama's name was Alfreida Rabbit. I was three years old when Emery came along. Seven years later, Mama gave us a sister named Abigail. My mama only seventeen when she had me. My daddy, if you can call him that, stayed around for a spell after I born, but he couldn't waste no time on a young'un—or so my mama said.

I lived with Mama and her parents on a farm in south Georgia. Running in cotton fields on hot summer days be what I remember most. Granddad Rabbit was a cuss of a man who worked in the fields all day and, near as I recall, Nana Rabbit always either cooking in the kitchen or hanging up the wash. Mama had a job cleaning for some white folks. She'd go off to work and I'd stay home with Granddad and Nana. They'd make me do chores to help around the farm, but I was just a young'un and wanted to play.

Can't say I knew back then where Emery came from. He didn't know his daddy neither. I do remember Granddad used to yell at Mama all the time and make her cry. I spect it due to her having us babies and not getting any help from the daddies.

We all lived together in this old rickety house, rags stuffed in corners to keep the wind out. Mama and I slept in the same room and when Emery came along, Mama fixed up one of the dresser drawers for him. First time he cried, I told Mama to just shut the drawer. She gave me what for and had me stand in a corner til I said sorry. I stood there a long time. Finally gave in when I got hungry, though I think I spent that whole summer wishing I could shut that drawer.

So it was Emery and me and Mama on the farm with Granddad and Nana. Mama would go to work and Nana and I would take care of little Emery while Granddad and his men worked the fields. I don't remember much of those early years other than we was hungry a lot and didn't have nothing extra for anything. I had a doll Nana made for me out of cloth and stuffing and twine. I named her Cynthia. Emery was too little to play with me, so Cynthia and I went everywhere together. Nana would make me hand over Cynthia on wash day. I would sit by the washtub until Nana finished then follow her outside while she put Cynthia on the clothesline. I'd sit there talking to Cynthia, waiting while she dried in the sun.

I once built a fort out of sticks in the field so Cynthia and me could have tea parties just like the ones Mama told me her white lady had. But then Granddad came and plowed it down. Granddad never had time for what he called my foolishness and he would shoo me out of his fields whenever he caught me and Cynthia there. Nana always told him it wasn't my fault and then they would argue about me and Mama. Then they'd argue about me, Mama, and Emery. Seemed like they was arguing all the time. They'd stop when they caught me listening, tell me to go somewheres else, but I would sneak back, and Cynthia and me would listen around the corner.

Granddad used to say my mama was nothing but a common hoe. Can't say how long I tried to picture my mama as a rake for the field weeds before I knowed any better. Every time Granddad called my mama names Nana would start to cry. Granddad would get mad and slam the door. I'd run away quick so Nana wouldn't see I'd been listening. Cynthia and I would come back later and Nana would be busy with Emery and house chores. She be acting like nothing ever happened. Granddad would show up for lunch, or for whatever made him come home, and both of them would act like ain't no one else in the room, like there weren't no reason to talk. I don't think they was happy with us living with them.

Mama would come home after a long day of working. She'd no sooner be in the door and Nana would hand her Emery. He always got to fussing when she came home too, like he was sickly or something. Emery cried so much that Mama didn't pay no mind to me. Lots of times I'd find Mama rocking Emery in the back room, tears be running down her face the same as Emery's. And once he got too big for the drawer, I was plum out of ideas.

Emery got big enough to play with about the same time I had to start my schooling. Nana made me leave Cynthia behind to keep him company after Mama told me big girls couldn't take their dolls to school. I didn't much like the way he sucked on Cynthia's arms, just made her dirty, but Nana promised she'd get Emery to stop. She never did though, so I'd have to take her for a swim in the creek when I got home from school. I'd hang her out on the line to dry, tell her 'bout my day, and Emery would jump up and down like a crazy fool, trying to get her down.

That's mostly what I remember from when it was just Emery and me and Mama and Nana and Granddad. Mama going off to work, Nana taking care of Emery and the house, me and Cynthia playing in the fields while Granddad worked. Granddad would come in dirty and smelly and grumpy, then Nana, hurrying to get his supper fixed, would shoo me and Emery out the way.

Abigail came along, the only one of us who had a daddy. We all might been better off if she hadn't, though. Her daddy, a big man name of Luther, worked Granddad's fields. He sure wasn't one of those young boys who worked for Granddad neither. Luther was old, all wrinkled like. He had him a son, too. Worked in the fields with him. Must have been about twelve or thirteen—older than me and taller. Name of William, but we called him Billy. Long skinny legs and knock-kneed, he looked like a gangly old Billy goat, too.

Once Abigail came, we was squeezed pretty tight at Nana and Granddad's house. Abigail went into the drawer, Mama and I shared a bed, and Emery slept on the floor. It sure was hard to sleep with all of us in that little room. Mama would get up with Abigail in the middle of the night, step on Emery, and he'd start to hollering along with Abigail. Mama would hush Emery, but it'd be too late.

Granddad would bellow from his room, then Nana would yell at Granddad. There was lots of times Mama would just take Abigail out the room, go into the kitchen so we could get us some sleep. I don't know how she did all that and still go to work the next morning, but she did.

Luther and Mama never did get hitched, even after Abigail was born. I heard Granddad tell Nana he was fixing to let Luther go, but Nana told him that wouldn't help nothing. Granddad grumbled, but Luther and Billy stayed working the fields.

Luther spent time with Mama and Abigail in the evenings or on weekends. He'd make Billy play with Emery and me, but Billy wasn't any fun. He'd be grumpy all the time, just like Granddad. Guess he didn't want to stay with us while his daddy went off with my mama and the new baby, but Luther didn't give him any say so. Every time they'd come, Nana would feed us then shoo us all outside while she did her chores. Granddad disappeared every time Luther and Billy showed up. He'd stay gone, too, until Luther brought back Mama and left again with Billy. I don't suppose Granddad had use for a man who wouldn't do right by his daughter.

Granddad didn't talk much anymore to Mama after Abigail came, either. He didn't talk much to any of us. The old crowded house, all his farm chores, must've got the better of his spirits. Can't say I blamed him none. I know Mama seemed real unhappy with Luther, yelling at him like she did. They fought all the time. I'd leave Emery and Billy outside then sneak around with Cynthia to listen through the window. I tell you, I didn't much like their fighting, but they were a whole lot more interesting than playing with those two boys.

I heard Mama once ask Luther why we couldn't come live with him.

He told her he couldn't be paying to raise another man's seeds. I give you money for Abigail, he said. That's enough. I already got Billy to worry about.

Things between them got real quiet. Then later on I heard noises, like they was wrestling or something, like Mama was struggling. Back then, I didn't know what was going on in that room. Even when I stood on my tiptoes, I couldn't see into the window.

I didn't like Luther much, didn't like not knowing what he was doing to make my mama so unhappy. And I liked him even less the more he and Billy hung around. Ain't nothing I could do to change it though. Not like I had anywheres else to go.

CHAPTER 19

Emma Jean shut the book and tucked it under the table when the kitchen door opened and Darnell walked into the room.

"How'd you do?" she asked him.

"I got me a deal on some burgers they hadn't sold before they was closing up." He held the brown paper bag aloft for her inspection. Grease stained the bottom.

She raised an eyebrow. "Bring enough for us?"

"Aw, Maw, you didn't give me enough money for that." He held the bag closer to his chest, as if he thought Emma Jean might steal it.

"Then go in the TV room to eat. And here," she said, reaching over to a pile of napkins. "Take these. Don't you make a mess in my front room."

When Darnell took the napkins, his bag of cheap burgers, and disappeared through the doorway, Emma Jean stood.

"Hey," I said. "Aren't you going to keep reading?"

"That's enough for one day. You need to head home before it ain't safe."

"But I don't know any more than I did before. Won't you even tell me how you got her journal, what you're doing with it?"

"I done told you all already. Mable gave it to me for safekeeping."

"But what are you supposed to do with it? Why doesn't she just talk? You can't make me wait." I smacked the table, but only Emma Jean's empty glass jumped.

"I can and I will, child. I done told you when I started reading. I have reasons for what I's doing. If you don't like it none, you can go on and forget everything you've learned up 'til now."

"But I haven't learned anything!"

She looked at me, long and hard. "Think on that a spell, child. You be changing your mind."

More riddles. "And you call me a stubborn donkey?"

Her laugh made it clear I had no chance of winning the argument.

"Then when do I get to hear more?"

"You get more when I think you ready."

"When *you* think?" Her cat and mouse game got the bells on my socks to jingling. "And when will that be?"

"Never, you keep at me like this."

Eyeing Miss Rabbit's book, I reached for my keys.

"Don't even think about it."

Defeated, I collected my things. Emma Jean carried the book as she walked me outside. Past the broken fence, a dog feasted at a tipped garbage can. His meal now disturbed as we approached, he ran down the alley toward another under one of the few illuminated streetlamps. This trashcan had spread its contents across the pavement in an evening buffet. A beggar unable to be choosy, the dog jumped right in.

I climbed into my car and rolled down the window. A loud pop shattered the night's silence. Emma Jean ducked and did a three-hundred-sixty-degree turn.

"Just a car backfiring," she finally said, pushing down the lock on my door. "Go on now. Get yourself home."

I drove down the alley and glanced in my rearview mirror. Emma Jean, the dog, as well as Miss Rabbit's book, had all disappeared. If that big old Crazy Sunday full moon hadn't been smirking, I might have thought it had all been a dream.

Retracing my route out of her neighborhood, I could almost hear Emma Jean laughing as I prayed. Without her in the car, everything outside took a step closer. Tract homes muscled up against each other at the pavement. Streets narrowed. Graffiti screamed. More sidewalks buckled and thinned. In spite of the hour, people still gathered on porches or corners. Piercing eyes followed me as I hunted for my turns. At one stop, a man approached, whistling and gesturing. I floored the gas pedal, leaving him to rant in my rearview mirror.

Twenty minutes later, after two wrong turns, I reached the highway and arrived home still in one piece. My heart didn't slow until I walked into the kitchen. With the events of the evening cowering behind the anxious ride home, I'd had no chance to think about Miss Rabbit.

On a normal day at this time of night, the table would have been cleared of even the tiniest crumbs, yet dirty dishes, leftover food, burnt candles, and discarded napkins had all been pushed aside to make a spot for my mother and her steaming cup of tea. In the center of the mess, a vase of drooping tulips let loose a petal as she said, "Thank goodness you're home."

Her words, like the unusual mess in the kitchen, set off alarm bells. Had she somehow found out where I'd been?

"You okay, Mom? What's going on?"

"I lost track of time, didn't realize how late it was. Mrs. Parker left just awhile ago." Her hand fluttered to her face, smoothed back a strand of hair. "You should've been home by now."

"I had to work a double shift. Don't you remember I called?"

"Of course, dear, but in all the commotion, the details slipped my mind. I started to worry."

"Why did Mrs. Parker stay so late?"

"Oh, she...needed someone to talk to." Again with the fluttering hand. "Woman talk is all. Are you hungry? Want me to make you something?" She pushed aside her teacup and stood. A little unsteady on her feet, she reached to the table for support before making her way to the counter. Black marabou-topped shoes I'd never seen before graced her feet.

"Where did you get those?"

"Mrs. Parker." She stuck out her foot for my inspection, lost her balance from the effort, and had to grab hold of the counter. "Aren't they divine? Really not anything I'd buy for myself. I don't even know where I'll wear them, but sure sweet of her, wasn't it?"

"Why are you wearing them now?" They really didn't say nice things about her pink fuzzy robe.

"Just for fun, dear. Mrs. Parker said we ladies should live a little. Do you know she even brought a bottle of champagne for us to drink?"

Champagne? The late hour? Fancy shoes?

"Where's Dad?"

"He's still out with Mr. Parker."

"Dad is out?" He always fell asleep watching the evening news. Had the world gone mad?

"Yes, dear. Now, stop asking so many questions. You're making my head swim. Do you want something to eat or not?"

"No. I think I'll take a shower and go to bed. I'm beat."

I should have helped her clean up the mess, wait for my father to come home, but the day's events, besides skewing reality, had sapped my energy. I needed Crazy Sunday to end.

CHAPTER 20

The next morning, when the sound of my name dragged me from a heavy sleep, I blinked and tried to swallow. Subtle reminders of the previous day arrived in bits and pieces: my tongue a wad of cotton; the polyester pants of my uniform plastered to my skin; a back complaining it hadn't been moved an inch all night. I propped up on an elbow and glanced at the clock. Not much past six.

"So-So, you up?" my mother yelled from somewhere far too close. "Come on. I made us all breakfast."

I croaked out a yes.

"So-So, did you hear me?"

"Yes, Mom. Me and the neighbors."

Ten minutes in the shower woke me. I spent another five on my bed, searching for a reason not to go to work. After my mother yelled a fifth time, I managed to get dressed and go downstairs.

Except for the marabou still gracing my mother's feet, all evidence of last night's events had vanished. My father, who believed it his job to engage me in conversation over meals, looked up when I joined him at the table. "Good morning.

How's the nurse's aide feeling today?"

Far more stable on her new fancy shoes, my mother flitted around the kitchen. "Let her wake up first. She hasn't had her breakfast yet. Would you like toast with your eggs, dear?"

I nodded at her and turned to my father. "I'm fine. Yesterday was nuts, though."

"How so?"

Could anyone who hadn't lived through it possibly understand Margaret's pudding, the ride in a police car or–oh God, they'd kill me if they knew–Emma Jean's neighborhood? I opted for something generic.

"They call it Crazy Sunday. Something about all the visitors and the full moon sets the residents on edge. Every single one of them was just out of control."

My mother set plates full of eggs, bacon, and hash browns in front of us. She never gave up trying to change my father's simple breakfast preferences. "Out of control how, dear?"

"Just acting up more than normal." I racked my brain for a palatable example. "Like this one lady named Mama. She only speaks Italian. It's normal for her to swear, but yesterday, she swore all day long."

"Oh my." Still too much information for my mother's ears. "She doesn't curse at you, does she?"

"She curses at everybody."

"I guess if I had to live in one of those places, I'd curse, too."

"Oh, you would not," my father said. "You couldn't say the word if your mouth was full of it."

She brushed his comment aside with a wave of her hand. "Oh, pooh."

"It sounds like you're getting quite the education and experience, Sophie. Do you still think you'd like to go into the medical field?"

"I don't know. There's just so much icky stuff the nurses have to do. Some of it is just plain gross."

"Well, honey," my mother said, passing me a napkin. "Maybe you'll meet a nice boy one day, get married and have children. Then you won't have to worry about these things."

My mother's definition of a career. A clerk once upon a time at the local dime store, she hadn't worked since she had married, and she'd done 'just fine, thank you very much'.

My father, the only one who championed my future, intervened. "Do you like the people you're working with?"

"I really like Emma Jean."

"The colored lady?"

"The *black* lady, Mom."

"Yes, her. Same thing." She shook her head like I'd said something stupid. "Don't you work with anyone your own age?"

My father winked at me and removed himself from the conversation to sneak glances at the folded newspaper. I think he knew better than to get in my mother's way so early in the morning.

"I met a girl yesterday who seemed close to my age, but she's leaving."

"Are you getting along better with the one nurse?"

"Smith? Yeah, she's okay now."

"You know, Mrs. Welch down the street is a nurse," my mother said. "She had to go back to work at the hospital after her husband passed. She's raising those two kids all by herself. Poor woman."

"Good thing she had a career to fall back on." I glanced at my father and caught the tail end of his smirk.

"Oh, I think it's just terrible she has to leave her kids and go to work." She clucked the words. "God only knows how those kids will turn out. I heard the oldest boy already got into trouble for playing with matches out in the field. See what happens when a child doesn't have their parents around?"

My father, likely finished with the part of the paper he could see, patted her hand. "We're very lucky to have you to take care of us, honey."

She smiled and got up for more coffee.

"By the way," I said. "What was with you being out with Mr. Parker last night?"

"Just finish your breakfast, So-So," my mother said. "You'll be late for work if you dilly-dally."

"No, really. What was that all about? You drinking champagne, Dad out late." I shook my head. "Talk about Crazy Sunday."

"The Parkers are having some...problems." She picked up my father's plate and took it to the sink. "They needed our friendship and we offered it. Nothing crazy about that at all."

"Problems?" I looked to my father for interpretation. He often understood Mom-speak better than I.

"She'll hear about it soon enough." His words stiffened my mother's back.

"Hear about what?" I asked.

My mother stopped fussing with the dishes and sat down. The kitchen clock ticked in the background while she gathered her thoughts. "So-So, the Parkers are...they're getting—"

"Oh, for Pete's sake, just spit it out." My father's patience, normally his strong suit, had failed. "The Parkers are talking about getting divorced, Sophie. That's why I went out with Mr. Parker last night and your mom spent the evening with Mrs. Parker."

"Divorced? Really?" The news didn't sit well on eggs. I swallowed hard.

"Yes, dear. But I don't want you to worry. They'll patch things up."

My father set down his cup a little harder than usual. "Now why would you say that? They're obviously—."

"No one knows what the future holds, dear."

He shoved away from the table, his chair screeching against the linoleum floor. My mother chewed her lip and tapped her marabou-clad foot.

I wanted no part of this discussion. "Dad, you driving me to work?"

"You can take my car," my mother said. "I'm having lunch with Mrs. Parker today."

While my father questioned the motive behind her plans, I grabbed the car keys and left for work. I had enough material from the last twenty-four hours to sort through.

What should have been a quiet drive to work turned into a

mind-numbing recap of the previous day's headlines: Man in Vegetative State Kept Alive; Woman Eats Poop; Resident Escapes over Cigarette Battle; Aide Nearly Kills After Being Spit Upon; Young Girl Ventures into Ghetto; Mute Woman Writes Memoir; Parker Family Splits Up. Before I could take my hand off the wheel to rub my throbbing temple, an entire column devoted to my mother's new love for marabou-topped shoes and champagne reared its ugly head.

Who has this kind of day and survives to tell the story?

My reflection peered from the rearview mirror, but too tired to see the irony, I focused on the coroner's van now parked in front of Sterlingwood's entrance.

THE SECRET MISS RABBIT KEPT

CHAPTER 21

I'd watched enough television to know what the presence of a coroner's van meant. Pulling into the parking lot, I reviewed names and faces of the residents. I barely knew them, but had become attached to quite a few, and the realization one of them might be dead knocked the wind from me. I prayed, but for whom I didn't know.

On my way up the walk, the front doors opened and two men wheeled out a gurney. I stepped aside to let them pass. Neither man made eye contact with me. The zippered body bag they carried offered little clue to the person inside. A knot formed deep in my throat. A fleeting vision of my mother making the sign of the cross lifted my right hand, but embarrassed, I scratched my head instead. The moment called for more grand a gesture than tending to an imaginary itch, but absent any idea of what that could be, I waited until the van's doors closed, then hurried inside.

Inside the break room, Smith was tidying up the mess left by the previous shift. Though she didn't glance at me as I walked in, the time clock announced my arrival with a loud clank.

"Who died?"

She raised a questioning eyebrow, the dark circles under her eyes now bags.

"The coroner's van?"

"Oh, Mr. Monsanto. Three o'clock this morning." She wiped up someone's spilled coffee creamer then turned on the faucet. "What was it Fitzgerald wrote? In a real dark night of the soul, it is always three—" The running water and clatter of dishes she loaded into the sink swallowed up the last of her words.

Her transformation from woman of few words to one quoting an author I'd studied in freshman English caught me off-guard. "Excuse me?"

She waved a soapy hand. "Ah, just a line I'm reminded of every time someone in here dies in the middle of the night." She rinsed a dish under the running water and placed it on the counter. "By the way, you're working alone today. I'm putting you on A-wing. And thanks for staying last night. Appreciate the extra effort."

How could she so easily dismiss Mr. Monsanto's death?

"Was anyone with him when he died?"

"I imagine not. But if it's any consolation, I don't think he knew the difference."

My shift officially begun, I should've moved on, but I stayed while Smith finished washing the dishes. After all, I'd waited days to talk to her. I assumed Emma Jean and I were the only ones who knew about Miss Rabbit's book, but I still wondered what Smith knew. As she dried the dishes, my mouth recognized an opportunity before my brain had time to stop it.

"Why do you think Miss Rabbit doesn't talk?"

Smith looked at me long and hard. "You're a curious one."

"Isn't it normal to be curious when someone refuses to talk?"

She wiped her hands with a towel then smoothed it out over the edge of the sink. "I've worked here a long time. Can't tell you how many folks I've seen come and go. Most people, especially ones your age, would've left after the first day you had. Too many discount the lives here, but you don't seem to have that in you." She headed towards the doorway.

"But—"

She turned, her eyes warning me to proceed with caution.

I took a deep breath. "You didn't answer my question."

"Ah, but I did. Listen to the silence, Sophie. You'll be surprised at the answers it holds."

"That's it?"

Her mouth hinted at a smirk before she shrugged. "Good luck with your wing today. Let me know if you need any help." At the doorway, she nearly collided with Emma Jean, who came plowing into the room like a freight train.

"Wouldn't you know it? I get on the slowest damn bus in the whole damn city this morning. I swear to God, I nearly pushed the guy out the way so I could drive. I ain't never driven no bus, but I tell you I could've gotten here faster blindfolded." Emma Jean shoved her card into the time clock. "Look at this. Fifteen minutes late. Crazy old fool got no business driving a bus."

Smith snickered and left the room, but Emma Jean continued to rant as she put her things away.

"Your wig's crooked," I said.

"No child, my whole damn head's crooked today. That's a fact." She reached up to straighten her wig, pulling one side then the other. "Ah, ain't no damn use." She blew her bangs out of her eyes then fidgeted with her bra strap. "You make it home alright last night?"

I nodded. No need to tell her about the imaginary goblins. "Mr. Monsanto died last night."

The information slowed her. "Well, that ain't exactly bad news. His suffering be over now, bless his heart. He gone yet?"

"Coroner's van left as I came in."

"And here I's bitching about a late bus ride." She shook her head, swiped again at crooked bangs. "Well, c'mon now then. The live ones still be waiting to get up and start their day." She threw an arm around my shoulder and gave me a big Emma Jean grin. "And we's fixing to make it a glorious one, ain't we, child?"

By the time we reached Mr. Monsanto's room, all signs of his existence had been stripped away. Although someone had opened all the windows and placed a fan in the room, the smell lingered. We had no good reason to be in the room. There was nothing to see, but my feet kept me rooted. I guessed that Emma Jean, standing beside me, felt the same way.

"You know, I ain't never seen him have a single visitor." Her words, spoken in the now-empty room, brought a knot to my throat. I brushed away a wayward tear before it could slide down my cheek, and headed for the door.

Emma Jean didn't follow. "See you at break. Holler if you need something."

I started towards A-Wing. A man I'd seen but never spoken to sat in the Day Room reading a book. He looked up at me as I approached. "Good morning."

Mr. Monsanto's lack of visitors still fresh in my mind, I stopped. "Hello."

"We haven't met. I'm Harold Baxter, but everyone calls me Porky." The man, skinny as a rail, bore no resemblance to the cartoon character.

"I'm Sophie. Your name is Porky?"

He leaned forward. "Here. Touch my nose."

I took a step back.

"It's okay. I don't bite. Touch this." He rubbed the top of his nose and leaned closer. Twisted scar tissue ran from underneath one eye, across the entirety of his nose, and over to his other eye. Reaching, my fingers met with short, wiry hairs.

"Pigskin," he announced. "Got injured in the war. Shrapnel tore me up and they used pigskin. Imagine that?" He laughed. "I got a pig's behind on my face."

"You're kidding, right?"

"Nope. That's why my friends call me Porky. That darn pig saved my face. Least I can do is carry around his name."

Still not sure I believed him, I touched the wiry hairs again.

"Guy next to me in the hole didn't have my same luck, though. Wasn't much left of him near as I remember, but missing part of my face like I was, I couldn't see too well. Probably a good thing."

"Did you know him?"

"Like a brother. His name was Charlie. Just a kid like me, but from Ohio somewhere. He was scared to death that day. Don't know why. All them damn days was scary. But it was like he knew his number was up or something. Kind of like Sam."

"Sam?"

"Mr. Monsanto. The guy they wheeled out a while ago. I didn't know his first name and felt kind of funny calling him Mr. Monsanto when we talked, so I just called him Sam."

"You two spoke?"

"Well, I talked and he listened, but yes. I been in there just about every night since he showed up here. I remember what it was like being laid up in bed, feeling so alone. My face was so bandaged I couldn't talk for a while neither. Sam never said so, but I know he was glad I was there."

I swallowed hard. "What did you mean by Mr. Monsanto was like Charlie?"

"Just like Charlie the day he died, Sam was restless last night. Hard to put into words. It was almost like they was afraid they would miss their ride or something."

Mrs. Kowalski walked up to us, saving me from a search for words I couldn't find. "Piece a bread and a cold potato? Come on, I'm hungry."

Porky reached into his pocket and pulled out what must have been a day-old roll he had wrapped in a napkin. He handed it to her, turned back to me and winked. "I know what it's like to be hungry, too."

Mrs. Kowalski, whose vocabulary in my presence hadn't ventured past her requests for food, offered a few clumsy pats to his forehead. "You're a good man, mister." She walked away eating her roll. Porky, now a bit misty-eyed, re-opened his book.

"Need anything before I go?" I asked.

He scratched his whiskers and leaned closer. "A shot of whiskey be good, if you can find one. Been a tough day."

"Little early, isn't it?"

"At my age, honey, ain't never too early for anything."

Laughing, I told him I'd see what I could do. I hadn't been serious about my offer, but as I headed down the hall, I realized a little whiskey might be what the veteran with the pigskin nose needed after losing the friend he'd named Sam. I went downstairs to find Dorothy Crumble.

CHAPTER 22

The stale aroma of cigarette smoke hung outside Dorothy's room much like the smell of decaying flesh lingered in Mr. Monsanto's. Nothing pleasant about the odors in Sterlingwood, they served as warning flags. A new appreciation for Emma Jean's baby powder habit formed as I knocked on Dorothy's door. A loud cough preceded her invitation to come in.

If such a thing existed, I'd have sworn I was looking at a snapshot of yesterday. Dorothy's clothes, her seat placement, and the pile of butts in her ashtray remained the same. Only her particular cigarette had changed.

"Howdy, Sophie."

"Oh good, I didn't wake you."

"Nah, I been up for hours. Who can sleep around this joint? Too many people, too much commotion. What can I do you out of?"

I took a seat on her bed. "I'm wondering if you have a certain something. It's not for me and, whether you have it or not, my asking has to stay between us."

Leaning closer, she lowered her voice. "This have anything to do with Mable Rabbit?"

"No. Why?"

She relaxed into her chair and shrugged. "I heard some things last night. Just figured that's what this was about."

"Heard some things? Like what?"

"Really ain't my place to say. Not like I was eavesdropping or anything. Person can't help what they overhear in the normal course of business."

"What are you talking about?"

Her smirk said she wanted her arm twisted—just a little bit.

I moved to the edge of the bed and dipped my head near hers. "What was it? Come on, you can tell me. I won't tell anyone."

In a bit of irony, she looked over her shoulder as if afraid someone might be listening. "Emma Jean was asking Mable something last night. I didn't quite catch what it was, but I tell ya, Emma Jean sure did a sell job."

"Did Miss Rabbit speak?" I hadn't realized until then that I wanted Miss Rabbit to speak to me, not someone else.

"No, no, no." She exhaled her smoke into my face then quickly waved her hand to clear the air. "That's just it. I only got Emma Jean's side of the story. I couldn't see inside the room, couldn't see Mable's reaction—you know, as I was passing by."

"Of course."

"Funny that you show up this morning, so early and wanting something. I could've sworn it had to do with Mable." She shook her head like she couldn't believe she'd been wrong.

My mind raced with thoughts of Miss Rabbit and the possibility she had spoken. Not my place to put Emma Jean's or Miss Rabbit's confidence in a stranger's hands, I needed to get Dorothy off the topic.

I straightened my spine. "I'm here for whiskey."

Dorothy broke into a coughing fit. "W-what?"

"A resident is in sore need of a drink. He specifically asked for whiskey. I'm wondering if you have any." I spoke as succinctly as I could, hoping the effort would make me sound more grown up. "I'd like to do something special for him. I'll pay whatever it costs."

She threw back her head and let go of one of those deep-belly Emma Jean laughs. "Well, why didn't you say so? Of course I got a little hooch for a fellow soldier in these here trenches." Laugh spent, she leaned over and whispered. "But I can't be getting into trouble passing it to you. Tell me who it is and I'll make sure they get taken care of."

I didn't have the time to argue. "Do you know Mr. Baxter? Porky?"

She nodded like she had figured as much.

I asked how much I owed her, but she shook her head. "This one's on me. I'm guessing it's his friend Sam he's mourning."

The woman's breadth of knowledge amazed me. "Exactly."

"Consider it done. I'll tell him it came from you."

"I don't want to get into any trouble either. Just get him the whiskey. That'll be enough."

When I stood she took hold of my arm and pulled me closer. "Now don't you be telling Emma Jean or Mable what I said. A woman's got to protect her sources. You never know when they'll come in handy." She gave me a conspiratorial wink and let go of my arm. "Us broads have to stick together."

I assured her and left the room.

Behind in my schedule, I shuddered to think what awaited me upstairs. I opted for Miss Applebee's room first. Of all the residents in my charge, she and her unfed cats posed the biggest concern.

She paced naked between bed and closet. "Oh, thank goodn—"

"I just spoke to Fred. Your cats are fine. How about we get some clothes on now?"

She stopped and looked at me. Then she looked down at herself. The realization she was naked seeped into her features like a spreading bloodstain. Her eyes grew wide. Her shoulders rounded. Embarrassed hands reached to cover private parts. "Oh my..." Her face collapsed. "I had clothes on just a minute ago."

The transformation of the Martha Applebee I knew to the one crumbling before my very eyes moved me across the room. I grabbed her blanket as an interim cover. "Martha, it's okay. You didn't know."

"I *am* losing my mind." Sobs racked her boy-chest.

I'd never held a trembling woman, let alone a naked one. Her cries washed away my hesitation. Instinct guided me. "You're just fine. Come on, we'll get you dressed."

I shuffled us to the closet, grabbed her favorite purple hat and the first dress I could reach with one free hand. A few days earlier, a naked woman wrapped in a thin cotton blanket, crowned with a lavish purple hat, would have made me laugh. Now it made my heart ache. Where was that Fred when we needed him?

I sat her on the edge of the bed and did my best to talk her through the fear. When nothing else I said seemed to calm her, I asked about the cats.

"Cats?" She put a hand to her cheek. "Why, I haven't had any cats in a long time." Although pets weren't part of her new reality, the thought seemed to console her a bit. After a moment, she cocked her head. "I used to have one named Missy. Big white Persian. I loved her so. She'd come running every time I pulled out the can opener. The little stinker, it was like she knew."

I took the hat off her head, gently laid it beside us. "So Fred didn't always feed the cats?" I kept my movements slow, unbuttoning the dress I had grabbed, before placing it over her head.

"No." She pushed away the garment. "I had Missy before Fred. Fred was my second husband. No, wait. My third. I married Mathew before Fred. Arnold was first, I think. He and I had Missy." She took the dress from me, threaded her arms through the sleeves then brushed the hair from her face "Oh goodness, it's been so long now I can't remember."

"That's okay, Mrs. Applebee."

"You know," she said, reaching for a tissue on the nightstand. "I think I would like another cat some day." She wiped her runny nose. "Do you think we could have one?"

I laughed aloud at the thought of a box full of cats on one of Dorothy's shelves. "I'll see what I can do."

She smiled along with me and patted my hand. "That would be delightful. Now, be a dear and let me lay down for a bit. Your visit has worn me out."

"Don't you want to go to breakfast?"

"No, I'll ask Fred to get me something if I'm hungry later." She pushed the purple hat out of her way, spread herself across the bed, and closed her eyes. "I'm going to think about names for our new cat."

And just like that, the tragedy ended.

I wiped the perspiration from the back of my neck.

One room down, eleven to go.

Later that morning, Emma Jean poked her head into my last room as I helped Mama in the bathroom. "You doing alright getting people up and to breakfast, child?"

Even after eleven rooms, I was unable to make sense of what had happened with Martha Applebee–and unwilling to share the experience with Emma Jean. "Yes. What a difference a day makes. Everyone is cooperating so far. What time is it?"

"Little after nine." A watch-less Emma Jean always knew the time, almost to the minute.

"You sure?" I'd somehow made up most of the time I'd lost dealing with whiskey and imaginary cats, which reminded me of what Dorothy had said earlier. "When do I get to hear more of Miss Rabbit's book? Making me wait is just plain mean."

Mama, getting between us before Emma Jean could answer, pointed a finger. Angry Italian words flew. At one point, it sounded like she was calling Emma Jean some sort of beast.

"Calm yourself, Mama." Emma Jean held up her hands in mock surrender.

Hands anchored on her hips like she dared Emma Jean to disobey an order, Mama gave the impression she was a whole lot taller than her four-foot-something.

"What I was 'bout to say was I decided you can't be coming to my house at night anymore like you done. It be too dangerous. Can't be having that on my conscience."

The experience still fresh in my mind, I didn't argue. "So what are you saying?"

Mama, eyes still fixed on Emma Jean, didn't budge.

"What I's saying—to the both of you, I guess." Emma Jean laughed. "I done brought it with me."

"You brought the book here?" I exchanged a quick glance with Mama even though she hadn't been part of the conversation, then for reasons that made no sense, I whispered to Emma Jean. "Do you think she even understands what we're saying?"

"Child, don't nothing surprise me anymore."

Mama alternated her gaze between the two of us.

"So you'll let me hear more later?"

"Yes. Stay after work, I'll read then." Emma Jean turned to Mama. "That okay with you, too?"

Mama smiled and relaxed her posture.

"You won't make me wait to hear the rest of the story? You changed your mind just like that?"

"Less you do something to tick me off. Then I'll beat you silly."

"Mio dio!" Mama slapped her own forehead and marched out of the room.

A belly laugh later, Emma Jean followed her. "See you at break."

The good news/bad news hit me. Though I'd get more of Miss Rabbit's story I had to wait six hours to hear it. I'd have laid odds Emma Jean had planned it that way.

CHAPTER 23

In spite of Emma Jean's attempt to ensure otherwise, my day never dragged its feet. Working alone, I had to skip both breaks and hurry through lunch. By the end of the shift, my appearance reflected the battles I had waged. The spray of a leaking catheter had stained the hem of my pant leg yellow. A thrown cup had left a brown splatter of coffee on my sleeve. Dried blood streaked my arm where a confused resident had scratched me. A purple bruise, caused by a collision of wheelchairs, formed on my ankle. The last eight hours had been difficult, but I'd somehow finished on time. At the time clock, I bent to tie my shoelace and discovered the slimy traces of an earlier blind step into someone's impatient bowel movement. Leaving the laces to trail, I punched out.

Emma Jean had asked me to meet her at the picnic table at the far end of the property. Brilliant sunshine and the sharp aroma of fresh cut grass held me in the doorway. After hours of artificial daylight and bad smells, my senses needed time to adjust.

Emma Jean reclined on one of the benches, her pant legs rolled up and her face pointed the sky. Her reasons for tanning eluded me, but fearing another white girl remark, I let my question go.

She turned to me as I sat down. "Beginning to think you forgot." Her devious giggle confirmed she had taunted me earlier on purpose.

"Very funny." I flashed a counterfeit smile. "Here, I brought you a soda."

"Mighty kind of you. How'd you do today? Ain't seen you much."

A million stories came to mind, but one stood out. With all day to think about it, I'd come to the conclusion I had done all I could. "Mrs. Applebee did something weird this morning."

"Weirder than normal?"

I explained what had happened. "And then, just like that, she went back to her crazy self."

Emma Jean shook her head. "Don't sound like she even got much time to enjoy her old self, neither. Seems to me, if the good Lord takes a mind, He should just keep it. Too hard on these folks to go back and forth." She sighed and shrugged. "But He didn't ask me, did He?"

The world according to Emma Jean. I laughed aloud. "No, but maybe He should've."

"Uh-huh, I done heard that."

We sipped our drinks in silence until I couldn't wait another second. "So?"

She belched.

"Emma Jean!"

"Ha, I's testing your patience, ain't I, child?" She reached underneath the table for her purse, where papers, hair products, makeup—nameless things—all threatened escape. Like a magician with a hat, she pulled Miss Rabbit's book, now wrapped in plastic, from deep inside. "Alright, here we go."

"I really appreciate you doing this, by the way."

"I know you do, child." She opened the book and flipped to where she'd placed what looked like an envelope. "Now, where was we?"

When I look back now, my always feeling responsible for everyone be what got me into trouble. Nana used to tell me it weren't no good to try and please folks all the time, said I should stand up for myself more. I did try sometimes, but I always got scared folks wouldn't like me none. Sure didn't help when Granddad called me his scared little rabbit neither.

My trying hard to be good done paid off with my schooling though. I used to be a terrific speller. Even won the Spelling Bee when I was nine. Had to spell the word 'arithmetic.' It done come down to me and this little girl name of Gladys. When it was her turn, she said 'a' instead of 'e.' They asked her twice if that was how she wanted to spell it. My stomach twisted all up in knots. I knew she done spelled it wrong. Can't say how I knew, but I did.

When my turn came, I spelled it loud and slow, just to show all them folks how smart I was. A-r-i-t-h-m-e-t-i-c. The lady in the fancy dress asked me twice if that was how I wanted to spell it and I said yes, ma'am, twice. All the folks clapped and carried on so, poor Gladys started to cry and ran off. I felt kind of bad about her doing that, but at the same time I was real happy. Funny thing, I didn't win nothing but a red ribbon, but I was mighty proud. Nana put it up in the kitchen for weeks after. Then one day it just went missing. Nana didn't notice, but I did. And I figured Emery had something to do with it being gone too. Turns out he had went and buried it in the back yard so he wouldn't have to look at it no more. By the time Nana got him to tell us where it was, made him go dig it up, it was all dirty and ruined. Nana cleaned it up best she could, but she wouldn't hang it in her kitchen no more. Reckon she didn't want to have Emery steal it again, so she gave it to me, told me to put it with my things.

Emery got in a heap of trouble that day. Think Nana and Mama both skinned his behind with the switch. If you ask me, that weren't near enough for what he done. That ribbon my pride and joy. Nana tried to tell me winning the ribbon something all by itself, but that didn't make no sense to me back then. Way I figured, what good was winning if you didn't have nothing to show for it?

I stayed mad at Emery for a long time after that. I know he just be a young'un, but he should have known better. I don't remember now what happened to that old ribbon. Think it just got lost over the years. Maybe Emery stole it and buried it again, got away with it this time. Never know, I guess, but I do know I never did win any more red ribbons.

Be right after that when Mama must have won her argument with Luther. We moved out from Nana and Granddad's house to one closer to town with Luther and Billy. Mama and Abigail moved into a room with Luther, upstairs next to Billy's. Emery and me shared the sleeping porch downstairs. I was happy I didn't have to share no room with my mama and baby sister anymore, but I sure didn't think it fair Billy got a room all to hisself. Me and Emery didn't think much of him anyway so it was okay us sharing a room, but there weren't no places for Emery and me to play except for an empty lot across the street. I missed Granddad's fields, but weren't no use in arguing. I did as I was told.

After we moved, Luther got hisself work washing dishes in the kitchen at some fancy restaurant and Mama got work cleaning at a hotel. Me and Emery and Abigail got looked after by an old lady name of Mrs. Marbly who lived next door. Luther slept during the day, so Mama made us go over to Mrs. Marbly's house even when we didn't have school. I liked going to Mrs. Marbly's. She fed me and Emery real good. Played games with us, too.

Luther would come fetch us later in the day, but there was nothing much for him to do and he didn't do that very good neither. He always acting like he had his hands full with Abigail, but he made me and Emery watch her most the time. If she was asleep, Luther made us go outside and play. Don't think he ever paid us much attention. His friends be over, they'd sit on the back porch laughing and telling stories while we inside watching Abigail. Mama would come home from work and Luther would fuss about how hard his day had been. He'd ask Mama all the time why Mrs. Marbly couldn't just take care of us til Mama got home from work. He'd say we kept him from doing chores around the house. My stars, that man could tell some lies.

Emery and me tried tattling on him once to Mama. She got real mad, told Luther right out that he was the daddy and to stop his fussing. She couldn't afford to have Mrs. Marbly watch us all day while he was home doing nothing but watching weeds grow, is what she said. Luther didn't like her talking back and they got into it something fierce. Emery and me be sitting on the front porch and heard them hollering inside. I's pretty sure the whole neighborhood done heard them carrying on. They never did try to keep their voices down.

Next day, Luther turned around and gave us both a good licking. Took a big old wooden paddle to both our behinds. Said if we ever told stories on him again, we'd get it worse the next time. After that, I ain't never told Mama about what Luther be doing any more, but he always gave me the ugly eye anyway. He downright scared me, so I did what he said. Didn't like it any, but I did it.

Billy another one who made me mad. He never did nothing around the house and he sure never did nothing to help with Abigail. Luther let him go out with his friends and made us stay home and do chores. He treated us like we was little slaves. Mama never seemed to notice it happening neither. She'd let Luther boss us around, never say nothing to defend us, never say nothing about Billy being lazy neither. I guess she was so happy to be out of Granddad and Nana's house she was willing to let things pass. Went on a long time like that, too.

The year I turned thirteen everything changed. I was still doing like I was told, trying to please folks, but I reckon now that's how the trouble started. Luther lost his job, started drinking too much. That's when Granddad's little rabbit got herself a real reason to be scared.

Emma Jean shut the book.

"Why'd you stop?"

"We's done for the day."

"Are you crazy? You can't stop there."

"I can and I will. I gots to get home. You heard enough for now." She took extra care to rewrap the book and envelope in the piece of plastic. "I need me a rest."

149

"But what happens to her?"

"You'll find out next time."

"But Emma—"

Exasperation weighed down her exhale. "You getting anything out of what you hearing me read?"

Any argument was useless, but I didn't want to get her mad by saying the wrong thing. I thought an extra minute before I answered. "Miss Rabbit didn't have a very easy childhood."

"What else?"

"Her life was different than mine?"

"That ain't the one I hoped you'd latch onto."

"Then tell me what I'm missing."

Emma Jean rubbed her eyes a long time before she spoke. "Mable's mama had three children with three different men and Luther was a no good lazy ni— Negro."

"Yep, I'm sort of seeing that part now."

"She struggled for her young'uns."

"Yes."

"She couldn't have been much older than you when she had Mable."

"But those were different times," I said.

"Having babies at that age ain't no different from now. A young, poor mama still a young, poor mama."

"So Miss Rabbit's mother struggled to raise three kids by herself. Is that the point?"

Emma Jean finished her can of soda and stood. "You getting closer, but I's going home."

No sense arguing. My mother was probably wondering where I was and Emma Jean still had a bus to catch. "But you'll keep reading to me, right?"

"Yep, but not today."

I followed her across the lawn, stopping when we reached the sidewalk and expecting to part ways. Instead, she headed in the direction of the parking lot.

"Where you going? I'm not supposed to drive you home again, am I?"

"I's driving myself." She grinned and pointed to a convertible parked in the far corner of the lot. "Like my new ride?"

"Wait a minute. I thought you took the bus this morning."

"Little white lie–no offense. My husband done surprised me with it this morning. Had to take me a little joy ride before I came into work."

We walked to the car and, even though it had to be the biggest one in the lot, she petted it like a baby kitten. "1965 Cadillac De Ville convertible. Baby blue, just like I's always wanted."

How they could afford such a thing?

"That's a nice gift."

"Well, it ain't all mine. It's ours. We have to share, but he done got it special for me."

I thought of Mrs. Applebee and her harsh visits with reality. "Won't it be hard to take the bus again?"

"Damn straight, but today I be living large, child." She unlocked the door, climbed in, and started the engine. "Oo-wee, that's music to my ears."

We said goodbye and I walked to my car. By the time I turned around, she had the top down and the radio turned way up. I waved my arms and yelled, "You working tomorrow?"

"I's working another double," she hollered, head bobbing in time to the music. "Gots to pay for this beauty somehow."

I doubted she heard the noise her rear tire made as it scraped the curb or the other car's angry horn when she pulled into traffic. I also suspected she couldn't have cared less. As I got into my own car, it dawned on me that for a woman who could barely see over the steering wheel, Emma Jean sure made do with what little view she had. Maybe I had been looking at things wrong all along.

THE SECRET MISS RABBIT KEPT

CHAPTER 24

My mother met me in the kitchen doorway. "Where've you been?"

I glanced up at the wall clock as the hands struck five o'clock. "Sorry. I didn't realize the time. I stayed to talk to one of the people at work."

"I expected you home earlier." Her voice hit those worrisome high notes. "I thought something happened to you—"

"Mom, I'm okay." I put my arm around her shoulder. "What's the matter with you?"

"You have to call Penny Parker. She's called several times."

I set my purse on the table and grabbed an apple from the bowl of fruit on the counter. "You're acting weird."

"I'm a little out of sorts right now, dear." She brushed a stray strand of hair from her face, picked up a dishtowel, and began to wipe the counter in repetitive circles. "Can you please go call Penny now? She really needs to talk to you."

I raised my hands in defeat. "Okay. Okay. I'll call her right now. Jeesh." I tossed my uneaten apple back on the counter and climbed the stairs. I couldn't imagine what Penny wanted, but nothing could stop me from getting off the day's stench.

The phone rang as I headed to the shower. My mother answered before it rang a second time.

"So-So, pick up the phone. It's Penny."

"Can't you tell her I'll call her back?"

"No, you need to talk to her now. It's important."

I took my time to find a robe then grabbed the extension in the hallway. "Hello, Penny. You can hang up now, Mom."

Penny's voice barreled over the line. "Where have you been? I've been calling for hours."

"I got held up at work. Let me call you back after I take a shower."

She started to sob.

More drama. Just what I needed after my long day. I slumped into a sitting position on the floor. "What's wrong?"

"My mother's left us."

I sat up straighter and tightened my robe. "She what?"

"Didn't you hear me? She's gone."

"Yes, I heard you. What do you mean she's gone?"

Her voice hit my mother's same earlier high notes. "She left a note saying she couldn't live like this anymore, couldn't be a wife and mother. Oh, Sophie, why's this happ—" A moan cut off her words.

My mother's mindless circles on the counter now made sense, but I couldn't believe she hadn't even warned me. "Where's your dad?"

More sobbing.

"Penny, shush." I waited until she quieted. "Where's your father?"

"He's downstairs. He came home after I called him when I found the note."

"What did he say about all this?" These details wouldn't help her, but I needed some blanks filled.

"Told me not to worry. Said he'd figure it out. She'd eventually come to her senses is what he said. But I don't think so. All her stuff is just...gone."

"I'll talk to my mother, see what she knows. Do you want to come over? Or want me to come there?"

"No. My dad said he doesn't want me to leave the house. He doesn't want anyone over, either." She blew her nose. "But will you call me after you talk to your mom?"

"Yeah, just give me some time. And don't worry. Everything will be okay."

"She just dumped us. Do you even know how bad that makes me feel?"

I knew exactly, but didn't say as much.

Downstairs at the kitchen table, my mother still clutched the wadded up dishtowel. I wondered how many laps it had gone before she'd given it a rest. The smell of a cooking roast told me the potatoes boiling on the stove would later be mashed. Her idea of Sunday comfort food. But it was Monday night. She never broke from routine.

"What the heck? Why didn't you tell me before I heard the news from Penny?"

She gestured to a chair. "Come. Sit down."

"You should've given me a heads-up, Mother." I yanked out the chair and sat.

Her eyes flitted across the room. "Don't be angry with me, So-So. I'm just at a loss. I had no idea Mrs. Parker...I knew how she...but I didn't know she...I mean—"

"You're not making any sense. Would you like me to make you a cup of tea?" In need of something to do, I didn't wait for her answer. Making her tea would be a new experience, but I'd watched enough times to fumble my way through the process. I hunted through several drawers for the tea before she pointed to the one next to the refrigerator. The cup and saucer she used were in a cabinet next to the sink. She'd always said the china, a delicate rose pattern she'd inherited from her mother, was the only 'proper way' to drink tea.

I turned on the burner beneath the kettle of water and sat down. "Now, tell me what's going on."

"She just up and decided she couldn't stay anymore. I thought I'd talked her out of it last night, but today, when she took me to lunch, her bags were already packed. There was nothing I could say to stop her." The fragile china clinked as she pulled the cup and saucer closer.

"But where did she go? How could she just leave like that?" I moved the china before she could break it.

"She wouldn't tell me, only said she'd be in touch," she said, her voice cracking. "How does a woman just walk away from her husband and child? I thought I knew her, thought she had better morals than that."

I rubbed my forehead, more out of confusion than anything else. My turn to toy with the teacup.

"Don't. You'll break it."

"Won't she send for Penny at some point?"

Her head popped up like it sat on springs. "No, that's the part that gets me. Mr. Parker read me the note. It said she hoped they forgave her, but for her own welfare she had to leave. For her own welfare? Imagine that. Since when is a woman's welfare more important than her own family? Once you make a commitment, you stick to it—whether you want to or not."

When the teakettle whistled I filled her cup with the hot water.

"Thank you, dear. How did Penny sound when you two talked? That poor girl. I can't even begin to imagine how she feels."

"How can you say that?" The kettle I slammed down on the cast iron burner helped make my point. "I know exactly how she feels. Haven't we talked about this very same thing for, oh, I don't know, about a hundred years?"

She walked up behind me and forced me to turn around. "Oh, So-So, I don't mean to dismiss your feelings. This is a little different, though, honey. Penny has spent sixteen years living with her mother. You never knew your birthmother."

"Yeah." I pushed her away. "She rejected me without even knowing me. How do you think that makes *me* feel?" I reached for a glass and slammed the cabinet door. "Why can't you, just for once, understand that?"

As my harsh words propelled her backwards, my father walked in from the garage. He glanced at her, then at me. Eyebrows raised, he dropped his briefcase on the table. "What in the world is going on here?"

The last time he'd used that tone of voice he'd caught me trying to smoke a cigarette with a girl from down the street.

My mother rushed to him. "You'll never believe what's happened."

When he turned to me, I held up my hands. "Don't look at me. Mrs. Parker left."

With no hint of whether he was relieved or sad, he pulled out a chair and sat. "When did this happen?"

My mother, her words fast and breathless, filled him in on the details. Stirring the potatoes, I wondered if she would include how I'd blown up at her. When she finished without a mention of my behavior, I exhaled and turned around. "I'm going upstairs to call Penny again. She's pretty upset."

My mother closed her eyes for a moment then walked over and hugged me. "I didn't mean to involve you in all this, So-So."

"I'm sorry, too." This time I hugged her back.

The corners of my father's mouth turning up in a smile, he loosened his necktie and unbuttoned his collar. "Something smells good. What's my lovely bride making us for dinner tonight?"

As my mother began to recite the dinner she had planned, my father winked at me. We both knew the Sunday menu by heart. I headed up the stairs to call Penny.

"That's it? That's all she said?" Penny's voice resumed her normal 'well, aren't you worthless' tone.

"Sorry, I thought she'd know more. Do you want to come over? My mom's making dinner."

"Well, mine isn't."

I fought the urge to rub her nose in the fact her mother dumped her. "I'm sorry—"

"I'm sorry, too." The line went dead.

Unable to solve all the world's problems, I replaced the receiver and went to take a bath.

I'd just settled into a mountain of bubbles, the stench of Sterlingwood almost a memory, when my mother knocked on the bathroom door. "So-So, did you invite Penny for dinner?"

"Yes, Mom."

"Is she coming?"

"No, Mom."

"You need to go visit with her. I'm sure she could use a friend."

I contemplated drowning.

"So-So?"

"What?" I had now hit the high notes.

"Don't use that tone of voice with me, young lady." She jiggled the locked doorknob.

"Just give me a couple minutes. I'll go over there."

"Okay, but don't dally. Dinner will be ready soon."

She hadn't told my father about the way I'd spoken to her. The least I could do was go see Penny, but unwilling to give her the satisfaction, I counted to a hundred before I pulled the drain on the tub.

When I arrived at the Parkers, Penny's father, involved in a heated phone conversation, pointed to the living room. I found Penny curled up on the sofa. She acknowledged me with an indifferent nod. Piles of used tissues littered her lap and the floor. I sat in a chair across the room and tried getting her to talk about something besides the absence of her mother. Moody and silent, she acted like she didn't want me there. It took all my willpower not to say, "Now you know how I feel."

In the next room, Mr. Parker made phone call after phone call. He yelled and paced, all the while using horrible names for his wife. Uncertain I should be privy to such private conversation, I told Penny to let me know if she needed anything. She responded with a distracted wave.

I showed myself out and returned home. My mother had dinner on the table. She started again on the Parkers as soon as we sat down and, no matter what we tried to tell her, she wouldn't listen. At first, I thought she took Mrs. Parker's leaving as a personal attack on her abilities as a friend, but then I sensed what sounded like a bit of jealousy. I left the table as soon as I could.

In the morning, I woke up to my alarm, groggy and

exhausted. A long hot shower later, I dressed and went downstairs. Several times during the night, from the living room below, my parents' loud voices had disturbed my sleep. How one subject could be so thoroughly beaten up escaped me. Now, the stillness of the house struck me. For the first time ever, my parents had slept in. No hot breakfast awaited me, but at least I didn't have to listen to any more of my mother's 'poor Penny' comments. I grabbed some fruit and found a note by the bowl, telling me to take my mother's car to work. My work shoes, now outfitted with new laces, sat by the back door. I could just picture my mother in her yellow rubber gloves, trying to get out the old poop-encrusted ones. I drew a smiley face on the note and left.

Light traffic at six-thirty in the morning allowed me to get to Sterlingwood in record time. The near-empty lot offered me a choice place to park right up front. All signs indicated a good day waited.

In need of a big dose of Emma Jean humor, I hurried downstairs to punch in then walked to the nurse's station. Neither a for-once-silent Mama nor a calm Mrs. Applebee acknowledged me. As I turned the corner, Nurse Smith said, "I think she'll take it pretty hard."

"Who'll take what hard?" I asked.

The night nurse, the home's administrator, Smith, and two other aides were all gathered. No one spoke. The night nurse averted her eyes. The two aides walked away. The administrator took a step closer, but Smith raised her hand. "No. Let me."

My heart started a tap dance against my ribs.

Smith gestured to a chair. "Sophie, sit down."

The night nurse, whom I didn't know very well, grabbed a tissue from a nearby box and she, too, left. She blew her nose a few seconds later. The expressions on Smith's and the administrator's face grew more serious.

Had I done something wrong? The names of the people I'd taken care of the day before ticked through my brain. Had Dorothy ratted me out for Porky's whiskey? There was no coroner's van in the lot; I couldn't have killed anyone. I backed down onto the nearest chair, swallowed hard, and prepared to be fired.

Smith cleared her throat. "Sophie, there's been an accident."

"Wh-what kind of accident. Wh-what happened?" I'd acquired a stutter. My mother would kill me for losing my job.

Smith moved to the seat beside me. Her closeness unnerving, I scooted over to create distance. She put her hand on my shoulder as her red-rimmed eyes searched mine. My heart pounded in earnest.

"Honey, it's Emma Jean. She was in a car accident yesterday."

I pictured Emma Jean behind the wheel of that big blue Cadillac, her head bobbing in time to the loud music. My mouth shaped words, but the voice that came out of me belonged to someone else. "But she's okay, right?" I swiped at my cheek. My hand came away wet.

"Her husband called this morning. She didn't make it."

CHAPTER 25

Emma Jean's family planned her funeral for Saturday. According to my mother, who had formed a telephone friendship with Nurse Smith when I refused to communicate with the outside world, the service would be held at Ebenezer Baptist Church.

"*The* Ebenezer Baptist Church, So-So." She pronounced the words like they should mean something to me. "The one where Martin Luther King Jr's mother was shot by some lunatic last year as she sat at the organ playing The Lord's Prayer."

Her history lesson sounded vaguely familiar, but I had no idea what difference it made. I rolled over on the bed to tune her out.

"It was just tragic. Things like that make a person wonder what the world is coming to."

What indeed.

Ever since Tuesday, when my mother arrived at Sterlingwood in her housecoat and silly marabou-topped slippers, then proceeded to sit on the floor outside the bathroom stall until I agreed to come out, I'd not been allowed a moment of solitude to grieve. Like the lump in my throat, she refused to budge, and her daily updates only served to remind me of my lost friend. I covered my head with a pillow.

"Honey, you can't hide forever. Life moves on. As hard as that is sometimes, you have to pull yourself up and go on."

Only the hundredth time she'd said those words. I pulled the pillow tighter. Nothing she could say or do would make me feel better and had it not been for the ringing phone, I'm certain she would have kept up the lecture until I imploded. When she ran to answer the call, I could only wish for the energy to get up and lock her out of my room. My pillow couldn't keep her voice contained to the hallway.

"Hello...Yes, it is...oh, hello...yes, of course she's here. Will you hold the line a moment, please?"

The floor creaked as she neared. I buried my head deeper.

"So-So, the phone. I think you ought to take this one." She took a deep breath and tugged at my pillow. "It's Emma Jean's husband."

I relaxed my hold on the bed sheets. "Her husband?"

"Yes. That's what he said. Come on now."

I tossed the pillow aside and climbed out of bed. In the hallway, I motioned for her to go away. She hesitated, but I stared until she went down the stairs. Stretching the phone cord as far as I could, I sat on the edge of the bed and tried to steady my nerves. "Hello?"

"Sophie? This is Clifford Williams. Emma's husband."

"Hi."

"I know we haven't met, but I heard a lot about you."

A heavy heart kept my mouth shut.

"Sophie? You there?"

"Yes." The knot I'd had in my throat since Tuesday threatened to explode. "I'm here."

From somewhere on the stairs, my mother spoke in a tone that failed as a whisper. "So-So, talk to the man."

"Shh!" I waved in her direction.

Clifford cleared his throat. "Excuse me?"

"Sorry, I was talking to my mom. What were you saying?"

"I was just sitting here going through some of Emma's things. Still can't believe she's gone."

That made two of us, but I couldn't speak the words.

"Well, there was something I couldn't make heads or tails of, but then I found a note inside with your name and phone number. Says this should be given to you in case something ever happened to—" His voice caught. "Sorry. This seemed like a good idea when I picked up the phone, but it's harder than I thought. Ain't like any of this stuff will bring my Emma back."

Nothing could fill the silence that followed. The acid in my stomach started its hourly climb up my throat as I tried to imagine what Clifford had found, what Emma Jean could have been thinking. Miss Rabbit's book? No, she wouldn't.

"I figured I better call, tell you I had it. I just know Emma would have my tail otherwise."

For the first time in days, the corners of my mouth turned up. "Yes...she would."

"Appears to be a book of some kind. Mable Rabbit is written on the cover."

His words sucked the air from my lungs.

"Does this belong to you?"

Did I dare lie? Emma Jean must have had her reasons. Tears filled my eyes. "It does."

"I wasn't sure if I'd see you at Emma's service on Saturday. That's why I called. I want to get this back to you—for Emma. Can I bring it to you then?"

My tongue, thick and heavy, struggled to move. "Yes, I'll be there. Thank you, Clifford. I...I didn't think I'd ever see that book again."

"I'm glad I called then. Emma spoke kindly of you."

"I miss her." In the three days she'd been gone, I hadn't once said those words.

"Me, too, Sophie. I'll see you Saturday."

CHAPTER 26

The church where Mrs. King had been slain could barely contain the crowd come to say goodbye to Emma Jean. As I scanned the room from where I sat in the third row with my parents, I wondered what she—or Mrs. King for that matter—would have thought about all the different colors of people gathered in sadness. For all of Emma Jean's white girl remarks, I had expected to be in the minority, but the number of Sterlingwood people alone diluted my whiteness. Their presence also made me wonder who had been left behind to take care of the place. My mother had told me they were renting a bus for transport, but I hadn't anticipated residents like Dorothy Crumble or Porky to attend. I even spotted Mr. Messina against the far wall when he waved to me. I turned and faced forward, but still unprepared to see Emma Jean in her casket, I focused on the worn hymnal in my lap.

The choir and its lively piano opened the service. Words of praise erupted all around. Several people stood and openly wept. Only when the preacher approached the podium did they quiet, but the silence didn't last. With every sentence he spoke, someone shouted an 'Amen' or nodded with a 'That's right'. One woman even went so far as to throw herself on the floor. As if her actions were normal, everyone let her be. My wide-eyed mother silently passed me tissues, and my father, who had also insisted on coming, sat with his hand on my knee. He lifted it once to check the time, but only when the preacher appeared to get his second wind.

After what seemed like forever, the preacher shut his Bible. Lifting his arms, he closed his eyes and recited the rest of the passage from memory. His deep voice resounded above the crowd. "Surely, my brothers and sisters, goodness and mercy shall follow me all the days of my life."

The choir broke into the first verse of Oh Happy Day and the crowd came alive. Women raised their arms and rolled their hips. The men clapped and swayed. Strolling down the center aisle, the preacher hugged the guests as he passed.

Unwilling to participate in their incomprehensible joy, I leaned over to my mother. "I need to use the bathroom. I'll meet you outside." Much to my surprise she let me go. I don't think she wanted to miss any part of the spectacle.

My intention to find a side exit faded as duty and momentum carried me to Emma Jean's side. I needed to say goodbye before I lost my nerve.

Outfitted in a lace-covered purple dress and a wig I had never seen, she lay in a casket of tufted white satin. Her bangs were all wrong and her skin looked like she had been dipped in wax. Had she been alive, she'd have been cursing. Had I not been crying, I would've laughed.

The urge to jiggle her, wake her, overcame me. Before last week, I'd never touched a dead body. Had those experiences been preparation for this moment? Laying my hands on Emma Jean's folded ones, I was surprised at how cold they were. Her knuckles, creased and worn, held no life, but spoke of her hard living. She had wiped noses and behinds, lifted grown women twice her size. I'd seen her cradle the dying and tend to the dead. In the little time we'd spent together, those hands had given more than they had taken.

There were no signs of injury from the car accident and I had never bothered to ask what had killed her. The details didn't matter. She had been so happy the last time we were together, living large in her final moments and making the most of what little view she'd had. She had left this world–left me–better for having been in it.

My heart, filling with gratitude for the memories, threatened to burst. I bent and whispered in her ear. "Thank you, Emma Jean. I'll never forget you."

Giving her wig a final little tug before I stepped away, I knew, like Clifford, she would have my tail if I let her go off all crooked to Heaven.

THE SECRET MISS RABBIT KEPT

CHAPTER 27

I shielded my swollen eyes and scanned the crowd of people streaming from the church. Why God allowed the sun to shine escaped me. Thunder and rain clouds far better suited my mood. I spotted Tanya in her bright red dress. An oversized hat tamed her hairdo, but her girth, threatening to swallow up the man beside her, couldn't be concealed.

I stopped a couple passing behind me. "Excuse me. Do you know the man standing beside Tanya?"

They stared like I was trespassing, then the woman answered. "Why, child, that's Clifford."

Her voice, so much like Emma Jean's, startled me. As if sensing danger in further interaction, the man then led her away.

I waited until most everyone had greeted Clifford and moved on before I walked over to him. Only then did I spot Emma Jean's son, Darnell, standing behind his father. His face, awash in grief, resembled nothing of the hungry, hamburger-toting kid I'd met the previous week. Afraid I'd start to cry, I took a deep breath and bit my lip.

Clifford's face lit up when our eyes met. "Sophie?"

My young, whitegirlness must have given me away.

"Hi, Clifford."

Tanya glanced at me, but in Tanya fashion, she moved to greet someone else. Without her bulk to dwarf him, Clifford stood at least a foot taller than me. I imagined his broad shoulders and big arms around Emma Jean. As if he'd read my mind, he wrapped me in a hug. The heat of his sweat reached through the back of his suit jacket. I could smell the fresh starch in his shirt.

The air now squeezed out of me, he stepped back and smiled. "It's nice to finally meet you. You're even prettier than Emma said. I'm real glad you came."

Words failed me.

He acknowledged my struggle with a nod. "Come on. Your book is back inside the church."

He told Darnell to wait and motioned for me to follow. I hoped we wouldn't run into my parents or anyone from Sterlingwood. An explanation for our actions wouldn't be easy.

Led to a small room off the church entrance, I stayed in the doorway while he retrieved the book from a corner shelf. As if Emma Jean were reaching down to put her seal of approval on the moment, a spotlight of sun streaming in through a leaded glass window blanketed Clifford and the book with its rays. He looked up at the light for a second and smiled before he held out the book. "Here you go."

A thank you caught in my throat.

"There's an envelope inside addressed to you. I didn't open it." Kind eyes, like Emma Jean's, studied me. "I don't know how a young gal like you stands to do the work Emma did. I never could figure what made her stay."

The book, wrapped in plastic and crinkling as I clutched it to my chest, supplied the words I sought.

"The residents. They kept her coming back."

"She used to tell me she was earning points for Heaven."

"Yes, she told me that, too."

He stepped outside into the sunlight. Closing his eyes, he tilted his face to the cloudless blue sky and whispered, "I know you made it, Emma."

His words propelled me into the shadows of the church's vestibule; my tears kept me there as he walked away. When he disappeared into a throng of mourners, I struggled against the sob threatening to split me in two. With Miss Rabbit's book tucked inside my purse, I went in search of my parents.

The Secret Miss Rabbit Kept

CHAPTER 28

My mother and Nurse Smith stood huddled in conversation at the edge of the church's parking lot, about ten feet from where my father, arms crossed and foot tapping, leaned against our car. His face brightened as I approached. "There she is."

The first I'd seen of Smith since she'd broken the news of Emma Jean's death, her black dress, heels, and dark hosiery revealed delicate bones; something her boxy white uniform didn't allow. The transformation from nurse into woman surprised me.

"Hi, Sophie," she said. "Nice to see you again. We've missed you."

Her words reminded me of all I hadn't missed. "Thanks."

My mother put a protective arm around me. "I was just telling Nurse Smith how much you were looking forward to going back to work, So-So."

I could only wonder on which planet she lived. My father's eye-roll as he walked over to join us said he shared my same thought.

"Let's not get into all that now, dear," he told her. "Sophie's had a rough week."

My mother started defending herself, but Smith interrupted.

"That's okay. We'll welcome Sophie whenever she's ready. But I better head off now. The bus to Sterlingwood is probably ready to leave. It was nice talking to you all." She smiled at me before she walked away, but I had no energy to do the same.

I waited until she was out of earshot before turning to my mother. "We haven't even talked about my going back to work. Why did you say that to her?"

"Well, dear, you've had the whole week off now. Getting back on the horse will do you a lot of good."

"But, Mom—"

"I'm just saying, So-So, you can't avoid your life."

"How can you say that? My friend just died."

Always the referee, my father eased in between us and herded us toward the car. Once inside, my mother laid her head on the seat. "Enough of all this talk. Let's go. I'm about to melt in this heat."

My father concentrated on the road, but when the silence dragged on, he began fidgeting with the radio dials. My mother slapped his hand. "Let that be now. The quiet is good."

His eyes in the rearview mirror pleaded with me to speak up and vote for the radio, but after the commotion of the service, the quiet *was* good. My brain had been spinning for hours and needed the break. I closed my eyes to the sound of passing cars.

Emma Jean's service had resembled no funeral I'd ever attended. We should have been mourning the loss as opposed to rejoicing. Though the festivities mimicked her zest for life, they all seemed a bit disloyal.

Oh Happy Day, my butt.

With nothing to celebrate, my gut clenched. I missed my friend. I missed her laugh. But most of all, I missed her interpretation of the craziness all around me. Without her, crazy would go back to just plain sad. Her outlook had given me hope. Her humor had brought me to work each day. How could I ever go back to Sterlingwood without her?

My eyes filled with tears for the millionth time. I hugged my purse, the book inside the only thing still connecting me to Emma Jean.

At home, my parents and I drifted to separate rooms. Telling them I planned to change clothes and nap, I locked my door. With trembling hands, I removed Miss Rabbit's book from my purse.

A trespasser. That's who I was. I had no business with the book. Why hadn't Emma Jean left instructions for Clifford to give it to Miss Rabbit's brother Emery?

The questions futile, I unwrapped the plastic before I could talk myself out of it. The envelope with my name and phone number scrawled across the front lay inside. I took a deep breath and opened the note.

Sophie—

This might be the craziest thing I ever done, but you leaving my house tonight, the fool out there shooting a gun, got me to thinking that if something happens to me, I don't want this book lost. It ain't mine and I ain't taking any chances. I need to do right by Mable. I made a promise.

You're the only one besides me and Mable who knows about this book. She gave it to me for safekeeping and now I's making sure you gets it. You need to know Mable suffered her whole damn life, blamed herself for something weren't her fault. After she's gone, her kin—or what's left of it—needs to know what really happened. Hell, maybe everybody needs to know what happened. But not until she's gone. Being poor, being a woman, being black—ain't no excuses for what she done had to go through. I know this book won't change no history, but if I knows anything about the importance of truth, I know it can change a life.

Take this, read it, and hold on to it. If she's still alive, let Mable know, best you can, that you understand. If'n you can't do that, child, at least learn from the words. See how a heavy burden bends a person, how no one be fit to judge a woman til they walk in her shoes. Mable, like your mama, did what she could with what she knew. Ain't no blame in that.

Now I's trusting you with this, child. Don't let me down. If you be reading this, I's no doubt in a better place and living large.

See you when you get here,
Emma Jean
P.S. Lordy, I hope they bury me with my good wig!
For the first time in a week, I laughed.

Had the new wig she'd had on been her good wig? I hated to think otherwise. Some fool shooting a gun? I had no idea. Even faced with danger, Emma Jean had looked after me. Hard to believe I owed ownership of this book to a gunshot.

I refolded the letter and stared at Miss Rabbit's book.

What had Emma Jean meant by 'like your mama, she did what she could with what she knew'?

I searched the pages for the last sentences Emma Jean had read to me. Words flew past. Mable's Spelling Bee ribbon...their moving in with Luther...his drinking...his job loss. I found the last familiar sentence.

I wasn't sure why Luther lost his job at the restaurant. Later, I heard him and Mama talking one morning, fighting really, before Mama went to work. Only bits and pieces, something about him looking sideways at some white lady. He swore up and down he hadn't, but I'm not sure Mama believed him. So he was out of a job and Mama was mad.

She went off to work and we didn't get to go to Mrs. Marbly's house because Luther was home. Cross as a woke up bear, he kept yelling about any little thing we did. At lunchtime, Abigail pulled something off the table, made a mess, and Luther yelled like we all done broke the law. He got so mad he picked up a dish and throwed it up against the wall. Pieces scattered across the kitchen. 'Bout scared me half to death.

When Luther told me to clean it up Emery high-tailed it back into our bedroom with Abigail. Luther sat there, giving me instruction on what to do the whole time, never once offering to help clean the mess he and Abigail done made.

You ain't good for nothing around here anyway, he yelled. If you been watching the baby like you was supposed to, this wouldn't have happened.

I knew to keep my mouth shut and just do what he told me, but I was fighting back my tears—

A knock on my locked bedroom door and I hid the book under the bed covers.

"So-So, you still awake?"

"Yes, Mom. I'm just laying down now."

"Well, try not to sleep too long. You'll never sleep tonight if you do."

"Okay, I won't. Wake me in an hour if you don't see me."

Her footsteps faded. My heart found its normal pace and I picked up where I'd left off.

Now don't you go and be a crybaby, Luther said. You know this is your fault, Mable. Clean it up and clean it up good. I don't want to see any mess when you're done.

Broken glass be everywhere. Milk had done splattered all over the table, cabinets and floor. I grabbed a towel and tried to mop it all up, but it be a bigger mess than the one little towel could handle. I must not have been working fast enough because Luther yelled again.

You're such a spoiled little Mama's girl. You ain't never gonna amount to nothing. You know that, Mable? You ain't nothing but an ugly, fat girl who ain't got no idea how hard your mama and I work to put food in your mouth.

His words hurt so much I wanted to run away, but I kept trying to wipe up the mess, not saying nothing. I cut my hand on some glass and he never moved. He just got madder and madder, no matter how fast I worked.

He hollered for Emery, told him to bring Abigail.

Eyes not looking at Luther, Emery led Abigail into the kitchen. She had my Cynthia's arm in her mouth, sucking on that doll just like Emery done as a young'un.

Take the baby outside, Luther told him. Me and Mable is fixing to have us a little talk.

He asked where Billy was and Emery told him Billy had left.

Speak up when I'm talking to you, boy.

He backhanded Emery right across the face. Seeing Emery was

*only nine and still as skinny as an autumn scarecrow, he couldn't take
no blow like that. Knocked him right off his feet. I made a move to
help him up.*

*Stay right where you are, child, and finish cleaning up that mess,
Luther said. Then he turned to Emery crying on the floor. Stop your
whining and be a man. Get up or I'll smack you again.*

*Emery stood, wiping his snotty nose with his sleeve. His little chest
be heaving up and down inside his shirt. I thought he was fixing to
faint.*

Look at me when I'm talking to you, boy.

*I remember thinking Luther could kill Emery right then and
there. It only take Luther a second to snap Emery's neck, just like
Granddad used to do with the chickens.*

I couldn't watch.

*Moving fast as I could, I wrung out the towel in the sink and
grabbed a dustpan for the broken glass. Luther bellowed at Emery,
getting down right close to his face.*

*You get outside. And don't you come back until I call for you.
Understand? And don't you be running over to old Mrs. Marbly's
house. If I hear you said anything to anybody about me slapping you,
I'll see you can't walk for a week. You got that?*

*Luther grabbed Emery by the throat, picked him up until his feet
came clear off the ground. Emery's eyes got as big as supper plates. A
big dark spot grew on the front of his pants. I wanted to kill Luther
right then for hurting my brother, but I was so scared, I reckoned if I
moved he'd kill us both.*

*Luther let go and Emery collapsed into a heap on the floor. Luther
kicked him and told him to get out. Without even a glance at me,
Emery scrambled to his feet, grabbed Abigail, and flew out the screen
door. The sound of that door slamming felt like a death sentence.*

*I had nearly all the broken dish and milk cleaned up when Luther
yelled at me.*

*You ain't done yet? What'd I tell you? You ain't gonna listen
then I'm gonna have to teach you a lesson.*

He crossed the room to me cowering against the icebox.

You lay hands on me and I'll tell Mama, I told him.

Thinking back, those words probably be what got me in trouble. He pulled me by my braid and when I tried to scratch his face, he twisted my wrist behind my back. Hurt so bad I thought my arm broke. His leaning in real close to my face, I could smell the liquor on his breath and his old man body odor. Made me sick to my stomach.

He threw me over his shoulder and carried me to the back bedroom. He closed and locked the door then tossed me on the bed Emery and I shared, told me not to move. He said if'n I made a sound he would kill me, that my mama or Emery would never miss their fat ugly girl. I squeezed my eyes as tight as I could, prayed he would drop dead right there in front of me.

I shut my eyes to stop the words. My brain couldn't process such cruelty. Little Mable attacked by a grown man? Emery backhanded as a nine-year-old? What kind of man does that to children? And why would Emma Jean want me to read such horrible things?

There must be a reason. I had to keep going.

All these years later, I can't even make myself remember what happened after the last thing he said. I don't know what I focused on to get through what he did to me. I do know he nearly split me in half. I also know I wished he would die.

Before that day, my girlfriends and me used to talk about where babies came from, but we didn't know the details about the business boys did to girls. Mama had sat me down when I got my monthly at age twelve, but she didn't tell me much. She said I had to stay away from boys til I was grown, but nothing she said prepared me for Luther. His big, old fat body pressing me real hard. His hand shoving my face into the bed pillow so no sound could come out of me. Every part of me hurt. His stink filled my nose.

Then at some point it was over.

He was careful not to leave any marks—least not on the outside. I remember he stroked my hair and dug his fat fingers into the back of my neck.

179

You ain't gonna to tell anyone about this, he said. It gonna be our little secret and if I hear of you telling anyone, that kitten you keeping under the porch is gonna be strung up from the nearest tree. Maybe I'll even go after your brother. You hear me, girl?

The kitten was the first animal I got to call my own. We had chickens at Granddad's farm, but those didn't count. The kitten's mama must have left her under the porch. I heard her there one morning after a rainstorm. No bigger than my hand, fur all dirty, it meowed something fierce. I asked Mama if I could keep it. She told me I couldn't bring it in the house, but she must have felt sorry for it, though, because she gave me an old milk crate and a towel to keep the kitten warm. I fed it scraps—even named it Scrappy—and it wound up hanging around. Luther hated that little kitten so I knew he weren't fooling when he said he'd string it from a tree. The thought of Scrappy hanging from a tree kept my mouth shut, all right. Luther must have figured as much because he finally climbed off of me.

You go on now get yourself cleaned up, he told me. Get that bed sheet washed up, too, and finish up with that mess in the kitchen before your mama and brother get home. And I don't want to see your ugly face outside until it's done neither. You got that?

I remember the screen door slamming, him yelling for Emery, but I didn't hear nothing after that. Don't know how long I laid there neither, but I know I stayed still as I could, afraid some part of me would break off if I moved. Funny thing, I don't remember nothing until later on when I was outside hanging up the sheet to dry. I must have cleaned up the kitchen too because the mess was gone and I know no one else would have done it.

Mrs. Marbly's voice is what I remember next. She yelled over to me from her yard next door.

Hey child, where ya been all day?

A row of wooden pins all stuck to her white apron, she was hanging up her washing and looking just like my Nana. I wanted to run to her, but I was too scared. I didn't know where Luther was, didn't know if he was watching.

Whatcha doing, she yelled. Helping your mama? Aren't you a good girl, Mable. You okay, child? You don't look well. Something wrong?

She started to walk over, but I shook my head. I could just see little Scrappy or Emery hanging from a tree. I hurried up with them sheets and scooted back inside. I didn't want Luther to see me talking to her. I laid down on the mattress and think I stayed there until I heard Mama's voice when she came in the back door from working.

Where's my sweet little Mable, she called. My little washing helper?

I ran towards the sound of her voice, but ran smack into Luther instead. He grabbed me by the hair.

I will hurt you, child, he whispered, his voice so low Mama wouldn't hear. Not a word, he said.

He let go and I cowered against the wall, my underpants wet from the pee and Lord knows what else that sneaked out.

Mama found us in the hallway and thanked me for helping her with the washing. I threw my arms around her, but she wriggled out of my hold and went back in the kitchen. Just like the scared rabbit I was, I ran after her.

I flipped through the remaining pages. Part of me wanted to keep reading, but Emma Jean had been right–too much for one sitting, too much to comprehend. My head hurt and my heart ached. Miss Rabbit had been three years younger than me when Luther raped her. He deserved to be strung up from the nearest tree–if he wasn't dead already. And poor Miss Rabbit. Her living with the memory all these years made me sick.

Was there any point now in getting her to talk? Would it be better to just finish the book, tuck it away, and let her live her last years in peace?

I reopened Emma Jean's note to search for an answer. Her voice spoke to me, loud and clear.

Let Mable know, best you can, that you understand. If'n you can't do that, child, at least read the words. See how a heavy burden bends a person.

But they don't have to stay bent, right?

Now I's trusting you with this, Sophie. Don't let me down.

Never, Emma Jean.

I tucked the book under my pillow. It was time to get back to work.

CHAPTER 29

By the time I dressed and went downstairs, my resolve to reverse the damage done by Luther had only strengthened. With no plan, no clear idea what Emma Jean's intention had been, blind faith moved me forward. These events—the book, Emma Jean's dying, my work at the nursing home—had come together for a reason. I just had to figure out what that reason was.

Conversation in the kitchen stopped my descent on the stairs.

"This whole week has been hard on her," my mother said.

"Hard on *her*? My mother hasn't even called me since she left."

Penny's trademark whine triggered the hair on the back of my neck. Just like her to turn the day into one about herself. I straightened my shoulders and entered the kitchen.

My mother, at the table with Penny, raised an eyebrow at the sight of my uniform. "So-So, you're dressed for work?"

My father, bent over to peer inside the refrigerator, straightened up too fast and bumped his head. Penny eyed me from top to bottom and snickered. "Nice outfit."

I resisted slapping her. "Like you said, Mom, time to get back on the horse."

"Oh, So-So." Hand to her heart, she smiled. "I'm so proud of you."

My father put an arm around me. "Honey, you sure you're ready? No one is forcing you to go back."

Leaning into the strength he offered, I nodded.

Penny pushed from the table. "Geez, I wouldn't work in that place for all the money in the world. You're crazy, if you ask me."

"But I didn't ask you, did I?" The temptation to wring her neck drove me a step closer, but my father grabbed my arm.

Mouth agape, Penny returned my glare for an instant before she stood, her long, California blond hair flipping with attitude over her shoulder. "Fine, Sophie. Be that way. I need a friend right now, but I can see you obviously don't care that my mother is gone and still hasn't called."

My mother, eyes widening, rose from her seat. "Now, Penny, let's not get carried away. We've all had some tragic news this past week. I don't think So-So intended to make you feel bad—"

Penny pulled from my mother's outstretched hand. "Sophie doesn't care about my feelings. All she cares about is some stranger dying–and a colored lady no less!"

My father released his hold on my arm. I guessed he'd had enough of Penny's nonsense, as well, but my mother held up a hand. "Penny, that's not true. We all care about your feelings."

I took a deep breath so I wouldn't yell. "Mom, please. Don't speak for me." I leaned into Penny's face, forced her to meet my gaze. "Yes, I care that your mother's gone, but ever since you found out I was adopted, you haven't said anything nice. You act like you're better than me. Well, now you know what it's like to be...what did you call it? Dumped? I lost a friend this week. Not a stranger. Not *a colored lady*. A friend."

As if unwilling to be party to my conduct, my mother sat down hard on her chair and averted her eyes.

Her actions weren't going to stop me. I pressed a finger into Penny's chest. "And not once since my friend died have you shown me a bit of friendship. You come over here whining, telling me I'm not paying enough attention to you, then you have the nerve to tell me I'm crazy for going back to work. You accuse me of being selfish? Look in the mirror." I spit the last words like venom.

Penny eyes filled with tears. She took a step back and looked to each of my parents in turn. I suspect she assumed they would come to her defense, but neither of them spoke. My mother didn't even look at her. I waited for my heart to stop pounding while Penny sniffed and wiped her eyes.

My father cleared his throat. "Okay, Sophie. That's enough now. We've all had a very stressful week. I don't think any of us are thinking clearly. Let's stop before we say things we don't mean." He walked over to Penny.

She shoved him before he got close enough to comfort her. "Don't touch me!"

"Pen—" He reached for her flailing arms.

Like an unleashed yo-yo, she swirled from him. "I hate you stupid people! I don't want to speak to any of you ever again."

My mother, now on her feet, stopped Penny on the rebound and caught her in a body hug. She held on, shushing her with whispers, until big, heaving sobs replaced Penny's angry words. She inched over to a bench along the wall and pulled Penny to sit beside her. "It's okay, honey. Everything is going to be fine."

I didn't budge. The whole spectacle left me speechless. Once again, Penny had turned events to suit her needs. My father and I exchanged glances, his saying "Give a little," mine saying "Over my dead body." A moment passed before I caved in to the plea in his eyes.

"Penny, I'm sorry."

She buried her head into my mother's neck and refused to look at me.

"Penny, I said I was sorry," I offered, louder this time.

"So-So, it's okay," my mother said, stroking Penny's hair. "She's just upset. You go on now, get to work. She just needs some time."

Frustration filled my father's face as he hugged me. "We're all proud of your decision to go back to work, Sophie," he whispered. "Don't worry about Penny. She'll be fine."

"Thanks, Dad."

My mother smiled and made a kissing gesture. Penny, eyes still closed, and nestled tight against her, obviously intended to milk the moment for everything she could. It took all my strength not to thump her thoughtless head.

My father handed me his car keys from his trouser pocket. A box of cookies on the counter caught my eye. "Is it okay if I take these?"

When my mother nodded, I grabbed the cookies, the car keys, and slammed the door behind me.

I hadn't driven anywhere in the last week. It felt good to be out of the house, all by myself and away from Penny's drama. On a whim, I drove a different route to work. Stopped at a red light, I spotted a floral shop up ahead. The sign—Pick Me Up Some Posies—reminded me of Emma Jean. When the light changed, I pulled into the parking lot.

As I entered the store, bells tied to the shop's door jingled like Dorothy Crumble's holiday socks. Would I ever be able to wear those again and not think of Emma Jean?

A girl about my age set down an armload of flowers. "Can I help you?"

"I'm here to pick me up some posies."

She laughed, though I guessed she'd heard the line more than once. "Have anything particular in mind?"

I pointed to a pot full of purple flowers sitting in the front window. "Those, please."

"Good choice. They're on sale today."

Another sign of things meant to be, I paid for the flowers and left the shop. With thirty minutes before shift change, I had plenty of time. No one knew I planned on coming in, but I couldn't imagine they'd turn me away. Hadn't Smith said they'd welcome me back any time I was ready?

Now or never. I threw the car in reverse.

CHAPTER 30

A screaming baby greeted me at Sterlingwood. A young woman, bouncing the child in her arms, stood as I neared. "Sorry. I can't seem to get him quieted."

"Doesn't bother me. This place gets pretty noisy all by itself."

She pulled a pacifier from her pocket and put it into the baby's mouth. As if someone had hit a power switch, the room fell silent.

"I guess I should have thought of that first," she said, laughing.

I smiled and walked away, but she showed up beside me and kept pace. "I'm Sarah. Sarah Chilton." She recited her name like she expected recognition.

I couldn't place her. "I'm Sophie."

"You're an aide here. You must know my husband Tommy."

My feet slowed. The details of Sarah Chilton's letter flashed through my mind. Car accident. Coma. Vegetable. I didn't know whether I should pretend I hadn't heard her or stop and give her a hug.

"I know it's tough," she said. "I'm used to people freezing up like you just did. No one knows what to say to me. It's okay."

"I'm sorry. I'm not very good at this stuff yet." I swallowed the lump forming in my throat. "The letter you wrote about what happened? Thank you for that. It's good to know things about the people here. I'm very sorry about your husband."

Her eyes misted.

Too soon to deal with anyone else's tears, I juggled my flowers and box of cookies, put my free hand on her back, and encouraged her to walk with me. When the silence turned awkward, I asked, "What's your baby's name?"

"Tommy Junior," she said as we reached her husband's room.

I brushed my fingers against the now content baby's head. His hair matched his father's cinnamon color—a fact that, days before, would have made me cry or curse my choice of jobs. This time, I weighed this woman's burden against my own and offered a smile. "Nice to meet you both."

Downstairs, the door to Miss Rabbit's room sat open a crack. I listened for voices before I knocked and walked in.

Miss Rabbit looked up from the Bible in her lap. The silence between us filled with words neither of us could speak—mine announced the battles I'd fought the last week, hers affirmed a stubborn determination. I placed the pot of flowers and cookies on the bedside table and bent to hug her. She smelled of baby powder and old yarn. Her frail shoulders stiffened at my touch. When I refused to let go, she raised her one good arm to my back. I hadn't cried in over two hours, convinced I'd shed my last tear, but this woman's touch threatened my resolve. Her tiny body quivered as she pulled me close. The first sound I heard from Miss Rabbit was her weeping.

In the moments we held each other, an English class lesson I'd once had came to mind. The teacher had introduced us to the word catharsis. When I had raised my hand for clarification, she defined the process of emotional release. At the time, the word played through my brain like a song set to repeat. As I scribbled the word in my notebook, its syllables and cadence suggested a liberation of sorts. I had imagined what it would be like to let go of feelings held too long, but wondered how purging one's soul could be good when vomit left an aftertaste.

Now I was convinced that living happily ever after had to be a myth, release a contradiction. Miss Rabbit served as proof. Cleansing her soul hadn't worked. I doubted it would work for me either. No matter what happened, both of us would forever carry the sour bile of past events.

I held on to Miss Rabbit until her shoulders stilled then leaned back to meet her eye. Now that I could pair her written words with the tone in her cries, the weight of her features was obvious. The furrow between her eyes screamed of worry. The lines at the corners of her mouth could only have been etched by a lifetime of sadness. How had I been so shortsighted? Why hadn't I taken the time to consider reasons for her silence? Like Penny, I'd never seen beyond my own needs.

I grabbed tissues for both of us and wiped my eyes.

"This is a hard day for me, Miss Rabbit, coming back to work and all."

Her hand trembled as she blew her nose.

Should I mention her book? Tell her I was now in charge of its safekeeping?

Emma Jean's words—let her know you understand—echoed, but not yet ready to go that direction, I took a deep breath. "I'm back because of you, Miss Rabbit. I'm still not sure how I'll get through this day, but I'm here for you. Emma Jea—" Her name tripped me. "I'm sure she'd want me to be here."

A tear slid down Miss Rabbit's cheek.

"I didn't see you at her funeral. I don't know if anyone asked you at the time, but I should have made sure you got there. I didn't think. I'm sorry."

Miss Rabbit shook her head and turned her gaze to the window. With her good hand, she reached for mine, her bony fingers stronger than I imagined.

As her thumb fretted the skin on the back of my hand, the sounds outside her room reminded me of other things I had to do. "I should probably get upstairs now and tell Nurse Smith I'm here."

Her hand tightened around mine before she nodded and let go. I gestured to the cookies and flowers on the table. "Those are for you. Save me a cookie. I'll come back during break."

Her tiny smile had to be a good sign.

When I reached the door, I turned around.

"Sophie." A single word spoken in little more than a whisper.

I glanced down the hall, but found no one there.

Could it be?

I poked my head inside the room. Miss Rabbit still faced the window. She couldn't have intended to get my attention. And yet...I'd clearly heard my name.

Was my mind playing tricks? The last few days had been brutal, but imaginary voices?

Shaking my head, I eased out of the room.

CHAPTER 31

At the nurse's station, Nurse Smith, once again in her standard uniform, looked up from a chart when I approached the desk. Recognition focused her eyes. "Welcome back."

"Thanks." I ran a nervous hand through my hair. "Sorry I didn't call. This was kind of spur of the moment."

"Not a problem. We're short-handed anyway, what with Em—" Her mouth snapped shut. A second passed before she moved to touch me. Her hand stopped halfway and returned to its place by her side.

"It's okay. I won't break."

"I'm sorry. This is hard for both of us." She cocked her head and studied me. "You sure you're ready to be here?"

"No, I'm really not, but like my mother said, time to get back on the horse."

She stared at me a moment, then slid a chart back into its slot in the carousel. "Okay. How about you take A-Wing? I can go help out on D."

"Sounds good. Thanks." A-Wing held most of my favorite people.

Smith walked around the desk and placed an arm around me.

Shoulder to shoulder, she squeezed, then stepped back and looked me in the eye. "I've told you this before, but it bears repeating–especially today. I'm impressed with you, Sophie. Returning speaks to your character. I just want you to know that the residents and I appreciate it."

I hoped either the blush creeping up my face or my fidgeting would change the subject. Mrs. Kowalski intervened instead. "Hey lady, piece of bread or a cold potato? C'mon, I'm hungry."

I'd forgotten my candy stash.

Mrs. Kowalski put her hand on me. "C'mon lady, I'm hungry. Just a piece of bread or a cold potato."

Smith opened a drawer. Pulling out cigarettes, matches and assorted other things, she laid them on the counter. Digging further, she located a candy bar and handed it to Mrs. Kowalski. "Here you go. A gift from Tanya."

"I wouldn't do that if I were you."

Smith looked at me like I'd said something stupid. "We both know the last thing Tanya needs is more candy. Besides, between you and me, I got Pete to tell me Tanya was the one who took away his cigarettes that day he left. Her word against his, I know, but giving away her candy is the least I can do for the trouble she caused." She winked at me. "If she ever asks, we'll just tell her Pete took it."

In my absence, Smith had grown a sense of humor.

Mrs. Kowalski fumbled with the wrapper until I came to her aid, then she stuffed the bulk of the candy bar into her mouth and left. Smith already preoccupied with another chart, I headed to A-Wing. The sound of laughter and blaring music had me peek inside the Day Room. A disgruntled Ruby wheeled into my path.

"What's the matter?" I asked her.

"Oh, these morons are watching some stupid cartoon. You'd think none of them had any brains. I'll turn into a blithering idiot if I stay in here any longer."

Caroline, sitting amongst the others, laughed the loudest. The action in cartoons transcending the language barrier, even Mama smiled.

"They seem to be enjoying it."

"They're all nuts, that's why." Ruby shook her head. "Put me to bed. I'm tired now."

"It's a little early for bed, isn't it?"

"Hogwash. I can go to bed if I want."

Unsure if I should indulge her lazy tendencies, I hesitated.

"Never mind, I'll find someone else to help me." She nearly ran over my foot maneuvering her chair past. Determination drove her down the hall. Stubborn as a mule, meaner than a snake, she made it difficult to be nice.

"Good night, Ruby. Sleep well."

She raised an arm. "Ah, go to hell."

A memory of a tough Emma Jean stayed my feet. "Not after all I been through. You can take that," I snapped my fingers, "to the bank."

Mr. Messina, pushing Cynthia in her chair, rounded the corner in front of Mrs. Applebee's room. "Good afternoon, dear."

Cynthia raised her head and mewled. Drool slid from her mouth.

"Hi." I grabbed the towel he kept on her shoulder and wiped her mouth. He didn't like people to see her drool. "How are you two?"

"Thank you, dear." He refolded the towel. "We're good. Aren't we, Cynthia?" The smell of alcohol accompanied his words.

Unsure of what else to say, I moved past him. Better to avoid talk of the funeral, anyway.

Mrs. Applebee charged out of her room. "My goodness, I have been looking all over for you. Where on earth have you been?"

Flattered, I wrapped an arm around her shoulder. "Hi, Mrs. App—"

She brushed past me and grabbed Mr. Messina's arm. "Fred, I've been worried sick about you."

Mr. Messina, his face now crimson, patted her hand. "I'm sorry, Martha. I had to take Cynthia for a little walk."

Ignoring the slight, I snickered. "But have you fed her cats?"

He didn't answer, reaching instead to wipe Cynthia's mouth. Mrs. Applebee stared at me. A few seconds passed in uncomfortable silence.

"Well, I need to get people down to dinner." I patted Cynthia's hand and headed down the hall. "I'll talk to you all later."

After I'd taken a few steps, Mrs. Applebee whispered, "Fred, who is that woman? And why in the world does she think I have cats?"

Somewhere, Emma Jean had to be just peeing in her pants.

CHAPTER 32

For the next couple of hours, I helped the residents on A-Wing. Thoughts of Emma Jean accompanied my every move. Her absence turned out to be as hard to ignore as her physical presence. Her laughter ringing out in the hallways, I kept chasing the lingering aroma of her baby powder. Though I couldn't expect someone like Mama to notice the difference, others, like Mr. Messina and Porky, should have commented on her absence. Did life just go on like my mother said? The same sense of disloyalty I'd experienced earlier in the day returned. This 'going on' made us all traitors to her memory.

When break time arrived, I walked to the porch. I had no sooner closed the door behind me when Emma Jean's empty spot on the steps sent me scurrying inside. We'd had our best conversation on those steps. I couldn't sit there alone.

Taking the stairs two at a time, I went to visit Miss Rabbit. Maybe she had saved me a cookie.

Dorothy's hoarse voice greeted me from the shadows of a doorway. "I didn't think we'd see you back here."

I shrugged and kept walking.

Cigarette in hand, she propelled her chair to keep up. "Boy, sure has been quiet around here without Emma Jean."

I had been wrong. Not hearing Emma Jean's name was easier.

"I tell you, Mable sure has been broke up." Short on breath, her words wheezed out like steam. "Have you seen her yet?"

I stopped and faced her. "I thought you knew everything around here, Dorothy."

"No, not everything."

"Yes, I saw her when I first came in. What do you mean she's been broke up?"

A long ash fell from Dorothy's cigarette. I scattered the remains with my foot.

She wiped a piece of stray tobacco from the corner of her mouth. "She hasn't left her room. I hear she isn't eating, either. I tried going in there a couple of times, but she just ignores me. Granted, she doesn't ever talk to me, but now, seems she won't even listen. I'm worried."

"What do you think I can do?"

She glanced down both ends of the hallway then tugged on my arm. "Come to my room a minute. I don't want anyone to hear us."

With no doubt the invitation to her room promised something of interest, I did as she asked.

"Close the door." She set her ashtray and cigarettes on the table then maneuvered her chair around to face me.

Her overflowing shelves and the shopping bags scattered over the floor hinted of a recent shopping trip. A stuffed animal with big, blue glass eyes peeked out from the top of one of the bags.

"What's with the cat?"

"Mr. Messina ordered it special for Martha Applebee. She has a birthday coming up."

The cat's long white hair matched the description Martha had given me during her one lucid moment. "Why didn't he just go buy it?"

"I don't ask questions, Sophie. A buck is a buck. I take 'em any way I can get 'em."

Dorothy's shopping on behalf of a fully capable Mr. Messina

made no sense, but little did as of late. "Okay, so what's this big secret you don't want anyone to hear?"

"I'm concerned about Mable now that Emma Jean is gone."

"You said that, but I'm not sure what you think I can do about it."

She leaned forward. "Sophie..."

I met her gaze, but the light reflecting off her glasses hid her eyes and kept me at a disadvantage. I shifted my position to reclaim a sense of space between us.

"Mable used to talk to Emma Jean."

Her announcement propelled me like cold water thrown in my face. Though I'd suspected Miss Rabbit spoke to Emma Jean, I'd had no proof, and Emma Jean had misled me every time I'd brought up the subject. "She talks?"

Dorothy slumped back in her chair, as if the weight of this secret had fallen off her shoulders. "Only to Emma Jean. And not a soul knows this."

"Except you. And now me."

Dorothy nodded. With an unsteady hand, she reached for a cigarette. "I swore to myself I'd never tell anyone. I mean, Mable doesn't have to talk if she doesn't want to, but now with Emma Jean gone..." She took a deep drag of her cigarette and closed her eyes. The slow, steady stream of smoke she exhaled enveloped us in a blue cloud. "I've been torn up about this all week, wondering what to do."

Questions flooded my brain. "When did she start talking?"

"Not long ago. I couldn't sleep one night. Got up to find a nurse for a sleeping pill. That's when I heard voices in Mable's room. The door was open a crack. I stopped." She shrugged. "Can't blame me. Pretty rare to hear two voices in Mable's room, especially that time of night."

"What was Emma Jean doing in her room at night?"

"Working night shift. Right after that big to-do with Mrs. Riggler's bedsore. When the aides got the boot, she filled in."

"Did you hear what they were saying?"

"Not really."

"Well, what *did* you hear?"

"I didn't listen for very long, afraid someone would see me. I didn't want to let the cat out of the bag."

When she snickered I followed her gaze to the stuffed animal in corner of the room. The cat's eyes, barely visible at the edge of the sack, stared back. A shiver slid down my spine.

"She spoke to me."

Dorothy's eyebrows climbed her forehead. "The cat?"

"No. Miss Rabbit. This morning when I went in to see her. She said my name as I left the room."

"See, I was right," she said, spreading her arms wide. "You're the one she'll talk to now. You'll take Emma Jean's place."

I laid my head on Dorothy's pillow and studied the cracks on the ceiling. All her talk about Miss Rabbit made me nervous. If she'd told me, who else would she tell? I feared Miss Rabbit's secret wouldn't stay secret for very long.

CHAPTER 33

The clock on Dorothy's nightstand confirmed I had been on break too long, but I still didn't have any idea what to do about Miss Rabbit. Coming to work with a mission to encourage her to talk, I now had the sense some things might just be better left alone. Things were getting too complicated and I doubted I had the strength. Who was I to try to make her speak? She could talk and did–just not to me. Couldn't Emma Jean giving me the book be enough? In time, Miss Rabbit might come out of her self-imposed shell. Who said I had to push her?

While the hand on the clock inched forward, I rubbed my stomach, trying to unravel the painful knots inside. I had people to take to dinner and no time to figure out this new problem Dorothy presented.

"Are you going to go see Mable?" Her eyes said she had no plans of backing off.

"When I get a chance." I stood and smoothed the bedspread. "But can you swear you haven't told anyone else about this?"

She nodded with enough emphasis that her glasses slid down her nose. "I didn't even tell Emma Jean."

"We have to keep it that way for now. You realize this, right?"

"Why do you think I haven't told anyone?" She lowered her voice. "Answer one thing for me, though. Did Emma Jean ever mention anything about a book?"

Her breadth of knowledge amazed me, but I kept the surprise from my voice. "Book?"

Averting her eyes, she dismissed my question with the back of her hand. "Something I once heard Emma Jean saying. Don't really know what she was talking about." She mumbled, as if doing so would make the words less of a fib.

How much of the story did she know? Better not to go there yet.

"If you figure it out, let me know. I have to get folks to dinner. I'll see you later."

"You'll talk to Mable soon though, right?"

"Soon as I can, Dorothy. In the meantime, can you just let her be?"

Emma Jean's very words to me. Now I understood them.

Upstairs, wheelchair residents lined up for dinner choked the hallway. Two aides were doing their best to quell the chaos. One whose name I couldn't remember gestured to me. "Give Mrs. Applebee a nudge, will you? Last I looked, she didn't know what she wanted to wear. I'm afraid she'll miss dinner and get all worked up. I've got my hands full here."

Mrs. Applebee, sitting in a chair in her room, stared at her open closet. Several articles of clothing lay scattered across her bed.

"Mrs. Applebee, it's time for dinner."

No recognition in her eyes.

"Mrs. Applebee? Do you want to get dressed?"

"I am kind of hungry."

"Which dress would you like to wear?"

"This is fine," she said, gesturing to what she had on.

"You can't go to dinner dressed in a slip. How about one of these outfits?" I pointed to the pile on her bed.

"Those aren't my things."

I rummaged through her closet and pulled out a pink dress. "How about this?"

"It's lovely, dear, but it's not mine."

"But Fred brought it today as a surprise for you."

She cocked her head, eyes flickering as her brain tried to process the information. "Who's Fred?"

It was like a chalkboard being slowly erased. Another memory gone with each tick of the clock.

She finally agreed to wear the dress, but left the room without her purple hat.

The cats, Fred, and now her hat? Hours earlier, I had laughed at the absurdity of her questions. Now the weight of what they meant slowed my feet. How much longer did she have before every memory disappeared? Could the same thing happen to me one day? I'd never had a more dismal thought. Sterlingwood had begun contaminating my mind.

"Sophie, can you take those people down?" The aide whose name I couldn't remember pointed to the full elevator then turned her attention to two male residents in a quarrel over a set of locked wheelchair brakes.

The man with the locked wheels, his face the same shade of red as his shirt, slapped her hand when she reached for the brake lever. "I'm sick and tired of these people trying to budge ahead of me in line. They can just wait until I'm good and goddamned ready to move."

I jumped into the elevator before anyone could involve me.

As the doors shut, the second man yelled, "Go straight to hell!"

One of the ladies beside me in the elevator put a hand on my arm. "Let's not push *that* button, okay?"

Someone else who still had a sense of humor.

Downstairs, I helped everyone off the elevator and found each of them space at a table. Returning to the elevator with every intention of riding back up, I jumped out, too tired to deal with the turmoil upstairs. After I made sure no one needed anything, I went to check on Miss Rabbit. She turned to me as I walked into her room, but looked away just as quickly. The cookies I'd brought earlier sat unopened on a bedside table.

"Aren't you going to dinner?"

She gestured to a dinner tray on the top of her dresser.

I removed the metal cover and cringed. Fish sticks swimming in grease, cold potatoes, limp broccoli topped with what looked like a frozen pat of butter, and a flattened roll.

She wrinkled her nose and turned back to the window.

"How about I go out to find us both something to eat after everyone is finished with dinner?" I said, betting I could get away with such a thing on my first day back at work.

She ignored me.

"There's a pizza place right down the road. You have to eat. Emma Jean would be giving you hell right now if she were here, you know?"

Her good hand fidgeted with the hem of her housecoat.

"Since she's not here, I'll come every day, even on my days off, just to see you. I'm never going to let you be." I sat on the bed and grabbed her hand.

Her lips pursed. The muscle in her jaw twitched. The eyes of the young, abused girl met mine. Pain, fear, and anger cowered inside the deep espresso color. My imagination brought these things into view, but I couldn't dream of her years of silence or all her self-blame.

I used a softer tone, aiming for the least threatening and most convincing words I could find. "You can talk to me. I'll do everything I can to make you feel better."

With no intention of becoming a savior, I hadn't planned this, but the scared child needed attention after all these years. I expected she would cry or at least pull her hand from mine, but she didn't. Outside the room somewhere, a tray of dishes clattered to the floor. The jangle of a dancing metal lid echoed a second longer than the rest.

"I don't like pizza."

As if it were something palpable, the sound traveled from my eardrum to brain, hop scotched across the connections there, and registered with the rational portion I still possessed. Breath filled my lungs before I could give name to the noise.

"Miss Rabbit, you spoke!"

My outburst startled her, but she quickly straightened her

glasses and resettled her gaze outside the window.

I don't like pizza? Was this all I would get?

"You said my name this morning, didn't you?"

After a moment, she nodded.

"And you didn't expect me to answer?"

A shake of her head.

We stood on the edge of a precipice. One push too hard might edge her back into silence. I needed a question requiring more than a head movement, but less than full disclosure.

"What do you have against pizza?"

She smoothed the afghan on her lap, released a deep breath, and turned to me, her face unchanged. "It gives me gas."

The days of confusion, sadness, and fear let loose in a loud snort of laughter I couldn't stop. The corners of Miss Rabbit's mouth edged upwards and, in the brief moment before she raised her hand in an attempt to prevent it, I think I even heard her laugh.

THE SECRET MISS RABBIT KEPT

CHAPTER 34

A little happy dance in order, I grabbed Miss Rabbit's hands and swung them side-to-side. The chair wheels didn't allow for much movement, but my efforts propelled her body in ways I imagined it hadn't moved in years. Her face lit up like fire in a breeze. I held her arms aloft as far as they would reach. "Oh, Miss Rabbit, I can't tell you how happy you've made me–gas or not."

The moment of unguarded happiness faded from her face. She pulled her good hand away to straighten her afghan and glasses.

"What's the matter?"

Her eyes shut, like she'd swallowed something sour.

I asked again.

Her tiny unpracticed voice did its best to convey weight. "I...don't want...to talk."

"But you are talking. Don't you see? We've made progress. That's all I wanted."

I couldn't explain why her lack of speech had eaten at me, but it had, and now, for every word she didn't speak, Luther gained one more piece of her.

A grunt of displeasure escaped her.

"We don't have to talk anymore now if you don't want." When she continued to stare out the window, I had to let go of my desire to pursue the matter. "Okay, how about you just tell me what you'd like to eat tonight?"

She pointed to the tray of cold food on her dresser.

"I can't let you eat that. It's been sitting too long. Why don't you let me surprise you? I promise it won't be pizza."

A wave of her hand told me she didn't plan to argue, or even speak, so I saved the remainder of my happy dance for the hallway.

Rounding a corner upstairs, I nearly collided with Porky. "Sorry, wasn't looking where I was going."

He shot out a hand to steady me. "I'm glad I ran into you. There's something I've been meaning to tell you." He glanced over his shoulder then whispered. "I wanted to thank you for the whiskey."

So much had happened since the day Mr. Monsanto died, a second passed before his words registered. "I told Dorothy not to tell you it was me."

"She didn't. I just knew." He gave my arm a little squeeze. "I didn't want to say this earlier in front of Mr. Messina and I haven't seen much of you since then."

"That's okay, Porky. You don't have to thank me."

"Seeing as how you just lost a friend, thought I'd return the favor." He pulled a wrapped package tied with a pink ribbon from beside his leg. "Here you go. I haven't shopped for a young girl in a long time. Dorothy helped me get it."

Heat rose to my cheeks. "You didn't have to do this."

"Go on. Open it. I won't be offended if you don't like it."

With hands beginning to sweat, I fumbled the unwrapping of a wooden box with an inscribed metal plate affixed to the top. The paper and bow fluttered to my feet as I read the words.

Porky recited the inscription aloud from memory. "'And those who were seen dancing were thought to be insane by those who could not hear the music.' Isn't that great? Dorothy came up with the saying. It's a little music box. Open it."

My hand trembled as I lifted the lid. A tiny ballerina dressed in pink stood in the center of a small mirror. With one graceful arm raised above her head, the other out to her side, she pirouetted on tiptoe to the clinking notes of a song I didn't recognize. My breath caught. "Porky, it's beautiful."

"Turn it over. There's a sticker on the bottom to tell you the name of the song."

I read through tear-filled eyes. "Dance, Ballerina, Dance." The gift touched a raw spot in my heart. I used the back of my hand to wipe my eyes. "This is so sweet. I can't believe you—"

"Dorothy and I weren't sure if it'd be ready before, I mean, *if* we saw you. She said you'd be back, but I wasn't so sure. Do you really like it?"

"This might be the nicest thing anyone's ever done for me."

"Well, that whiskey was the nicest thing anyone's done for me in a long time. Hit the spot, you might say." He laughed. "If you were a drinker, you'd know what I mean."

I closed the lid and wrapped my arms around him. "Thank you, Porky." His musty, old-man odor filled my nostrils when he raised an arm to pat me on the back.

"I'm glad you like it. I wasn't sure how to repay your kindness and, after losing Emma Jean, I thought you needed a little pick-me-up. Sure won't do like whiskey, but maybe it'll help. Dorothy said the words might remind you of all of us. I'd like to think some of us aren't crazy—at least not yet."

I ran my hand over the polished wooden box. "This is perfect."

Porky graced me with a smile so large I thought his scars might pull apart.

"You're the best." I brushed my fingers against the pigskin on his nose.

"Aww, shucks," he said, cheeks flushing. "You make me wish I was sixty years younger."

My turn to blush, I looked away.

Nurse Smith called from the end of the hallway. "Come help me, would you?"

I turned to Porky. "Thank you again for the gift."

"My pleasure." He leaned over and picked up the paper and bow. "I'll throw this away for you. Go on now. Somebody needs you."

"Can you keep this for awhile? I'll come by later to get it."

He nodded and put the box on his lap.

Smith motioned for me to follow her. "We've lost Mrs. Riggler. I want to get her cleaned up a bit before they take her away."

For the first time, the news of death didn't bring me to my knees. "When?"

"One of the aides went in there and realized she wasn't breathing. Frankly, I'm surprised she lasted this long, what with her backside so eaten away."

The memory of Mrs. Riggler's hollowed-out bedsore sent an electric shock across my chest. As we walked, Emma Jean's words and tone channeled through me. "Damn shame is what that was."

Smith stopped and cocked her head, her expression saying she recognized the words. "Yes. A damn shame *is* what that was."

A heavy silence coated Mrs. Riggler's room. Someone had pulled the sheet up over her head and unplugged the air mattress. With the drapes closed, the only light entered through the doorway. The thought of fiddling around with a dead body in near darkness didn't excite me.

"What are we doing exactly?" I asked.

"Crazy as it sounds," Smith said, flipping on the lights, "I want to change the bandage and get her hair brushed."

Nothing sounded crazy anymore.

From the opposite side of the bed, I helped turn Mrs. Riggler. Smith moved with a calculated swiftness, but the odor of the exposed crater serving as a reminder of Mrs. Riggler's unnecessary suffering, I kept my breaths shallow and my eyes averted until she finished.

"Go get wet a washcloth so we can wash her face," Smith said, grabbing a hairbrush to tidy Mrs. Riggler's white hair. When

Mrs. Riggler's mouth sagged open, I turned to my chore. The water in the bathroom took a minute to warm, but I let it run until I had to pull my hand from the heat.

"Come on, Sophie. That's good enough. Let's get this done."

When I returned with the wet towel she waved it off. "Just wipe her face. You won't get past this if you don't try."

Making sure no dead flesh touched mine, I pressed the cloth to Mrs. Riggler's forehead. I imagined her eyes closed in pleasure, the moisture coming as relief, and with each stroke, the task got easier. Dreadful imaginary bugs still crawled over my skin, but their footsteps lightened.

"See, it's not so scary. You're doing just fine." Smith smoothed the sheets as I worked.

After one last swipe at the corners of Mrs. Riggler's mouth, I stepped back. "There. How's that?"

Smith nodded. "When in doubt, Sophie, put yourself in their shoes."

I returned to the bathroom to rinse out the washcloth.

"I'm sorry. This shouldn't have happened," Smith said. "And I'll make sure nothing like this ever happens again. Not on my watch."

I poked my head out of the bathroom, but Smith hadn't been speaking to me. Her eyes, squarely focused on the still body in the bed, held a determination and sadness I hadn't seen before in her. The ultimate responsibility for Mrs. Riggler's bedsore lay in her hands as head Day Nurse. I couldn't imagine how such a thing made her feel.

A knock on the open door broke the silence. The same two men who had taken Mr. Monsanto stood in the doorway. One of them nodded my way in greeting. "Excuse me. We're here for the body. The girl at the desk sent us to this room. Coroner is on his way."

"Come on in. This is the right place. She's ready now," Smith said, patting Mrs. Riggler's hand before she turned to me. "Thanks for your help. You can go on back to whatever you were doing."

I glanced at Mrs. Riggler one final time. The fourth person to die since I'd starting working at Sterlingwood, she, like Mr. Monsanto, had never been able to say a word. Their deaths, the speed with which people left the world, scared me. Had Mrs. Riggler, Mr. Monsanto, Mrs. Steiner, or even Emma Jean, been allowed a conscious thought before they left? Did they speak of gratitude? Regret? Or did death come so fast they hadn't had time for the smallest exclamation? I knew the answer would only come when it was my time, but I envisioned Emma Jean yelling something like, "Oh Lord, not in this wig!" The thought made me laugh aloud.

In her honor, I forced my feet to do a little dance step across the threshold. One of the men with the gurney looked at me sideways. I shrugged and smiled. He just couldn't hear the music.

CHAPTER 35

My little dance, however well intended, didn't make me feel better for very long. Too many people dead. Many more sick or crazy. Although no amount of music could change those facts, I headed to Porky's room to retrieve my jewelry box.

The words etched on its lid brought Mrs. Applebee to mind. How much longer before she didn't recognize anyone? According to Dorothy and a certain cat in a bag, she had a birthday approaching. Maybe a celebration, an actual party instead of the ones she imagined, might be one of the few things she could still enjoy. I made a detour to the nurse's station to check her file for the date. The home's administrator, raising her head as I neared the counter, refocused on her stack of papers without a word.

"Hi," I said, and though it wasn't my place to ask what brought her into work dressed in grass-stained jeans on a Saturday evening, I peeked over her shoulder for a clue. A completed admission application sat atop the pile of papers.

"Hey, how you doing?" She picked up the phone and dialed.

She had forgotten my name again and her lack of interest in me said she didn't much care if I answered.

Mrs. Applebee's chart could have easily been scanned for her birth date and replaced in the carousel. I could have just walked away and not said anything, but how long did this woman plan to ignore me?

I grabbed the chart, took a seat along the wall, and waited for her to hang up the phone. Such pettiness had never been my style, but tired of people's thoughtlessness and reminded of life's brevity every place I turned, I stayed put. After all I'd been through, her inability to address me by name seemed rude. I'd taken on Penny and her bad behavior earlier in the day. I'd even gotten Miss Rabbit to talk. Seemed high time my days of being overlooked and tossed aside should end. I straightened my spine and waited.

When she replaced the receiver, I raised my voice to a volume unwarranted for the distance between us. "How are *you* doing?"

Her shoulders twitched. She looked sideways, then turned in her chair. "I'm just fine. Why do you ask?"

"It's the polite thing to do." I waited for my words to sink in. "You seem very absorbed in what you're doing and you're frowning. Thought maybe you could use the distraction."

A question formed behind her eyes. I guessed she didn't know how to converse with someone whose name escaped her.

"I'm Sophie. We've met several times. In fact, you interviewed me for this job."

"Of course. Sophie. I remember."

I might have imagined how her shoulders relaxed, but the way her eyebrows rose when she spoke my name told me she had located familiar ground. "Welcome back."

"Thanks. It's good to be here. I think."

Mumbling something about the aide who passed, she turned back to her papers.

I used my loud voice again. "Emma Jean."

"Pardon?"

"The aide who died. Her name was Emma Jean."

"Of course. Yes, I'm sorry." No eye contact accompanied the apology.

"Are you admitting someone new?" Her lack of manners

deserved my prying.

Another question in her eyes, I pointed to the form on the desk.

"Yes. We just lost one. I need to fill the bed."

"Mrs. Riggler."

"Excuse me?"

"The woman we lost. Her name is Mrs. Riggler."

The ringing phone interrupted us. She never looked up from her call as the coroner and the two men with the gurney wheeled Mrs. Riggler's body past. No pause, no moment of silence, nothing. One out, another one in. A revolving door full of dead and dying bodies.

The men gone, her call completed, she set down the receiver.

"How did you get here so fast?" I asked. "Mrs. Riggler only died in the last hour or so."

"I live just down the street. I'm called to deal with the vacancy."

"Who's going to fill the vacancy?" I made no effort to mask my dislike of her terminology.

The details already gone from her mind, she scanned the form in front of her. "A Miss Jane Cornwall, age sixty-four." She flipped a page. "This is interesting. Last known weight–four hundred seventy-five pounds."

The magnitude of the number didn't register until I multiplied my own weight–then I imagined having to lift it. "How's that going to work?"

"We'll manage." She collected the papers and stood. "Have a nice day." The squeak of her gardening shoes accompanied her rapid pace down the hall.

I slid into the chair she had vacated. We'll manage? I'd never seen her touch a resident, much less bother with the ones who died. Sterlingwood had an aide shortage, what with Emma Jean gone and several of the night aides fired. If past behavior indicated anything, Tanya wouldn't last long, either. The entire place held up by a few strong arms, four-hundred-plus pounds would topple the load.

THE SECRET MISS RABBIT KEPT

CHAPTER 36

My jewelry box sat on Porky's bed, but there was no sign of Porky. I stowed the box in my locker then went to help the residents during the last of dinner. Once they were all fed and out of the dining room, I received the okay from Nurse Smith to run to the corner store–the same place we'd retrieved Pete. Before the clerk had time to recognize where I was from and start asking questions, I paid for fried chicken and a container of raspberry-flavored gelatin I thought Miss Rabbit would enjoy.

When I returned to her room, she didn't acknowledge the containers I set on her tray table.

"I think you'll like what I brought."

She gave the food a cursory glance.

I handed her a chicken leg on a napkin. "Here. I'll go find something for us to drink."

Ignoring the curious looks from the kitchen staff, I pulled a container of sweet tea from the refrigerator, grabbed two glasses, and returned to Miss Rabbit's room. She greeted me with a small, but greasy smile.

Now that I'd managed to get her talking, the urge to fill the silence between us disappeared. We could be two old friends, passing the time over a meal and reflecting on our day. Emma Jean had once remarked how Miss Rabbit's silence was a nice change from all the yelping souls in Sterlingwood and, for the first time, I understood what she had meant.

"Do you have my book?"

Swallowing before my tea could spray across the room, I tried envisioning a lie that would work.

In a quiet, determined voice, she asked again.

My imagination failing, I had no choice but the truth. "Yes, I do have your book. Emma Jean made sure someone gave it to me."

Her jaw muscles tightened. "Just so you know, I ain't going to talk about it."

"Just so you know, I haven't read all of it yet."

She closed her eyes and nodded.

I searched for words, magic words, anything to make this whole thing right. "You didn't do anything wrong, you know."

"You ain't done reading."

Acid gurgled in my gut. I slid over on the bed to get out of the setting sun's eye-level glare only to have the creak of the bed frame call attention to my movement. Everything conspired to have me respond. Where was Emma Jean when I needed her?

"Nothing I could read from this point on would convince me you did anything wrong, Miss Rabbit." My posture sagged from the effort of the words. My tired legs turned to dead weight. "We don't have to talk about this now–or ever–if you don't want. You were only a young girl. He's the guilty one, not you."

"I'd like to go to bed now, please." Her voice cracked. Tears welled in her eyes.

I'd pushed things too far.

We went through the steps to get her into bed, her breath laboring from the efforts. Lack of food for the past few days, as well as our conversation, had taken a toll on her. By the time her head hit the pillow, a film of sweat had broken out on her brow. I wiped it away and pulled the covers up under her chin. "You need anything else before I go?"

She grabbed my arm and pulled me close. "Promise my book is safe with you. I don't want Emery reading it while I's still alive."

"Cross my heart and hope to—" I swallowed the last word, disgusted with my thoughtlessness.

Her eyes, no doubt closed to shut me out, flickered when I patted her hand.

"Thank you for spending time with me, Miss Rabbit. I'll see you tomorrow."

The silence added weight to the room's shadows. The lack of fresh air threatened to choke me. I collected our trash, opened the door, and found Dorothy scurrying down the hall as fast as her chair would take her.

THE SECRET MISS RABBIT KEPT

CHAPTER 37

I waited until Dorothy turned the corner before I stepped out of the room. Let her think she'd gotten away with something. Better yet, allow her mind to run wild like mine had done for days. She would bring up the subject of Miss Rabbit soon enough. With people to get to bed and Miss Rabbit's book to read when I got home, I didn't want to be sidetracked.

Settling residents in bed went much easier than I expected. With no full moon to jumble their brains or twist their moods, they cooperated. Either tired from the monotony of their day or from the sheer act of living inside timeworn bodies, most welcomed the opportunity to lie down and go to sleep. The normally passive Caroline, whom I located in the Day Room, turned out to be the one exception. She refused to budge.

"But it's late, Caroline."

"This is the first peace I've had all day. No nasty Ruby. No Pete pacing with his cigarette. Nobody's begging for food. Mama isn't ranting. It's finally quiet. Can't I just sit for a while and watch this?"

She never stood up for herself, much less refused to follow

whatever lead she'd been given. Arguing with her about bedtime didn't feel right, so I took a seat. "What's on?"

"The Mary Tyler Moore Show."

When Mary threw her hat into the air, as she did at the start of every episode, Caroline shook her head. "This woman acts as if being single is a gift. It isn't, you know."

"It's just a show, Caroline."

"Well, all I'm saying is these programs shouldn't glorify being unmarried. People were put on this earth to be paired up, to multiply. Those who don't get married go through life feeling as if they aren't normal."

"Is that how you felt?" How a comedy inspired such a serious subject escaped me.

"Yes." Her tone showed no hesitation, the words said as if in confession. "Ruby and I were always the spinster aunties. I guess I got along alright in spite of it, but life sure would've been easier with a husband."

Remembering her tale of a love lost in war, I searched for another means of comfort. "You had family, though. I mean, you had Ruby, right?" I couldn't imagine such a nasty woman for a sister, but I guessed their relationship must have held some special bond.

"She's been a rattlesnake long as I can remember. Gotten worse as she's aged. Has it almost down to a science now." A bitter laugh escaped her. "I often wonder how things would have been if I hadn't needed her, if I could have somehow cut the ties between us. Sometimes I think she practiced unkindness just because neither of us had anywhere else to turn."

Boisterous canned laughter erupting from the television jolted Caroline from her thoughts. A subtle change to shoulders and jaw, now straight and tight, revealed a defense mechanism learned through a lifetime of criticism.

I stifled an urge to hug her. "Yet you're always so kind. They say what goes around comes around, Caroline. Maybe Ruby will get hers one day."

"God better hurry if He intends to pay her back for all she's done to me. I'm running out of time." She directed her mumbled words at the television. Her way of deflecting ownership of the revenge she imagined? I suspected her docile nature, embedded like a decades-old tattoo, wouldn't allow her to claim such thoughts.

"Someone once told me a person earns points for Heaven. If that's true, Caroline, I think you have enough now."

Without turning, she patted my hand.

"I need to finish up some things while you watch your show," I told her. "I'll help you to bed when I'm done, okay?"

She laughed with the television audience when I stood to leave. I left her to her show and decision about bedtime. It was the least I could do.

Within the hour, Dorothy found me at the nurse's station making notes in charts. Her fuzzy bedroom slippers schlepped across the linoleum floor as she scooted toward me. "You're still here, huh?"

"Yep."

She sidled up to the counter. "What's new?"

Eyes focused on a chart, every facial muscle in use to contain my smirk, I offered my father's standard reply. "New Mexico, New Jersey, New York, New Hampshire—"

"Ha. Ha." She coughed from the effort of the forced laugh. Catching her breath, she leaned in and failed at a quiet whisper. "Cut the crappola, kid. I thought we made a deal."

I swiveled to face her. "What deal?"

"You promised you would talk to Mable and let me know what happened." The woman's ability to stretch the truth knew no bounds.

"I don't remember any such thing. I said I'd try to talk to her. Period."

"And?"

"And nothing. I haven't had a chance to talk to her yet." I suspected she just wanted confirmation of what she already knew, but I needed to know what that was.

"Bullshit. I heard you—"

"See. You're not being straight with me."

Interrupted by Smith lumbering in between us, Dorothy sat

upright, pushing her chair to get out of the way.

Smith tossed a chart on the desk. The metal binder's clatter punctuated her accusatory stare. "Why isn't Caroline in bed yet?"

"She asked if she could stay up and watch a television show. I told her I'd put her to bed when it ended. Is that a problem?"

"It wouldn't be if Ruby would stop carrying on. Can't you hear her? She's about to drive me nuts. She made me so mad I told her Caroline moved out."

"Moved out, as in left Sterlingwood?" I asked.

"Yes. I thought Ruby could stew on that for awhile, maybe feel some remorse for how she's treated her sister."

Not a humane ploy for Smith, but not one I could argue. Maybe Ruby deserved to experience a little unkindness. "Sorry. I didn't know it'd cause a problem. Caroline just wanted some alone time."

"Ah, don't we all? Please either put Caroline to bed or get Ruby up. I don't care which, but I can't stand any more nonsense today. She's beside herself and now I feel guilty." Smith grabbed a different chart and knocked a stack of papers off the desk. Without bothering to pick them up, she stomped off. Never one to show highs or lows, Smith had been seething with emotion.

Dorothy nudged me. "Ask her what's wrong."

"Why me?" I whispered.

She pushed on the small of my back. "Go on now. She'll answer you."

"Smith?" I called. "Is something else wrong?"

A loud exhale preceded her returning footsteps. She walked to the front of the counter and shoved a chart at me. The name on the inside cover told me all I needed to know, but Smith explained anyway. "Four hundred seventy-five pounds is what's bothering me. Do you have any idea what this will involve?"

A spectator until then, Dorothy perked up as she inhaled the aroma of new gossip. "Four hundred seventy-five pounds of what?"

"Three hundred too many pounds of resident is what–and a stroke victim to boot."

"Holy shit." Count on Dorothy to sum things up.

"She'll be here in the morning. I don't know what management is thinking. We aren't capable of taking care of a woman this size." Smith's normally pale complexion mottled as she spoke. "The biggest mechanical lift we have can't even handle that much weight. It'll take ten of us to move her and we never have that many people on hand."

Words failed me as Smith massaged her temples.

Dorothy shook her head. "Hey, maybe you can get two lifts? One for each half."

The image made me laugh.

"Hey, don't dismiss me. Might just work. You better come up with something, otherwise you'll have another Mrs. Riggler on your hands."

Mention of the bedsore sobered me right up. "We won't know until she gets here. I'm going to put Caroline to bed so I can go home. It's been a long day."

"You're coming in tomorrow, right?" Smith's serious expression provided no room to turn her down.

"Wouldn't miss it for the world," I said, heading for the Day Room and hoping my sarcasm would be forgiven.

Dorothy wheeled up behind me, but waited to speak until we were far from Smith. "You going to tell me about Mable, or what?"

I stepped in front of her and lowered my voice. "Are *you* going to tell me, or what?"

"Yes, I was eavesdropping." Her head hung with the open admission of guilt, but only for a second. "I couldn't hear if she answered you, though. Did she talk?"

Her need for information would outlast my ability to keep the secret. "Yes, she spoke. She told me..." I leaned over, waited for her excitement to build, and then whispered, "Pizza gives her gas."

Emma Jean would have howled at the shocked expression on Dorothy's face, but the memory of her hearty laughter turned mine bittersweet.

Dorothy slapped the arm of her wheelchair. "Well, doesn't that just beat all? Hasn't spoken in God knows how long and that's what she has to say? Surely she said something else."

"Nope, that's pretty much it."

"You're lying, aren't you?"

Caroline wheeled up behind me. "I'm tired now. Can you put me to bed?"

My conversation with Dorothy would have to wait. "Did you enjoy your show?"

"Yes. Nice to be by myself."

"You've been gone so long, Ruby thinks you've moved out for some reason. She's so worked up that she's been hollering at everyone. She misses you. Isn't that something?"

"Oh pooh, she just misses having someone to yell at."

"No, honest. She's been in tears because you aren't there." By osmosis, I'd acquired Dorothy's ability to stretch the truth.

Hand to her heart, Caroline's eyes welled up with tears. "Really?"

"Yep, heard her myself," Dorothy said, stretching my lie. "She's beside herself with worry."

"Oh my goodness, I'm an awful person for upsetting her. I should get in there straight away. Will you help me, Sophie?"

With Dorothy trailing, I pushed Caroline to her room. Ruby shot up in bed the moment we crossed the threshold. "There you are."

Like a good and selfless sister, Caroline wheeled to Ruby's bed and gave her the best hug she could manage from a seated position. "I didn't leave you. A television program in the Day Room caught my eye."

Ruby leaned back on the bed. I detected relief, but one never knew with her.

When I motioned Dorothy out of the room so they could have a few minutes alone, a loud cry echoed down the hallway.

"What the hell?" Dorothy stopped her chair, tripping me in the process.

I untangled my feet and ran toward Lucy's room. The screams, now almost at a pitch only a dog could hear, were those of a person being threatened. Was it too much to hope that someone had Lucy by the throat this time?

CHAPTER 38

My wish didn't come true. With not so much as a fingertip on Lucy, an exasperated Smith stood at the side of the bed as Lucy flailed and gasped for air like an oxygen-starved guppy flipped out of its bowl. "Ahhhhh! She's killing me!"

Her familiar lyrics slowed my feet, but my irritation ratcheted up a notch with their volume. Smith, her features drawn, turned my way to reveal the pink liquid smeared down the front of her uniform. Lucy's face and hands, adorned with the same blast of pink, told of yet another medicine battle.

"Do you want me to hold her down?"

"Forget it. I've had enough today. She complained about an upset stomach earlier, but if she doesn't want to take anything, she doesn't have to. I'm done fighting."

I tuned out Lucy's unwarranted calls for help and left the room.

Outside the doorway, Dorothy sat shaking her head. "She's an ornery old cuss, ain't she? I don't know how you gals put up with half the nonsense in this place."

From a housecoat pocket no bigger than my hand, she pulled a lighter, a full pack of cigarettes, and an ashtray. Having watched

Mary Poppins and her magic bag, I half-expected a lamp would follow.

"Whatcha staring at?" She flicked her lighter multiple times before a flame appeared. Rubbing the raised callus on her thumb, she mumbled. "Nothing's easy."

Her problems bigger than a difficult lighter, she didn't need me to point out that fact. I walked back inside Ruby and Caroline's room.

"I don't want the door open," Ruby said. "Shut the goddamn thing."

Caroline looked at me with doe eyes as she maneuvered her wheelchair around the open bathroom door. "She doesn't like the door open when she sleeps."

"C'mon, I'll get you into bed now." I closed the bathroom door harder than necessary and wheeled her over to the bed.

She gestured to a nightgown folded on the pillow. "I'm a little cold tonight, so I picked a flannel one."

Ruby barked from her horizontal position on the other side of the room. "You know you'll be too hot. It's about a hundred degrees in this damn place. Wear a different one."

"She said she's cold, Ruby." Irritation slowed my words.

"Fine." Ruby turned her head in disgust. "Let her suffer then."

I counted to five before walking over to her. "No one is going to let her suffer. Worry about your own self and go to sleep now."

Caroline's nightgown now stuck on her head, I untangled her arms and helped her into bed where she collapsed like a ragdoll. Her eyes shut so fast I thought she might have died. "Caroline, you okay?"

She nodded, but didn't open her eyes.

"You've had a long day. Time for some rest."

"Thank you for your help. Will you be going home now?"

"Yes. I've had a long day, too." I gave her a kiss on the forehead. "Sleep tight." At the doorway, I took one last glance back at the sisters. Despite Ruby's earlier scare, nothing between them had changed.

Still parked in the hallway, Dorothy extinguished her cigarette and gestured for me to come closer. "Hey, you did good tonight, Sophie."

"I didn't kill anyone if that's what you mean."

"Ha–that *is* a good day."

"Oh, in all the commotion, I forgot to tell you Porky gave me the music box. He said you helped him."

"He wanted to do something special for you and couldn't manage alone."

"It's beautiful. Thank you."

"What goes around comes around. The whiskey meant a lot to him. Big old burly guy even teared up–all because of a glass of whiskey. Imagine that."

"Where'd you come up with the saying on the box? The 'those who couldn't hear the music' line?"

"I found it in a book, after I first moved into this joint. Stuck with me. Helped me understand some of these folks here, if you know what I mean."

I did.

"I read those words to Emma Jean once. She got all misty-eyed, just like Porky with the whiskey. Figured they might stick with you, too."

I couldn't imagine Emma Jean tearing up about anything–unless of course she laughed too hard, but that memory just made me miss her all the more. There were so many things I'd never get the chance to know about her. I bit the inside of my cheek to focus on a different pain.

"Anyway, I hope you like it. Porky was thrilled we were able to pull this off. And even more thrilled you came back so he could give it to you in person. He was afraid he wouldn't see you again." She pulled out another cigarette. "We all were."

Watching her struggle again with the lighter, I decided we'd both had enough for the day. "Why don't you skip one and go to bed instead? It's late. I'm going home now."

She motioned me to go on ahead. A big inhale later, she coughed hard enough for me to fear she might just hack up a lung. I waited until she caught her breath. No doubt one day we'd find her dead in her chair, clutching a lit cigarette, but not on my shift.

I arrived home to a quiet house. Unlike my mother not to wait up for me, but maybe her day had been a long one, too. I climbed the stairs and found a note stuck to my bedroom door. Penny wanted me to call no matter what time I arrived home. The words made my already tired limbs heavier. A replay of our earlier battle didn't thrill me, but my mother would never forgive me if I'd ignored her note. I'd hang up if Penny didn't answer after four rings.

She picked up on three, her voice reeking of panic. "God, where have you been? It's after eleven."

"It's called work." I plopped down on the floor and closed my eyes. Maybe I could sleep through the conversation.

"Don't all those old people go to bed at like six o'clock? You have to watch them sleep or something?"

1...2...3...4...5. "What do you want? I'm tired."

"My mother finally called."

"And?" The news should have excited me, but tired of her and my day in general, I could only manage the single word.

"She just wanted to know how I was doing."

"So what did you tell her?" I sensed an upcoming punch line, but resented her stringing out the story at the late hour.

"I barely spoke to her. What's to talk about? She left me, remember?"

How could I forget? "Did she say if she's coming back? Or why she actually left?"

"No, I didn't ask, but I overheard my father..." Her voice faded and dissolved into a sob.

The day refused to end. I contemplated suicide by phone cord strangulation.

"She has a boyfriend."

"What?" I sat up so fast the phone fell from my hands. Returning the receiver to my ear, I repeated the question.

"You heard me. Is that not just the grossest thing ever? She's actually cheating on my father." She strung out the word cheating as if it were spelled with a dozen e's.

I pictured Penny's mom at my birthday party. In tight pants, high heels, a drink in her hand, and giggling silly, she batted her eyes at every man within twenty feet. Still, she was pretty old. And married.

"Are you sure you heard right?"

"I'm sure. Guess he's some guy my father knows." She started to cry again.

Had my parents known this? The single act of Mrs. Parker's leaving had set my mother spinning. What would news of a boyfriend do to her?

"Now, my father says there's no way he'll let me live with her, even if she wants me."

"Do you even want to now?"

"No. I hate her."

I knew about hating an absent mother and as much as Penny annoyed me, I couldn't help but sympathize. I repeated Emma Jean's words—not that Penny would or could grasp their meaning. "Someone once told me you can't appreciate the weight of a load until you pick it up. You don't know why she left your dad. Maybe she had good reason."

"Geez, Sophie. How profound. You've been hanging around those old people too long. You're starting to sound like a real freak."

This time I aimed my count for ten.

Penny interrupted at eight. "Stop talking like you're a hundred years old. You're creeping me out."

"I'm tired, Penny. Can we talk about this tomorrow?"

"God, you *are* a hundred years old." She slammed down the receiver.

Promising I'd never speak to her again, I threw the phone on the floor where carpet muffled the noise. Not quite as satisfying as if I'd tossed the phone against the wall, but my parents asleep in the next room didn't need to be rousted from bed. My mother would hear Penny's news soon enough.

I stretched across my bed, unable to muster the energy to undress. Until I couldn't stand the uniform any longer or I fell asleep, I would ponder all the evil things I could do to Penny.

When I shifted my head, Miss Rabbit's book poked out from under my pillow.

"Here, child," Emma Jean whispered. "Someone has a life worse than yours. Stop your damn whining and read."

The hour or my exhaustion had me imagining things, yet I couldn't let another person have the last word. "Of course. Only normal people count sheep until they fall asleep, right? Crazy people read horror stories."

Afraid I'd hear her again, I opened the book. The last section I'd read fell somewhere past the halfway point. Miss Rabbit's oversized handwriting, scrawled across the book's small pages, created an artificial sense of length. Closer now to the end than the beginning, I addressed an absent, but oh-so-present Emma Jean. "Please tell me Luther gets what he deserves."

Met with silence, I took a deep breath and focused on the page.

CHAPTER 39

I wish I could say Luther never touched me again, that Mama somehow found out what happened, that a lightning bolt done come out the sky and struck Luther down, but I can't say none of those things. What happened that day was just the beginning.

Oh God.

I made sure I'd locked my bedroom door. Now imprisoned by my own will, and with no sign of my parents, I looked for another excuse–anything to distract me from the horrors the next pages contained.

Emma Jean, bullying my conscience for consent, spoke each direction I turned. "Quit being such a baby and finish up now. Time's a wasting." Her impatient foot, tapping at my brain, accompanied each second I stared at Miss Rabbit's book.

Some months before, my father and I had come upon a traffic accident. At the bottom of a gulley and smashed beyond recognition, one of the four cars lay eerily still. No one could have survived. Fire trucks, police cars, and ambulances blocked much of the scene, but as my father and I drove past, I craned my neck out of the window to steal a glimpse.

Eyes on the road, my father reached with a free hand to pull me back. "Stop, Sophie. You don't need to be looking at that."

"Why?"

"Because you'll never be able to un-see it."

I guessed what I'd read of Miss Rabbit's book had already found a way to reassemble itself at a moment's notice, like a Polaroid in my brain. I'd never be able to un-see it, but did I need to enhance the picture with more horror?

Before the Emma Jean of my psyche could further justify her reasons for giving me the book, I read on. Like staring at the car wreck, I couldn't bring myself to look away.

I don't know why Luther did what he did to me. Maybe losing his job. Maybe his drinking. Maybe he just done gone crazy in the head. Even after all these years, I ain't never quite come up with a way to wrap my brain around his sort of evil. Best I can figure, he knew exactly what he be doing. He ain't never showed no regret for the pain he done caused me. Went on for too long and happened too many times for me to try and understand it none.

Just when I be thinking he'd had his fill of me, after weeks passed and he stayed away, he'd get all liquored up and come after me again. With Mama working all day, he had nothing better to do. Easy for him to send Emery and Billy out the house with Abigail and be alone with me. And Mama, much as I loved her, sure acted like she blind. But I never said nothing to nobody—just like Luther told me.

Wasn't long after the first time Luther touched me when he asked if I done said something to her. I told him no, but he didn't believe me none. No matter what I said, he just got madder. Slapped my face and stormed out the house, saying he'd show me what happened to ugly, fat liars. I hid in my room, about scared to death, knowing he be fixing to do something awful. I spent the whole night scared.

Woke up the next morning, thinking Luther been all talk. Least that be what I wanted to believe. Then I found poor little Scrappy on the front porch, her head cut near clean off. Reckon it could have been coons or possums, but I knew it be Luther sending me a message.

Something in me changed right then. Fight gone out of me, I'd just close my eyes, let Luther do his business, quick-like, and leave me alone. Long as I didn't fight, it didn't hurt so much, and after so many times, I stopped hurting altogether. Guess I just stopped feeling.

Months and months it went on, but he ain't never showed no sorrow or regret. Never left me alone none, neither. Least til my belly started growing bigger. And if truth be known all these years later, that big belly a mine, keeping Luther away like it done, be the only reason I waited so long to try and get rid of it.

My vision blurred.

Miss Rabbit's words flew around my brain like a trapped bird in search of an exit. Eventually tiring of the dizzy path, they sought refuge in a space once previously reserved for a woman I'd never known and found comfort in the decade-old fissure burrowed in a corner there. With no space to spare and little tolerance for more bad news, my gut protested. I ran to the bathroom just in time to throw up.

"So-So? You okay in there?" My mother stood outside the door, no doubt awakened by the noise echoing off the tiled surfaces of her no-longer-clean bathroom. I pictured her tousled hair, sleepy eyes, and a face etched with concern for her only child. She would no doubt break down the door if I didn't answer.

"Yes, Mom, I'm fine. Just a stomachache, but I'm okay now. Sorry I woke you."

"I wasn't really asleep, dear. I heard you on the phone with Penny earlier and couldn't get back to sleep."

"Oh, sorry." I flushed the toilet and opened the door.

Just as I'd pictured her, but marabou-topped slippers added to the mix.

"You think it might've been something you ate?" She placed her lips on my forehead–her way, for as long as I could remember, to measure body temp. "Gosh, I hope you haven't picked up something from the home. Anyone else at work sick?"

"No, they're fine." I steadied my knees before they could give way. "I'm fine. We're all fine."

"Well, you don't seem to have a fever. Maybe you're just overtired."

My father called from their bedroom. "What's all the racket?

Everything okay out there?"

"Yes, dear. So-So wasn't feeling well, but she's okay now. Go back to sleep. I'm coming." She patted my arm. "Get yourself into bed. You've had a long hard day. Hopefully, you'll feel better in the morning." Hesitating when her antenna picked up another signal, she added, "So-So? You look so sad. Is something else wrong?"

Penny's mother has a boyfriend. Miss Rabbit got pregnant after being raped. Pick one, I wanted to say, but didn't. Entrusted with these secrets, I needed to find a way to deal with them by myself. "No. Just tired, I guess."

"We all are, honey. Why don't we get some rest?"

I hadn't yet let go of the table still filling in for my weak knees.

"A wise man once said—"

"Stop, Mom. I don't need one of your quotes right now."

"Just listen, So-So. You never know." Despite the late hour, her long-standing devotion to overworked proverbs remained absolute. "A wise man once said, 'Though you can't prevent the bird of sorrow from flying around your head, you don't have to let it build a nest in your hair.'"

I tried not to laugh at the paradox of marabou and wisdom.

When we exchanged our own versions of frustrated sighs she must have decided whatever else she felt compelled to say could wait until morning. She slipped inside her bedroom and shut the door.

My stomach now settled, knees stable, I headed back to my room to read the rest of the book. Maybe the pain would be lessened if I didn't linger over the words. You have to rip off the bandage quickly, my father always advised. It'll be over before you have time to think. Unlike my mother's brand of wisdom, his offered more practical uses.

CHAPTER 40

Imagine me still calling that baby an it after all these years done passed. Ain't like I trying to ignore the truth. I know it don't make the truth any less true. Guess I talked myself into believing Luther's seed ain't got a right to no name. Luther didn't care a lick about me none anyway. Suppose I be going to hell for thinking this way, for doing what I done, but nothing can change that now. Been too long passed.

It was Emery who figured out something going on with me back then, that I weren't acting right. He waited until Mama had gone, one day when Luther out somewhere with Abigail and Billy, when it be just him and me. He set me down and asked me straight out, real quiet-like, Luther messing with you?

I about fell over. Could be he intended something else, but seemed we both knew what he be asking. Part of me wanted to up and tell a lie, but most of me just relieved somebody seeing things not be right. But instead of answering, I started to cry. I didn't say nothing, but Emery put his fist right through the back screen door. Never seen him get mad like that. Scared me about as much as anything Luther done.

I ran out the house, just like the scared rabbit Granddad said I was. Emery had to chase me down and tackle me. Don't know what I figured he was fixing to do, but I fought him hard. He laid on me, held my arms down until I quit, then he stayed holding on while I cried some more. Snot running out my nose, all over Emery's shirt, I remember thinking how mad he'd be when he done see the mess I made on his clothes. Funny how I be more worried about that snot than what I just let on to.

Had about cried myself out when Emery said we needed to let Mama know what Luther done, but no way I be telling Mama. I told him so, too. Luther already done killed Scrappy. I figured me or Emery be next.

Don't recall now how I got Emery to see things my way, but he finally quit saying we had to tell. I made him swear right then and there not to say nothing to nobody or Luther sure kill us both. Emery tried telling me he'd take care of Luther, that I wouldn't have to worry no more, but I knew Emery, skinny as a autumn scarecrow, couldn't do nothing. He was just all talk, wanting to protect me. I knew better. Wanting and doing be two different things. Emery weren't no match for a man like Luther.

So Emery crossed his heart, hoped to die if he ever broke his promise, and I finally stopped crying. Then just like we been talking regular like, I helped Emery fix up his hand where he put it through the screen door and set about seeing to our lunch. Guess I so used to acting like nothing wrong, easy for me to pretend.

I must a had Emery about convinced he imagined the whole thing because, though his jaw be working like one a Granddad's old cows, he didn't say nothing after that. Might have been Emery didn't figure Luther be doing all he be doing to me, or might have been, like I say, he pretending, but near as I could figure, he kept his word to not tell Mama. He made sure, best he could, Luther and me never alone in the same room again though. He followed me around at home like Scrappy used to when she hungry. About ran hisself ragged trying to make the truth go away.

He nearly let Mama know something up just by his acting

different. She so used to us squabbling like two roosters, she didn't know what to make of Emery being so nice. Truth be known, I didn't neither. But Emery watching out for me, pitiful as it might have been, did make me feel better. Ain't like no one else cared about me. Maybe Nana, but she didn't come round none. And forget Mama. She too busy to see what right under her nose. I never knew a seeing person who couldn't see things all laid out for her. But that be Mama. She had no business being with a man like Luther in the first place, but I guess she done had to live with that herself. Suppose the good Lord give us all our own set of worries.

Luther let me be after that day Emery and me talked. Don't know if it be because of Emery or because Luther just done had his fill of me. Now I think maybe Luther knew what his seed done and didn't want to be taking the blame none, but back then I just be grateful something keeping him away.

Everything went on regular like that until one day Emery and I out in the yard taking Mama's washing off the line. My shirt lifted and Emery pointed at my belly, teased me about how fat I be getting. I ain't paid no attention until then, but right away, I knew something weren't right. Of course I didn't say nothing like that to Emery. I just told him to mind his own business and leave me be. Fat ain't no crime, I said. Besides, him being so scrawny, he just jealous I bigger than him.

Don't know how it be that Emery didn't figure my belly wasn't no fat. We both seen Granddad's cows having young'uns, seen Mama get fat with Abigail. I guess it be like Granddad used to say, no one notice a dog's mess until it be stuck to they own shoes. Emery no different, I suppose.

I pretended nothing wrong that day, but the thought of Mama knowing what I done, her finding out I had a baby coming and that it be Luther's, set me to fretting like nothing I ever done. I left Emery to finish the clothes on the line and ran inside. Mama be standing at the sink washing dishes while Abigail on the floor playing. Brought to mind one of them advertisements for washing soap I seen once. Can't *say if the folks in the advertisement be happy for real—though they was white folks—but that picture sure made it seem like if you bought that soap, everybody end up smiling. Well, I couldn't afford to be buying no fancy washing soap, and I sure didn't know how to get rid of what growing inside me neither. I did know I couldn't let Mama find out what I done. Figured the only choice I had be to run away.*

I thought on that idea a long time. Nana had kinfolks living nearby and they seemed real nice, but I had me no idea where to find them. I thought of everybody, even that nice lady in the fancy dress who gave me the red ribbon for winning the Spelling Bee. She seemed to think I be somebody special, but I didn't know where she lived neither.

Weeks went by with me fretting and my belly growing bigger. I tried all sorts of crazy things to get rid of that baby, too. Took some of Mama's castor oil, thinking if it about killed me to swallow, surely it get rid of that baby. Another time, I bet Emery he couldn't punch me in the belly hard enough to make me cry. Don't know about the baby, but I sure had a hard time not crying. Also tried jumping rope, but my legs done give out long before my belly did. I even stuck things up inside me there to poke that baby out. All sounds silly when I write it now.

Be a lot of work keeping that belly a secret. The dresses Mama got me, the ones she said I'd grow into but done never fit me right, sure came in handy after awhile. I also took to not being with my friends, spending more time doing my schoolwork, and staying out the house much as I could. No one seemed to notice much neither. Mama thought I just being a good girl. Luther already staying away like I had me the plague, so my secret stayed safe near as I could tell.

I know I should've thought my plan through longer. Young'un like me trying to deal with all that by myself, but my belly be getting harder and harder to hide each day passed and I weren't feeling so good neither.

Day finally came when I scrapped together a plan and enough loose change to get me a bus ticket, but only place I knew to go be Nana and Granddad's. Figured as much as they hated Luther, they'd be willing to hide me. Or they'd know a way to get rid of my belly. Don't make no sense now, but that belly a mine had me so crazy, be a wonder I didn't go find me a bridge to jump off.

Here I doing all this soul cleansing the lady on the television spoke of and I sure don't know what good it be doing. Truth be told, my belly all tied up in knots just like back then.

Now I see, clear as day, how I should have told Mama soon as Luther first laid hands on me, should have screamed or something so Mrs. Marbly would come running. I could have said something the minute I took to hanging those sheets to dry. Luther might not have tried to kill that sweet old lady like he done with poor Scrappy. He'd been out our lives, gone for good. Then I might have growed up a regular girl instead of spending all these years without my kinfolk. Then there'd been no dead baby to find me in my sleep every night.

What's done is done, I guess. I's an old lady now, counting the days until the good Lord decides what he doing with me after all this. I always hoped He busy that day I ran away, maybe looking after another poor young'un what needed Him. I's guessing I had his full attention, though, scared as I was.

I waited to leave the house until everyone be gone that day, Mama at work, Luther and the rest of them out somewhere. Pretended to be sick, so they left me at home. Didn't have to pretend too much, with my belly troubling me and all. After they gone, I put dresses on, one after the other, so I wouldn't have to carry nothing. Didn't leave a note and sure didn't look back. Knew if I did, I'd chicken out. My knees shaking so bad by the time I got to that bus stop, the driver had to help me up the steps. I's sure he thought I had no business riding that bus, but I told him about me visiting my Nana for the first time, showed him my ticket, and gave him my best smile. Think he took pity on me. Or maybe he just be in a hurry to get on home to his own young'uns. Not sure what I would have done if he stopped me.

The minute that bus got to going down the street, the sweat starting pouring off of me. Figured it just be my nerves, or all the clothes I had on, but then my belly started cramping. Lady sitting across the aisle *asked if I be feeling okay. I told her I's fine, didn't need no attention even though I bout to be sick right there on the man in front me. Wanted to get off that bus right quick, do my business in private, but didn't know how to get the bus to stop. I stayed real still, hugged my belly and did some right serious praying.*

Seemed like hours before that bus stopped, but soon as them new folks got on, I scooted out the door quick before anyone could stop me. Didn't know what I'd do after, but knew I had to get off that bus.

I stood there, nothing but a farmhouse down the road a spell. Fresh air felt good, but my belly still be aching. Didn't know what else to do, so I walked. My worn out shoes had me feeling every pebble and bit of glass on that road, too. Figured when my belly stopped hurting, I could catch the next bus, or maybe a car would pass. Didn't have no plan, but staying in one place didn't make no sense.

Weren't long before the pain had me about bent over. Knew I'd found me some real trouble when I couldn't walk no more. About had to crawl off the road to get into the field. Figured everything be better if I could find a soft spot to lay down and catch my breath.

Soon as I laid in all them corn stalks, I felt something wet running between my legs. Lifted my dresses and, Lordy, I ain't never seen so much blood. I knew then, plain as the color of my skin, my actions had done killed that baby. Also knew it be true. Wanting and doing really be two different things.

My stomach tied into knots, the images imprinted on my brain, revulsion set in. Unable to read any more, I pulled the blanket around me and closed my eyes.

"Damn you, Emma Jean."

This time, she had nothing to say.

CHAPTER 41

I shut off the alarm clock. The kinks in my back told me what little sleep I'd gotten had likely been spent frozen in a fetal position. The bells down the street, announcing another Sunday, reminded me I hadn't been to church in weeks. My mother would soon nag me. Given what God had put Miss Rabbit through–what He'd put me through–any future attendance on my part would likely happen later than sooner. What kind of a supreme being piled so much onto one so young?

Emma Jean's theory about the reciprocity of life now shot to hell, and God's good intentions appearing to be based on nothing more than useless assumptions, the reality became what I could do for Miss Rabbit. At a tentative knock on the door, I tucked her book under the covers.

"Sophie, you awake?"

"Yes, Dad."

"May I come in?" He waited for permission before opening the door. His Old Spice aftershave preceded him into the room. "Good morning, Sunshine." He loved mornings. Best time of the day to do anything, he always said. "Have you been up long?"

"No. Didn't get to sleep until late."

"I know. I heard you and your mother in the hallway."

He awakened the memory of Old Man wisdom and bird nests. I ran a hand through my hair just to be sure nothing had formed overnight. "Sorry we woke you."

"None of us have been sleeping very good these days." He took a seat at the end of the bed, something he never would have done when I was a little girl. His morning ritual of snuggles and tickles were acts he had restrained as I matured, but ones my heart missed. Perhaps a mind reader, he reached over to give one of my toes a yank. At his sudden move, thoughts of a perverted Luther struck me. Startled, I pulled away. Confusion, mixed with what looked like hurt, crept over his face.

"Sorry. Got a cramp all of a sudden." I tried to relax, straighten my leg, but I couldn't erase the ugly images. Too late, anyway. Dad's spontaneity had passed.

He shrugged off my curious behavior and scooted closer. "I want to talk to you about something while your mother is at the market. She's worried about you."

"Why? I'm fine."

He rolled his eyes.

"Really, Dad. I'm fine." The words didn't convince even me.

"It's okay to not be fine. A lot has happened in the past couple weeks. We're worried you're holding too much inside, not talking about how you're feeling. That incident with Penny yesterday? Let's just say we've never seen you explode like you did. I'm not saying it wasn't warranted but—"

"She pushed too far, acting like she's the only one who's lost someone. I'm tired of her being so mean and selfish."

He thought a moment then nodded. "How did your return to work go?"

His change of direction catching me off-guard, I offered my generic answer. "It was fine."

"And?"

"Well, kind of hard, what with Emma Jean gone." Speaking her name still hurt.

"Not many kids your age would be willing to work in a place like that, much less go back after what happened. I'm proud of you."

"It's not as bad as people think. Sure, no one likes to wipe dirty butts or deal with oozing bedsores, but it's not all like that."

His face crinkled like a prune, but in his defense, how many daughters discussed hygiene and bedsores with their fathers?

"It's all part of the job, Dad."

"I know. Just hard to imagine my baby girl doing those kind of things."

Did I dare tell him about Margaret's pudding or Mrs. Steiner's manual enema? If I shared Ray's erection stories? Good Lord, he'd lock me in the house for good.

He poked me in the leg. "Did I say something funny?"

"No. Just thinking about some of the people who live at the home."

"They make you smile?" He eased back on his elbows. "Then you must have favorites."

I slid over to give him more room. "There are a few people I like more than others. Yes."

"Are they nice to you?"

"One of the residents gave me that last night." I gestured to Porky's music box on the dresser.

My father walked over to get a closer look and ran his hands over the words engraved on the top. "Does this quote have some kind of significance?"

A familiar knot formed in my throat. "It kind of describes the people at the home. Emma Jean, too."

He nodded, but he couldn't possibly understand.

"You didn't know her, but she was a little...different. I mean, she always had a good attitude, never thought anything of all the bad stuff there. She somehow managed to find the humor in things, even when all of it was just really sad. It's hard to explain. She heard music no one else did."

"Your mother and I have tried not to bring up her name since the accident. Figured it would be too hard on you, but maybe we were wrong. Sounds like maybe you do need to talk about her."

A tear slid down my cheek before I could blink it back. To my father's credit, he didn't call attention to it, waiting instead for me to speak.

Like riding on a carousel, images of Emma Jean floated past. The half-cocked wig; her sunbathing on the porch; the wrestling matches with Lucy; her rants on a mother's love and explanation of points in Heaven. All good stuff—until she drove off in her new blue convertible. The ache I'd tried to stuff deep inside sprang to life. The days of trying to be strong collapsed into one loud sob. "Why'd she have to die, Dad?"

His Old Spice and strong arms encircled me before I could take another breath. Unlike my mother who would have filled the space with well-intentioned words, he cradled me and waited until my chest stopped heaving.

When I found the will to pull away, the snot I'd left on his shirt triggered another harsher memory. The burden of Miss Rabbit's secret transformed into one I could no longer carry alone. Time to come clean. I silently asked Emma Jean for forgiveness.

"Dad, if I tell you something, can you promise not to tell Mom?"

His sudden uni-brow suggested I might have rung the alarm a bit too hard.

"It's not about me. Don't worry. Just something about a resident."

"And why don't you want to tell your mother?"

"You know how she gets upset about stuff, the way she won't let things be."

"That's an understatement."

"If she hears this story, she'll never understand."

"She'll never understand what? How can I make a promise without knowing what it's for?"

"I don't want her to know about this, at least not until I've figured it out for myself. But I *need* to tell you. Only if you promise to keep it between us, though."

As he studied me, I guessed his sensitivity to my mother's needs versus mine weighted his thoughts. He glanced down at the music box on the bed and opened the lid. The ballerina sprang to life, spinning to the music until he closed the box and looked at me. "Alright, Sophie. You have my word, but if this is serious, all bets are off. Your mother would never forgive me for keeping something important from her."

When I agreed to his terms, he closed the bedroom door. "Just in case she comes home."

One small consideration offered and the last bit of the dam crumbled. Like when I'd told Miss Rabbit about my birthmother, this story, now set free from the bindings of a promise, surged from my lips in one long stream of consciousness.

The Secret Miss Rabbit Kept

CHAPTER 42

I liked to think my father the strongest man I knew. Rarely, if ever, losing his temper, his patience dwarfed what I imagined a saint's. Unkind words never crossed his lips. He'd teared up at the news of his mother's death, but only briefly. For these reasons and more, my decision to share with him, instead of my mother, seemed obvious, but for a man I'd just entrusted with a secret, the way his eyes avoided mine when I finished with all the details of Miss Rabbit's story didn't fit. The fresh creases in his forehead brought no comfort, and the never-before-seen tremors in his hands were a dead giveaway that I'd miscalculated.

"Soph..." The rest of my name disappeared in the gust of his exhale. As if I'd witnessed the rumble of a nervous volcano, I didn't know whether to watch or seek cover.

"You stuck your nose in this lady's business? Why?" His words more of a reprimand than a question, they accompanied a foreign glare.

"Dad—"

"This is far too much for you to be involved in. You're only sixteen years old, for Christ's sake."

Not the reaction I expected or had ever experienced, I couldn't speak.

"This needs to be brought to the attention of professionals, people who know how to deal with this kind of thing. You know nothing about this stuff, much less how to try to fix it." His voice, hoarse with emotion, sucked the air from the room.

The emotion I'd been fighting came in a rush. "I thought you'd understand."

Emma Jean, an almost satisfied smirk on her face, stood on a nerve at the edge of my brain. "I done *told* you not to tell anyone, child."

Whether my father believed my tears inevitable or earned is unclear. He kept his distance and let me cry. His face didn't soften until I finished blowing my nose, then he took a deep breath and put a hand on my leg. "I'm sorry I lost my temper. This took me by surprise. This woman's horror, the fact you've kept it all to yourself..." He ran a hand through his hair and stared at the ceiling. "Let's just say I would've preferred you'd taken me into your confidence sooner."

Another of his deep breaths had me believing he'd finished, but they only served to fuel his lecture. "No father wants this for their child. I guess I'm just angry for being unable to spare you."

"It's not like it happened to me."

"No, of course not, but this kind of stuff changes a person, Sophie. It's like punches to the gut. Leaves a mark where you can't see it. Get hit too many times and, before you know it, you accept the bruises, almost expect them. You're just too young."

Neither his explanation nor his concern made sense and I still had no idea what I'd done wrong. My head about to explode, I blew my nose for the second time and wound up sobbing into the tissue again.

"Oh, honey. Come here." He pulled me snug into his chest. The steady beat of his heart, the strength in his arms, conveyed what his words hadn't. "I hate the fact you got yourself into the middle of all this."

I didn't say as much, but I hated it, too.

"Hello? Where is everyone?"

At my mother's voice, Dad and I drew back from each another. I snatched a fresh tissue while he called to her. "In Sophie's room. Be down in a second, dear."

Footsteps hurried up the stairs. Dad and I looked at each other and, in that brief second, his eyes told me he intended, at least for the moment, to keep his word. I tucked Miss Rabbit's book deeper under the covers.

They met at the doorway and, intentional or not, my father blocked my mother's entry. She stood on tiptoe and peered over his shoulder. Curiosity etched her forehead. "What are you guys up to in there?"

"Just coming downstairs to see if you'd make us a late Sunday breakfast," he said, enveloping her in a bear hug no doubt intended to distract. He smothered her neck in kisses, making exaggerated smooching noises, and stopped at her flushed cheek.

Her throaty giggle, enough to make me blush, faded when she pushed him away and smoothed her hair. "Quit now."

I cleared my throat to remind them of their audience. "Yeah, Mom. How about some waffles? I'm starving." Food the farthest thing from my mind, I hoped my contrived sense of urgency would not only divert her attention, but also stop their making out in my doorway.

"Eggs and bacon, too?" Her eyes lit up with a sense of purpose.

"That'd be great," I said. "I'll come down and help you in a second. Just let me get dressed first."

My father gestured for me to stay put. "That's okay. *I'll* help your mother in the kitchen today."

Skepticism raising her eyebrow, Mom glanced at both of us in succession. "Okay, now I *know* something's up."

"Nothing's up. It's a beautiful Sunday morning and your family is hungry. That's all you need to know, little lady. C'mon, maybe I can show you some new tricks in the kitchen." Dad coaxed her from my room, keeping her busy with conversation as they made their way down the stairs.

Drained from my impromptu performance, my nerve endings in need of a break, I laid across my bed. Waffles would take awhile.

After my father's reaction to Miss Rabbit's story, I couldn't imagine what my mother's would have been. The subject wouldn't end here, either. Breakfast preparation would only give my father more time to think about what I'd shared. I hoped he would keep his promise, but I guessed he would do so only until he'd had a chance to further discuss the topic with me. He'd insist I share with her. Even if I did, I'd still hold full responsibility for not having told her from the onset. She would first blame me, then him, and then herself; the reason being something crazy like her not having raised me right. The same thing happened whenever I did something wrong, as if my actions were somehow connected to hers. Were all mothers this crazy?

Miss Rabbit's mother certainly didn't sound anything like mine. My mother would've known in an instant if someone did to me what Luther had done to Miss Rabbit. At least I hoped so. Even considering how much I hated my mother knowing all my business, as hard as I tried to keep things private, wouldn't I have gone to her if I had been in the same situation? Aren't mothers just wired to understand everything?

Yet I sat with this secret, unwilling to share.

Maybe Miss Rabbit and I were more alike than I thought. Maybe the fear of being judged or blamed made girls hold their secrets tight. If nothing broke the cycle, fearful young girls turned into silent old ladies. I never wanted to tell anyone the story of my adoption. Caroline's fear kept her from standing up to her sister Ruby. Miss Rabbit cared more about what people would think than she did about her own safety. All proof that scared little rabbits live up to their namesakes—and the bullies win.

I dug out Miss Rabbit's book, ran my hand over her name scrawled across the front by an old woman's shaky one. Not the story of a lifetime, but enough of one to provide definition. What would a book with my name scribbled across the front contain?

Miss Rabbit, without knowledge or intention, had written herself into my story, my life. Same with Emma Jean and the people of Sterlingwood. If a stranger picked up my story one day, would they read about what I had done to make these lives better? Or would they find that I, too, had stayed silent? Would my management of Miss Rabbit's secret define me?

I shut my eyes and tried to envision what a happy ending looked like for both of us.

"So-So, breakfast is ready." Nothing in my mother's singsong voice indicated her day had been spoiled with my story.

"Coming." I covered Miss Rabbit's book, grabbed clothes from my closet, and dressed. A swipe of a hairbrush, a dab of blush to get some color back into my face, and I headed to the kitchen.

Waffles, a plate of both bacon and sausage, another of eggs, a pitcher of juice, whipped cream, strawberries, and a pile of hashed brown potatoes awaited my scrawny appetite. My mother should have had more kids. "Holy cow, when do the other ten people arrive?"

My father and I looked at each other and eye-rolled in unison. "Your mother has outdone herself this time."

"You said you were hungry. Better too much than not enough."

"No one's complaining, honey. You did a wonderful job." He pulled her in for a kiss. Buttering her up for bad news?

"Your father whipped the cream and made the juice, So-So." She announced the accomplishment as if an award would follow.

I filled my plate with as much as I could stomach, but my mother placed an extra slice of toast atop the eggs for good measure. Seemingly satisfied none of us would starve, she returned to the sink and began washing the dirty pans. As I took my place at the table, my father glanced her way and whispered to me around the food in his mouth. "You okay now?"

She turned before I could answer. "Everything alright with you two?"

Like marionettes held by the same string, Dad and I both nodded and reached for the bowl of strawberries as she wiped her hands on the kitchen towel and came to sit between us. I started to hand her the plate from her usual seat at the table, but she waved it away. "No, not just yet. I want to talk about something first."

The strawberry I hadn't yet swallowed lodged in my throat. Giving no sign he sensed the brewing storm, my father squirted ketchup onto his eggs.

"I'm a little concerned about you, So-So. Your father and I are both a little concerned. The way you lost your temper with Penny yesterday was so unlike you."

"The way I lost *my* temper? She goes crazy and you comment on how *I* acted?"

"I've already spoken to Penny about the way she behaved. Now I'm speaking to you."

"You don't think she deserved to be told off?"

"It's not up to us to decide what a person deserves, but it is up to us to be kind. Do unto others as you would have—"

"I know, Mom." I swear she had a quote for everything.

Dad gestured at me with his coffee cup. "Don't use that tone with your mother, please."

"Sorry." Somewhere between my bedroom and the kitchen, I'd lost him as an ally.

"Penny and her father are going through an awful time. No, I don't condone her behavior. I think it's deplorable, but without a mother around–or at least not one who seems to care one iota about her family–Penny isn't getting the guidance she needs. Her father has his hands full. The least we can all do, as friends, is be a little more understanding."

Her lecture would go on forever if I didn't give her what she wanted. "Okay, fine."

"I'm not siding with Penny, dear. It's just that I raised you to know better. I worry that everything happening in your work life has become too much for you."

"Dad already talked to me about this. I'm fine. Can I have the butter, please?"

"Dad talked to you?" A single eyebrow climbed her forehead.

"While you were at the market, honey," my father said. "I let Sophie know how concerned we are. She insisted she's fine, though." His gaze focused on his plate–until he handed me the butter dish. "Isn't that what you told me, Soph?"

I prayed he'd stop talking.

"Why don't *you* tell your mother what you told me?"

His words, more of a cue than a question, placed me center stage. Chewing my syrup-soaked waffle as slowly as I could, I sensed my mother's antennae rising to pick up any signal I might give.

"So-So, *are* you fine?" Facts weren't facts until she heard them herself.

As the wall clock's pendulum methodically ticked off the seconds in the background, my father's thoughts telegraphed across the table. If I didn't speak up soon, he would find a way to discharge his burden by bringing Miss Rabbit's story into the conversation.

Emma Jean made a guest appearance in my brain. Hands on hips, devilish sparkle in her eye, she wagged a finger. "Lordy, child, you sure done opened up a big fat can of worms now. What'd you think would happen? You can't make your daddy keep no secrets."

Conversing with ghosts wouldn't help me with my mother's mental health inquiry. I bit my tongue.

"Well, go on then," Emma Jean prodded. "Spew them guts of yours."

If the real Emma Jean could have spoken, she would have plied me with shame, tanned my hide for breaking her trust. This guilt turned the remainder of my waffle to concrete. I choked down the lump and muttered an apology to both the real and imaginary Emma Jean.

"No, I'm not fine, Mom. I need to tell you something."

THE SECRET MISS RABBIT KEPT

Chapter 43

Cold waffles, congealed bacon grease, and wilted whipped cream were all that remained when I finished retelling Miss Rabbit's story. This version, made longer with details I had failed to share with my father, also included her actual written words. I'd gone upstairs at one point and retrieved the book, knowing nothing I paraphrased could have conveyed the horror as well.

My mother's hands shook as she pictured the dreadful things my father warned we couldn't un-see. I knew this because of the way her spoon clinked against her teacup when she pushed it away, the way her chin quivered and eyes blinked as she fought to hold back tears. All of us sat motionless, these awful images imprinted on our brains, as the clock's pendulum continued its sideways sway on the wall. My heart beat twice with every second that ticked past.

My father made an awkward attempt at lessening the tension in the room by reaching for my mother's hand. "Quite a story, huh?"

Their skin hadn't touched before she pulled away to wipe her eyes. "You knew about this?"

He glanced at me with what I read as frustration and regret.

"Only minutes ago. Sophie told me while you were out."

Afraid to upset what I predicted would be her normal chronology of blame, I didn't make a sound. My turn in the spotlight would come soon enough.

"And Emma Jean entrusted you with Miss Rabbit's book? Just you, no one else?"

"Her husband Clifford gave it to me at the funeral. She left a note telling him what to do."

"Will you read me this note, please?" The earlier singsong quality of her voice had slipped away, replaced now with an eerie rhythm I'd never heard.

I pulled Emma Jean's note from between the pages of the book, unfolding it for what must have been the thousandth time. The realization that the paper no longer smelled of her baby powder stuck in my throat as I began to read aloud. Only when I fell into the rhythm of her dialect did my voice find strength, but it faltered as I read the part about her hope to be buried in her good wig. Even my father cleared his throat at those last few words.

My mother faced me, but her gaze focused on something distant. Her voice still held the peculiar rhythm when she finally spoke. "But not until she's gone."

Emma Jean's words, but why my mother had repeated them escaped me. "What?"

"That's what Emma Jean wrote in the note. 'Maybe everybody needs to know what happened. But not until she's gone.'"

Where did she plan to go with this? The haunting beat of scary-movie music played inside my brain. The tune amplified when my father's chair screeched across the linoleum as he stood.

My mother put a hand out to stop him. "Sit. We *all* need to discuss this."

His posture appeared to slump under the weight of her words, but his role as peacekeeper forced him to sit without argument. He offered a muted apology amidst a clumsy clatter of silverware.

My mother redirected her focus in an instant. "Emma Jean trusted you with Miss Rabbit's private thoughts, the story of her horrible experience, and the reasons she's stayed silent. All of this has been handed to you, So-So–no one else. I don't think you realize the importance of that."

Now rousted from his side of the fence, my father laid a hand on her arm. "Honey, I think she understands."

She pulled back and drew a breath. "Call it a mother's instinct, but I don't think she does. What sixteen-year-old can grasp the *courage* it took for this woman to write these words?"

"What makes you think Sophie hasn't?"

"Because she's never lived it."

"None of us have. That doesn't mean we can't understand or sympathize."

His words straightened her back like a hot iron on a cotton shirt. "Empathy is no substitute for experience. Nor is sympathy a proper tribute to courage."

I had no idea what she meant or which Old Man she quoted, but the way my father set down his cup told me he wasn't pleased. "There's no need to raise your voice," he said. "You're getting all worked up for the wrong reasons. Don't cloud this issue with everything else that's troubling you."

The evil eye she shot him announced he'd crossed a line, but she turned to me before he could speak. "Please tell me you haven't shared this story with anyone else."

To get back into my mother's good graces, I shook my head. I hadn't actually *told* Dorothy, had I? I eased back in my chair, wishing I could crawl into a hole instead.

"Good. These are Miss Rabbit's private affairs." She glanced upward as if she'd find strength on the ceiling. "I just can't believe you chose to discuss this with your father rather than me." Tears welled in her eyes, but they seemed more likely a result of a bitter taste the unacceptable words had left in her mouth.

Dad grabbed her hand and this time she let him. Now welcomed into her space, he wrapped his other hand over the top of their clenched ones. "Honey, she only told me because I got it out of her first. Don't worry, you haven't failed as a mother."

His words crumbled the last of her reserve and she started to cry. He pulled her up as he stood, wrapping her in his arms.

Her tears my fault, I expected Emma Jean to reprimand me, but neither the wagged finger nor the 'I told you so' ever came. I guessed her disappearance served as punishment for my thoughtlessness. Losing this last bit of her only magnified my pain.

Dad handed Mom his handkerchief. "You know, I expressed my concern about our lack of qualifications to deal with this sort of thing. I told Sophie she should go to the authorities."

Mom gave him a look like he'd lost his mind. "Absolutely not. Miss Rabbit never intended her story to be made public until after her death. If I have anything to say, that's the way it'll remain." Her hand froze in mid-air as she lifted the tissue to her nose, almost as if she had overlooked a step. Her eyes burned with determination as she recited another bit of Old Man wisdom. "Trust is like an icicle. Once it melts, that's the end of it."

Any relief I'd hoped to gain from having unloaded my burden evaporated, but a niggling voice in my brain, reminding me that fearful young girls turn into silent old ladies, urged me on anyway. I gripped the sides of my chair. "Mom, I didn't mean to make you cry. So you know, I *do* realize how serious this is. These experiences aren't mine, but that doesn't mean I can't understand them. And telling Dad first has nothing to do with you. Some things happen for a reason. Just like how this book found me and not someone else.

"All I ever wanted was to get Miss Rabbit to talk. What Luther did was awful, but what she's gone through since is just as bad. Nothing will make it all better, but keeping this a secret doesn't help her or me." My lack of control exhausted me as much as the search for my mother's understanding.

Surprise etched her face as she eased into a chair. Our eyes stayed locked until my father picked up his breakfast dishes.

"Okay ladies, how about a break now? We'll talk more about

this later, after we've all had some time to think. C'mon, sweetie, I'll help you wash the dishes."

The ding of the front door bell saved us from further discussion and provided him with an excuse to leave the room.

"Who's here?" I asked my mother as she smoothed the front of her blouse and fussed with her hair. Heaven forbid someone see her not primped and perfect.

"I don't know, dear. We're not expecting anyone."

Loud enough to serve as a warning, my father's gracious welcoming of Penny at our front door ratcheted the tension in my jaw. My mother shot me a 'be nice' look before she moved our dirty dishes to the counter.

Sink now piled high, but table clean, she called into the other room, the singsong quality of her voice returning. "Hi Penny. Come join us in the kitchen."

I grabbed the bowl of remaining strawberries and stuffed them into the refrigerator. They wouldn't be offered to Penny if I could help it. My parents might have forgiven her, but I hadn't.

"Hi Sophie."

Penny's voice tightened my spine. With no intention of answering, I reorganized the refrigerator shelf: ketchup by mustard, jar of jelly next to dill pickles. A near-empty quart of milk, crowding the full one beside it, caught my eye as the doorbell rang a second time.

At the sound of her father's voice in the front room, Penny and I locked eyes for the first time. Nothing like intrusive parents to force friendship. A heavy sigh escaped her lips. "Why did he have to follow me here?"

Her discomfort providing a touch of guilty pleasure, I tried not to gloat.

Mom hurried over to the doorway. "Such a nice surprise, Jim. What brings you to our humble home?"

Wearing grass-stained jeans and a frayed sweatshirt turned inside out, Mr. Parker gave my mother a hug before nodding in my direction. "I apologize for interrupting your Sunday. Penny has something to say to you all and I came over to make sure she does so."

The groan of frustration from his red-faced daughter couldn't have been any louder. "Dad, I told you I would do it. I don't need you here watching."

His glare did nothing to stop her.

"Why do you have to butt into this anyway? You wouldn't even have known what happened here yesterday unless I'd told you. You're embarrassing me. I'm not saying anything until you leave. Just go home."

A deathlike silence filled the room. Baseball-sized eyes announced my mother's shock, but with the kitchen emptied of kindness, and in keeping with her southern manners, she put an arm around Penny. "Let's all take a deep breath, shall we? How about something to drink? Coffee? Juice?"

In a replay of the previous day, Penny recoiled and slapped her away.

Mr. Parker barreled across the room, grabbed Penny, and spun her so fast her head caught up a second later. He roared into her face. "Enough, young lady. I won't tolerate behavior of this sort. You'll apologize this second."

I shoved the empty container of milk into the refrigerator, wishing I could find space there large enough to accommodate me.

Mr. Parker gained volume. "We're not leaving until you apologize."

Penny crossed her arms and tossed her long, loose hair over a shoulder. Chin pointed in defiance, she sneered. "Fine. I'm s-o-r-r-y. Is that better? Now will you go away?"

Her ability to spell a word she so rarely used stunned me almost as much her nerve. How much attitude could she fling at her father before he snapped?

The thought no sooner entered my mind when Mr. Parker's hand connected with the soft rosy skin of Penny's California cheek. The loud crack of flesh against flesh preceded the silence like a misplaced exclamation point.

CHAPTER 44

The slap sucked all the air out of the room, making the escape I longed for impossible. While Penny's problems, once again overshadowing mine, placed her in the spotlight of my parents' attention, her own father stood at the sink, back turned and head in hands. To Penny's credit, she didn't utter a sound as my parents helped her into a chair. She stared straight ahead, never glancing at her father or me.

I kept waiting for him to speak, but much like Penny, his stubborn nature ruled. He didn't move until my father put an arm around him.

"C'mon, Jim. Let's go have a seat in the other room for a minute."

With no intention of being part of a plan that left me alone with Penny and my mother, I found a spot up against the wall closest to the doorway. I'd make my break behind the men when they left the room.

"So-So honey, could you give us a few minutes?" my mother said, her plea wrapped in a distracted smile.

Her desire to exclude me diluted my resolve to leave, but only for a second. Who wanted to hear any more of Penny's whining anyway?

I took the stairs two at a time before either of us could change our minds. With Dad busy in the front room with Mr. Parker and Mom tending to Penny's nightmare, no one acknowledged my departure.

Once I was upstairs, being alone with Miss Rabbit's problems proved to be more uncomfortable than the drama downstairs. I'd again be drawn into her story if I didn't get the book out of sight. Stuffing it under bras in my drawer seemed a bit of an insult, though, and also likely to be the first place my mother searched. I knew she would search, too. She'd want to study it, just as I had. But her hands had no business on Miss Rabbit's book. After I'd betrayed the words inside, the least I could do was safeguard the path they traveled. On tiptoe, I found a spot behind boxes on the top shelf of my closet.

Porky's gift still lay at the foot of my bed where my father had left it. On its side, the top not opened enough to start the music, the box brought to mind Mama's rants in Italian; Mrs. Kowalski's hunt for a piece of bread and a cold potato; Roy's erection galloping down the hall; Pete's need for another cigarette; Mr. Messina's one-sided conversations with his wife. Not least of all, Miss Rabbit's silence. Whether I served as witness or not, their routines endured.

I lifted the lid. The ballerina, her hand held high and straight, twirled as the notes plinked out their tune. Like the residents' at Sterlingwood, she would dance until the music stopped. I opened and closed the lid several more times, recalling the names of those who'd died since I'd started working at Sterlingwood. When the list ended with Emma Jean I slammed the box shut and closed my eyes. Neither the darkness or silence made me feel better.

My father called from downstairs. "Sophie, it's safe to come down now. Penny's gone." Only he knew the words to get me out of my room.

I found him alone in the front room. "Where'd everybody go?"

"Penny's house. Your mother went to make sure everything is

okay over there. You know how she is."

Made perfect sense. Concerned as she'd been about Mrs. Parker's leaving, I wouldn't have been surprised if she packed a bag and moved in with them for a few days. A home wasn't a home without a mother, she'd say. I guessed the Parkers needed her more than we did. "What'd I miss?"

Running his hands through his hair, he sat down on the sofa and let loose a deep sigh. "Good Lord. I could use a drink." Then, as if my mother had just announced her five o'clock rule, he added, "Surely, it's five o'clock somewhere."

Uncertain whether to try to make him a drink, or enforce my mother's laws, I asked about Penny instead.

"She's still a bit shaken up, though she did finally apologize for her behavior yesterday. Boy, she's a tough cookie."

"She deserved to be slapped."

"No one deserves that. He could have handled her better, but it looked like he regretted his action the second he slapped her. He seemed more shook up than her." He patted a spot on the sofa. I sat down and laid my head on his shoulder.

"I'm sorry you had to witness such behavior. Before he left, he asked that we extend his apologies to you."

"Why? I'm not the one he smacked."

"Just another thing you can't un-see, Soph."

I nestled against him, inhaled the Old Spice-waffle-bacon-fried-egg aroma on his shirt. Neither Penny nor Miss Rabbit had this luxury of a man who brought such simple comfort.

"Dad, what should I do about Miss Rabbit?" I listened to him breathe in the interim before he spoke.

"As I see it, there's not much you can do," he said, fiddling with a strand of my hair. "Your mother and I would love nothing more than to keep you from being exposed to this kind of stuff, but we can't. Obviously you feel a need to help this poor old Miss Rabbit, but I don't want you to be under the false impression you can fix her. Her troubles date back to long before you were ever born, honey. After all these years, she might just be broken for good."

I started to object, but he pulled me back into the crook of his arm. "Just wait. I'm not saying you can't try to help her. We can't stop you, but I want you to at least recognize the possibility of failure. I still think getting professionals involved might be a good idea, even though your mother would have my hide for saying so."

"She did get pretty upset about that suggestion of yours, didn't she?"

"Yes, but I think there's something more there."

"Like what?"

"Since Penny's mother left, your mother's world has been a bit...how shall I say it? Upended?"

"Then I'm not imagining things. She's been acting like she was the one left behind or something."

"Sort of looks that way, doesn't it? I think she feels the sanctity of her own commitment being questioned."

"The what?" I loved when he spoke to me as an equal, but what he said often escaped me.

"Remember her icicles and trust line? That's the second time I've heard her say it in the last week. I think the combination of Mrs. Parker's sudden departure, Penny's behavior, and your sharing Miss Rabbit's story with me first, have all made her question her role as a friend and mother. Just bad timing is all. Don't take her reaction personally. You know she loves and supports whatever you do."

"Well, that sure isn't what she said."

A few seconds ticked past, convincing me he agreed. I relaxed into his shoulder and closed my eyes.

"Sometimes you just have to listen to the silence, Soph."

Not the first time I'd heard those words yet I still didn't know what they meant.

"Sure would be a lot easier if people just said what they meant," I said. "Like you and I do."

"If everyone were like me and you, I wouldn't feel the need for a drink right now." He nudged me forward and held out a hand for me to help him up. "Let's go clean the kitchen before your mother gets home, shall we?"

"You know we still haven't come up with any ideas on how to

help Miss Rabbit."

"I'm guessing, by the time your mother comes home, she'll not only have the Parkers reunited, she'll have a plan for Miss Rabbit, and at least twenty more...what do you call her quotes?"

"Wise Old Man quotes?"

"Yes." He snickered. "She'll have twenty more of those to support her theory. Like she's said on more than one occasion, no man was ever wise by chance. I'm beginning to think she may be right."

I grabbed a dishtowel off the counter while he rummaged through the refrigerator for a beer, then a drawer for an opener.

"Five o'clock already, huh? Dang, I must be late for work."

He winked and put the bottle to his lips, drinking until he'd finished the beer. The empty bottle tucked into the trashcan under the sink, he turned on the faucet. "I'll wash, you dry?"

"Sounds like a plan."

We worked side-by-side in silence. Claiming he couldn't get the top off with his wet hands, he handed me the bottle of dish detergent. "I think both your mother and I would prefer if you gave this Miss Rabbit thing some more thought before you did anything."

How much more thought could I devote? I tilted the container of soap under the running water, watching as the bubbles formed and popped. In the bigger picture, we were all on this earth for mere seconds. Did any of us have time to waste?

"Sophie, you listening?"

I nodded, but couldn't bring myself to meet his eyes. I'd made up my mind to have a discussion with Miss Rabbit whether my parents approved or not. After all, her book had been given to me, not anyone else, and the balance of the story should come from her. The lessons to be learned—whatever Emma Jean presumed them to be—were mine to decipher. Maybe Miss Rabbit would never heal. Perhaps the damage done had created a permanent scar. Regardless, I couldn't let her go to the grave having wasted the last bits of her life. The expectation of failure had to be considered, as my father warned, but I wouldn't know unless I tried. Still, at her age and after so many years had passed, what did I expect to accomplish?

The dishes finished, I dressed for work. My mother hadn't come home by the time I needed to leave. I couldn't imagine what she did at the Parkers' for so long, but with my head already wrapped around what awaited me on a Crazy Sunday, I didn't have the extra space in my brain to worry about her, too.

Downstairs, my father had his feet up on the coffee table, a pen and Sunday crossword puzzle in hand. On my way out of the door, I tossed the bottle cap he'd left on the kitchen counter into the garbage. No doubt my mother would notice he'd broken her rule, but I felt better knowing I'd tried to keep one secret.

CHAPTER 45

"Piece a bread and a cold potato? Lady, c'mon. I'm hungry."

I handed Mrs. Kowalski the cookies I'd tucked into my pocket.

No smile, no look of surprise, she shoved one cookie into her mouth and held the other to her lips, as if any distance would subject the treat to theft.

"C'mon. I'm hungry." The words tumbled out of her full mouth.

"Didn't you just have your big noon meal?"

"A piece a bread and cold potato?" She wrapped her hand around my arm, her short, thick fingers tight to my skin. The wedding band she wore floated between two arthritis-enlarged knuckles.

I spun the ring until the tiny stone embedded in the gold sat on top. "Did your husband give you this?"

She pulled her hand from me. "Hey lady, you got a piece of bread or a cold potato? I'm hungry."

I guessed after however long she'd been in Sterlingwood, a stranger's interest no longer registered; the need for human connection replaced by an obsession with food. "I'll see what I can find, hon. I'm just now getting to work."

The words meaning nothing to her, she set her sights on Mr. Messina walking through the front door. "Hey mister..."

Digging into his pocket, he winked at me like he had the solution. Silly man. I smiled at him and went to punch in.

Downstairs, clanks and clatters from kitchen staff cleaning up from the day's big meal, and voices of visitors overcompensating for not-so-hard-of-hearing relatives, echoed across the linoleum floors. The break room sat empty except for the lingering aroma of roast chicken and cornbread. Dirty dishes had been left on one of the tables—despite the hand-written signs posted in multiple places to remind everyone their mother didn't live there. Someone with the nerve to address the repeat offender had penciled Tanya's name at the top of each sign.

I hadn't thought about her in days. Did this mess signal her return to work?

The time clock answered with an ambiguous thunk.

Upstairs, the nurse's station was also deserted. Unusual for a Sunday, considering management insisted the desk be staffed during visiting hours—another one of the cosmetics used to disguise an ugly face.

I followed the voices coming from D-wing and found everyone in Mrs. Riggler's old room. Smith and a handful of aides stood in a circle around a woman sprawled across a no-longer-visible mattress. Four hundred seventy-five pounds of new resident had arrived.

A man who normally worked in the kitchen addressed Smith, his arms spread wide. "This just ain't going to work, I'm telling you. Y'all gots to get a crane or something. They don't pay me to do this shit."

Smith grabbed him by the arm and ushered him into the hallway. "You don't talk about the residents in front of them like that, Donny. That poor woman feels bad enough without you adding to it."

Smith's anger failing to keep the reprimand private, the other aides and I, still gathered inside the room, looked at each other and snickered.

"I just calls 'em like I sees 'em, ma'am. It's going to take more than the folks you got, is all I'm saying. No offense intended."

"I'm quite aware of the difficulties involved. We'll figure out something else. Thank you anyway." Smith breezed past me, shaking her head. "Okay everyone, a new plan. We'll roll her over. Sophie, go get me another set of sheets."

"Another set of sheets?" By the looks of things, another set of anything wouldn't help.

Smith directed Tanya and the others to surround the bed. Everyone in place, she turned to me. "A set of sheets. Now."

Her voice jabbing like a hot poker, I raced to the supply closet and back.

The bed-ridden woman, whose name I couldn't remember, wept. Her pumpkin-sized face scrunched into layers with the effort. Spittle ran down several of her chins. "I'm so sorry. I'll be fine. Please just let me be."

Why was that voice so familiar?

"You cannot lay on a wet bed, Mrs. Cornwall," Smith told her. "Don't worry. We'll be as gentle and quick as possible, but you need to help us as much as you can. Fair enough?"

Mrs. Cornwall used the top sheet to wipe her eyes and nose. "Oh my. Alright."

The helium-filled voice of the Oz Munchkins!

Affected by the stroke she'd had, or by the massive weight she carried, her vocal cords had likely been squeezed within an inch of their lives.

Battling the urge to laugh, I handed Smith the sheets. She passed them around, then rolled and twisted one into a sort of rope. Handing one end of her sheet to me, she told me to bunch it under Mrs. Cornwall's shoulders, then directed the others to do the same underneath her legs. "We'll use these to help get her to one side."

The sheets in place, on Smith's count, we all pulled. Tanya's groans to my left accompanied someone else's errant fart to my right as we strained against the dead weight. Mrs. Cornwall's shoulder slowly rose. Her enormous breasts slid sideways under her hospital gown. At their momentum, she cried out.

One of the orderlies, sacked by a large breast, muttered a not so quiet, "Holy crap."

"Easy now," Smith said, the words straining with her efforts. "You all got her?" In one quick swipe, she replaced the wet pads. "Okay, let's lower her. Slowly now."

Unable to imagine this exercise every time I had D-wing, I broke out in a sweat.

On her back once again, Mrs. Cornwall adjusted her out-of-place parts the best she could with one good hand. "Oh, that feels better. Thank you." Her labored breaths echoed our own.

Smith patted Mrs. Cornwall's arm and straightened the top sheet. "We'll get that catheter back in and you'll be good to go. I think Tanya and I have this handled now. The rest of you can go."

Everyone scattered but me. "Tanya, how come you're working swing shift?" I didn't have the strength to address what had kept her away so long.

She wiped the sweat from her forehead, while trying to wedge herself onto the only available seat in the room. When the arms of the commode wouldn't accommodate her massive hips she leaned up against the wall. "Don't get no money if I don't work." She said the words as if she thought the concept unfair.

"How've you been?"

"S'pect like you been, only worse."

I never thought about how Emma Jean's death might have affected others. "How are Clifford and her son doing?"

"Same." Her eyes focused on the ceiling, she waved a hand in front of her face to create a breeze.

My efforts on her wasted, I turned to Smith. "What wing do you want me to work?"

"Miss Rabbit's." She'd never used the name as reference to a wing.

"You sure you don't need any help?"

Smith gestured to a sleeping Mrs. Cornwall, who squeaked with each snore, and whispered. "She's so worn out she might not wake up for awhile."

I lowered my voice to match hers. "When did she arrive?"

"Right after noon. They wheeled her in here, bed and all. Her catheter sprung a leak somewhere during transport–hence the mess. Poor thing. I just don't know what we're going to do with her. The administrator is looking into a special lift suited for these cases."

"Not to be rude or anything, but am I the only one who thought of the Munchkins?"

Tanya slapped her thigh and let out a loud hoot. "Ooo, girl, I been trying to place that voice ever since I walked in here."

Smith's expression acknowledged that she, too, recognized the reference, but she waved at us to be quiet. "Let's get to work. Sophie, go."

I'd somehow landed on Tanya's good side, even if just for the moment, and with no full moon in the near future and only the crazy part of Sunday to tackle, my day appeared to be on the upswing. I left the room to start my rounds.

Miss Rabbit's room first on my list, I knocked and eased the door open. "Hello, Miss Rabbit."

Her empty wheelchair, at an odd angle in the bathroom doorway, sat too far away from the toilet. Had she gotten stuck and been waiting for help? Why hadn't she pushed the alarm button on the wall?

"Here, let me help you." I tried to shove her wheelchair into the bathroom ahead of me, but its wheels struck something solid. I peeked around the corner. My startled gasp failed to rouse her from where she lay unconscious on the floor.

THE SECRET MISS RABBIT KEPT

CHAPTER 46

On my first day of training, Emma Jean had pointed out the alarm panel located in every bathroom. Time and again she'd told me, "When in doubt, smack the button." I silently gave thanks for her foresight as my hand moved to the wall. A split second stretched to an eternity before the alarm sounded.

I knelt between the toilet and where Miss Rabbit lay. No matter how many times I repeated her name, her eyes didn't open. Squeezing her good hand did nothing. My limited medical know-how would do more harm than good in the passing minutes, but the need to occupy my trembling hands and distract my overactive imagination led me to straighten the housecoat scrunched high atop her crooked legs and retrieve the lens from her glasses laying against a baseboard beside her head.

As I wiped the trail of spit from her mouth, Smith plowed into the tiny space behind me. "What happened?"

"I—I don't know. I found her like this." My voice, thick with dread, struck the walls of the cramped bathroom and bounced back at me in a sad chorus of indictment.

Smith placed a hand at Miss Rabbit's jaw line–something my

panic hadn't allowed—and barked orders.

"She's still with us. Get that chair out of the way. Stay here, but don't touch her. I'll go call for an ambulance."

I stood over Miss Rabbit, willing her to wake. The beat of my heart kept track of the time until paramedics arrived.

Two strong men worked on her as I sat on the edge of her bed. Neither the insertion of tubes or placing her onto a gurney stirred her. When they wheeled her out of the room, my legs wouldn't let me follow. Like Emma Jean before her, Miss Rabbit had capsized my lifeboat, paralyzed me with an ominous fear of loss. Although Smith had said Miss Rabbit wasn't dead, I guessed that the parts she'd kept from me, the pieces I hadn't yet gotten to know, would be changed for the worse. The blood on floor where she'd hit her head, now congealing into dark brown smears, whispered of lost opportunity.

Dorothy appeared in the doorway. "Sophie, you okay? I heard you're the one who found Mable."

I nodded.

"She didn't look too good when they took her outta here. Heard the paramedics say she might've had another stroke."

If I nodded again, the tears welling in my eyes would fall.

Dorothy leaned over the arm of her chair and patted my hand. "She's a tough old bird. Bet she'll be okay. You just might have saved her life."

The attempt to make me feel better didn't work. I guessed she realized as much when she leaned back in her chair.

"Hey, you seen the big gal in Mrs. Riggler's old room yet? Holy smokes—" Her words, tripping over the phlegm in her throat, paired with a barked cough.

I stood and slapped her on the back. "Holy smokes is right, Dorothy."

"Yeah, yeah." She struggled to catch her breath. "Like I was saying, I'd hate to be the one to try to move that woman. Gives me a pain in the back to even think about it. I sure would like to know how she let herself get so big. Damn, once you lose sight of your feet, wouldn't you think to push yourself from the table?"

Unable to focus on fat ladies or bad habits or Dorothy's incessant cough, I stood. "I have to find Smith."

"You know she's going to have to call Emery, don't you?"

I hadn't even thought of next of kin. Of course Miss Rabbit's brother would have to be told, but why did Dorothy think this fact mattered to me?

She spoke louder as I walked away. "I wonder if he even knows what happened to Emma Jean. They were tight, you know? He'll take all this pretty hard. Guessing he'll be in need of some good news when all this hits him, don't you think?"

The implication, like a smack to the back of the head, stopped me.

She held up her hands, palms out. "I'm just saying. Poor woman might die. She hasn't spoken to her brother in years. Might be a good time to bring them together. Least give him some peace of mind. No need for him to think she hasn't reached out to anybody."

"Miss Rabbit's life is none of my business." After having done everything in my power to the contrary, had I really said those words?

"But what if she dies? Do you want her going to the grave silent? Seems to me, with Emma Jean gone, you hold the only insight poor old Emery might get."

I sensed Emma Jean in my peripheral vision. Silent and unmoving, she stood ready to pounce if I broke my promise. Didn't she realize Dorothy knew almost as much as I did? There was no such thing as news to this busybody.

As Dorothy tilted her head to study me, a light coming in from the window flashed onto the lens of her glasses. Like a traffic signal, the flicker warned me to proceed with caution. Stop and look both ways, it said.

"Wouldn't it be nice if Emery heard some good news?" she said.

"Are you saying I should tell him Miss Rabbit has spoken to Emma Jean?"

Dorothy's voice dropped to the level of gravel. "Cut the crap, kid. I know Mable talked to you. I also know you have something of hers."

The image of her scooting down the hall the previous night when I opened Miss Rabbit's door had me point an angry finger. "You *were* listening."

"Someone had to make sure this didn't go to the grave with Emma Jean." Impatience crossed and uncrossed her arms before she leaned closer. "Listen, we're all on our way out, kid. No time like the present to make things right."

"Just how much did you hear?"

"Enough to know whatever has kept Mable silent is long past gone. This stroke, or whatever of hers, is a wake-up call to put an end to this nonsense."

"Shouldn't you be saying all this to her?"

"Don't think I haven't tried. But you're the one."

"The one what?"

"The one to fix this."

I sat on the bed, pulling her chair closer to make my point. "And just how am I supposed to do that? You think years of silence will end just because you and I say it's time? Even I'm smart enough to know that's not how things work."

She sat back and rubbed her chin. Somewhere among the wiry whiskers there, she found a new angle. "Tell me. How bad is it?"

"How bad is what?"

Her narrowed eyes and puckered mouth dared me to ask more stupid questions.

Could I? Should I? Where the heck was Emma Jean when I needed her?

"Okay, Sophie, let me come at this another way. If you were about to die—"

"Stop saying that. She isn't going to die."

Smith, now at the doorway, cleared her throat. "Everything okay in here?" As she glanced from me to Dorothy her eyebrow arched. "You get all the dirt you needed, Mrs. Crumble?"

Dorothy sat tall and met Smith's stare. "You people fail to consider what you'd do without me. Somebody's gotta stay on top of things around here. Did you call Mable's next of kin yet?"

Smith wrapped her hands around Dorothy's throat. "You do know you're not in charge here, right?"

When Dorothy stuck out her tongue, pretending to gag, Smith laughed, but didn't let go until Dorothy nodded.

"Not that it's any of your business, but yes, I called the next of kin."

How they could laugh escaped me. "Any word on Miss Rabbit?"

Smith shook her head. "Looks like she might've had a stroke. We'll know more after they run tests. By the way, in light of what's happened, Tanya has offered to help you with your rooms, believe it or not."

Dorothy put a hand to her chest. "Well, which cold day in hell would this be?"

"Hush now. This might be short-lived, but let's enjoy the moment while we can. Sophie, accept her offer, even if you don't need her help. I'm curious as to what this new, improved Tanya wants."

"Sure. Will you let me know what you hear about Miss Rabbit?"

"Of course." Smith turned to Dorothy. "That okay or should I come to you first?"

"You just wait til I'm dead and gone. You'll see how this place falls apart." She pulled a cigarette and lighter from the pocket of her housecoat. One strike of the flint and a tall flame kissed her forehead, causing a clump of her hair to crackle. "Son of a bitch!"

"Give me that damn thing before you kill yourself." Smith fiddled with the lighter until the flame shortened, then handed it back. "At this rate, it won't be long before you're dead and gone."

Dorothy ignored the remark and took a drag from her cigarette. Blue smoke slithered between her lips as she spoke. "Sophie, give some thought to what we talked about."

Smith questioned me with her eyes. I shrugged, playing dumb the best I could. "Cigarettes finally got to her brain. I'll see you guys later."

Dorothy called after me. "You don't do it, I will."

I still had no idea what 'it' was supposed to be, and until news of Miss Rabbit arrived, I guessed none of us would.

CHAPTER 47

As I worked my way through the wing, I couldn't stop thinking about Miss Rabbit and her fall. My absentmindedness came to a head when I pulled Roy away from one of the women residents, but forgot to zip his fly. I went after him to correct my mistake, but a few steps later, threw my hands in the air. How much damage could one old, freed penis really do in a place like Sterlingwood? I changed direction, chuckling at how Emma Jean would've appreciated my newfound rationale.

Martha Applebee, outfitted in a combination of brilliant orange plaid and bold teal stripes, popped out of the doorway to my right. "There you are, dear. I've spent hours looking for you."

Her sudden appearance didn't startle me as much as her color selection. To remark on the outfit would only fluster her, but the longer I studied her the more sense her choices made; the purple, feathered hat actually pulled the ensemble together. Only Mrs. Applebee could manage such a feat. "You sure look bright and cheerful today. What's up?"

"Someone told me I have a birthday this week. I don't know how it slipped my mind, but we must arrange a party and I need your help."

In all the commotion, I'd forgotten about my plan for her birthday, but chances were she'd forget hers as well. "A party it is. What'd you have in mind?"

Finger to mouth, she pondered my question.

Mrs. Kowalski approached. "Hey lady, piece of bread and a cold potato?"

Mrs. Applebee clasped her hands and held them against her chest. "That's it! We'll arrange a dinner for all my dear friends and we'll reserve a fine dining hall, so there'll be plenty of seating."

I held up a finger to silence Mrs. Kowalski, and addressed Mrs. Applebee. "That sounds like a wonderful idea. What do you need me to do?"

"Well, for starters, we must decide on the menu."

"How about if I take care of that? Pick a day and I'll make arrangements for the location and food." Sterlingwood posted a monthly menu. My job would be to convince her she'd made the selection and steer her away from soggy fish-stick day.

"Oh, you're such a dear. What would I ever do without you?" She patted the top of my head, leaned closer, and lowered her voice. "I think a nice prime rib with lobster tail would do nicely, but I don't want my guests thinking me ostentatious."

"You? Never. But let me surprise you. Have I ever failed?"

She drew back, hand to her face. "Of course not, dear. You're my very best assistant."

Mrs. Kowalski stopped moving in and out of my line of vision and tugged on my sleeve. "Hey lady, c'mon, I'm hungry." She smacked her lips as a visual aid.

"It's almost dinnertime, Mrs. Kowalski. Why don't you start heading that way?" I pointed toward the elevator. "Go. I'll help you in a second."

"I'll take her, dear. You're far too busy planning my birthday gala." Martha put a tender arm around Mrs. Kowalski and coaxed her down the hallway. A few steps later, she called over her shoulder. "Now don't forget, I like dark chocolate cake with butter cream frosting."

Her lucid moment offering hope, I turned my attention to

Ruby and Caroline's room.

"About damn time you showed up."

"Hello to you, too, Ruby." I introduced my exaggerated smile to her scowl.

"No one has given me a shower this week." Her tone turned the announcement into an accusation.

In the corner with an open book on her lap, Caroline muttered, "I keep telling her today is Sunday, but she won't believe me."

"I don't give a shit what day it is."

I fought the urge to yell. "It's almost dinnertime. Wouldn't it be better to wait until tomorrow?"

Caroline shook her head and closed her book. "That's what I tried to tell her. One of the girls offered to bathe her the other day, but she didn't want to miss her television program. Now she wants you to drop everything on a Sunday."

"Mind your own damn business. If I want a shower, I should be able to have a shower." With each word, Ruby's voice climbed in volume. Her neck and cheeks mottled a deep red.

"Tell you what," I said. "After dinner, if I have time, I'll get you into the shower. Fair enough? But right now, you need to head downstairs."

Always the good girl, Caroline wheeled over to where I stood, but stopped to let her sister go through the doorway first. In an unusual gesture of goodwill, Ruby motioned for Caroline to move ahead of her. When Caroline proceeded, Ruby smacked her on the back of the head.

Ruby's surprise attack sent Caroline sideways in her chair. Blinking away her initial shock, Caroline raised her hands to her face and began to cry.

"Oh my gosh, are you okay?" I put an arm around her and turned to Ruby. "You should be ashamed of yourself."

"Maybe she'll learn to mind her own business now." A smug smile had replaced her previous scowl. "Besides, I hardly touched her. Now get out of my way, I'm hungry."

Keeping her chair in Ruby's path, Caroline pointed a shaky finger. "First chance I get, I'm moving out of here."

Ruby responded by ramming the wheels of her chair into Caroline's.

I stepped between them. "Enough now. I'm getting Smith to deal with you. Don't you dare move a muscle."

I pushed Caroline down the hall to the nurse's station where her cries slipped into sniffles. Smith sat at the desk with the phone to her ear.

"Yes, that's right. She doesn't talk...No, there's no physical reason we know of...Okay, I'd appreciate an update as soon as you know something." Smith replaced the receiver and turned to me. "That was the hospital. Miss Rabbit is conscious now, but they're still running tests."

Flopping onto one of the seats against the wall, I said a little prayer of thanks to the God I'd doubted earlier in the day.

Smith gave us both the once-over. "What's going on here?"

At the question, Caroline erupted into sobs. "M-my sister hit me."

Smith's face puckered so tight her eyes shut. The phone rang before she could have made it to a count of three. Pete showed up in front of the desk, cigarette in hand, and with phone to ear, Smith reached into the top drawer. She pulled out a lighter before he could ask. He didn't make eye contact, but an uneasy, crooked smile turned his mouth.

Caroline's sniffles once again tapered off. Her injuries, more emotional than physical, weren't urgent. I handed her a tissue from the box on the desk.

"Th-thank you, dear."

Still on the call, Smith leaned over the desk as if trying to avoid my stare. "Yes, Mr. Rabbit, there's been an accident. One of our aides found Mable unconscious on the floor. She's been taken to St. Joseph's hospital. Looks like she may have had another stroke, but we don't know yet for sure. She's conscious now from what I understand, but they're running tests."

I walked to the front of the desk to listen. When Smith waved me off, I moved an inch or two sideways, then crept back when she refocused on her conversation.

"I know. I'm sorry to break this news to you over the

phone...Yes, that might be a good idea."

Patiently waiting her turn, Caroline blew her nose. I placed my hand on her leg and whispered. "We'll deal with Ruby in a minute, but I need to talk to Nurse Smith about this phone call first, okay?"

Smith glanced at us, but continued with the call. "I'll take care of that right away...Yes, St. Joseph's. Keep us posted." She hung up and turned, her expression giving nothing away. "No, tell me what happened. This other business can wait."

Caroline recited her version of the incident, managing to hold back her tears until the very end. "I want to switch rooms. I just cannot live with her any longer."

"We'll get you moved immediately. I promise. In the meantime, I'll go speak with your sister." Smith examined the side of Caroline's head. "I'll need to file a report on this, as well."

Caroline brushed away Smith's hand. "I'm fine. I don't want to get her into any troub—"

"There needs to be a record in case any injury shows up. Don't worry. Ruby's days of hurting you have officially ended." While Smith's jaw worked inside her cheek, the air around her threatened to combust at any moment. "Why don't you eat in the Day Room tonight? Stay as far away from Ruby as you can. Sophie and I will get your stuff moved out of your room while she's at dinner."

"Not eat with my sister?"

At the absurdity of her question, Smith and I exchanged glances.

"I guess I shouldn't do that, should I?" Caroline's posture wilted. Her eyes welled with fresh tears. "I just don't understand why she has to be so mean."

Smith laid a hand on Caroline's shoulder. "Strokes–even mild ones–do funny things to people. Ruby might've been mean all her life, but her stroke likely affected her brain and exacerbated her tendencies. Don't take anything she does personally. But you should know, I won't stand for any violence. I'd have moved you after this even if you hadn't asked. If it'll be easier on you, we can make this my decision."

"Could you do that? I mean, would you? I don't want to give her any more reason to pick on me."

"Consider it done. I'll go speak to her right now. Sophie, get Caroline settled in the Day Room and we'll have dinner brought up. In the meantime, we'll move Mama in with Ruby. The language barrier might be a good thing. As mobile and feisty as Mama is, Ruby won't stand a chance."

Suppressing a giggle at the thought of Mama's Italian curses directed at Ruby, I wheeled a forlorn Caroline through Pete's haze of smoke toward the Day Room.

"Hey, you got another light?"

"Ask the woman at the front desk, Pete. She's giving 'em away today."

Smith called from behind the desk. "Sophie, once you've gotten Caroline her meal and the rest of your people to dinner, come see me, please. I need you to go to St. Joseph's hospital on a quick errand."

CHAPTER 48

I had never been in a hospital before Nurse Smith asked me to bring Miss Rabbit her Bible. The unfamiliar surroundings, combined with the reason for my visit, had my knees, as Emma Jean would say, knocking like coconuts on a tree in a windstorm. Certain the woman at the front desk would hear the clatter of my bones, I spoke much louder than necessary when I asked how to find Miss Rabbit.

She offered a sympathetic smile and shuffled through a pile of papers. Once she found what she needed, she raised her voice and enunciated her words like I was deaf. "Looks like she's just been moved to room 212. But visiting hours are over now."

A doctor on his way out the door waved in our direction. "Good night, Sheila. See you tomorrow."

Like one of the goofier girls in my high school, Sheila wiggled a couple of her fingers at him and blushed. "Good night to you as well, Dr. Finder. Enjoy your evening." Her eyes followed him as he disappeared around the exterior of the building.

"I'm sorry," she said, her focus finally returning to me. "Who did you want to see?" With the interruption, she'd forgotten about my hearing problem.

"Mable Rabbit."

"And you said you were a...relative?"

Prepared to be Miss Rabbit's granddaughter if pressed, I hoped my smile wouldn't count as a lie. I couldn't afford to lose any more of my points for Heaven.

Between glances at the exit door, she shuffled more papers. Tempted to tell her that even I knew Dr. Heartthrob wouldn't be back, I drummed my fingers on the desktop and acted as nonchalant as possible.

She met my gaze and pointed. "I really shouldn't, but...the elevator you need to take to the second floor is just down that hallway. The room will be on your right-hand side."

I mumbled my thanks before she could change her mind then followed her directions.

Bible tucked under my arm, I stopped in front of Miss Rabbit's closed door. What had God intended with this errand? Of all the people He could have sent to deliver His book, why me? Smith hadn't said whether or not Emery specifically asked for me, but I couldn't imagine he had; we barely knew each other. As apprehensive as the request made me, my thoughts skipped clear over the why, rushing to the how and when. With no time beforehand to question Smith, God, or anyone else, I stood at the doorway questioning them all. Neither the closed door nor the book I held provided any answer.

"Is there something I can help you with?"

I jumped at the intrusion. Who in the world had known what I'd been thinking?

A woman popped her head above the divider at the nurse's station. "Sorry, I didn't mean to startle you. You looked lost."

"No, I'm fine. I found the room I need."

"Are you visiting Mrs. Rabbit?" Her hesitation pointed to my skin color not matching the Relatives-Only visitation rule.

"Just here to drop something off. I work at the place she had her accident." If it hadn't been for the long day she wore in wrinkles on her forehead and dark circles under her eyes, I would have asked just how many visitors or relatives came to call dressed in nurse's aide uniforms and carrying Bibles.

"Oh, you're from Sterlingwood. I spoke to a Nurse Smith."

"Yes, she's the one who sent me."

"Go on in then. Her brother is in there." She disappeared behind the divider.

The door to Miss Rabbit's room opened as I turned.

Emery had aged in the weeks since we'd last laid eyes on each other. Stooped more than I remembered, he straightened only slightly to put a hand on my shoulder. "Well, hello there. Miss Sophie, right?"

"Hi, Emery. I brought Miss Rabbit's Bible, like you asked."

He took the book from me and, after a second's thought, pulled me in for a hug. "Ah, it's good to see a familiar face around here. Thanks for coming. I hoped Miss Emma might've showed up, but I'm happy to see you. Hate to be troubling you ladies, in light of all you gots to do, but I know Mable be real glad to see her Bible when she wakes up."

God had planned this terrible punishment for me, but my gut told me to fudge the truth. "I was all caught up with work, so Nurse Smith asked me to come. Your sister sleeping?"

"The tests they ran done wore her out. Doctors think her blood pressure just got the best of her. The bump to her head knocked her out. Weren't no stroke like they first thought."

Relief flooded over me. Maybe Miss Rabbit would be okay after all. "That's wonderful news."

"Why don't you come on in for a spell? Mable is in the bed by the window." He stepped aside before I could decline his offer.

I slid past him against my better judgment. An elderly woman lying in the first bed, her eyes fixed on the ceiling, didn't acknowledge me. Almost as if Emery knew I might change my mind at any moment, he kept a hand on my back until we reached the curtain separating the space between the two beds.

I peeked around the curtain and a steady landscape of peaks and valleys on the heart monitor confirmed Miss Rabbit's good health. Her eyes flickered open and she stared at me as if I were an apparition. I laid my hand on the part of her arm not disturbed by IV's or equipment. "Hi, Miss Rabbit. It's me. Sophie."

She blinked several more times before the corners of her mouth edged higher.

"You gave us quite a scare, you know?"

Her silent stare reminded me of our secret.

Emery walked to the opposite side of the bed. "I remembered how much you like to read your Bible, so I had Miss Sophie bring it. Thought it might get you to healing faster." He set the book beside her.

Miss Rabbit never took her eyes off me. She pulled the book closer, tucked it under her hip and, as if fearing its disappearance, kept a hand on the cover. Emery had chosen wisely.

"Sounds like you'll be getting out of here sooner than later, Miss Rabbit. You might be back in time for the party we're having for Mrs. Applebee's birthday." I doubted Miss Rabbit cared anything for parties or Mrs. Applebee, but silence would have stuck out more than my idle chatter. Maybe if I kept talking, she'd jump in at some point and save me from having to surprise Emery with the news of Emma Jean.

"You sure used to love parties, didn't you, Mable? Remember that one Ma had for you? Think it was your tenth or eleventh birthday."

Miss Rabbit's gaze never shifted.

Emery didn't allow her slight to stop him. "Ma invited all the neighbor kids. Surprised Mable so much she cried." He laughed and slapped his knee. "I know that sure don't sound like a good thing, but it was Mable's way. Funny, she ate so much of Ma's chocolate cake that day she got herself a bellyache and had to lay down. Later, Ma made me go check on her. Remember what you said to me, Mable?"

Keeping her eyes trained on me, Miss Rabbit shook her head.

"You said folks should eat cake first. That ways there always be room. Makes a whole lot a sense, don't it, Miss Sophie? We shouldn't be saving the best for last. Might not get the chance later."

Like a reminder from God, the intercom system came alive in the hallway and announced a Code Blue. When hospital staff and clanking carts flew past the doorway, Emery and I exchanged frowns. He rubbed the whiskers on his chin until the noise in the hall faded. "Sure hope theys had their dessert."

His comment poked at my unease. "You know I should probably get back to work now."

"Okay, Miss Sophie. Let me just use the facilities first and I'll walk you out. I'll be back in a bit, Mable. I'm thinking a nice piece of chocolate cake might taste good right about now."

A spark of interest ignited in Miss Rabbit's eyes.

"I bet he'll bring you some, too," I said.

Emery smiled at her from the foot of the bed. "I'll bring back a big piece and we can share just like the old days."

Miss Rabbit looked at him for the first time.

"I'll take that as a yes." He laughed and headed toward the bathroom, whispering to me as he passed. "We're making progress. Yes, indeed."

Once the bathroom door closed, I leaned over and kissed Miss Rabbit on the forehead. The scent of baby powder, reminding me of who should have been standing in my place, kept my lips pressed to her skin. I whispered into her hairline so I wouldn't have to look into her eyes. "He doesn't know about Emma Jean and I don't quite know how to tell him."

She let go of her Bible and put her hand on my back.

"I should tell him, right? I mean I have to tell him, don't I?" I straightened, in hopes she would answer.

Her red-rimmed, espresso-colored eyes, for once not shielded by her glasses, offered no insight to her thoughts.

"Oh, Miss Rabbit, I wish you would talk."

"I been telling her the same thing long as I can remember." Emery, now at my side, shook his head. "But near as I can tell, wishing don't make nothing so."

Her hand atop her Bible again, Miss Rabbit set her gaze outside the window, refusing to look at either of us.

Emery shrugged and picked up his pork pie hat from the chair. "C'mon, Miss Sophie. I got me a bad hankering now for that chocolate cake."

"Goodbye, Miss Rabbit. I'll see you soon."

Her hand tightened on her Bible.

When Emery ushered me out of the room, the sight of the woman at the nurse's station reminded me of something I should have said earlier. I leaned over the glass divider. "By the way, her name is *Miss* Rabbit, not Mrs. She doesn't like when people make that mistake."

The woman looked up with a blank stare. She'd moved on to other things since we'd spoken. "Alright."

"*Miss* Mable Rabbit. She'd very much appreciate if you got it right." I waited until a light of understanding went on in her eyes before I turned back to Emery.

Emery smiled. "You sure is a sassy little thing, ain't ya? Been spending too much with Miss Emma, I reckon. She do tend to rub off on people. How she been, anyway?"

I swallowed hard and took a long, deep breath.

Emery stopped walking and tilted his head. "You okay, Miss Sophie?"

"Let's go have that piece of chocolate cake now."

CHAPTER 49

In the hospital's cafeteria, Emery studied me with eyes nearly the color of tar. They weren't so much black as they were bottomless. A speck of gold, like a pinprick of light, peeked from the edge of his iris. Uncomfortable with its hypnotic effect, I shifted my gaze to the chocolate cake sitting untouched on the table between us. I suspect his manners prevented him from starting before me, but I couldn't bring myself to lift my fork. If any more time passed in silence, he would soon know I hadn't joined him to eat cake. Much as I wished I could stop the hands on the clock, prevent things from moving forward, it was as he'd said: Wishing don't make nothing so.

"Miss Rabbit is going to be okay then?"

"Seems like it, but she sure done gave me a good scare." The recollection had him shaking his head. "The news ran me out my house so fast, I ain't sure I even locked up my front door."

"Was she awake? I mean, was she conscious by the time you got here?" I could only imagine the fright Miss Rabbit must have felt, waking up among strangers.

"Yes, but some of the newer doctors couldn't figure out why she wouldn't talk. Good thing I was there to explain." Emery's focus left me for the first time, traveling, I suspect, to a place in the past with no more answers than he already had.

"I don't mean to be nosey, but my curiosity can't take it anymore. How long has it been since Miss Rabbit spoke?" My nerve with a man I barely knew had me back pedal. "You don't have to tell me if you don't want to."

"Naw, ain't no secret. Mable ain't spoken, to me or anyone else least I knows, for a good long time." He rubbed the stubble on his chin, continuing to fuss with the whiskers as he spoke. "It'd be back when our sister died. Ain't done the arithmetic lately, but I figure a good twenty-some odd years passed now."

"She was an adult when she quit talking?"

"Yes, ma'am."

Something didn't add up. "But it wasn't her stroke, right? I read her chart. She had the stroke just a few years ago."

"That's right." Eyes averted, he picked up his fork only to lay it back down again.

"Luther, go ahead and—" The name, embedded in my brain cells since I'd learned of it, spewed off my tongue like it had a mind of its own. Heat rushed up my neck the second the word announced itself. A wide-eyed Emery stared back.

"I-I mean Emery, of course. Emery." Repeating his name wouldn't erase Luther's, but I kept saying it anyway. "Emery, go ahead and eat your cake." I gestured to his plate, only to tip my glass of water. I reached before it toppled, but water and ice sloshed onto the table. The vase of plastic flowers sitting between us fell when I grabbed my napkin. No water in there, but the flowers flew to the floor. As I struggled to right everything, my cheeks tingled with the heat of embarrassment.

He laid a firm hand on my flailing one and squeezed with enough pressure to quiet me. Our eyes locked for what became several beats of my heart.

"Miss Sophie, I ain't heard Luther's name since Mable quit talking. Like to think it be a coincidence, but the way you carrying on now, I'm guessing this ain't no such thing."

The walls of the cafeteria drew closer. Dishes stopped clattering. My peripheral vision disappeared as I peered into this old man's eyes. "I-I don't know what you're talking about." My new stutter and blank stare, announcing my big fat lie, could have been a sign plastered to the center of my forehead.

Emery let go of my hand and sat back in his chair. Unable to meet his stare, I bent to pick up the one flower remaining on the floor.

His quiet voice, now heavy with emotion, reached all the way under the table to find me. "You know you ain't fooling me none. And I gots a right to know."

When I bumped my head on the edge of the table I knew Emma Jean had come to knock some sense into my skull. "Child," I could hear her say. "Too late to be trying to cinch the sack. Cat's outta there now."

I took a deep breath and sat upright. Now mindful of something more pressing than news of Miss Rabbit, I folded my hands in my lap to stop them from trembling, and met Emery's gaze. The light in his eye would surely extinguish the minute he heard what I had to say.

"Emma Jean..." I closed my eyes to speak the words. "She was killed in a car accident."

His sharp intake of breath hit me in the center of my chest. Bouncing like an echo along my spine, the ping reverberated until the sound sank into my gut and lay there like day-old road kill.

"No..." The word seemed all he could manage as tears filled his eyes. The sudden slump of his shoulders turned him into half his usual size. His wobbly hand rose to linger over the short gray hairs on the crown of his head. The seconds ticked past as he stared at his piece of cake. "How did it happen?"

My next breath hurt, but the pain seemed only fair when compared to what I had just caused him. Did he need to know about Emma Jean's new shiny Cadillac? The blasting music when she pulled out of the parking lot? Would it matter that they said she'd died instantly, or I had been the last one to see her alive? Could giving him more details to grieve lessen my pain? I didn't think so.

"I really don't know much. I couldn't bring myself to ask. She was buried last week."

"Poor Miss Emma. So full of life." He shook his head and wiped a tear from his cheek. "Losing friends be the worst part about getting old, Miss Sophie. Done it too many times now for my liking, and it don't never get any easier."

I couldn't imagine.

"Dang, this news sure does break my heart. Wish someone had told me sooner. Would've liked to pay my respects to her kin."

"Her husband is a real nice man." Not that this mattered, but any fact sounded better than the last one I'd shared.

Nodding like I'd told him something he expected, Emery stared at his cake. He turned the plate one way, then the other, before he looked at me. "Sure don't feel much like eating this now, but I reckon Miss Emma wouldn't have it no other way." He picked up his fork. "You know, this just be another lesson on how the good Lord can call us home any time He sees fit."

Home...nursing home...Sterlingwood. Smith was going to kill me. I searched the room for a clock.

Emery tapped his fork on the plate. Not hard, but enough to get my attention. "Miss Sophie, you know I ain't letting you go til you tell me how you heard of Luther."

"But they'll have my hide if I don't get back soon."

"Then your boss lady can come down here and holler at both of us if need be. I been waiting twenty years to hear my sister speak, and if I gots to hear her through you, then that's what is going to happen."

The cat had managed to find its way out of this bag. Why couldn't I? Maybe misdirection would work. "Will you tell me something first?"

"If I'm able." His calm unnerved me.

"Do you know *why* Miss Rabbit stopped talking?"

He leaned close and whispered. "This ain't no subject to be discussing with a girl young as you. Just tell me how you knowed Luther's name." His words slowed like they were climbing uphill. "Did Mable talk to you?"

My turn to play with the silverware. "No, she didn't exactly *talk* to me."

Confusion and weariness weighted his sigh. "Miss Sophie, think you could see it in your heart to save this old man some time?"

Despite the days of dread and rehearsing what I'd say, my mind stumbled over the choices. When nothing I'd previously considered sounded suitable, I opted for the truth cloaked in a whisper. "Your sister wrote down the entire story."

Emery's bottomless black eyes filled with disbelief.

"She gave it to Emma Jean for safekeeping and when Emma Jean died—" The last word stole my breath, forcing me to pause. "Her husband gave it to me. That's how I know about Luther."

"Mable wrote down all that stuff?"

I nodded.

He exhaled like a tire with a slow leak. "I don't believe it."

"Emery—" The truth would dawn on him soon enough. Better I leave him to his own pace.

Dishes shattering on a hard floor turned everyone's head but Emery's. No doubt trying to wrap his brain around the truth, he didn't move or speak until a passing stranger accidently bumped his chair. Startled from his thoughts, Emery offered the man a smile, edged his chair closer to the table, and returned his attention on me. "Mable know you have this story of hers?"

"Yes."

"So everyone but me knows about her writing?"

"No, just me and Emma Jean. She made me promise I wouldn't tell a soul." Emery didn't need to know about my parents or Dorothy.

He shook his head, like he was trying to ward off an unwelcome intruder and grasp why they'd come calling in the first place. "And Mable wrote everything down? All of it?"

"I only know what I read."

A sigh escaped him as he clenched a fist. "So Luther's done changed another life now."

As if he knew exactly how Miss Rabbit's story affected me, his matter-of-fact words had me looking for a way out of the room. I stopped a passing doctor to ask the time. This little errand of Nurse Smith's had cost me almost two hours in travel and discomfort.

"Emery, I really need to go now."

He didn't lift his gaze from the table.

The intercom above our heads clicked on to page someone. A man in scrubs, at a table in the corner of the room, jumped and grabbed a phone off the wall. Juggling a chart and cup of coffee in one hand, pen in the other, he cradled the receiver with his shoulder while he took notes. He still hadn't spilled his coffee by the time Emery cleared his throat to speak.

"Listen now. What Luther done wasn't right, but his name brought up after all these years ain't right, neither. I didn't do by my sister like I should've and, Lord knows, I ain't proud, but that man, and what he done, needs to be put to rest now. Young'un like you shouldn't know of such things, and I'm real sorry about that."

"You don't need to—"

"Hold on, child. You all of what...fifteen, sixteen years old? Not meaning any disrespect, but you have no idea what an old man like me needs, and I'm fixing to tell you." He leaned back and crossed his arms. "What you ain't said yet–and I been listening real close–is if Mable talked or not." He took a bite of his cake, chewed it slow and deliberate. "Now just remember, before you go and tip your glass or drop more flowers, ain't none of us be getting any younger."

I waited for a sign–a prod from Emma Jean, a bright light, something. When nothing arrived, I took a deep, steady breath and shared the only thing I knew for certain. "She told me pizza gives her gas."

A moment passed before Emery laughed, but then he laughed until tears rolled down his cheeks. I grabbed the opportunity like a scared rabbit and headed for the nearest exit.

CHAPTER 50

In the hospital's parking lot, Emma Jean jabbed a finger into my conscience. "Child, what *is* you thinking? Letting Emery know his sister done spoke, and you scoot outta there like your pants on fire? Mable lying up in bed, not having a clue you opened your mouth. Shoot, ain't you got no sense at all?"

She had a point. Miss Rabbit would never forgive me if she learned of my betrayal from Emery. I had to go back.

In the lobby, the elevator doors closed before I could reach them. I took the stairs two at a time. Deep in thought about what I'd say to Miss Rabbit, praying Emery hadn't yet finished his cake, I didn't spot the wet floor until I lost traction and one leg skidded sideways. My arms cart wheeling, I collided with a hunched janitor's backside. His mop handle stabbed me in the forehead as I toppled. His strong, well-placed hand on an adjacent wall stopped both of us from hitting the floor.

"Whoa there, girl. You okay?"

More embarrassed than injured, I nodded and rubbed what felt like a dent where the mop had poked me. "Sorry, didn't see you."

"They should give me a sign or something. People be sliding

all the time when I'm mopping. You sure you okay?"

The ding of the nearby elevator brought my mission back into focus. "Yes, I'm fine. Sorry again for being so clumsy." Leaving him to his work, I headed to Miss Rabbit's room.

"What you doing back up here?"

The voice spun me. Emery, now off the elevator, walked toward me, holding a piece of chocolate cake.

"I came back because...because I—" The new dent in my head slowed my thinking.

He laid a hand on my shoulder and lowered his voice. "Don't set yourself to worrying none, child. Your secret's safe with me."

Relief unknotted my tongue. "You aren't going to tell her?"

The janitor worked his mop along the floor, averting his gaze only when I stared back. Seeing no need for another person to be party to our conversation, I motioned for Emery to follow me to a sitting area in front of the elevator.

We took seats side-by-side in scuffed plastic chairs. He moved aside a discarded magazine to set down the cake. The cover, declaring Elton John 'Rock's Captain Fantastic', reminded me not only of Penny's claim I hadn't heard of the singer, but of her tendency to stick her nose where it didn't belong–which brought me back to my point.

"I came up here to warn your sister I'd opened my big mouth. I couldn't let you be the one to tell her."

"I won't tell her, Miss Sophie. I figure if she's seen fit to not speak to me all these years, the first words out her mouth shouldn't be ones telling me to go to hell–excuse the language."

I waved off his unnecessary apology. "I only told you so you'd have some hope. Seeing as she spoke to me, you might be next."

"Now that's a right good way to look at things, but can't say I'm as optimistic. If our falling out done lasted this long, I'm thinking it be powerful enough to carry her to the grave."

"Falling out?"

The pork pie hat twisted in his hands. "If'n you don't mind, Miss Sophie, it be family business. Happened long time ago. I don't see fit to bring it up now, especially with a young'un like you."

"This the reason Miss Rabbit quit talking?"

"Yep, but it be between her and me."

"Does this falling out have to do with Luther?"

"Everything what happened has to do with Luther. He done more damage than just what he done to my sister."

My need to interfere propelled me. "Would my knowing what happened help me get Miss Rabbit to talk more?"

"Right now, if'n you don't mind, I'd like to let this go."

We stood at an impasse and time was wasting.

"Okay then," I said, though I hated giving up. "You won't tell Miss Rabbit about this, though, right?"

"You have my word."

"Thank you. I have to go. Miss Rabbit is probably waiting on her cake, anyway."

Emery smiled, but his thoughts appeared to be somewhere else as he turned to leave.

"Thank you, Emery."

"No, thank *you*. Mable's pizza remark be the first good laugh I've had me in quite a spell. Reminded me of her as a young'un. She used to pass some wind from time to time. Big old noise come from her, but she'd always try to blame our baby sister Abigail. She'd get so mad when I never believed her none. She'd say, Emery, can't no one see where wind comes from."

He let out a belly laugh and wiped his mouth with the back of his hand. "Silly, I know, but it just tickles me. After all these years she finally owning up to her own wind."

I smiled, knowing enough not to question the music to which some folks danced.

As I waited for the elevator, Emery headed toward Miss Rabbit's room, nodding to the janitor on his way past. The janitor returned his gesture and, mopping with a little more gusto, started to whistle.

I hated to think what awaited me at work. Surprised Nurse Smith hadn't resorted to having me paged at the hospital, I hustled to my car and drove back to the home as quickly as traffic would allow.

Once inside Sterlingwood, I hurried down the hall. Each room I passed, the lights were out, the beds occupied. Someone had worked very hard in my absence. The first corner I turned brought me face-to-face with Tanya.

Eyes wide, hands on hips, she blocked my path. "Girl, where the hell you been at?"

Her tone, part question, mostly accusation, had me take a step back. "Smith sent me on an errand."

"I know that much. Where'd she send you? Chicago, for Christ's sake?"

"I got tied up at the hospital. Who put all my people to bed?"

"Who do you think? Been working my damn ass off." She wiped her brow, as if to show me just how much of a sweat she'd worked up. "I ain't getting paid to do both our jobs, you know?"

"Sorry. I didn't think I'd be gone so long. What's left for me to do?"

"What's left is you can rub my aching feet. Captain Smith been barking orders since you left. I never even had me time to eat."

"Go take a break. I'll find Smith, tell her I'm back, and cover for both of us. Anything I need to know?"

"You need to know I ain't doing this for you again, but since you asked, Martha Applebee be having a fit over the menu for her birthday party. Dorothy 'bout set fire to her dress after dinner. Ruby pegged Mama in the head with a throwed fork after we moved Mama into the room. Mr. Messina be in his wife's room, drunker than a sailor on leave. Pete smoked hisself a pack a cigarettes after dinner, and Lucy done threw a bedpan at me. So, no, ain't nothing new you need to know about." She crossed her arms, daring me to say something.

Not all the names she had rattled off were my residents and, as evidenced by her still present massive rear end, she hadn't worked her ass off either, but unwilling to poke the monster, I kept my mouth shut.

"They's all yours now. Have fun." She kicked aside an empty wheelchair and sashayed down the hall. I didn't move until she was out of sight.

At the nurse's station, Smith argued with someone on the phone. "I don't care how much money it takes. We need something to move this woman. Find the money. There's no excuse. I'm telling you she'll wind up with an ulcer like Mrs. Riggler...Yes, the patient we just lost...All right. Let me know first thing in the morning. Goodbye." She slammed down the receiver a little harder than necessary and put her head in her hands. A moment passed before she looked at me. "What took you so long?"

"Miss Rabbit's brother kind of kept me. Think he needed somebody to talk to. Sorry. I couldn't be rude."

"I understand." She gathered some papers on the desk and stood. "Where's Tanya?"

"Getting something to eat."

"God forbid she should starve to death." Smith rolled her eyes.

"She said she did all my people and had no time for a break."

"Don't let her fool you. Getting her to do more than her share took some convincing."

"But that's more than she's ever done in the past." Although Tanya had helped me, the reason for my need to defend her escaped me. "If it's any consolation, she is being a little nicer."

Smith's expression said she didn't find my defense agreeable or believable. "That's all well and fine, but her job here isn't to win congeniality contests. Not that she ever would, anyway."

"Don't you think she deserves a little slack, what with Emma Jean gone and all? I mean, like how you were explaining to Caroline why Ruby is so mean, maybe Tanya has something going on we don't know about."

Her hesitation told me my words might have found a soft spot. I added an apology for good measure. "I should've come back sooner."

"No, your absence was actually a good thing."

"Lady, can I have a light?" Outfitted in pajama bottoms and a shirt buttoned incorrectly, Pete gestured to his unlit cigarette.

Smith raised her hand to stop me from opening the drawer where we kept the lighter. "Pete, you can't keep this pace with these cigarettes. When we said good night a while ago, I told you that cigarette would be your last."

"Yeah, but can I have a light?" His cigarette danced at the edge of his mouth.

I looked to Smith for an answer. When she shrugged, I opened the drawer. Lighter in hand, I waited until Pete's eyes met mine. "Tell you what. I'll light this if you hand over your pack and go to bed when you're finished."

"Okay, good. Can I have a light?"

Keeping a close eye on both of us, Smith put a hand out once Pete's cigarette was lit. She had to gesture a couple times before he relinquished the pack. The pack empty, she shook her head, but not to be outsmarted, she snatched the full one peeking from his shirt pocket. Without acknowledging her maneuver, Pete puffed on his cigarette and walked into the Day Room, where he began pacing in his obsessive circles.

Smith stuffed the pack into the pocket of her uniform and headed down the hall. "Now when he asks, you can tell him you don't have any."

"But where are you going?" I called after her. "You didn't tell me why my not being here was a good thing."

Back turned, she held up a hand to hush me.

CHAPTER 51

I needed a quiet minute alone. The abandoned wheelchairs outside the Day Room as good a place as any, I sat down in one and put my feet up on another as Pete continued his laps around the room. Cigarette smoke trailed him like engine exhaust. Reclining my head, I closed my eyes and tried to relax my shoulders. Emma Jean appeared out of nowhere, intruding on my thoughts and space.

"Hell of a place, ain't it, child?" Perched on the porch steps like she'd done countless times, she splayed her bare brown feet in a patch of nearby grass. "Bet you never imagined what you was getting yourself into when you signed up to work here, did ya?" Her belly laugh rang out in the summer sky.

Her physical presence baffling me, goose bumps lifted on my arms. I stayed quiet, afraid words would cause her to vanish.

"I done never told you, but I's mighty proud of you. I sure didn't make things easy on you with Miss Rabbit's book and all, did I?"

My involvement in Miss Rabbit's affairs did rest on her shoulders, but there was no point in saying as much. I still trusted she'd had her reasons.

"You right, child. I had my reasons. You ain't figured them out yet, but you will. Everything happens for a reason."

Did she know something I didn't?

"Don't you be questioning me now. This one time, just trust I's smarter than you."

But—

"Ain't no buts about it." A softer, less devilish version of her trademark smile accompanied her words. "The hard part is over now, child. The rest will take care of itself. Just don't give up."

But Emma—

She laid a cool hand on my knee. Her swollen, calloused knuckles I remembered had softened as well. "You heard me. You gots to trust your instincts. They been working out pretty good so far, ain't they?"

I opened my mouth to question her, but something poked me in the leg. Startled, I banged my ankle on the wheelchair frame as I sat upright. Dorothy sat beside me, smirking.

"Somebody's had a long day," she said.

"I must have fallen asleep."

"You okay, kid? You look a little pale."

"Yeah, I'm fine," I said, but couldn't shake the fog. "You ever have a dream that seemed so real it was almost creepy?"

"Yeah, I'm hoping I'll wake up one of these days." Laughing, she reached into her pocket.

Dorothy's sense of humor leaving a lot to be desired, I rolled the wheelchairs against the wall. "I'm going for a soda."

Pete quit circling and headed our way.

"Fresh out, Pete." I shook my head. "No more until tomorrow."

When his gaze went to Dorothy, she put a hand on the pocket where she kept her cigarettes and told him no as well. Resigned for the moment that he'd had his last smoke of the day, he left. I headed in the opposite direction.

Dorothy called after me. "I wouldn't go in the break room if I was you."

I kept walking. "Why's that?"

"Smith and Tanya are going at it pretty good in there."

The news stopped my feet.

"Yep, you heard right. Smith is holding a Come to Jesus meeting down there."

"You heard them?"

"I'm surprised *you* didn't. Only ones downstairs still sleeping must be deaf."

"Smith? You sure? She never yells."

"I guess even she has limits when it comes to Tanya. Go listen for yourself if you don't believe me. They were still at it when I left."

Curiosity and common sense stretched me in a tug of war.

Dorothy motioned for me to go ahead. "If you stand just to the side of the door they won't see you. Scoot into the kitchen if you hear them coming."

No one would suspect this sweet old lady to be such a devil. One had to believe her hairdresser charged extra to hide those little red horns. But I'd be a fool not to take advantage of the information. I hustled downstairs.

Other than thunderous snores coming from Porky's room, the lower floor was quiet. I crept along the wall, careful not to let my rubber-soled shoes squeak on the linoleum. I stopped just outside the break room door. What sounded like a chair slid across the floor.

"We done here?" A trace of attitude choreographed Tanya's words.

"The question remains, are *you* done here?"

Tanya didn't answer.

Seconds later, Smith spoke again. "Alright then. There'll be no more of this nonsense on my shift. If you need this job as much as you say you do, then start acting like it. Your sister isn't here to stand up for you and, if you keep this up, I'm not sure how much longer Sophie will stay on your side."

Smith's words didn't have time to register before the sounds of the two of them getting up to leave had me scrambling for cover. I scooted into a resident's room one door down, wondering how on earth Dorothy thought I could've ever made it to the kitchen. My heart pounding with fear, I sucked in a breath and pressed my back as close to the wall as I could.

Tanya's voice reached me in the shadows. "Hey white girl, I can see your shoes."

Unable to explain my presence any other way, I stepped forward, mumbled an apology, and waited for the inevitable tongue-lashing. Instead, Tanya shook her head and snickered.

Smith stepped around her. "I see we have a little Dorothy-in-training."

"Sorry." Nothing I could do about the rush of heat in my cheeks, but I could try and explain. Neither Smith nor Tanya could know my words would be a lie. "I heard you yelling."

"The matter is settled now." Smith adjusted her cap and smoothed the wrinkles out of her uniform. She glanced at her watch, then at Tanya. "I'll let you two be for a few minutes. Come upstairs when you're finished. We need to tend to Mrs. Cornwall once more before we all go home tonight. Hopefully, it'll be the last time without mechanical assistance."

She turned to leave and I started to follow, but Tanya reached out a hand. "Come and sit a second."

Her touch, foreign and unexpected, startled me.

"Quit acting the fool. I ain't fixing to hurt you." She lumbered into the break room, to the far side of the table, and gestured for me to take a seat.

My curiosity would've had me follow, but fear of this woman's capabilities, the fact that she outweighed and out-muscled me, kept me rooted in place.

"Come on, we ain't got all night."

Her tone enough to propel me forward, I angled a chair to face the door then straddled its seat. If she decided to jump me, she'd have to first climb over both table and chair.

"You's a jumpy thing, ain't you?"

At my lack of answer, she smacked her hand on the table. I flinched, which only proved her point and made her laugh.

"Settle down. I'll save the beatings for some other time. I'm only here to apologize."

Another person beside Penny whose vocabulary I hadn't expected to include the word.

"Apologize?" I gave the word as much attitude as I dared.

Her eyes averted, she fiddled with a paper napkin already riddled with holes. "Smith done told me how you stuck up for me."

Heeding Emma Jean's advice to trust my instincts, I kept my mouth shut.

"I know you and me ain't gotten along so good in the past. But you ought to know it bugged me how my sister always be talking about you, acting like you something real special, when all she done was give me nothing but grief."

"Tanya, I—"

"No, wait. Ain't no need to explain none. That be my problem, not yours. She gone now and, like Smith said, I gots to keep living." The first hint of emotion creeping into her voice, she cleared her throat. "What I saying is I need this job, and now I know I would've lost it if you hadn't said something to Smith. So...I owe you for that."

In spite of what felt like a web still clinging to my feet, I inched closer to the spider. "Did Smith make you say all this to me?"

A glimmer of kindness and humor reminiscent of her sister's sparkled in her eyes, and in that instant, a person appeared whom I guessed I could come to like. Who knew Tanya had it in her?

Then she blinked.

Sitting up tall and proud, a snap of her fingers to accompany her words, she tilted her head. "Girl, nobody *makes* Tanya do anything."

I had to admire her spunk. "Of course not. What was I thinking?"

"Damn straight." She tossed her wadded up napkin at the trashcan some ten feet away. Once it fell dead center into the open container, she stood and pushed her chair under the table. "Okay, we good now, white girl?"

Instinct told me Smith had everything to do with this. Maybe even Emma Jean had thrown in a little something extra, as well.

My feet no longer stuck, my tongue untied, I stood.

"Yeah, black girl, we're good now."

THE SECRET MISS RABBIT KEPT

CHAPTER 52

For the rest of the evening and throughout a fitful night's sleep, my agitated brain chewed on, but refused to swallow, the day's events. In the morning, my father pulled me aside to say Miss Rabbit's issue should sit for a while; Mom didn't need the extra worry. More than happy to oblige, I read his newspaper at the breakfast table while she prattled on about the Parkers. According to her, she and Mr. Parker had spent hours together the day before, discussing not only his absent wife, but his disrespectful daughter, as well. The entire subject exhausted me.

I stuck my head deeper into the paper only to find a full-page advertisement for a movie my friends had seen without me the previous night–another reminder of just how badly my life sucked. A movie about a shark whose jaws were large enough to warrant top billing didn't interest me, but anything would have been better than work.

I really needed to get a life, but when I tuned back into my parents' conversation, I sensed that wouldn't happen any time soon. They still hadn't reached a conclusion on the Parkers. Though my father believed everything would work out, my mother now held firm to the notion that nothing short of a good spanking could cure Penny's bad behavior. I guessed that, like Smith with Tanya, even my mother's reserve of kindness had limits.

Breakfast finished, I left them to their endless debate. I had used up the extra time Smith had given me and I still needed to get dressed for work.

Less than an hour later, I pulled into Sterlingwood's parking lot. A medical transport vehicle drove in behind me. With the last admitted resident being Mrs. Cornwall—who had already filled more space than allotted—there were no available beds. The van's presence meant a current resident had to be either coming or going. Both options made my heart race.

I slammed on the brakes to prevent a climb up the parking curb then jumped out of the car to get a quick peek inside the van's back window.

Sitting hunched between medical equipment, Emery smiled. Even Miss Rabbit, peering through taped-up eyeglasses, offered a small grin.

The driver motioned for me to step aside as he and his helper opened the doors. Emery climbed out first, grunting from the strain of straightening. I offered a hand when he stumbled. The two attendants slid the gurney from the van, unhinging its legs in one swift motion. Miss Rabbit, head bandaged and eyes shut at the jostling, held tight to the Bible lying across her lap. Against the backdrop of the big outdoors, she looked tiny and frail.

I laid a hand on her bruised arm. "How are you?"

She squinted at me through bright sunlight and gave a weak thumbs-up.

"I bet you're anxious to get to your own room."

One of the attendants raised an eyebrow. "We're trying very hard to make that happen, ma'am."

"Oh, sorry." I moved to let them pass. "Emery, I have to get my purse out of the car. I'll come see you both after Miss Rabbit is settled."

"Actually, Miss Sophie, hold up. They don't need me right now. You have a minute?"

"Sure." Just steps from my car, I had little time to consider what he wanted.

"Get your pocketbook. I'll wait."

"How'd everything go at the hospital?"

"Mable enjoyed the cake. I went home for a while. Came back early this morning. That place sure drags its feet with discharging folks, though. Hurry up and wait is what I been doing."

"You both must be tired."

"Mable slept for a few minutes on the way here. Think I would've too, if'n I'd had more room. Can't complain, what with them giving me a ride and all." He moved like one of his legs didn't want to cooperate and, when we reached the porch, he grabbed hold of the railing and took a deep breath.

"You okay?"

"Been a long couple days is all."

He seemed to be in no hurry and I had to get to work. "Do you want to go inside?" I asked, reaching for the door handle in hopes he'd get the message.

"What I want is to see what Mable wrote."

As I wrestled with a proper response, Emma Jean took a seat on the porch step. Before I could determine if her arched eyebrow signified a question or a challenge—or if her continued appearances meant I'd lost my mind—Emery eased down into her place and she vanished.

Could it be that I, like crazy Mrs. Applebee, just didn't realize I actually lived here?

"Miss Sophie, did you hear what I said?"

My shift not even begun, my shoulders strained under the day's weight. "Yes, I heard you, but I can't do that. I broke my promise by even telling you about the book."

"This here be family business. I need to know what Mable said."

"But you told me you knew about Luther, about what happened after."

His head tilted like a dog offered a walk. "After?"

Oh no. There were blanks he expected me to fill.

"I just mean after all. You know about Luther—after all."

Gaze focused on the ground, he scratched the whiskers on

his top lip. "I done me a lot of thinking last night. Come to the conclusion this needs to be settled once and for all. I ain't seeing the reason this hornet's nest been stirred up again after all these years."

The vision of a young girl bleeding in a cornfield stood in the way of my voice. Without consideration of his need, I tossed out a weak apology and left him on the steps.

Inside the lobby, Mama shook her fist at an invisible demon perched somewhere high above her head. Though spoken rather than shouted, enunciated rather than mumbled, her words were still foreign. Unable to help battle her ghost even if I tried, I moved on.

I passed Tommy Chilton's room. His wife, an open book on her lap and a baby carrier at her feet, had fallen asleep upright in a bedside chair. Tommy lay in bed with dull, lifeless eyes. My feet never slowed.

I darted past Mrs. Kowalski's hungry reach, stepped over a swath of toilet paper and God knows what else trailing from Margaret Bjorn's slipper and, avoiding eye contact with a frantic Mrs. Applebee, waved off Pete's request for a light. All at once, their neediness and helplessness assaulted me like unrelenting stabs to my gut. Tears threatening, I held my balled fists high above my head and unleashed a loud screech of frustration.

None of the residents around me so much as blinked.

A second later, Pete took a step backward, but I guessed his recoil had more to do with a belief that one of us lunatics might steal his cigarettes.

"You got a light?"

My irritation percolated just below the surface of my skin. If I had a nickel for every... "No, but if you go to the nurse's station, I'm sure someone will have one for you."

"Okay, thanks." He averted his eyes, took a few hesitant steps then stopped midstride. With a trembling hand, he extended his unlit cigarette. "You want one?"

His extraordinary effort needed little time to shame me. "Thanks, Pete. Maybe later."

Visibly relieved, he palmed his cigarette and walked away.

In the seconds before my anxiety had time to rekindle, Emma Jean's familiar words arrived in a whisper.

"The hard part is over now, child."

I couldn't see her, but I hoped, with a vantage point I suspected to be a great deal higher than mine, she would get me through what I needed to do next.

The Secret Miss Rabbit Kept

CHAPTER 53

I knocked before pushing Miss Rabbit's door open. Her bed sat empty.

"She's in the dining room."

How Dorothy always managed to sneak up on me would be a discussion for another day.

"She just got back from the hospital," I said. "How'd she get in the dining room so fast?"

"How do ya think? In a wheelchair, of course."

With no patience for her sarcasm, I turned to leave, but she held up a hand. "Hold on. After all the commotion between Smith and Tanya last night, I never got a chance to ask you about—"

"Too much to keep track of these days, Dorothy?"

"You ain't kidding. Who needs soap operas with all that goes on around here?" A phlegmy laugh later, she pointed. "You didn't answer my question."

"What question?"

"How'd your talk with Emery go?"

"How do ya think?" Attitude worked both ways.

"You wisecracker, what's that supposed to mean?"

Her coughing fit allowing me to leave, I caught up with Porky in the hallway. Recognition took a second, then a smile lit up his face. "Well, hello there, young lady."

I slowed to the pace of his chair.

"You enjoying the music box?"

"I am. You should see how nice it looks in my room. My father couldn't believe you gave it to me."

He stopped his wheels and whispered. "You didn't mention the whiskey, did you?"

Laughing at his misplaced concern, I mimicked one of my father's winks. "That can stay between us."

"Good girl. Some things are better kept secret, don't you think? I've always said upsetting the apple cart gets you nothing but bruised fruit." He resumed wheeling his chair. "That reminds me of the time..."

Bruised fruit? Quite the analogy for the mess I was in, and exactly how we'd all wind up if I filled in the missing pieces for Emery. What had he said? Twenty years had passed without them speaking? Emma Jean had done me no favors. That much was certain. If she'd had a plan, why hadn't she shared that as well? My brain hurt.

"And then she blamed me," Porky said, glancing up at me. "Can you believe that?"

Could I believe what?

"You're not listening to this old man's ramblings, are you?"

"Y—yes, I am. No, I can't believe it," I said, though I had no idea what I'd just agreed with. He disappeared from my peripheral vision and when I turned, I found him stopped in the middle of the hallway. "What's wrong?"

"You ever stop to think about what it's like to be old?"

Guilt had me lay a hand on his forearm. "Sorry. I'm a little distracted."

"Oh, I know you're busy. I'm just wondering when it was I got so old that I forgot people have better things to do than listen to my tired stories."

Shamed for the second time since I'd arrived at work, I

addressed my invisible friend. "I thought you said the hard part was over, Emma Jean."

Porky shot me a sideways glance. "Pardon?"

When he continued to stare, I laughed and offered what I hoped would be a believable explanation. "See, you're not the only one getting old. I've started talking to myself."

"Silly girl, you're not old." He waved me forward. "Get back to work now. I can talk to you another time."

Years of lessons in manners trumped my need to find Miss Rabbit, but I didn't have to practice them in the hallway. "Let's you and I grab a table. I'd like to hear how you upset the apple cart. Come on, I'll even give you a push."

His instant smile offered no argument.

In the dining room, Miss Rabbit zeroed in on me from twenty yards away. Emery turned a second later, but when our eyes met, he averted his. He could ignore me for keeping my promise if he chose, but with no reason to let him, I wheeled Porky to their table, set his chair next to Miss Rabbit, and took a seat beside Emery. "It's great to see you in here for a change, Miss Rabbit."

A mouthful of eggs excused her silence this time.

Porky exchanged a cordial nod with Emery then squeezed Miss Rabbit's hand. "Welcome home, dearie. We've missed you."

She blinked several times and pulled her hand from his. Sensing an awkward moment, I said, "Thought you two could use some company. Porky was just about to tell me a story."

Giving me a long, hard look for the first time since I'd sat down, Emery settled his coffee cup in its saucer. "I could use me a good story. Kind of quiet with just the two of us here."

Oblivious to the sarcasm in Emery's words, Porky proceeded and for the second time, my overburdened brain tuned him out. Snippets of a story about a world war and a woman all blurred as I studied Miss Rabbit. Her bandaged head and persistent silence, not to mention a brother who knew little of her past, had all the makings of one of Dorothy's soap operas and I didn't want the lead role—especially since my lines hadn't yet been scripted.

In another misplaced bit of punctuation, Emery and Porky

erupted in laughter. Miss Rabbit pushed her chair from the table, indicating she'd had enough, but of what I couldn't be sure.

"All done, Miss Rabbit? Here, let me help you." Pleased I'd been given an out, I maneuvered her into the aisle then addressed Emery. "Why don't you sit and enjoy your coffee? I'll get Miss Rabbit settled in her room."

Without looking at me, he nodded and turned to Porky. "So tell me, how'd you wind up with a name like that, young man?"

Convinced the tale of the pigskin nose would keep them busy long enough for me to accomplish what I needed, I pushed Miss Rabbit down the hall as fast as I could. Despite her grip on the armrest, I kept my pace. When I tucked her into bed and sat beside her, the way she scrunched up her face and squeezed her eyes shut convinced me she suspected my motivation. Though she wouldn't likely answer me, I asked anyway. "What's the matter?"

Her silence still a guessing game, I waited through the minutes that ticked past. She must have regretted the day she ever spoke to me.

"I ain't talking."

Though welcome, her still-unfamiliar voice startled me. "But I have to ask you a question before Emery gets here. And I need an answer."

The crepe paper wrinkles in her face gathered tighter.

"I thought you stopped talking because—" No need to further upset her, I tried another approach. "How long has it been since you've spoken to Emery?"

A raised brow opened her eyes, but I refused to let her penetrating stare intimidate. "He told me you stopped talking as an adult. Please tell me why."

Her intention couldn't have been more pronounced had she screamed.

I stood and rested my hand on her Bible. "I swear all I ever wanted to do was help you."

Eyes closed once again, she turned her head into the pillow.

Defeat official, I made my way to the door, stopping at the spot where, days before, I'd heard her speak my name. Could I again catch her saying something she intended no one to hear?

Emma Jean's too-loud whisper knocked me sideways. "Good Lord, child. Do I have to tell you *everything*? You got the damn book. Read it for yourself!"

THE SECRET MISS RABBIT KEPT

CHAPTER 54

Emma Jean's announcement, coupled with Miss Rabbit's continued silence, left me only one option. I had to go home and finish the book. But first, I needed a good excuse.

Scooting into an empty bathroom, I applied a hot, wet washcloth to my face and neck. I rubbed my eyes to smear the mascara, making sure they turned red, and as a final touch, messed up my hair. A glance in the mirror confirmed my transformation into flu victim.

Upstairs, when I found Smith transferring a for-once-subdued Lucy from commode to wheelchair, she took one look at me and frowned. "What's wrong?"

"I need to go home. I'm sick." I threw in a little of Penny's infamous whine for good measure.

Smith settled Lucy in her seat then walked over to put a hand on my forehead. "You are a little clammy."

"I know. I better get out of here before I make someone else sick, huh?"

Her gaze traveled skyward to calculate, I guessed, what one less person meant to everyone's workload. "We can't have that.

Although, if you do have the flu, chances are it's already too late for the rest of us."

"Sorry. I probably shouldn't have come in. I wasn't feeling good when I left home, but figured it would pass."

"Go. We'll manage without you." In Smith fashion, the decision made and nothing more to discuss, she left the room.

Lucy, who up until that moment had been quiet, shrugged. "*Where* does she think I'm supposed to go?"

"She wasn't talking to you, Lucy." The first time the woman had shown the slightest bit of self-control and I had no better answer for her. She made me wish I had come down with the flu earlier.

By the time I arrived home, my father had left for work. Since any mention of sickness would start my mother hovering, I explained my presence with a forgotten day off. The suggestion I go back to bed came from her.

Pleased with what a little determination and whole lot of desperation could accomplish on such short notice, I locked my bedroom door and climbed into bed with Miss Rabbit's book.

The last entry I'd read about her being certain her actions had killed the baby, her knowing that wanting and doing were two different things, ended at the bottom of the page. As if words had eluded her, the next couple pages contained crossed out lines and doodles. I skimmed to where her entries began again.

It wasn't the good Lord looking over my shoulder saved me that day. Be dumb fool luck got me to Nana and Granddad's house. A man who worked the field found me wandering, all lost and raggedy in them darn rows that all looked the same. He had hisself a house nearby and taking pity on me, I guess, he and his missus brought me inside. They the ones who knew where my grandfolks lived and they was nice enough to get me there.

Nana about fell over when she laid eyes on me, too. Though I'd had me the good sense to get rid of my soiled dress back in the field, explaining how I'd come to be standing at her front door with the neighbors be a different matter. Ain't like I was lying none when I told her I had ran away and got to feeling poorly on the bus. Still, she quizzed me real good, and better the blame for killing that day be on Luther, I told her what he had done to Scrappy. Soon as I got to the describing part, her questions stopped.

Mama showed up later with Emery and Abigail, but she spent most of her time talking to Nana in the other room. Though I got me the sense Mama was angry, she stayed real quiet-like. Wasn't until we was on our way home, when Emery got around to asking why I'd left, that she finally spoke. Even then, it only be to tell him to mind his own business. Scared as I was of seeing Luther again, I didn't care if nobody talked. Turned out my worry be wasted. Him and Billy weren't there, and if Mama knew where they was, she didn't tell us. She never said another word about what happened and I sure never said nothing either.

Wasn't long after when Mama announced we was moving back in with Nana and Granddad. Guess with the house we was living in being Luther's and all, she didn't see fit to stay. Us young'uns didn't put up no fuss, though. Mrs. Marbly be the only one who cried. She hugged me so hard when we was leaving, she about squeezed me to death.

Only good things that come out of that day, besides not being made to see Luther no more, was Nana getting me a new kitten and her making Mama let me keep it in the house. I named the kitten Scrappy after the one Luther done killed, but tiny as she was and much as she fussed, Abigail got to calling her Baby. I won't lie, the name didn't set right with me at first, but much as Luther hated cats, the name seemed fitting the longer I thought about it.

Time moved along, but the big old raincloud that parked itself on us the day Luther first showed up never did go nowhere. Mama and me weren't the same after that. It be like she only had herself two babies from then on, favoring Emery and Abigail like she did. She just ain't had no use for me, like nothing I ever done be good enough. When I think back, Nana and Granddad spent more time raising me than she ever done.

After that day I took the bus, something changed with Emery and me, too. Could have been he blamed hisself for what happened, but he acted like what I done might rub off on him. Reckon I just as guilty. Ain't neither of us wanted no reminder of what should have never took place. Be too much for a young'un like him.

I suspect we all knew Luther be to blame for the change in our family, but none of us talked about him. In fact, after a while, Mama and me pretty near quit talking about everything. Guess she figured silence be better than facing the truth. I did get me the nerve once to ask Nana about Luther, about where he had gone off to, but she told me we was never to speak his name again. That suited me just fine.

I'd been happy to go my whole life and never hear of Luther again. Might have happened, too, if Emery hadn't made it his business to bring it up at Abigail's funeral. After fifty some years of us all pretending it be distance, not Luther, that got between our family and kept us apart, I guess Emery couldn't see fit to let it be. Don't know what he was thinking either, what with us being together for the first time in years, and Mama already being distressed. He about put her, and me, in that grave with Abigail.

I reckon, with Abigail dying, Luther being her daddy and all, his name bound to come up, but the nonsense started with something silly as Emery recalling how Abigail as a young'un used to suck on my old doll Cynthia's arms. I laughed when Mama told how Emery used to do the same thing. Don't know if he didn't take kindly to my teasing or what, but next thing I know, that crazy old fool turned to Mama and got right serious. He said, seeing as all these years passed, ain't the time come to talk about what Mable told us Luther done?

Well, Lord, you ain't never seen a colored woman turn so pale. Mama acted downright shocked, like she never known Luther to do anything wrong. I didn't have the voice to tell Emery to just let it be, or the good sense to get up and leave, though now I know I should have. Mama just kept sitting there, not answering, so Emery asked her again. That's when she started hollering.

You know good and well Mable just be telling stories, she said. Luther never did nothing to Mable. Her lies be the only reason he left.

I couldn't believe what my ears was hearing. Those words of hers, the first ones out her mouth that had anything to do with what happened all those years back, and they the worst ones she could have picked. Then, as if I ain't been hurt enough, Emery turns to me and asks why I lied.

Why I lied. Imagine that. I tell you, colder words ain't never been spoken.

Emery always been a bit of a mama's boy, but after Luther out our lives, he never left Mama's side. I reckon running to her be all he knew to do as a child. I sure weren't in no shape to help him feel better. So it sure shouldn't have been no surprise when he accused me of lying that day, seeing as how he under Mama's wing all those years, but it still be the last thing I expected. Bad enough Mama took Luther's side. She always been blind when it come to him, but after all I ain't said over the years and could have, Emery getting in line with her to turn on me about finished me off. I spent me a lifetime thinking we ain't talked about all this for good reason and, here, I come to find it weren't that way at all. They both just believed I be lying.

There weren't no forgiving Mama or Emery for what they done, though I reckon anyone reading this will have to decide that for they self. Much as I'd like to think Mama's pretending be her way of trying to make the hurt go away, I know better. She punished me with that silence of hers my whole life, beat me down to believing I done wrong. Them calling me a liar be what finally shut me up for good. Ain't like there be sense in talking if no one listening anyway.

When Mama died after I had me my stroke a few years back, she still believed it be me who done wrong. I know because Emery told me. Same as he done told me a hundred times since how sorry he was for taking Mama's side all those years. I don't suspect he means it none, though, seeing as he waited until Mama dead to say as much. Seemed to me a sorry like his, so long after, weren't gonna make up for what he done anyway. Just like how me being sorry about Luther's baby now don't make me no saint. Ain't no taking back history.

I ain't proud of this here story. Only reason I writing is because of what that lady on the television said about souls needing to be cleansed. I can't lay blame on anyone else for what I done in that cornfield. No one there but me. Ain't no amount of scrubbing gonna change that fact. We all be meant to make our own decisions. That's what I done back then and what I still be doing now. Silence the decision Mama made. It worked for her. I suspect it'll keep working for me, too.

Blank pages filled the rest of the book. The deliberate nature of their emptiness, paired with Miss Rabbit's silence, had me wiping my eyes.

"Sophie honey, you okay in there?" The doorknob turned with my mother's words.

When I unlocked the door, she walked in and scanned the room. Her gaze traveled to Miss Rabbit's book lying on my bed. "Have you thought any more about that poor woman?"

My mind still wrapped around that very thing, I could only nod.

"What are you planning to do?"

For the first time in weeks, I knew the answer.

CHAPTER 55

My mother did the one thing I never expected. She let me walk away without answering her question. I'm certain the reprieve would have proved temporary had the phone in the hallway not rung, but I still scored her immediate lack of response as a victory. Free from further interrogation, I headed back to Sterlingwood.

During the drive, somewhere between self-congratulation and misgivings, Emma Jean appeared in the seat beside me. I resisted the urge to touch her to make sure she wasn't something I'd simply conjured for strength.

She laughed and leaned against the passenger door. "Keep your hands on the wheel, child. You ain't crazy just yet."

Her definition of crazy, as well as an explanation of how she could read my mind, would have to wait. What I needed involved Miss Rabbit and, hallucination or not, Emma Jean could provide the answer.

I said the words aloud to make sure there wouldn't be any misunderstanding. "I've finally figured this out, haven't I?"

To my left, an angry car horn hollered and pulled my attention from a smirking Emma Jean. By the time I glanced back, she had vanished. I touched the seat and addressed the empty space. "Emma Jean, I'm right, aren't I?"

Her silence for the remainder of the trip told me I would have to find the answer on my own.

Arriving at Sterlingwood, I waved off a hungry Mrs. Kowalski, ignored a frantic Mrs. Applebee, walked past a gloomy Tommy Chilton's room and down the stairs to Miss Rabbit's, but this time, managed to get there without shrieking. I nudged open the door and found her in bed with her Bible. Prepared to persevere, I pulled up a chair and sat down hard. "You knew Emma Jean was going to share your story with me, didn't you?"

With eyes closed, she moved her lips soundlessly, as if whoever would listen had no need for volume. When she didn't acknowledge me, I prayed to her same God, asking for either Him or her to answer, but the minutes passed in silence.

Just as I reached the boundary of my faith, she placed her glasses on the closed Bible and cleared her throat. I held my breath.

"The day—" Her words, ending in a startled high note, seemed to surprise her as much as they did me. Slower and in a quieter voice, she began again. "The day you told me how your mama left you on them church steps?"

I nodded, afraid any sound would silence her courage and her new voice.

"I got me the sense you was hurting real bad that day."

The succinct summary, along with being offered by one who had spoken so little, forced me back in my chair. "I didn't need you to feel sorry for me. I was just trying to get you to talk, remember?"

"No, you don't understand." She whispered like a child forced to relinquish a best friend's secret. "I ain't never met anyone...adopted. Everyone I knew–except me–kept their babies."

Feel-better words for this situation didn't exist in any language I knew. The ones I selected tasted foreign and inadequate. "Maybe they didn't have another choice."

She couldn't have understood how difficult my statement had

been, for her voice strengthened. "I had me a choice I didn't know at the time. I could've done like your mama and had me that baby for someone else to love. What I done was wrong."

"No, what Luther did was wrong. Your family didn't know. You can't blame yourself for what isn't your fault."

"But that's what you been doing, ain't it?" Her eyebrow dared me to disagree.

This accusation, from her of all people, slapped me in the face. "But it had to have been my fault. She tossed me aw—"

"That's exactly what Emma Jean said you'd say about your mama."

"Neither of you know anything about my mama." Dangling at the edge of an unfamiliar cliff, I used the words as a lifeline. The irony of the effort left me breathless.

She replaced her glasses and stared hard at me through cockeyed lenses. "What we *know* is that she loved you."

My parents had used a thousand variations of these words for as long as I could remember. Although I couldn't explain their sudden clarity any easier than I could my ability to see Emma Jean all these weeks after she'd died, I knew without a doubt that their messenger had been hand-selected. Emma Jean's pulling me into Miss Rabbit's history had never been about learning what one sick man had done to a child, or about witnessing a family's disbelief. She hadn't intended for me to save anyone or patch up a relationship. She knew my invention of a murdered birthmother mirrored Miss Rabbit's refusal to let go of her secret. In Emma Jean's eyes, we were both liars. Her mission— and the reason she stayed to taunt my sanity—had been to make sure we spoke the truth out loud.

Who would have thought a dead woman with a fondness for wigs could accomplish so much from such a great distance? The realization startled me. "Do you know what Emma Jean's done?"

Fussing with the edge of the bed sheet, Miss Rabbit twisted a stray thread between her fingers. "She done left me with a mess, is what." A final yank, and she tossed the hard-won thread over the side of the bed. "I swore I'd never talk about this again. And here I am."

"She got us together for a reason. She meant for you to not spend the rest of your life in silence and for me to stop blaming my birthmother. Don't you see? What you did is no one's business. You were just a scared young girl."

"Just like your mama might've been when she left you on them church steps?"

A snicker from the corner of the room announced Emma Jean's arrival. "Speak up, child. We all wants to hear the answer to this one."

Emma Jean's wide grin so lifelike, her voice so distinctive, I expected surprise from Miss Rabbit. Instead, she grabbed my hand and repeated her question. "Just like your mama, right?"

After journeying to this climax together, neither woman in the room would relent until I said the words aloud.

"Yes. My mother could've been a scared young girl like you."

No bells went off, no one applauded, and for once, Emma Jean kept quiet. My statement gained weight in the ensuing silence and, for the first time in my life, I understood what might have been an explanation for my birthmother's actions.

Miss Rabbit made no attempt to hide her smile as the same gold fleck she shared with Emery lit her eyes. "That's right. Now don't you forget it none, neither."

"What about you?" If we were on the same maiden voyage, she needed her turn at the helm. "Isn't it time you talk to your brother? I'm pretty certain he understands now that you weren't lying. Your mama just didn't want to face the truth."

A loud knock on the door, followed by a familiar hacking cough, preceded an uninvited Dorothy into the room. Appearing oblivious to what she'd interrupted, she parked a few feet from Miss Rabbit's bed and nodded at me. "I thought you went home sick."

"I had to come back for something."

With lips pursed, she studied Miss Rabbit and me. Neither of our expressions offered her a clue as we returned the stare. She accepted the stalemate, shrugged, and waved a disgusted hand. "Keep your damn secrets then. Just thought you'd like to know, this place is going to hell in a hand basket since you left."

"What do you mean? I haven't been gone that long."

"Long enough to convince Martha Applebee that her assistant–that'd be you if I'm not mistaken–forgot all about her birthday party. Ruby told her, and I quote, 'No one's throwing a party, you goddamn old loon.' If that wasn't bad enough, Roy came to Martha's rescue with good 'ole Mr. One Eye–if you catch my drift."

She paused long enough for me to catch her drift.

"Mr. Messina would've smacked him if Smith hadn't pulled them apart. Now the whole joint's worked up." She shook her head and pulled out her pack of cigarettes. "It ain't pretty, I tell ya."

"But we never set a date for her party."

"Just telling you what I know. Don't shoot the messenger."

Planning a party was the last thing on my mind, but I'd made a promise and I'd broken one too many of those already. Having had my say with Miss Rabbit, I wasn't sure what else I could do for the time being. A break might be good for both of us–especially if the place was going to hell in a hand basket. "Do me a favor. Go tell her the party is tomorrow. I have to get out of here before Smith sees me."

The smoke Dorothy exhaled floated in a perfect circle between us while she considered her reply. "Only if I can tell that nasty old Ruby she ain't getting any damn invite."

Miss Rabbit's hand flew to her mouth too late to conceal her smirk. The lighter mood in the room convinced me it would be okay to leave.

"Looks like someone approves of your idea," I told Dorothy. "Do what you have to do. I have to go."

Dorothy rolled her chair out of my way, whispering to me as I passed. "You ladies get things all squared away?"

Recalling my recent lesson on choice, I opted to ignore her question. "I'll see you both tomorrow. I have a party to plan."

THE SECRET MISS RABBIT KEPT

Chapter 56

Finding a dark chocolate cake with butter cream frosting took me all afternoon. The lady at the last bakery I stumbled upon, who was kind enough to add wording on the top of the cake while I waited, kept apologizing for the slope in the middle. "This one was an experiment and I'm not very happy with the way it turned out, so I'll just charge you my costs. Fair enough?"

I didn't tell her the guests wouldn't notice the difference.

Party plates, a banner, balloons, and candles were all on sale at the dime store down the street. The birthday menu wouldn't be the prime rib and lobster Mrs. Applebee wanted, but like the uneven cake, it wouldn't matter.

Down to my last few dollars and still in need of a gift for the birthday girl, I stopped at a thrift store. In the bottom of the discount bin, a hat embellished with beads, feathers, and netting so resembled Mrs. Applebee's taste in millinery, it might have once been hers. Like the lopsided cake and incorrect menu, a few missing beads would be overlooked, but unlike the baker, the sales clerk offered no discount, stating the item was one of a kind—a fact Mrs. Applebee would no doubt appreciate.

All my errands complete, I arrived home and walked into the kitchen, my arms laden with purchases. "Can you grab this before I drop it, please?"

My mother ran from her place at the sink and grabbed the cake seconds before I lost my grip. "What's this?"

"A birthday party for someone at the home."

No more questions. No comments. Not even a peek into any of my shopping bags.

"What's the matter, Mom?"

She tried denying there was anything wrong, but gave up with a heavy sigh. "It's just been a very stressful day."

Resisting the urge to tell her the same, I made space for the cake in the refrigerator. When she grabbed another pot to scrub, I headed to my bedroom. No sense pushing if she didn't want a discussion. My day had been enough by itself. I'd nearly cleared the kitchen doorway when she changed her mind.

"I think I've convinced Mrs. Parker she needs to see a counselor."

The Parkers. Again.

As much as I would have liked to ignore her statement, I couldn't. But I didn't have to encourage her, either. I stayed outside the doorway, hoping she'd get the message. "And why is that?"

"Someone needs to talk some sense into that woman's head."

"No offense, Mom, but haven't you done enough? I mean, is this really any of your business?"

She pulled a chair from the table and sat down. "Someone had to make it their business. Besides, she called me. That was her on the phone this morning. She's the one who insisted on telling me about—" Her cheeks flushed.

My curiosity piqued, I set down my bags and joined her at the table. "About what?"

"Her man problems."

Not something I wanted to discuss with my mother, but I'd already ruined any chance of escape by sitting down. She'd be hurt if I didn't continue. "And?"

"And we met for lunch. After our long talk, I think she

realized how foolish she's been acting." Closing her eyes, she rubbed her temples. "I just don't know how much more of this I can take. It's given me a terrible headache."

"Why don't you go lay down? It'll make you feel better and Dad won't be home for awhile, anyway."

"Oh, you're probably right," she said, but made no move to stand.

In an effort to coax her along, I told her I needed a nap and asked if she would wake me in an hour. For the second time in a day, she let me go without argument.

I woke up two hours later, which contradicted everything I knew about my mother. Sensing something amiss, I headed down the stairs. My parents' conversation in the kitchen made it clear that the subject of the Parkers had not only come up again, but also must have been the reason for my mother's lapse. I stopped on the bottom step.

"You've done enough," my father said. "Let the Parkers figure out their next move. Besides, I'm not sure I want my wife associating with a woman like her anyway."

"But don't you see?" My mother's voice hit its distressed high notes. "She needs a friend now more than ever."

"All I'm saying is that leaving her family the way she did, having a man *friend*, and the whole notion she might've been pregnant. What kind of woman even *considers* having an abor—"

"No! Don't even say the word out loud. I can't bear the thought of it. Besides, she'd kill me if she knew I'd told you."

My butt found a seat in a hurry.

Into what alternative reality had I wandered? Good God, no wonder Mrs. Parker had left. Penny would just die if she knew. Though I'd never be mean enough to tell her, just how many secrets should one person be expected to keep?

"Enough with the lessons now, Emma Jean. I get it."

Met with silence, I retraced my steps to bed where I tossed and turned until morning. This time, my mother woke me.

"Sophie, get up. The phone is for you."

Squinting at the sunlight coming in through my open curtains, I stumbled into the hallway and picked up the receiver.

335

My brain had fogged from too many hours at rest, and the absurdity of Smith calling to see how I felt didn't help. I asked what she really wanted.

"We're in a jam here. There's a shortage of people on both shifts. Any chance you could work a double?"

Karma had come to call. I agreed to be there within the hour. As an afterthought, I mentioned the party I'd planned for Mrs. Applebee. Too busy, distracted, or not interested, she simply thanked me and hung up.

My mother, hovering while I took the call, followed me into my bedroom. "Don't you think you're working too much?"

"Can't help it. They're shorthanded." I pulled a uniform from the pile of clean clothes.

"Don't make a mess now. Those are all neatly folded." She straightened the pile and took a seat on my bed. Her eyes zeroed in on the music box sitting on my dresser. "Where'd you get that?"

The stress created by the Parkers had obviously taken a toll on her detective skills.

"It's a gift from one of the people at the home."

Running her hand across the wooden top like my father had done, she let loose her motherly cluck. "Isn't this lovely? And, goodness, what a special quote that is."

"I know. Open it up. Can you believe someone gave that to me?"

The ballerina twirled a few times before she shut the lid. "Yes, of course I can, dear. You're a very special person, but *why* did someone give it to you?"

I brushed my hair and recounted the story, including the part about the whiskey. The minor infraction seemed harmless after all we'd shared as of late, but her eyes filled with tears anyway.

"What's wrong?"

"Your getting that man his whiskey after his friend passed, the words on the box. Everything, honey. It's all very touching. You've grown up so much in the last few weeks."

She'd had a rough few weeks as well. Holding responsibility for some of it, I owed her some kindness. I set my hairbrush aside, wrapped an arm around her, and placed a rare kiss on her forehead. "That's no reason to cry, you goof."

"One day when you have children of your own—"

"I know, Mom. I know." She'd start with her Old Man quotes if I didn't stop her. "I have to get to work." I threw in another kiss for good measure and left the room.

Trying to keep pace, she called after me on the stairs. "Not that this is a good time, So-So, but you haven't said anything more about Miss Rabbit. Your father insisted I let you be, but I'm afraid you'll never tell me anything unless I ask."

Not by coincidence, I stopped on the bottom step–the same place where, the night before, I'd overheard her and my father discussing Mrs. Parker. "I've decided some secrets are better off kept."

"But what are you going to do with the book?"

Count on her to bring up the one thing I hadn't considered.

THE SECRET MISS RABBIT KEPT

CHAPTER 57

Throughout my entire first shift, Mrs. Applebee, in one of her rare days of clarity, hounded me about her party. Did I order the food? Was I certain there would be enough? Had everyone RSVP'd? At one point, Mr. Messina took pity on me and distracted her with the stuffed cat he'd had Dorothy buy. The gift, bringing back memories of her furry family members over the years, reduced her to tears long enough for me to escape and decorate the dining room. At four thirty, when the residents began to gather near the elevator for dinner, Emery walked into the lobby, hat in hand.

"Hello, Miss Sophie."

I suspected his manners prevented him from ignoring me, his sense of privacy from asking again about the book.

"You're back." Not the most tactful thing I'd ever said, but afraid any conversation would lead to another standoff, these words already represented more than I wanted to say.

"I reckon if I keep at this, she'll just have to talk to me before one of us sees the grave." His heavy sigh belied the new optimism of his words.

The man needed hope, and though I couldn't provide such a thing with any certainty, my gut said I should try.

"She just might surprise you," I said.

"You telling me there's something *else* I don't know?"

Unable to look him in the eye, I bent to tie my shoe. My next lie would be a whopper. "No, I told you everything."

Judging by his frown when I stood, the way the muscles in his jaw bulged, I'd disappointed him. The uncomfortable silence between us grew.

A few doors down, the administrator stepped out of her office. "Mr. Rabbit, there's some paperwork we need to review. Could I trouble you to come in here for a minute?"

Short on words or long on frustration, Emery left me and followed her into the office. When the door closed, Ruby hollered from her room for an aide. I found her on the verge of tears, her face screwed up in her trademark scowl.

"I want someone to tell me why I'm not invited to the party," she said.

"You don't know why?" I had imagined Dorothy sharing an entire arsenal of reasons when she'd uninvited Ruby.

"Because that Crumble woman is a mean old bitch is why."

"See, it's comments like those that get you in trouble. You made a real effort with your sister the other day, then you hit her in the head. The second Mama moved in, you pegged her with a fork. Yesterday you called Mrs. Applebee a crazy old loon. When are you going to learn you have to be nice to people, and not just after you've hurt them?"

"I told you," she said, raising her voice. "Being stuck in this chair, stuck in this god-awful place, I just want to kill someone!"

"I know it's hard. You just have to try to make the best of it."

Spittle flew ahead of her pointed, angry finger. "What does a kid like you know about hard? Do you even realize I've been stuck in this chair for likely as long as you've been alive?"

With her defense growing roots, though not yet deep enough to win the battle, an idea dawned. Why hadn't I thought of this before?

"Come on," I said. "There's someone I want you to meet."

Before she could argue, I wheeled her down the hall and into another wing, praying I could accomplish what I planned without appearing as mean and callous as her. Lucky for both of us, the room I needed for this lesson sat wide open, no one beside its occupant in sight.

"What are we doing here?" Ruby gestured to the man in bed. "Who is this?"

"*This* is Tommy Chilton. You want to know how old he is?" I let the question taunt her for a second. "Twenty-four. He's also married and the father of an infant son." The immobile man focused in a vacant stare, anchored by tubes and penned in with bed rails, provided the remainder of the story.

Ruby's face drained of color when the words and scene settled in. A shaky hand went to her mouth. "Oh my God."

She didn't say another word, but she didn't take her eyes off Tommy either. I kept her there until I was certain she'd never 'un-see' what she'd just witnessed.

Back in her room, I sat on her bed, pulled her chair close, and waited until she made eye contact. "I'm sorry you're stuck, I really am, but near as I can tell, nothing is going to change. Miserable is a choice. I took you to that room so you'd never forget that there's always someone–like Tommy–who is worse off than you."

She dissolved into sobs, and though I couldn't think of a person who deserved compassion less, I hugged her.

Then I held on.

She smelled of sweat and greasy food and hair in need of a good shampoo. Being at the mercy of another's kindness could make a person want to kill someone, I guessed, and Ruby had created fewer options for herself than most.

I waited until she stopped trembling. "How about I take you to the party and, afterwards, I give you that shower I promised?"

She leaned back in her chair and, wiping her nose with the back of her hand, she looked me in the eye. "What's the catch?"

"You have to learn from this lesson and promise to start being nicer. No party otherwise," I said, using the sternest voice I dared.

Her gaze strayed to the ceiling as she pondered my ultimatum. "Is there any way you could talk Caroline into moving back in with me? Mama is driving me crazy."

"Talk to Smith. She's the one who made that decision."

Ruby had to know her only chance would involve serious groveling, but she nodded anyway.

"Alright then. Let's get you freshened up and downstairs to the party."

She let me wash her face and comb her hair. As I wheeled her out of the room, she set down her foot to stop the chair. With bloodshot eyes and a runny nose, she looked up at me. "Thank you, Sophie. I promise I'll try to do better."

Not a lot of words, but enough to tell me hope existed for a new, kinder Ruby. I bent and kissed her forehead. Her inexperienced smile, maybe afraid of being seen or, heaven forbid, associated with kindness, dissolved into a twitch–likely the best she could do in her ongoing battle of good versus evil.

Downstairs, Caroline spotted us in the doorway to the dining room and waved us to her table. "I'm so happy you made it on time. Look, Ruby, I saved you a space right next to me."

"Thank you. Sophie was fixing my hair."

"It looks beautiful," Caroline said, brushing a hand atop her sister's matching pixie locks.

Ruby patted Caroline's arm. "Yours does, too."

Had a higher power finally answered Caroline's pleas? A choice between faith and science hinged on what one believed, but Caroline made clear whom she trusted when she caught my eye and smiled. I gave Ruby's shoulder an encouraging squeeze before I went to check on the rest of the residents.

Roy and Pete sat at a table for two. Someone had dressed Roy in a clean blue t-shirt and given him a shave. Pete had not only managed the proper match of buttons to buttonholes on his shirt, he'd also combed his hair, but his repeated attempts to pull a cigarette from his empty pocket guaranteed Roy would be sitting alone sooner than later.

Lucy, Mama, and Mrs. Kramer, all chattering at once, occupied seats closest to the kitchen entrance. Their table full,

Mrs. Kowalski seated herself as close to the birthday cake as she could without being on top of it. Ethel Johnson, Viola Barnes, and Beatrice Walker sat trapped in a corner, forced to listen to Polly Stern's choruses of yes and no. Dorothy wheeled over to join Porky, Cynthia, and Mr. Messina by the picture window.

Son in her arms, Tommy Chilton's wife Sarah stood at the far entrance. Her gaze stopped at the banner I'd strung up earlier. The banner now loose on one end and the word Birthday hidden by the new fold created, 'Happy' hung like an ironic comment on the festivities. When she left the room moments later, I could only guess that happy wasn't yet a place she was ready to be.

I accounted for everyone except Miss Rabbit and Emery. Though he could have been still tied up with paperwork, someone should have brought out Miss Rabbit. I headed to her room and found Emery standing outside her closed door.

"You two are going to be late for the party if we don't hurry," I said.

"Aw, I didn't know about a party. I'll come back another time."

"No, you're invited, too, of course. Come on, let's get your sister."

"You know she ain't going to care none if I'm there, Miss Sophie. I'll just be on my way."

"No, how about if we find out what *she* wants?" I motioned for him to follow me into the room.

Miss Rabbit turned from her seat at the window. After a nearly imperceptible glance at her brother she fixed her gaze on me.

Emery smiled at her despite stooped shoulders, tired eyes, and what I knew to be a heavy heart. "Hello, Mable."

His words prompting no response, I walked over and took Miss Rabbit's hand in mine. "Mrs. Applebee's party is about to start. Emery thought he should leave. Wouldn't you like him to stay?"

Her fingers tightened around mine, but she remained mute.

Fiddling with his hat through the lengthening silence, Emery eventually shrugged and turned toward the door. "That's okay,

Miss Sophie. You all go along now."

"Wait." I knelt and locked eyes with Miss Rabbit. "You want him to stay. Don't you?"

When she refused to answer, the one person with insight whispered into my ear. Knowing better than to question Emma Jean, I repeated her words like a ventriloquist's puppet. "Time's a wasting, old girl. Giddyup."

Emery raised an eyebrow at my uncharacteristic prompt, but whatever he had intended to say was lost when Miss Rabbit straightened and cleared her throat.

"Course I want Emery to stay, but I *still* ain't talking."

I nearly peed my pants.

"You mean unless you feel like it," I said.

A quick glance at her startled brother and she smiled.

"That's right, child. I's got *me* a choice.

CHAPTER 58

If asked, I couldn't name a single thing more beautiful than Emery's smile when Miss Rabbit finally spoke. His joy alone would have had me linger—the triumph reason enough to have me stay—but the party in Mrs. Applebee's honor would have to suffice as celebration. The two of them deserved a few moments alone. I eased out of the room and headed back to the festivities.

The cake hadn't yet been destroyed, though frosting graced the corners of Mrs. Kowalski mouth. A not-so-secret flask could be the only explanation for the boisterous laughter at the table Porky, Dorothy, and the Messinas shared. Lucy, Mama, and Mrs. Kramer continued a three-way conversation—however little sense it made. Pete no longer in his seat, an orderly had joined Roy in an effort, no doubt, to ensure pants stayed zipped. With the kitchen staff beginning the dinner service, I made my way to the stairs.

Tanya stepped out of the elevator with Margaret Bjorn and called to me. "You getting Mrs. Applebee? She's waiting for her assistant to escort her, you know."

"I was just headed in that direction. Can you ask the guys in the kitchen to light the candles? I want her to see the cake right when we walk in."

"Sure thing." In somewhat of another miracle, Tanya took Margaret's hand and, matching the woman's slow pace, led her to choose her own seat.

I scooted into the elevator as the doors closed, leaned against the back wall, and shut my eyes in what felt like the first moment of reflection I'd had all day. Emma Jean arrived in the darkness, but her presence no longer surprising me, I addressed her first. "Did you see how happy Emery was? He almost made *me* cry."

"You done good, child."

"I didn't do anything. It was all you—and Miss Rabbit's book."

For once, she didn't smirk. "The book worked, didn't it?"

"You knew all along it would. I still don't know why my birthmother left me on those steps, but now I understand she must've loved me."

"We all do the best we can with what we know. Ain't no one fit to judge, child. Now I don't want to hear none of that 'my mother was murdered' stuff anymore. Agreed?"

I nodded. "What should I do with the book?"

"You'll know when the time comes. Just listen."

"Listen to what?" My exhaustion or the motion of the rising elevator had her fading in and out of focus. "Emma Jean?"

All but her whisper disappeared. "Trust me, child."

I opened my eyes to a frenzied Mrs. Applebee standing outside the elevator doors.

Adorned with a multitude of rhinestone bracelets, her arms flew skyward when she saw me. "Oh my, I feared you'd gotten stuck in traffic. We must hurry now. I don't want to keep my guests waiting."

"You look beautiful." For once, her go-to purple hat matched her dress and lace shawl.

"Thank you, dear. I didn't have time to see the hairdresser like I would've preferred though." After a quick fluffing of her hairdo, she threaded her arm through mine and pulled me back inside the elevator. "Now, you're certain we've ordered enough food?"

"Positive." I pressed the button for the bottom floor.

"And no one's been left off the list?"

"Nope."

"Have there been any last minute cancellations?"

"Your friends would never dream of missing the celebration."

Her posture relaxing with a satisfied sigh, she wrapped an arm around me and rested her head on my shoulder. "This will be a wonderful party, dear. I just cannot begin to thank you enough."

The elevator doors opened before I could tell her the pleasure had been all mine.

THE SECRET MISS RABBIT KEPT

ABOUT THE AUTHOR

Robin began her writing career as a child. Penning plays for neighborhood friends' performances, she was paid in popsicles. Though Robin's love of plays and popsicles continued into adulthood, she concentrated on writing human-interest articles and book reviews for a variety of online publications until a newspaper headline about a woman's body—found in a local lake and long unidentified—supplied the idea for her first novel. Spurred by the question, *What kind of man doesn't know his wife is missing?*, Robin wrote When Dreams Bleed.

A wife, business partner, mother, stepmother, and Ya-Ya (because she can't quite wrap her eternally youthful brain around the G-word), Robin also plays the role of alpha female to her family of horses, dogs, and a noisy donkey named Sophia. You've likely heard her bray (the donkey, not the author).

Born and raised in the Chicago suburbs, Robin currently resides in Scottsdale, AZ with her husband and her herd. If she's not working on her latest story, you can find her cooking, reading, watching home improvement television shows, or indulging in her unhealthy addiction to Facebook.

The Secret Miss Rabbit Kept is Robin's second novel. For

more information, visit Robin's website www.robincain.com

ALSO FROM ROBIN CAIN

WHEN DREAMS BLEED
A Novel

A software genius with a knack for business, Frank's been living the dream his whole life. He's amassed money, success, and is now accumulating women, but someone thinks he's gone too far. Who is seeking revenge and why? His wife? His mistress? Or the shadow who has been following his every move? Just when he thinks he has anticipated his opponent's next move a tragic car accident leaves him paralyzed, his life's work is being stolen, and his wife has disappeared. Just how far will someone go to teach him the correlation between deception and despair? *When Dreams Bleed* examines temptation and the ensuing consequences in a contemporary world. It's no secret that dreams come at a price, but what happens When Dreams Bleed?